Frankie McGowan began he
on magazines before going on to newspapers as a
feature writer and columnist. She launched and
edited *New Woman* and *Top Santé* and has twice been
nominated for magazine editor of the year. Frankie
lives in London with her husband, Peter Glossop,
and their children Tom and Amy. *A Better Life* is
her fifth novel.

A Better Life

FRANKIE McGOWAN

VICTOR GOLLANCZ

LONDON

The right of Frankie McGowan to be identified
as the author of this work has been
asserted by her in accordance with the
Copyright, Designs and Patents Act 1988

First published in Great Britain in 1999 by
Victor Gollancz
An imprint of Orion Books Ltd

Orion House, 5 Upper St Martin's Lane, London WC2H 9EA

A CIP catalogue record for this book is
available from the British Library

Typeset by Rowland Phototypesetting Ltd,
Bury St Edmunds, Suffolk
Printed and bound in Great Britain by
Clays Ltd, St Ives plc

To Tom with love

Acknowledgements

While I consulted various adoption agencies on the procedures involved in reuniting families, the interpretation of those guidelines is, of course, my own. I would like to thank those who shared with me their experiences of finding their birth families, which was truly helpful. I am indebted to Humphrey Price, Viv Redman, Hazel Orme and, as ever, Sarah Molloy, whose help in their different ways has been invaluable in the preparation of this book. My grateful thanks also to Norma Fraser, Chris Allen, various friends in Italy and, most especially, my daughter Amy, who all assisted my research.

Chapter One

The studio lights went down. Ben Goodwright raised his arms above his head and began vigorously to applaud, which he had told the audience was their cue to yell, whistle and stamp their feet. 'So obedient,' he muttered, as the noise erupted around him. At least as floor manager he was paid to endorse an hour of unadulterated crap. Those of the studio audience who had dodged past him – and there were always a determined handful who did – surrounded Max for autographs. The rest began to shuffle out, blinking in the sudden sunlight of the studios' foyer.

The six-strong line of human frailty who had ensured that Max Warner's acquisition of a second home in Manhattan and that his penchant for fine wines was secure remained seated on the podium looking around uncertainly. Three had entertained several million viewers with brutally painful revelations of the infidelity perpetrated on the others sitting alongside them, and they were all uncertain now of their role.

'Ben?' Anna Minstrel came through his earpiece. 'Make sure those people are looked after. No booze. Don't want a repetition of yesterday.'

'*Sun* been on?' Ben chuckled.

'Tell me about it,' she murmured. 'And get them out before Max erupts. He can't sign autographs for ever.'

'Will do. Stupid berk,' Ben muttered, without looking above to where Anna was sitting out of sight behind a stretch of black glass high above the studio floor. 'Just

I

ignores me. I might as well be signalling to the *QE2*. Oh, God, here he goes again. Vesuvius is erupting.' Much better to leave the fall-out to Anna, he decided, wincing at the first explosion from the silver-haired Max. She never let him get to her.

From where she sat in the control room, Anna could see Max Warner slamming his unread script against the floor manager's chest. If that was as bad as it got, Ben could handle it. After all, it was she and not Ben who would take the brunt of Max's fury. His was the name that lured the audience to switch on, but it was Anna who made sure that his performance was worth the effort. Max hated any suggestion that his thoughtful or provocative questions, his witty asides, the homily he delivered at the end of the show owed anything to anyone but himself. When an interview with him appeared in the papers analysing his knack of pushing his subject to even greater heights of intimacy, he would be quoted as saying it was down to a natural and instinctive feel for the hearts and minds of his guests. On such days he convinced himself that Anna would have read the article and was privately laughing at him. His resentment of her doubled. He had to hate someone.

Now Anna watched as Max stormed off the set on his way to confront her.

'Just look.' Anna leaned, with a mock shiver, towards the man next to her, who was nursing his head in his hands. 'Frightening me to death, he is.' Slowly she removed her headphones and stretched her arms above her head, wondering why she didn't search out something else to do, as Oliver constantly urged. Something more upmarket, something political that went out in the evening, instead of all this trailer-park trash in the morning. Maybe she would. But then again, maybe she'd think about it another time. Not thinking about it at all, of course, was easiest.

She smiled wryly at the dejected-looking Henry Spedding and linked her hands behind her head as the control room began to empty. Aggie Finch, Henry's deputy, got up and wedged her chair against the door to let in some air. Stuart, the director, had already vanished on a fruitless errand to head off Max.

Tessa, the show's PA, was collecting up styrofoam cups and discarded running orders. 'More coffee, Anna? Henry? Or something stronger?' She giggled, knowing what was coming and not wanting to miss it. She could see herself now sitting in the wine bar that evening regaling her friends, who in Tessa's view had dull jobs not worth hearing about, with descriptions of these thrilling clashes between Max Warner and his producer.

'Not for me, Tess.' Anna yawned, knowing it would take Max less than two minutes to reach her. 'So what's it to be, Henry? My resignation or his reputation? Don't look at me like that. You hired him.'

'I think,' Henry said, dragging his hands away from his eyes, 'I think I've lost the will to live.'

Anna grimaced. 'And they'll renew his contract,' she said.

'He's loved,' Henry moaned. 'Millions of viewers say so.'

'Shame millions of viewers can't see there's only a pulse where there should be a brain,' she retorted.

'They don't see it because you don't let them,' Henry objected. 'Why do you do it? Why don't you just let him fall flat on his smirking face and then we could be rid of him?'

'Because I'm paid not to.' She sighed, hearing raised voices through the open door. 'And the strange thing is, Henry, if he would just stop being afraid of accepting help, he'd probably be quite good. Oh, hell, here he is. Do me a favour, Henry? He'll be up here in a minute and I've got eight zillion phone calls to make before the meeting. I haven't got time for all this. Tell him you bawled me out and I'm sobbing in the loo. Tell him anything. Just give me ten minutes to get life restarted.'

Henry, balding, thin, and with the prospect of school

3

fees to find for three children out of his very average salary, shot out a hand and grabbed her arm.

He had planned to slip out to Boots for some aftershave before his lunchtime assignation with the PA on *Chic Chefs* with whom he was having the most unsatisfactory affair – or non-affair, really, since furtive gropings in discreet restaurants had been his lot so far. An hour spent soothing Max's monstrous ego – and it would certainly be an hour – would sabotage his hopes of anything more satisfying, something that would still the terrible sense of time rushing past in a chaotic tide of children, school runs and his own horizons, which seemed rapidly to be closing in on him.

He thought of the small hotel to which he had taken Charlotte, last year's 'final' fling, who now worked for CBS and who, in Henry's bitter view, had sunk her six-inch Prada heels into his back for the advancement of her career and little else. He thought of the concierge, who had asked no questions, and the room with its crisp cotton sheets and double bed, the heavy brocade curtains that blotted out daylight and reality. The vision of Melissa's legs gripping his frame as she gasped for more had sustained him throughout the torment of *Max Meets*. He couldn't bear to let it go. He gave a stifled moan. 'No. Oh, God, no,' he implored Anna. 'You? Sobbing in the loo? He'll never believe it. No one would. Anna, please, don't leave me alone with him. I'll hit him. And I can't afford to hit him. And I don't want your resignation. And you know you don't mean it. I'd have to go as well if you did. It's only knowing he hates you more than he despises me that keeps me here.'

Anna patted his shoulder as she got to her feet. 'And the only thing keeping me here is—' She broke off and frowned comically. 'Good heavens. Remind me what it is. I've for-gotten. Listen, if Oliver rings I'll call him later,' she said, gathering up sheaves of papers and hooking her bag over her shoulder. 'Uh-oh.' She groaned. 'Here he is. I'm out of here.'

She stopped at the door of the control room, which led

on to a corridor along which hung portraits of the station's most famous faces just as Max Warner reached it, blocking her exit. The benevolence of the on-screen host of *Max Meets*, who encouraged the stream of dysfunctional people he encountered each day to confide in him and confront each other, stretched only as far as the edge of the studio floor. Anna marvelled that a man with such a limited vocabulary had ever found fame on such a scale.

As he caught sight of her he unleashed a tirade liberally laced with expletives. Henry leapt to his feet in protest. 'Now, just a minute, Max.' He raised his voice. 'That's not on. Absolutely out of order.'

Max ignored him. 'Stay out of this,' he screamed, jabbing a finger at Henry. 'Are you listening to me?' He turned on Anna again, but she had wriggled past him and was already heading for the stairs.

'Show's over, Max. Look,' she clapped her bag to one ear and a folder to the other as she walked backwards down the corridor, 'can't hear you any more.'

'Let me remind you,' Max yelled, at her retreating back, 'that without me this show would die on its feet and you'd be out on the fucking street. Let me further remind you,' he bawled, following her to the head of the stairs and leaning perilously into the stairwell, 'that I could fucking well have you sacked.'

Anna turned her face up at him and blew him a kiss. 'You know you'd miss me, Max. You know you love me whispering in your ear.'

'Whispering?' He went an odd shade of purple. 'You call ordering me around like the fucking SAS *whispering*?'

Anna halted. Everyone waited for her to retaliate. Briefly she considered where it would lead and then, since none of the options open to her appealed, she shrugged and strode on to her office.

Later, she knew, there would be a bottle of champagne on her desk. After lunch Max would search her out and justify his behaviour by drawing her attention to his professionalism which, he would claim, demanded so much more of him than of anyone else. He would bend his head just a little to one side and say, 'Forgive?' with that hesitant, boyish smile and in the tone that made millions of women adore him and left Anna feeling queasy.

For Max the show was not about the emotional messes who paraded their untidy lives in front of the viewers each morning, it was about him. Especially him perched casually on a high stool at the end of the programme, delivering his lines about the quality of relationships, the importance of integrity, straight to camera. Written for him by Anna. Today when Anna had said that his line of questioning with a self-confessed wife-abuser sounded sympathetic and that he must stick to the script, he had ignored her for a further thirty seconds. Now he was convinced she had taken her revenge by cutting his closing address.

All of this Anna knew. She didn't care much about it. She wasn't sure she ever had. It was a job. That was all.

There wasn't much, these days, that she did care about, except her father and Oliver. All of it rolled around her and slid away. Which was odd because, when she thought about it, it was the future she had stopped contemplating and the past that preoccupied her.

Anna arrived at her office door and went in, realizing that Aggie had followed her and was muttering under her breath all the things she wanted to say to Max but had never summoned the courage to voice. 'I don't know why you don't just tell the stupid sod where to go,' she grumbled. 'He just doesn't read the brief. It's like watching a ventriloquist. Out of here,' she pointed to her mouth, 'and into here.' She tapped her ears.

'Or not,' Anna reminded her. 'Like today.'

'Honest to God, Anna,' Aggie shook her head disbelievingly, 'doesn't he get it? There are several million women watching him, and they don't want to hear a wife-beater getting a soft ride.'

'Tell Max, not me.' Anna glanced down a list of messages.

'Ag, be an angel and check with Charlie we've got hotels for all these people tonight. And if we haven't, check Henry hasn't nabbed one with you-know-who and get it back.'

Aggie rolled her eyes. 'The idea of bumping into him and bloody Melissa. Don't worry. Tess says his poor wife rang and left a message that he wasn't to forget parents' evening, so he's using up his lunch break. He's booked in at one.'

'In which case,' Anna kept a straight face, 'he'll be out by five past.'

Aggie giggled.

'What's that piece of paper you're waving at me?'

'Oh, sorry. About tomorrow. Good news. At least, I think it is. Tess says Freda – the one who was adopted at five and has now found her sister? – will come on and say . . . Let me see . . .' She consulted her notes. 'Ah, here it is. "I wasn't adopted. I was discarded. I was an inconvenience who got thrown out with all the other rubbish in their life."'

Anna looked up. 'Good Lord. What else?'

'Can't get Brenda Forsyth. Says her credibility as a leading psychologist is being damaged with all this soundbite therapy. Forgetting, of course, that we made her "leading" in the first place. And we've got a yes from Gordon, who's going to say he's never given up hope of finding his father and he's spent nearly ten grand in doing so and has just remortgaged his house so he can go to Australia and pick up a lead there.' Aggie put down the piece of paper. 'Why,' she demanded, 'doesn't he just phone or pay a detective? I think it's the search he's hung up on. Probably be a disaster when he finally gets to the old man and that's it, except we need to get Max to really wind up the rejected bit.'

Anna took the list from her. 'I suppose. On the other hand, not everyone feels rejected.'

'No, but they're not so interesting, are they?' Aggie objected.

Anna smiled. 'No, I'm not,' she teased.

7

'Oh, Lord. Sorry, Anna.' Aggie's hand flew to her mouth. 'Forgot. You know what I mean, though. You should be on this programme.'

'I'd need a brain transplant first. Tempting, though. Imagine what it would do to Max. He'd end up screaming, "And can you blame them for giving her away?" And anyway, I've had a great life. I just feel sorry for whoever was my real mother because she just couldn't keep me. So, as you said, boring. And now you'd better buck up, Ag.' Anna grabbed the nearest phone as she saw Max bearing down on her, and thrust a list into the other woman's hand. 'Give this to Henry,' she said, ignoring Max, who was now giving an elaborate performance of snubbing her. 'I've just got to call my father. He rang while we were in the studio.'

Aggie noticed the look on her face. 'Nothing wrong, is there?'

'Hope not.' Anna slid into a chair. 'But it's unusual for him to ring so early.'

'How is he?' Aggie asked.

'Okay-ish.' Anna frowned. 'He's been visiting an old friend in Scotland who lives near where he grew up. I expect it's helping. But it takes time – you don't get over someone like my mother in just eighteen months, believe me.'

'No, of course not,' Aggie said sympathetically. 'Poor man. Thank God he's got you.'

'Thank God, I've got him.' Anna meant it. Without her father her life might have been so different. She slotted a video into the machine in front of her then pressed her father's telephone number on the speed dial. While she waited for him to answer, she began to rewind Friday's programme, which the legal department said had libelled a cabinet minister and which she was convinced had not. She heard her father's familiar voice. 'Hi, Pa,' she greeted him. 'Hold on, just got to change this tape. Okay, I'm with you. Aggie,' she mouthed, holding out the tape. 'Urgento. Tell

8

Henry no way libel. Sorry, Dad,' she turned away as Aggie went off clutching the tape. 'Frantic? No, just the usual. Missed you. You're not to go off for that long again. Unless you take me too.'

Colin Minstrel had decided to break the news of his impending marriage to Anna over dinner at their usual meeting-place. The wedding would take place a month later, just before Christmas and eighteen months after the death of his first wife.

The small Italian restaurant just along the road from Anna's office was several blocks from where Colin got off the bus that had brought him from his home in Clapham to Waterloo. He made the same journey once a week and he liked to walk the last half-mile. If Anna had to go back to work afterwards he sometimes went on to a concert. Until about six months ago he hadn't been to one in years when Meryl had suggested it on a weekend she had spent in London. While Colin hadn't particularly cared for the performance, he had liked all the business of buying tickets, choosing where to sit, studying the programme. Meryl, he recalled, had dismissed the pianist as mediocre, which pleased him because he had thought so too.

On the way home he would walk along the Embankment, if the weather held, perhaps as far as Battersea Bridge, where he would wait for a bus to take him to Clapham. He had plenty of time: retirement had followed rapidly on the heels of widowhood and had left two chasms in his life that needed to be filled, which neither friends nor Anna could do for him.

Anna had become his companion, protector, house-keeper, but it wasn't what Colin wanted of her or of anyone. Sometimes when she had turned up three times in the same week, after only days in a new job, he could see the exhaustion on her face and wanted to say, 'I'm okay. Come again next week, not tomorrow. You have your life. You must live it. It's what your mother would have wanted,' but he had known she would take no notice. She was so kind, just like her mother, doing everything for everyone.

Now, of course, there was Oliver to be considered.

Colin quite liked Oliver. He had warmed to him on two accounts: first, he was encouraging Anna to move on from that ghastly programme, and second, he had encouraged Colin to retire, which had horrified Anna. 'Not now,' she had argued. 'Now, more than ever, you don't need another change. In a year or two when the pain's more bearable. Oliver doesn't understand. I do. I'm there too, remember?'

He could have continued to teach for a while longer but he did not want to. Colin had had enough of the boys who faced him each day in his maths classes. 'When I retire,' he had vowed, before Barbara's death, 'I shall never impart so much as the date to any child ever again. I shall take myself off around every historic castle in England then write a book. I shall be happy and become a total bore on the subject.'

'I'll come with you,' Anna had teased. 'I'll turn it into a series. You'll be famous.'

'No, thank you,' he replied promptly. 'You'd have that wretched mobile phone with you and cameramen telling me what to do and a soundman ordering me to speak properly. I shall make your mother come with me and she can take notes,' he had ended grandly.

Instead, Barbara had set off one morning to the parade of shops around the corner from the home they had shared for over thirty years and an hour later was pronounced dead of a heart complaint that no one had known she had. Colin could see that staying on at school would have filled his days. But no one seemed to understand how much pain it would have caused him. He and his wife had met at that school: Barbara had been running the headmaster's office when Colin arrived from Scotland to take up his first teaching job. It hadn't been long before she had been looking after him too: finding him a bedsitter, showing him where to shop, inviting him home to her own small flat for supper. Of course, he had fallen in love with her, and they had married three months after they met.

When they were told they could have Anna, Barbara had given up work. They first saw their daughter when she was just a few days old, lying in a crib, and Barbara had cried and said she could not believe that anyone, no matter what, could have given up such a beautiful child. And then she promptly thanked God for the Italian au pair who had been forced to part with her baby.

Small gusts of rain whipped at Colin's coat as, head down, he plunged towards the restaurant through the office workers surging either side of him. Punctually at seven he pushed open the outer door of Mancetti's. A low babble of voices met him, the scent of ciabatta wafted from the kitchen. Usually, at this point, Colin was assailed by a wave of comfort at its homeliness but tonight he felt mildly apprehensive. He smiled a greeting to the owner, who came towards him, hand extended, beaming with pleasure.

'Mr Minstrel,' Bernardo exclaimed, wiping his hands on the black apron wrapped around his ample waist. 'We missed you last week. How was your holiday? Come in, come in. Here, let me take your coat. As you can see we're busy tonight, but business is bad. I said to my wife just this morning that at this rate we'll have to sell up. But who would buy?' As Colin removed his coat and settled into a chair Bernardo grumbled about the state of the catering industry, which was not, he lowered his voice, what it once was. Colin enjoyed these exchanges, knowing that he was not expected to argue in favour of change – and change was what Bernardo would have to face up to if he was to survive – but to be a comrade in arms. They were both members of a generation who mourned falling standards. He ordered a beer, unfolded his paper and waited for Anna to join him.

'She's late,' Bernardo remarked setting down Colin's glass. 'Nothing changes, eh?'

Colin gave him a thoughtful look. 'Sometimes it does,' he said.

'You mean you live in hope?' Bernardo laughed heartily at his own joke.

'Something like that. Anyway,' Colin said, 'she says it's not that she's late, just that I'm always early.'

'Since when has punctual been early?' Bernardo threw up his hands. 'Take my business. They make reservations for eight o'clock and think that means nine and then wonder why I have to give the table away. I have to live.'

Of course she was late, Colin reflected, but she had warned him she might be. Each time the door opened he glanced up.

Twenty minutes after he had completed the sports section and read the concert reviews, which always demolished even the bravest performance, Anna arrived, full of smiles and hugs and apologies. He watched as she settled herself into the seat opposite, ordered mineral water and whipped her hair out of the band looped at the nape of her neck. 'That's better.' She grinned, massaging her shoulders.

'Tired?' he asked, as Bernardo brought her drink.

She shook her head. 'Just Max. As ever.'

'What was it today?' Colin asked sympathetically.

'Same as ever. Won't read the brief I give him, and when he gets it wrong he blames everyone else. I can only do so much from the gallery. Once he's on the studio floor he should know what he's meant to do – which he would if he read his notes. He shouldn't need me whispering into his earpiece. Which he ignores anyway. Ends up looking the prat he is. Ugh.'

'Oh dear.' Colin pulled the corners of his mouth down. 'I didn't watch this morning. Was it dreadful?'

'You missed nothing,' she assured him. 'Now, what was it that was so urgent? How was Scotland? It's lovely to see you, Dad.' She reached across the table and squeezed his hand.

Colin waited until Bernardo had moved away then told her that he was going to marry Meryl.

Chapter Two

Anna paused. 'I'm sorry, Dad? You're doing *what*?'

'Getting married,' he repeated steadily. 'I wanted you to know first. Well, obviously I did. I hope you'll be pleased. Although I'm sure you must have guessed.' Anna groped for her drink. 'We can spend Christmas together,' Colin pressed on. 'You know, all of us. One family instead of two.'

'Married?' She was unable to take her eyes off his face, searching it for a sign that this was just a joke. But even as she scanned the thick grey hair, the laughter lines fanning out from the blue eyes, she knew it wasn't. 'You're going to marry Meryl?'

'Of course Meryl,' her father said, with a hint of hurt in his voice. 'Who else have I been trailing home to see all these weeks?'

'But why? Why Meryl?'

'Oh, Anna.' He gave a deep sigh and laid the menu across the heavily patterned plate in front of him. He clasped his hands on top of it. 'I can see I'm doing this very badly.' He removed his glasses and rubbed the bridge of his nose. 'You must have guessed,' he said replacing them. 'No?' He looked faintly disbelieving as she shook her head.

'No, I didn't,' she replied, in a voice unlike her own. 'I didn't guess at all.' Her mind roved rapidly over the last few months, the two occasions when she had briefly met Meryl, the widow of Colin's best friend Giles Carlton. Small, neat, bustling Meryl Carlton lived in Scotland. She had grey hair cut into short wisps around her face, doll-like eyes and a dislike of inactivity that Colin personified. If there had been clues Anna had not seen them. 'When . . . when was all this – I mean, is it decided? Definitely?'

'Ah.' Bernardo swept up to the table. Anna stared at her father.

'You are here.' Bernardo beamed. 'Now you make up for keeping your father waiting by eating well, yes?'

'What?' Anna looked blankly at her menu. 'Oh, yes. Sorry. Just a salad. Dad?'

Colin folded the menu and handed it to Bernardo. 'The, er . . . the chicken. That's all. I'm sorry? Oh, yes. Vegetables, too.'

When Bernardo had bustled off Colin glanced at Anna and cleared his throat. 'Well, we were just standing there at the check-in yesterday afternoon and I said, 'This is silly. You're in Scotland and I'm in London and apart from being round the corner from Anna, what possible reason is there for me to stay in that empty house?'

Anna winced. He had changed, she could see that. He didn't look younger or happier, but, now that she looked closely at him, he had an air of well-being. As though he had just returned from a bracing holiday. He was clear-eyed, more purposeful. Clearly the change had come from inside. But it was too soon for marriage.

'Look, Dad,' she began carefully, leaning forward so that she would not be heard by the couple at the next table, 'are you sure that you, well, you know . . . ?'

Colin knew what she was thinking. 'No. I'm not off my trolley,' he said. 'I'm not that decrepit.' On the far side of the restaurant Anna could see Aggie engrossed in a conversation with her friend who worked in personnel and from whom no secret was safe. Henry was there too, staring morosely into a wine glass at a table by the door clearly praying that a bulging coat stand would camouflage Melissa's presence. If she could have guessed at what was coming she would not have chosen to meet her father in what amounted to the office canteen. She turned back to him, now and he tried to take her hand, but she lifted her glass and took a sip of water.

Colin's shoulders dropped. 'It's not the way it was with your mother. But it's every bit as good in a totally different way. I didn't think it would happen to me again. But . . .' he lifted his hands in a small, helpless gesture '. . . there you are. Smitten. We have no way of knowing when it's going to happen. I feel very blessed to have known it twice in my life.'

On a sensible, practical level Anna knew love could strike at any time, but now she felt neither sensible nor practical, only that her father was sixty-two and she did not want what was left of her peace of mind invaded by images of him with Meryl. She did not want to imagine her father involved in such intimacy with a virtual stranger. She could not have been more shocked if he had told her he had been unfaithful to her mother.

Suddenly she understood why all those people who pleaded to come on the show to unburden themselves to the dreadful Max Warner wanted to do it – why they wanted to scream abuse at the Other Woman, to unload the guilt of affairs, to rail at the injustices of fate. At that moment she felt like shouting herself, trying to talk him out of it. But as she studied her father's face, she knew she could not. His cautious statements were not negotiable. She gave it one last try anyway. 'Dad, please, it's none of my business – I mean, good God, how could it be at my age? And of course I'm pleased for you. But don't you think it's a bit sudden? After, you know,' she mumbled, 'Mum.'

He reached across the table and placed his hand over hers. This time she let him. 'I could never forget your mother,' he said. 'How could I? You must never, ever think that. And it *is* your business,' he said. 'You know it is. I wouldn't do anything that you didn't like, but you've never said you disliked Meryl—'

'I don't,' Anna broke in. 'Meryl's fine. I just don't know her.'

'No,' he conceded. 'You're right.' He sighed, squeezed her hand and let it go. 'I suppose it's because you've been busy – what with your job and poor Oliver wedged in between me and Max Warner. What odd men there are in your life.'

She smiled reluctantly. 'And,' he went on, 'I'm rather surprised myself. It just seemed sensible, the right thing to do. I've known Meryl since Giles and I were in our first year at Aberdeen.' He looked away. 'I was always fond of her. She's a good woman, Anna.'

Anna did not want to hear of Meryl's goodness. 'Dad, I'm sure she is,' she said abruptly. 'And you must do whatever you think is right. I just wasn't expecting this, that's all. Just let it sink in for a day or two, eh? Wow. Married. When? And where?'

'Middle of next month.' Relief flooded Colin's voice. 'A small church service. Just the family. Athol and Sheridan and their families. We thought it would be nice if you came up to Carrigh for a weekend first, to meet everyone before the day.'

Anna nodded mechanically. After Barbara had died, she remembered now, Meryl had sent flowers and an invitation for Colin to spend a week or two with her. And he had. They had gone walking in the hills around Carrigh, north of Perth, where Meryl had lived all her married life and only twenty miles from where Colin had been born. They had renewed friendships, revisited old haunts. They had talked about times they both remembered, happier times when Meryl had married Giles and Colin had come south to his first teaching job.

Of course Anna had been interested in his visits, but her own grief and shock at her mother's death had kept her from the realization that while she was still desperately missing Barbara, her father was moving on. While Anna had thought that this old friend and her family were helping distract him from the emptiness of his life without Barbara, the widowed Mrs Carlton had been intent on filling it.

They left soon after, neither having done justice to Bernardo's food. He had been especially reproachful of Anna who had eaten hardly anything.

'Meryl said you could fly up on the last shuttle from Heathrow on Friday,' her father told her, as they walked along the wet pavements towards the studios. Anna said she would get the midday flight on Saturday. She needed time to think.

Sitting at the front of the bus taking him back over the bridge to the south side of the river, Colin stared fixedly ahead. The roads were too familiar to be of interest and he had a lot to consider. Later he would call Meryl and tell her that he would be there on Thursday as planned and that work prevented Anna from joining them until after lunch on Saturday.

Anna was all the family Colin cared about, his and Barbara's only child. After they had been told that Barbara could not have children, it had taken them a year to decide on adoption. By the time she was seven, Anna also shared what little they knew of her birth-mother and, so that she grew up with no sense of having been rejected or any fanciful ideas about her parentage, they told her endlessly of how they had chosen her from all the other babies they could have had.

Anna, therefore, had always known that she had not been abandoned by the star of a travelling circus or a careless royal, but that she was the result of an ill-judged love affair between a teenage Italian au pair and an unknown man. One of her natural parents, Barbara and Colin told each other, had given Anna that restless energy, the self-deprecating sense of humour and that nose. In childhood, it had been too large for such a small face. The skinny little girl with the dark, serious eyes could never have been their natural child, but she was Barbara in every other way, resilient, strong and funny. And indeed Colin had loved them both. Anna had grown into an unusually striking, if not beautiful, young woman. By the time she was sixteen she towered over Barbara and could look Colin in the eye. Her nose looked strong rather than out of place, and when she smiled, heads turned.

Colin alighted from the bus at the end of his road. It had stopped raining, the air was damp and cold and for once he was anxious to be home. He began to walk quickly, turning away from the busy main road into the more dimly lit Granton Street, into which he and Barbara had moved when they brought Anna home at just a few weeks' old. At the time the house had seemed perfect if rather alarming when they looked at the monthly mortgage repayments. Now it had hardly changed, and the area was much the same, except for the butcher's, which was now a betting shop, and where there had once been a greengrocer there was now a mini-mart that hired videos and sold stamps and lottery tickets. It was owned by a pleasant man called Mr Viraswami, who liked to think that in the street among those he regarded as riff-raff there was a professional man like Mr Minstrel.

He was just starting to close up when Colin looked round the door. 'Ah, sorry to disturb,' Colin began, 'but is there time for me to . . . ?'

'Of course, Mr Minstrel.' Mr Viraswami ushered him in. 'Of course. Please. Take your time. I'll be a few minutes more. You're late tonight?'

'A little,' Colin agreed. 'Dinner in town with my daughter.'

'Ah.' Mr Viraswami nodded. He did not approve of *Max Meets* and was constantly rushing into the back room to remonstrate with his wife and daughters when he found them gathered round the set instead of sorting deliveries. Since they had also ignored his stricture that they should not wear jeans, he had little faith in his words being heeded. In Mr Minstrel he felt he had a kindred spirit. It was never quite clear to him why this was so, because Colin always met his references to the waywardness of young people with the response that they could be puzzling but that they had their own ways.

Out of respect for Colin's feelings Mr Viraswami never referred to Barbara's death but it was obvious to him that Colin was poorly served in the family department. He had just the one daughter, unmarried although she was at least thirty, and living alone – if just ten minutes away. What support was she to him? Should the same fate befall Mr Viraswami, he had numerous sons and daughters-in-law to tend his every need.

'Just some milk and a small loaf,' Colin said, placing them on the counter. 'And to say I'll be moving at the end of the month so I won't need my newspaper.'

Mr Viraswami looked dismayed. 'That is a shame,' he said, handing Colin his change. 'We'll miss you. Where are you going? To your daughter?'

Colin laughed and shook his head. 'No. I'm to be married and I'm going to live in Scotland. The house will be on the market tomorrow.'

'Married?' Mr Viraswami exclaimed, making a mental note to contact the estate agent first thing. His son could do with living nearer the shop. 'That is very good news. Very good. Your daughter will be pleased. You've been a very good father to her. She's done so well. Goodnight. Be sure to come and say goodbye.'

Mr Viraswami had taken over the shop when Anna was in her final term at university so he had no way of knowing that Colin felt he had played little part in his daughter's upbringing. Except to give her a good, loving home, the one he was going to now. And while Colin knew he loved Anna, he didn't really understand her. He had truly believed she would be pleased that he was to remarry. But clearly she was not. He paused, key in hand. No that wasn't right. She had been shocked not angry. But he had to move on. Only a few days before, he had made a solitary pilgrimage to Barbara's grave where in a private exchange he had sought her blessing. All he needed now was Anna's.

Oliver had been right. Anna needed a change, particularly from that job. Delving into the lives of people who were dysfunctional and exhibitionist was not Colin's idea of entertainment any more than it was Oliver Manners'. In Anna's present mood, he thought it wiser not to mention that Meryl had said the same thing.

Chapter Three

Later that night, in a crowded tube train Anna decided to be positive about her father and Meryl. She still thought he was making a huge mistake, but Oliver had said – and he was probably right, she sighed – that only her father could know that. The darkened windows reflected a jarring reflection of her face as the train rattled through the tunnel. Anna knew that her mother would have wanted him to be happy, but now she suddenly felt displaced in his affections. They roared into the station, and Anna hoisted her bag on to her shoulder, rummaging in it for her ticket.

When she walked in Oliver was opening a bottle of wine he had retrieved from the fridge. He was still in his suit, his tie loosened. Most people described him as glamorous, and he was, with his untidy blond hair and that Englishness that his background had ensured he would never lose. The moment she met him Anna had decided that she had rarely encountered anyone as handsome and could understand why a procession of left-wing political groups employed him to put the right spin on their public utterances. She had grown to love his private utterances too. And to depend on him. She had phoned him the minute she had left Colin after dinner.

'If he's wrong,' he said now, nuzzling her neck as she leaned against the kitchen table, 'he'll soon find out. And, besides, at their age it's much more likely to be companion-ship, nothing more passionate, so where's the disloyalty to your mother – which is what all this is about, isn't it?'

'No. Yes. I mean possibly,' she cried. 'How do I know? And he said smitten,' she reminded him. 'Smitten isn't a word normally associated with comfort, is it? And, Oliver, he *looked* smitten. There was a glow about him. That's it,' she said earnestly. 'He looked *pleased* with himself.'

'Well, I expect he was pleased.' Oliver sounded exasperated. 'Marriage isn't generally associated with misery. Well, not at first,' he added, with a grin. She didn't smile back. 'And anyway after all he's been through, and Meryl has been on her own for – how many years?'

'Ten,' Anna said. 'Two grown-up married sons. With kids,' she added, trying to remember all she could of the family that was now her father's.

'Well, there you are. I think it sounds perfectly okay. Anna, don't look like that. You said to me once that you hoped he'd marry again one day, so now he's going to. I do think he could have found a better way of telling you, though. But men of his generation are like that – a bit brisk where emotional stuff's concerned. My father's just the same.'

'But why's he got to do it so quickly?'

'Anna, you're being stupid.'

'I know, I know.' She groaned. 'It's just that he's lonely for my mother. And that's not fair on Meryl,' she added unconvincingly.

'That's Meryl's problem,' Oliver insisted, taking her wineglass from her and placing it with his on the draining-board. 'And it's not fair on me that you haven't made me feel at home and I've been here a good thirty minutes.'

'You *are* at home,' she objected, leaning against him. 'My home. And I *am* welcoming. Look,' she indicated the wine, 'and I've got the pizza-delivery number at my fingertips.' She flexed her fingers. 'See?' She was tired and the thought of a hot bath had sustained her all the way from the studio to Braverton Street. Even so, she felt a pang of guilt. Her father had said that poor Oliver was wedged in between him and Max. 'Sorry, sorry.' She rubbed her nose against

22

his chin. 'What a misery I am. I just haven't got over Mum. Sometimes I feel she's somewhere near by, and I can't handle it when I look round and of course she isn't there. Why doesn't he feel it?'

'Anna.' He gave her a gentle shake. 'Darling. Please just let it go. The wedding's in less than a month. I understand how you feel, you loved your mother, so did your dad, but he's got to move on. If you try to stop him, he might resent you for it. You might even resent yourself. Then you'd be impossible to live with. You're impossible now. I haven't seen you for three days . . . and you are doing unspeakably wonderful things to me in that shirt which I think would look better off.' He bent his head and kissed her tentatively, then more forcefully while he manoeuvred her on to the nearest horizontal surface – the table.

'You're right,' she agreed, helpfully pulling off his jacket. She just wished it were that simple. Instead she said, as solemnly as the moment would allow, 'I warn you, I've been in these clothes all day and I'm feeling very grubby.'

'What a coincidence,' he muttered thickly into her neck. 'So am I.'

On a good day, Anna usually reached her house in Braverton Street around eight, after a ten-minute walk from the tube. She had lived alone for the past eight years, three in this terraced house, in a road that contained a mix of aspiring young executives and ethnic minorities. The area was an eclectic jumble of affluent squares, worn-out streets and high-rise flats, not far from where she had grown up, and was what Oliver called real. Everything about Anna struck Oliver as real and everything about him had saved her. It was his stability, his decisiveness, that had given a shape to her life in the first awful months after her mother's death.

Oliver had been brought up in a Georgian rectory in Somerset, educated at Charterhouse and Cambridge and now lived in a smart block in St John's Wood, but he preferred Anna's terraced house in Clapham to his own conventional surroundings.

Anna had bought the house after a year of paying an exorbitant rent for a flat she had shared with Carrie Hunt until Carrie had gone to live with the father of her baby, Euan. Anna's mother had encouraged her to buy it, largely because it was less than twenty minutes away from her, and had asked a neighbour's son, who was looking for work, to paint the dingy grey outside white and the inside walls lemon. There were only two rooms downstairs and a tiny kitchen, so Anna had asked him to find someone to knock through the small dark room at the back to make a kitchen she could live in.

Books, paintings and cushions crowded every corner in a riot of colour but plans for anything more substantial had crumbled under the size of the mortgage repayments. But Barbara had been in her element, ferreting out bargains to furnish the house. Once it had been eight almost matching chairs for the kitchen, then a chance meeting in a local furniture shop had led to an odd-coloured second-hand blue carpet being laid for nothing. Now a deep blue sofa filled the window recess, flanked on either side by two round tables crammed with pictures of Anna's friends clustered round a central photograph of her mother. Anna loved that picture: Barbara had been engrossed in a book until Anna had called her then clicked the camera.

Behind the sofa, a large sash window was framed with green and blue curtains pulled back on cords to reveal window-boxes dripping with red geraniums. It looked, her mother had said, marvelling at Anna's fearlessness with colour, like a house that should be sitting in the sun, not wasted on a road like Braverton Street.

While her mother made curtains and filled the freezer, Anna embarked on restoring the little roof garden. It was the main reason why she had bought the house, and had been cleaved out of the space left when an attic room had been added at the top of the house. It overlooked what only the very generous called an interesting view. A high-rise block of flats could be seen to the immediate east, and to the west an uneven skyline of factory roofs, garages and a derelict park identified by a valiant but uninspiring cluster of trees. Anna didn't care: its pink-washed walls, the deep Mediterranean blue of the iron railings that surrounded it, the terracotta pots of all sizes crammed with hardy plants were the result of two weekends of her own hard work. It was where she did her best thinking. It also represented the only – minor – source of contention between her and Oliver: he felt it needed toning down with cream walls, black railings and a couple of director's chairs, rather than the rickety pair Anna had put there.

'But I've got Italian blood in my veins.' She laughed at him.

'Of course.' He looked carefully at her. 'I keep forgetting because you don't have a temperament at all, do you?'

'Yes, I do,' she said indignantly. 'And I'll demonstrate it if you mention tasteful white walls and black railings again.'

But otherwise Oliver loved everything about her, apart from her neighbour, Eamonn Bingham, who lived next door and worked tirelessly for the homeless. In Oliver's view he had an overpowering and quite irrational sense of social injustice. In his turn Eamonn felt Oliver's socialist leanings were more fashionable than fundamental. And then there was Dottie. Dorothy Fellowes lived next door on the other side and alarmed Oliver with her reliance on Anna. At eighty-odd she still defiantly proclaimed her independence to a series of exasperated social workers who retreated down her path composing paeans to their own forbearance in the face of her stubbornness in the reports they were obliged to write. Oliver thought Dottie should be in a home. Only Carrie, who had now been abandoned by the man she had thought she would love for ever, was regarded by Oliver as a delight, except when she wanted Anna to babysit Euan or have him to stay overnight. In this he had an ally in

Euan who thought poorly of being asked to sleep anywhere other than his godmother's bed.

Oliver and Anna had met when one of Oliver's clients, an MP with much to say about single working mothers, had – to Oliver's horror – accepted Anna's invitation to appear on *Max Meets* to confront the warring band of women who wanted to put an end to his career. Since he had recently revealed that he thought them the authors of their own misfortune, responsible for the breakdown of family life and the rise in juvenile crime, this was hardly surprising.

On that occasion Oliver had stuck valiantly by his client's side, ready to reverse any of his more insensitive comments, but found as the morning progressed that his eye strayed almost hypnotically to the programme's producer, white shirt tucked loosely into khaki combat trousers, loafers and her astonishing mane of hair pulled into the nape of her neck into which he wanted to sink his teeth. He could not recall that she had once raised her voice more than was necessary. He thought the control she exerted over the whole production was the sexiest thing he had ever witnessed. He thought he might be in love.

The next day he had phoned her and asked if he could take her to lunch. A month later he had parted from his long-term girlfriend, Rachel, and launched himself into making sure that Anna could not do without him. And she couldn't. His purposeful approach to life, the way he organized his clients and understood just how hard her job was, drew her to him at a time when any decision beyond what to wear each day seemed overwhelming.

Oliver liked her friends and his friends liked her, except perhaps Rachel, who had every reason not to. Oliver still had lunch with Rachel, and Anna wasn't sure she liked it, but of course they worked together. Even so.

More of a problem, but one she felt was Oliver's to resolve, were his parents. Or, at least, his mother, Christina. She had welcomed Anna warmly but was clearly nervous about her. *Max Meets* was bad enough but Oliver had swapped Rachel, whose pedigree embraced a diplomat for a father and a mother who was the younger daughter of an earl, for Anna, the adopted child of a schoolmaster from South London.

When Anna turned into Braverton Street she had been thinking about Oliver possibly having lunch with Rachel while Anna was in Carrigh over the weekend. If she had said don't, which Anna sometimes suspected he wanted her to do, she knew he would not. But she didn't ask because it was not in her nature to ask for anything.

Today had run relatively smoothly because Max had been in high spirits about going to New York, and the chief guest on the programme, Freda, who had been adopted at birth, had, as promised, complained loudly that she had not been given away. Chucked away, she had cried, like an old shoe. With no evidence that the nice couple who brought her up had mistreated her, she stuck rigidly to her view that as a result she had had a rotten life. '*Emo-shunally,*' she thumped her chest with a clenched fist, 'I've been damaged, know what I mean?'

Anna felt Freda had been more fortunate than damaged, and much preferred Gordon. 'I want to know where I come from,' he said simply. 'It's got nothing to do with my mum and dad – the ones who adopted me – it's to do with wanting to look at a family album and see my nose, my eyes. Now, take my dad. He loves sailing and I can't stand it. You could say that might happen in any family, and you're right, but my mum says to him, "Oh, you're so like your father. There'd have to be a hurricane to get him off the river." See? Whatever I do, no one can tell me where I got it from, except my real mother. Is that so hard to understand?'

Up in the control room Anna's eyes were fixed on him. 'No,' she said to herself. 'Not hard at all.'

Now she was glad to be almost home. Tomorrow she would fly up to Carrigh. The sight of the elderly woman, leaning heavily on a frame with one hand, made her quicken her step. Under Dottie's other arm was her skinny cat, Mister, legs dangling untidily as he mewed for contact with the floor. He was almost blind but this did nothing to deter him from making a bid for freedom if Dottie left the door open too long.

Anna groaned. If Mister got away, it behoved her or Eamonn to spend the next hour trying to retrieve him. And it was much too cold for Dottie to be standing outside but she always did if Anna was bringing her shopping for her. Eamonn had offered to help, but Dottie had spurned him: Eamonn got all the wrong things, she complained, butter when she'd said marge, sardines instead of pilchards. Hopeless, he was. How he ever found homes for the homeless when he couldn't find his way round her shopping list was beyond her. Dottie knew that Anna would simply bring her shopping and listen while she roundly abused the manager of the supermarket she refused to set foot in. Afterwards she would go to her own home next door and not bother her, until Dottie summoned her with an imperious thud on the adjoining wall.

'Can't find a damn thing in there,' Dottie had grumbled, when Anna had first offered to collect her shopping, 'and when I do I can't reach it. No, you do it, dear. Taller than me, you are. Give me the wrong change, he did. Waved a five-pound note at me saying that's what I'd given that cheeky little minx at the checkout. I might be slow but I'm not stupid. Course it was a tenner. She pocketed it. No, you go, dear. Much better.' Dottie had been widowed after the war and had never remarried. Years of independence had given her a fighting spirit that accounted for her survival and insistence on living alone. At first when Anna had moved next door she had been alarmed at Dottie's fragile strength but even more wary of her temper. Once upon a time Dottie's hair had been a fiery red, which had suited her in every possible way, and there were still traces of it in her strange, shaggy eyebrows. 'Fierce, I was.' She cackled delightedly. 'Still can be. You just watch.'

'When one of us notices she's started to sleep downstairs,' Anna suggested to Eamonn, when they had become friendly enough to discuss their joint neighbour's welfare, 'or that she hasn't washed up her cup, we'll do something about it.'

Dottie's only son, who lived on the other side of London, showed up perhaps twice in a good year and each time he left in a hurry. Once he had distressed Dottie so much by urging her to go into a home that when he'd gone Anna and Eamonn, on the way back from Carrie's, had found her standing in great agitation in the street. They had made her tea, found Mister, who had made his escape, and assured her that there was no way her son would be allowed to move her while they were around.

The only person who felt her son might have a point, even if it was self-interest, was Oliver.

'Is everything all right, dear?' Dottie asked, as Anna reached her. 'You look tired. That job getting you down? Freaks, aren't they?' She adored *Max Meets*.

'None bigger than Max,' Anna muttered. 'Now, I've got you two small sliced white, Dottie,' she explained, putting the fresh bread into the tiny bread-bin beside the sink. 'They didn't have any large. I didn't think you'd want ciabatta. Is that okay?'

'Honest, I don't know,' Dottie grumbled, leaning heavily on her frame as she followed Anna around, watching her deftly putting things in the right cupboards. 'Bloody foreign bread. No large indeed. Chibbawhat? Well, really,' she mumbled on, enjoying the mild annoyance which, in the end, was largely what kept her going.

It had been Meryl who had suggested a wedding before Christmas, Meryl who had opted for a family-only weekend a fortnight before the wedding so they could all get to know each other. It had been Meryl too who had quietly told Anna, when her father had driven to the village to collect some last-minute shopping, that he would not be retiring, after all.

'But he has.' Anna smiled, puzzled. 'He wants to do what he's always said he would do once he left teaching. Roam around historic castles, picnic lunches, long walks. He's had enough of grubby schoolboys.'

'Well, of course he can still find time for that.' Meryl's colour was just fractionally heightened. 'He'll only be working part-time, coaching for exams, that kind of thing. It's not good for a man like Colin to give up too soon.'

'He hasn't given up,' Anna protested. 'You don't know Dad. He truly loathed those last few years before Mum died. All those ambitious parents with unambitious little boys blaming him when they didn't get into Westminster or Harrow. Heavens,' she rolled her eyes in mock horror, 'don't suggest teaching to him.'

'Well, we'll see,' Meryl replied briskly. 'Now, I'm sure you want a rest before you change for dinner. Rose and Gordon are meeting us at the restaurant.'

'Rose and Gordon?' Anna asked politely, as Meryl led the way upstairs.

'Gordon Picard,' Meryl explained. 'He was in your father's year at Aberdeen. Now married to Rose, of course, not Janet. I must remind Colin in case he forgets. Here we are. Now, have I remembered everything?' Meryl cast a quick glance around the low-ceilinged room with its brown carpet and virtuous single bed covered with a pale yellow counterpane that matched the curtains.

'This is lovely,' Anna said. 'I'm sure you haven't forgotten a thing.'

'Then I'll leave you. Don't rush. It doesn't matter if we're a few minutes late. Gordon and Rose know we have a guest for the weekend.'

Anna blinked. 'Of course,' she said.

Chapter Four

On Sunday seven adults and five children, including Anna and her father, were squeezed round the rosewood table in Meryl Carlton's high-ceilinged dining room. With her family around her and lunch almost over, Meryl consulted a list clipped into a black-leather organizer. From where she was sitting, Anna could read the word 'Arrangements' typed across the top.

Meryl had said that this was to be a discussion but it sounded more like a briefing. Meryl had seen to it all. Anna wasn't surprised: in the short time she had been in Carrigh, dining the previous night with her father's old university friends, in church that morning where the banns had been read for the first time, it had not taken her long to recognize the major-general in Meryl. At first Anna had wondered if widowhood had created the spaces in her life that could only be filled with unremitting activity, but it rapidly became clear that, long before that unhappy event, Meryl had laid siege to Carrigh.

Each social event on the Carrigh calendar was addressed from her position as chair of the Carrigh Village Committee with the same vigorous spirit she had brought to her brief career in local government. Sheridan's arrival, a year after her marriage, had altered her horizons and ambitions but not her approach, so the spring fair, the summer picnic, the carol concert, which preceded the Carrigh Parish Council dinner, had become Meryl's triumphs and local government's loss. She also made her own bread.

The wedding would take place midweek, a small ceremony in the village church for just close family and friends, she announced, while Colin nodded agreement. It would be followed by a lunch in the Bracken Burn hotel, which was the last building at the edge of the village before the road wound on and up into the hills towards the west coast. 'So difficult to accommodate everyone's needs,' Meryl did not so much explain as report, 'but John – that's my cousin – will be away after that and can't make a weekend so I've compromised. Midweek to suit him, and an early lunch to suit Anna so that she will only have to take one day away from her desk. Now, what else?' She frowned down at her list while glasses were refilled, dishes passed around, small children distracted or rebuked as the lunch dragged into its second hour.

Anna gazed curiously at her. Consultation was a word that clearly did not trouble her soon-to-be step-mother. If it had, surely she would have discovered that religion and the Church were low on her father's list of priorities, yet here he was being led meekly to the altar. And what of her? If such a thought had occurred to Meryl, which it clearly hadn't, a phone call would have elicited the information that midweek for Anna was as much of a nightmare as the weekend for Cousin John.

Anna gave in. After twenty-four hours in Meryl's company, she felt unequal to opposing anything she arranged. She would have to square it with Henry that his meticulously organized schedule was going to suffer a hiccup. Somehow she'd manage it, but now she just wanted to go home. There was nothing of her father in this house: but then, he had wanted little of his old life – a few photographs, his books, some paintings, which Meryl said needed to be thought about so that they would blend with those that had hung on her walls for thirty years. The furniture had been sold except for Barbara's favourite chair, which was now in Anna's spare room. The sale of the house had paid off the mortgage and the rest was being invested in a small extension to Meryl's house, a conservatory, because Meryl had always felt it was what the house needed, with its north-facing garden. Also there was to be a small study for Colin, where the pupils Meryl was lining up for him would be coached for schools beyond their grasp.

Anna's mother seemed to be a closed chapter in Colin's life. It was as though she had never existed. But Anna knew on another level that that wasn't entirely true. If someone had just mentioned her name, acknowledged her, she would have willingly found that level. But they didn't, so she didn't.

'Now,' Meryl said, unscrewing a fat black fountain pen rimmed with gold and fitting the cap on the end while she scrutinized the list. 'Guests. All of us,' she began to make rapid little ticks against names, 'of course. John and Donald – my other cousin,' she explained for Anna's benefit, 'their wives and my nephews and nieces. Four of them. And we'll have to include Beattie. She lives with John and Maggie. My aunt,' she said to Anna, who nodded politely. 'Very infirm, but she'll be hurt if she's not sitting right there in the front pew. Dreadful, isn't she, boys?'

Colin had invited his cousin James and his wife, last seen by Anna, and for only the third time in her life, at Barbara's funeral. James was to be best man. There would also be the dozen friends who formed Meryl's immediate social circle. No one else. The few friends and colleagues Colin had mustered in his previously quiet life could not be expected to make the journey so far north. Oliver would be in Paris.

Meryl said they would not be going away: Christmas was too close. She and Colin would be going to Athol's for the day so that the children could spend Christmas in their own – new – home, of which Anna had already heard a great deal. 'You too, Anna,' Meryl said, 'if you can. I know that job of yours is very demanding. But, of course,' she added, with an emphasis not lost on Anna, 'you and Oliver will have made your own plans. You mustn't feel pressured by any of this. Your father is going to be well cared for from now on.'

Colin bestowed a beaming smile on his betrothed.

'How kind.' Anna sipped her wine, gripping the stem of the glass. She said deliberately, 'My own problem, Meryl, is that as I hadn't expected Dad's news, I assumed he would be at – home.' She dabbed at her mouth with one of the stiff pink napkins. 'And, of course,' she went on calmly, 'I'll have to let Oliver's mother know that you won't be there on Boxing Day. If you remember,' she turned to her father, 'you told Oliver you'd enjoy a long walk after all that eating on Christmas Day, so I said yes. I'll just have to see . . .' She trailed off, waving her fork in mute explanation. 'You know? Explain.'

She caught her father's agonized glance. The others had stopped speaking. Meryl's gaze held Colin's for just a brief moment. But it was enough, Anna could see that. Her father was going to underline the fact that the decision had been made, that this was the way things were going to be.

He didn't fail her. 'The children, you see,' Colin said quickly. She could not mistake the note of pleading in his voice. 'Anna understands, don't you, dear? So much easier with all their things around them.'

Anna couldn't bear it. 'Of course.' She caved in. 'Meryl, do you mind if I let you know? Is that all right with you, Dad? I have to talk to Oliver and, of course, Carrie. My best friend,' she explained. They were all looking at her, waiting. 'She's spent the last couple of Christmases with us, hasn't she, Dad? Since she had her little boy, Euan.' She knew she was rambling. They wanted to get on with their lives, not get bogged down in hers. 'My godson.'

'Of course, of course,' Colin said anxiously. 'Although it would be so much nicer for – for all of us, if you managed to get up here. But I do understand. Now, Sheridan, let me fill that glass. Athol?'

Under the guise of admiring the view through the long windows that led to the garden and beyond, Anna glanced furtively at the fireplace that filled the centre of one wall with only an elaborately heavy clock to adorn it. Like the room, it was a handsome piece. Trailing carved claws stretched out on each side and inlaid porcelain panels curved around the face, which depicted lovers in some eighteenth-century idyll entwined on wooden benches while champagne-coloured retrievers slumbered at their feet. Her gaze shifted to the heavy walnut sideboard that filled the opposite end of the room behind Meryl's place at the foot of the table. There were just three silver-framed photographs placed at exact intervals along its highly polished surface. Meryl's wedding to Giles was supported on either side by equally traditional wedding photographs of her two sons, married for nine and six years respectively.

The likeness between the sons and their father was uncanny. They stared back from their photographs kilted and smiling, their brides looking slimmer and jollier than the two women now seated at the table. Their children had all inherited, to varying degrees, the sturdy build of their paternal grandfather.

Anna's eyes strayed back to the clock. Surely more than ten minutes had gone since she last looked?

'It's wonderful, isn't it?' said Fenella, the younger of Meryl's daughters-in-law. She had followed Anna's glance. 'It's been in Athol's family for generations,' she explained. 'Athol, of course, has inherited his father's love of fine art and we think Fiona – fork, please, Fee,' she admonished the small girl seated beside Anna, who was picking peas off her plate between her thumb and forefinger, '– we think Fee has that little streak in her too.'

'Have you really, Fee?' Anna turned her attention to the child. 'I can't draw for toffee.' She wasn't expecting a reply. She had given up on Fee out of compassion: the child had stared fixedly at her plate throughout the meal, resisting all Anna's attempts to befriend her.

'Poor Fee,' Anna had said, as they sat down. 'Having to talk to a boring grown-up.'

'Nonsense,' Fenella contradicted crisply. 'She was asked and said she'd like to.'

'Well, that was kind of you, Fee,' Anna said, sounding suitably grateful. 'I was feeling a bit shy too.'

Fiona's cheeks burned. She shot Anna an embarrassed smile then quickly looked away again. Under cover of the table, Anna gave her hand a squeeze.

At Anna's other side sat Sheridan, the elder of Meryl's sons, who worked for the Land Registry in Edinburgh. Meryl's younger son, Athol, had recently been appointed head of a small village school, twenty miles the other side of Carrigh. The elder couple did little to help the conversation, although Sheridan answered Anna's questions with a good-natured laziness but asked none in return. His wife, Primrose, looked as though she was battling with sleep. But after an hour, Anna would not have cared if she never encountered Athol and his wife again. He was shorter than his brother but in every other way like him, from his cable-knit sweater over a checked shirt to his thick shock of hair and rimless glasses. Athol's decided views on education collided with Fenella's thoughts on her three children and the house they were buying on a new estate with a state-of-the-art waste-disposal system. Lack of parental co-operation jostled with patio barbecues, the inappropriate pastimes of the average seven-year-old with the merits of a guest bedroom with its own *en suite* shower. The entire meal was punctuated with injunctions from both parents to their small children on social graces beyond their grasp, designed more, Anna suspected, to cast them in a heroic light as parents than as an example to their offspring.

Fenella's face was devoid of makeup except for rose-pink lipstick that exactly matched the silk shirt tucked into the black wool trousers. Unlike her children, who had the Carlton reddish blonde hair, Fenella's was straight and brown, competently cut to frame her plump face. She was unremittingly anxious. Her irritation with her more languorous sister-in-law was plain in the gently complaining tone with which she addressed her.

Primrose largely ignored her. She was square-jawed and had allowed her straggling pale blonde hair to please itself. She wore a high-necked marigold sweater that did not quite cover her ample bottom, which was encased in black leggings tucked into short boots. She yawned sporadically and exerted no influence over her own two children who were, on the whole, reasonably well behaved.

They were all enclosed in their own world, too absorbed in their lives to feel any need to be part of anyone else's family. Ten of them against two of us, Anna thought ruefully.

Meryl sat at the opposite end of the table to Anna's father. Clearly she had lost no time in installing him as head of her house. Three more weeks and Meryl Carlton would be Mrs Minstrel. So what did it matter?

Bone china was massed on the highly polished surface. Sprays of winter jasmine and heather from the garden were arranged in slender silver vases and placed equidistant from each end of the table, whose leaves had been extended to encompass the group seated around it. A cut-glass bowl filled with enough fruit to rival Carmen Miranda's hat formed a centrepiece directly under a pear-drop chandelier, which caught the glow of the red wine in the narrow crystal glasses beside each plate.

Fenella's youngest child, Corin, who had just had his second birthday, had a plastic beaker with a lid which he waved at random at his mouth. From time to time he sucked at it noisily, and screamed delightedly when he banged it on the table and dark droplets of Ribena spurted across the surface. 'Corin,' Fenella scolded, mopping up each successive puddle. 'You're not a baby. *Corin*. What will Auntie Anna think?' Anna decided that Fenella was far more tiresome than her son.

It was not that the Carltons were unwelcoming, it was just that they talked constantly of people she had never heard of and in whom she had no interest. Eventually she remained silent, just smiling politely until she thought the muscles in her mouth would give out. She didn't blame them. Why should they care about her? She had been foisted on them, not sought out. She didn't mind that Fenella and Primrose had never seen *Max Meets* or that Fenella claimed she never watched daytime television. 'Not that I find anything wrong with it,' she added hastily, remembering it was Anna's livelihood, 'I just never seem to find the time, what with the children and moving house, do I, Prim?' She looked encouragingly at her sister-in-law for her agreement.

'What?'

'Daytime television, Prim,' Fenella repeated. 'I don't have time, do I?'

'Well, you like the cookery programmes,' Primrose pointed out. 'You watch those. Mad about cooking, she is,' she added, as an aside to Anna.

'Oh, but that was only when Fee had that awful virus.' Fenella glared at the indifferent Primrose and turned back to Anna. 'Just wait till you have three under-sevens, all throwing up at the same time.'

'Why wait?' Primrose interjected, yawning. 'Have mine.'

'Sounds grim,' Anna said quickly. 'I really don't know how you managed.'

'Oh, one does,' Fenella said. 'Fee, what is your fork for?'

'Oh, let her use a spoon,' said Primrose, 'or she'll be here till supper. Shona was five before she could hold a pencil, let alone a fork. And Alistair wasn't dry at night until he was almost three. Lazy little blighters.' She stretched out her hand for her wine. 'Takes after me, of course. Not Sherry.' Alistair chose that moment to slither off his chair and began to whimper when he couldn't get back up. Primrose gazed with mild boredom at the grizzling child. 'Honestly, Al,' she protested, 'do you want Grandpa to think you're still a baby?'

38

Grandpa? Anna glanced at him and then at Meryl, who gave her a bright smile as she rose from her chair.

'Of course he isn't.' Meryl scooped Alistair gently back into his. 'There,' she smiled, ruffling his hair, 'Alistair's a big boy. He's going to play football for Scotland when he grows up, aren't you, Al?'

'Yes.' The little boy nodded vigorously. 'And Nanna's going to come and watch every game and give me ten pence for every goal I score and I'm going to score hundreds,' he announced, wriggling his bottom more comfortably on the seat.

'Just the winning goal will be fine,' Meryl assured him. 'Now, Anna,' she resumed her seat and consulted the clock, 'I don't want to hurry you, but we'll have to think about coffee. Your plane,' she reminded her.

'You must come and stay with us,' Fenella said. 'When we move, I mean. We'll have a guest suite then, so it won't be any trouble.'

Meryl glanced at Anna and their eyes met. 'Lovely idea, Fenella,' Meryl said, 'but we mustn't monopolize Anna's time. You know how busy she is. And we'll see her in three weeks at the wedding.'

They were her father's family now. Anna's heart wrenched for her dead mother.

'Is Grandpa your grandpa too?' Fiona asked suddenly. She slid right off her chair and stood on one leg holding Anna's shoulder for support while she rose up and down on her toes. Anna smiled down at her, delighted to encourage this new burst of confidence. 'No,' she said. 'He's my daddy. Like your daddy is yours.'

'Mummy said Grandpa wasn't your daddy.'

'Heavens,' Fenella almost screamed. 'Is that the time? These children need a walk. Athol?'

Hours later Anna let herself into her darkened house. Suddenly she couldn't face being on her own, but Oliver was not back from his meeting in Birmingham. There were several messages on her machine, all of which she ignored except the one from Carrie. 'Come now,' Carrie urged in a whisper. 'I walked him round Battersea Park for two hours and he's comatose.'

Carrie's flat was in a mansion block in Battersea. Anna pressed the time switch and took the stairs two at a time, knowing that the light would last only as long as it took her to get to the second floor. Euan's buggy was folded in the hallway outside Carrie's door.

As she gave her usual signal, Anna thought – and not for the first time – that Carrie was truly remarkable. She left at seven each morning to take Euan to the childminder, then spent the day in that boring law office, unable to ask for promotion because the hours would not fit in with the childminder. When she got home, she couldn't relax until she had bathed, fed him and embarked on the nightly challenge of getting him to bed.

She answered the door in a pair of oversized pyjamas, which she had taken to wearing so that Euan would assume that she, too, was going to bed. However, the ploy had been rumbled. Her fair hair was pulled back into a pony-tail, she looked tired and she was far too thin. Anna's eyes travelled down Carrie's leg to Euan, who was gripping it with a fierce, proprietorial air, a plastic space-fighter in his other hand. At the sight of Anna he let go of his mother and rammed the toy into Anna's knee for her to inspect. 'You vile child,' Anna yelped, scooping him up. 'Why aren't you in bed?'

'Bed bad,' he pronounced. 'Bed smack.'

Anna growled at him. Encouraged, Euan repeated his joke. 'Bed gone.'

'Really?' she panted, dropping into the sofa, Euan on top of her. 'So how's Father Christmas going to know where to leave your presents?' Unimpressed, Euan wriggled on to the floor and began to take the spacecraft apart.

'Bad, eh?' Carrie asked, handing her a drink.

'Uh-huh. Dad belongs there and I don't. That's it.'

Carrie settled into a corner of the sofa, handed Euan a drink and Anna a glass of wine, and listened to Anna's description of her day. '. . . and not once,' Anna finished, 'did they ask about my mother. It was as though she'd never existed. They're just sweeping Dad up and me out.'

'Surely not?'

'Not in so many words. But think about it. She wants to marry Dad, not gain a daughter. She talks as though no one has ever cared about him, or has any say in the matter of their marriage.'

'You mean, you?' Carrie said.

'Yes, me. Who else is there? And I've never asked to be part of their family but I resent being deprived of my own. Sorry, does that sound ghastly?'

'Yes,' Carrie agreed amiably. 'And confused. But, then, you are a ghastly person, which is why you're my best friend. Tell me something. Just mild interest, nothing more, have you ever thought any more of tracking down your real mother?'

Anna groaned. 'You sound like Oliver's parents. When they're not forgetting and calling me Rachel. Bloody Rachel with her perfect pedigree. You know where you are with a diplomat's daughter with two columns of credentials in *Burke's* to let you sleep easy, but me? You can see it written all over her. What if Anna's real mother was on the game? What if the bloke who knocked her up was a Sicilian bandit? Drugs, sex . . . oh, my.' Anna rolled her eyes.

Carrie leaned forward, peering hopefully at Euan to see if he was showing signs of collapse. 'Did you ever find out anything else,' she asked, 'except teenage unmarried mother?'

Anna shook her head. Once, when they had been at university, she had made a tentative attempt to discover how easy or difficult it would be to find out about her parents. When she had told Barbara the flash of alarm in her mother's eyes had stopped her. But now Anna remembered the file. They had shown it to her, with its three pieces of paper. Sometimes, the woman said kindly, the birth-mother leaves a letter in the hope that one day her child might read it and know why she had to part with them, to forgive, to understand. Anna had picked up the papers, details of her birth certificate, the letter authorizing her adoption from the nursing home, and the letter saying that Colin and Barbara Minstrel had been passed fit to adopt. 'I don't need one,' Anna had said quickly, before the woman could tell her all the reasons why there was no such letter for her. 'I know all I need to know.'

Now she said to Carrie, 'Apart from being Italian? No. She had no money, poor cow. That much was obvious. Au pair living over here. But,' she tried to look virtuous, 'I have it on the reliable authority of my mother, who was assured by the good sisters at the maternity home, that my real mother was not of the criminal classes. Oh, I don't know,' she sighed, as she wiped Euan's face with the flannel Carrie passed to her. 'Of course I've thought about it, but today I've had a taste of trying to be part of what's meant to be my own family. And, besides, how do I know she'd even want to see me? Anyway, enough of that . . . Now, my friend,' she swung Euan over her shoulder, 'you have a choice. Bed or bed. Which is it to be?'

When she got home, Oliver was waiting for her. 'I don't like it when you're not here.' He kissed her. 'I want to come home to you.' He was feeling very energized after a successful business dinner and suggested solicitously that what she needed was a hot bath and bed. She kissed him and said he was a dear, but she could have done without him bearing a glass of wine into the bathroom just as she was wrapping herself in a towel. But neither could she disappoint him.

'Oli-ver,' she wailed, as he pulled her determinedly towards the bedroom, the towel falling behind her, the wine spilling. 'Don't you ever get tired?'

'Not of this,' he muttered. 'Nor of you.'

Anna woke at two then again at four. The second time, she turned her head and looked at his face, tousled blond hair, mouth slightly open. How unfair, she thought, that he should have a better profile than her. She reached up and ran her finger lightly down his nose. Oliver didn't stir. She was so lucky to have him. Gently she eased away his arm, which was lying heavily across her stomach, and closed her eyes. What was it her mother had said? 'It's not where you come from, it's where you're going that counts.' She could see Barbara removing her glasses, looking up from her book, grey streaking the once copper-coloured hair, her careless regard for fashion, which saw her pulling one of her husband's checked shirts over a skirt that wrapped itself around her ankles. So right. So very right. Anna would know when the time for change came. It just hadn't come yet. She sighed as sleep claimed her.

The wedding passed off uneventfully, which was not surprising after all Meryl's planning, and Anna spent Christmas with Carrie and Euan, having claimed reasonably truthfully to her father that she couldn't risk not getting a flight back on Boxing Day. He had sounded disappointed but Meryl was practical, and they made her promise to see them just as soon as the New Year allowed. Eamonn came round, bringing his friend Paul who was, like most of Eamonn's friends, recovering from a life on the streets and now had a job and a flat. But no family. Oliver had tried to persuade her to spend the day with his family, but another extended gathering of relatives would have been too much for her. Instead they agreed to devote Boxing Day to each other. Families, she decided, going through the wedding photographs her father had sent, were not what she was good at.

It was nearing the end of May. She had seen her father twice for long weekends, once when she had run out of reasons to postpone a visit to Carrigh, the second when he and Meryl had stayed in Braverton Street *en route*, for home after two weeks in Spain. They had gone to the theatre, dined out with her and Oliver, and, so as not to be alone with them and risk being blunt with Meryl, Anna had organized a small dinner party the night before they left. It was better that way.

She was racing as usual between studio and control room, having greeted that day's guests who were assembled in the Green Room. She had watched them demolish mountainous plates of sandwiches and found herself wondering as she ran if 'I'm big but I don't eat like a pig,' that day's slogan was as appropriate as she thought. Max's guests were living proof after all that delusion was the province of the overweight.

The studio audience was being warmed up by Ben Goodwright when she was waylaid in one of the corridors by a tall, well-dressed woman with highlighted blonde hair, who called her by her name.

'Sorry, let me show you the way.' Anna smiled and turned back. It happened all the time, members of the audience wandering off to have an illicit peep backstage. 'The audience go through here.' She pointed to the gangway that led up to the red plastic seats welded on to ranks of iron scaffolding and stood back to let the woman go through. But she didn't move. Instead she reached out a hand and held Anna back. 'No, please,' she said, with a strong accent. 'I must talk to you. Can we talk somewhere?'

'Talk?' Anna looked puzzled. 'I'm afraid right now the programme is about to start. Look, why don't you give your name to – here, Tessa,' she grabbed the PA by the arm as she rushed past. 'Can you show this lady to a seat and get her name? We'll write to you,' she added, and prepared to relinquish her to Tessa's care.

But the woman shrugged Tessa off. The corridor was crowded. Cameras and cables snaked past them. 'Please,' she begged. 'Just a moment. It will take only a moment.'

Something about her made Anna pause. Their eyes locked. The woman briefly closed hers. Anna took a step back and collided with Max, who was stabbing his finger at his script while a resigned director holding a styrofoam cup listened patiently. Coffee cascaded to the floor and a few drops splashed on to Max's script.

'Oh, that's right,' Max screamed, throwing the script into the air. 'Ruin my suit as well as my jokes.'

'It didn't touch you, Max,' the young man snapped.

Anna heard herself apologize. Her heart began to beat uncomfortably. 'Do I know you?' she asked.

The woman seemed lost for words, and just kept staring at her.

Anna's voice was urgent, breathless. 'Who are you?' she demanded. 'What do you want?'

'Don't you know?' The woman's voice was unsteady. 'Anna,' she clenched her fists, 'I'm your mother.'

Chapter Five

Afterwards Anna couldn't recall why she hadn't just called Security and had the woman escorted out. It was, she told Oliver, much later, an odd feeling. She knew, just *knew*, the woman wasn't lying. Instead she had grabbed her by the arm, pushed her into a small side office and ordered her, in a voice of barely suppressed panic, to stay there until the programme was over. The Green Room, which had been closer to hand and her first choice, had been filled with half a dozen cases of obesity. 'Here,' Anna gasped, almost hurling the woman inside the door. 'In here. Sorry.' She backed out. 'I have to go. Wait here.' She held up her hand as though preventing the woman from following her and was gone, racing along the corridor on legs that felt like rubber.

For the next hour it was not the programme that occupied Anna's attention. Not a moment of it registered. Even the name of the woman sitting alone just along the corridor in a sparsely furnished office eluded her. It was by no means certain she had even been told what it was. 'Your mother' had seemed enough. The roaring in her ears had seen to that.

On screen several unhealthily overweight women denounced two others who were thin as string as media pawns when they were not pandering to male fantasies. Two more collapsed sobbing when they saw a video of themselves that revealed unequivocally that years of fast food and watching *Max Meets* instead of taking a brisk walk every morning had left no place to hide. Max strutted about unchecked, offering help with weight loss via a regime devised by a young man in a muscle vest, earring and pony-tail. Without Anna's guiding instructions, he was out of control, hogging the microphone, lengthening his questions into what sounded like an address to a war-torn third world. Frantically Henry nudged Anna. 'Do something,' he hissed. 'He's in orbit.'

'Cut it out, Max,' Anna commanded curtly, through his earpiece. 'This isn't *Hamlet*.'

To his credit Max didn't flinch. Instead, he turned smoothly to the nearest thirty-stone mass, asked her to hold his hand and make him a promise to lose the twenty stone that stood between her and a beautiful life, after which he discreetly removed his earpiece and slid it into his top pocket. Anna felt sick. Before the credits finished rolling she had already fled back down the corridor. She half expected her visitor to have gone, but she was still there. The woman, almost as tall as Anna, with long, slender legs and impossibly high heels, was leaning against the window-frame looking down into the side-street below. At the sound of the door, she turned, stared intently at Anna and gave a helpless little gesture with her hands. 'I don't know what to say,' she whispered. And then, to Anna's horror, she began to cry. Helpless sobs racked her body and she sank into a chair.

Anna closed the door and leaned against it, her heart hammering painfully against her ribs. Not knowing what to do, she weakly urged the woman to stop crying. But her tears appeared unstoppable. 'Years, you see,' she gulped, looking up at Anna. 'All these years. I thought I would handle this so well. I thought I was prepared. But, as you can see,' her shoulders shook again, 'I'm not. Just tell me one thing. I must know. Are you happy?'

Anna nodded, transfixed by the woman in front of her. 'Happy? Yes. Why shouldn't I be? Absolutely. Yes.' She nodded quickly, impatiently. 'Of course I am.'

In the many secret moments in the past when Anna had

47

envisaged a meeting with her real mother, she saw them greet each other in a civilized way, with warning enough on both sides to make sure they were emotionally prepared. That's what the agency had said should happen. Letters would be exchanged and they would act as brokers, counselling caution against unrealistic expectations, until both sides felt equal to a first meeting.

She had seen herself being quite nice to a woman the world had treated badly, maybe even offering to do something for her. Now, the bit of her that was still functioning was instinctively aware that this woman was unlikely to require financial assistance from anyone, let alone an abandoned daughter. There was a gloss and glamour about her, a smooth polish that had nothing to do with the cream linen suit that heightened the olive skin or the discreet gold jewellery, but that came, quite clearly, from having had unfettered access to the best in life. Anna had foreseen a gentle, forgiving Anna, an understanding one, not an Anna who felt a sudden rush of bitter, though unvoiced, recrimination. It shocked her because she had never known she felt that way. Nevertheless it threatened to rob her of anything resembling dignity. Striving to remain calm, she sat in a chair, well away from the woman, behind the desk, which served as a shield between them. 'Look,' she said, 'please try not to cry. This has been a shock for me too. How did you find me? And why? No one contacted me. What's your name again?'

The woman blew her nose and cast around for another tissue. Anna pushed a box towards her. 'Sophia,' she said, blowing her nose. 'Sophia Grescobaldi. Did you not know?' Anna shook her head. 'Forgive me. I'm all right now. You?'

Anna nodded, studying her. There wasn't a doubt in her mind. This woman might have streaked blonde hair, a strong Italian accent, although she spoke almost perfect if stilted English, but she was her mother. They shared the same eyes, the same mouth, and she was almost as tall as

Anna. Only their noses were different: Sophia's was short and straight. They were both sitting with their arms wrapped around their bodies, Sophia rocking backwards and forwards in jerky, painful movements while Anna remained perfectly still.

'Lorenzo wanted to know,' Sophia said. 'All his life he has been – what do you say? Anguish? Yes, anguish about you. He is dying. He wants to know before he die that you forgive him – and – and me.'

'Who's Lorenzo?' Anna was bewildered. 'What are you talking about?'

'My husband,' Sophia pressed her fist to her chest. 'My husband. Your – your father.'

Tessa put her head round the door. 'Sorry, Anna,' she said, trying not to stare at the woman with a handkerchief pressed to her mouth. 'Meeting's about to start. Max is, er . . . you know . . .'

Anna lifted her head and stared blankly back at her. 'What? Yes. Yes, of course. Would you tell Henry I'll be along as soon as I can? Something's come up. Start without me.'

Tessa hovered for a moment, then reluctantly shut the door.

There it was, her history, laid out before her in this dreary office, with its stiff chairs and single desk and a window that overlooked a side-road into the tradesmen's yard. There was no longer any abandoned girl to feel sorry for. Just as her father had been swept along by Meryl's plans for him, a complete stranger had walked in off the street and reinvented Anna. She had had no choice. You couldn't change history, she thought fleetingly, just the spin that was put on it.

As Colin and Barbara Minstrel had been celebrating their daughter's second birthday with a trip to the zoo, Sophia had married Lorenzo Grescobaldi, already pregnant with their son, Andrea. Anna raised her head slightly to look at

49

Sophia. They were living in apparent affluence in Rome – but now Lorenzo was dying.

He wanted forgiveness, to know that the daughter he had given away was all right, not bitter towards him, and if she was, he wanted to make whatever amends he could in the short time left to him.

'Why didn't you keep me?' Anna whispered. 'You got married. You had another child. Why not me?'

Sophia closed her eyes. 'More than anything in my whole life I wanted to keep you,' she said. 'But it isn't as you think. We were both eighteen, but his family wanted so much for him, not a waitress from Naples.'

'Who did they want him to marry?'

Sophia gave a small laugh. 'A contessa.'

'A *contessa*?' Anna repeated faintly. 'Which one?'

'Any one. Italy's full of them. If he had been English they would have accepted no less than Princess Anne.'

Anna looked uneasily towards the door. She reached out and moved the phone a little nearer to her.

'They sent him away for a whole year to forget me. And all my letters and my phone calls are ignored. And I wrote and said I was pregnant. But they didn't care. They just cut me off and they tell Lorenzo I have just forgotten him and gone to London. Which was only partly true because my family think I am a disgrace. I go to London to stay with my aunt and her husband. They had a baker's shop in Soho. They said I was the au pair and made me work so that none of their friends would know I belong to them, and then when I began to . . . you know . . .' she extended her hands around her stomach . . . 'grow big, I was sent to the nuns at the home where you were born. Everyone thought they were Christian, but they were fiends. Oh, my God, those nuns. Every day they wanted me to repent. And I did not feel guilty of anything except being in love. I scrub floors until I pretend to be very ill so they let me stop. And I vow when I have baby I never work for anyone again. Ever.'

Sophia got up and began to pace around the room. 'All

they kept saying was "Give up your baby to a decent couple,"' she said, pulling a tissue into shreds. 'As though *I* wasn't decent. No one tried to help me keep you. No one. Right up until the moment I signed the adoption papers, signed you away, I believed myself to be alone in the world. Do you know what it was like for girls in Italy at that time? Girls,' she tapped her wedding ring, 'without this.'

Wordlessly Anna shook her head. Sophia sighed and sat down. She turned her head to look out of the window. 'Even here it would have been a nightmare to have kept a child on my own. But there,' she raised her hands, seemingly incapable of conveying the awfulness of the censorious world in which she had been raised, 'I would have been a slut and you would have had a terrible life. I couldn't do that to you. Even if I had the means, I had no husband. No father to give you – what do you say? A respectable life. Even now, you know, they would be appalled.' She tapped the desk top with a forefinger. 'Even now.'

Anna could only look helplessly at her. To have been given away in circumstances of such misery. Nothing joyous surrounded her birth. 'But you got married,' she ventured. 'Couldn't you have . . . ?'

'Got you back?' Sophia gave a sharp little laugh. 'I'm sorry. Forgive me. I never think about it because it makes me like this.' She gestured towards her red eyes. 'And how? You would have been almost two years old and I could not have done that to you, even if it were possible. I would not want to break your parents' heart, but I know I would not have been strong enough to leave you. But now . . .' She gave a helpless little shrug. 'Now, Lorenzo want to make sure you are all right and to help if you are in any trouble. Andrea insisted too. He adores his father, he is a good son.' She sighed and gave a small, wry smile. 'Good, but a little spoilt, perhaps.'

Anna stared at Sophia, trying to feel something for her: this woman had carried her inside her for nine months, had given birth to her, had given her away, but nothing stirred inside her, nothing that could safely be called anything but an overwhelming, fascinated curiosity. There was no envy and that first sense of rage had not been born of resentment, but once again she had been deprived of choice. It had been her right to decide if she wanted to meet this woman and that had been taken from her. She did not want to think about a brother either, the adored son, who had made up for the child Sophia had been forced to give away.

'I don't need any help,' Anna said curtly, knowing only that she had been the single obstacle standing between Sophia's life of poverty and a more attractive one. 'If I had been in trouble, which I never have, my parents would have been there for me.'

'I can see that,' Sophia said gently. 'Please believe me, I'm not going to allow anyone else to intrude on your life unless you agree. I wouldn't let them do to you what they did to me.'

'No, no, please,' Anna said. 'I'm truly fine. I never knew anything about you. I always thought you had been abandoned by – by the man who was my father. How could I have known anything about my real family? How did you come to marry him?'

Sophia delved in her bag – cream leather with an expensive-looking finish – and produced another tissue. 'I went back to Rome not Naples,' she said, snapping it shut and replacing it on the floor beside her. 'Not my own family. I never wanted to see them again. And I haven't.' She gave a disdainful, dismissive flick with her hand at some far-away despised group of people. 'They are history. In Rome, Lorenzo find me again and we meet secretly for some more months, and then I became pregnant with Andrea. This time there was nothing to stop us. Lorenzo was going to be twenty-one and he was a man. And they didn't want to lose him. But it was me. All me.' Sophia tapped her chest with her knuckles. Anna noticed her rings. 'I am to blame. I bring disgrace.'

'And he, I take it,' Anna remarked drily, dragging her eyes away from a sapphire, square cut, catching the light, the size of a stamp, 'had nothing to be blamed for?'

Sophia looked up sharply, eagerly. 'You do understand? You do. Oh, thank God. But it was too late to get you back.'

'But you have now,' Anna pointed out, curiosity calming her shock. 'And how did you find me?'

Sophia took a slim envelope from her bag and handed it across the desk to Anna. 'Giulio Farrini did it. He's a lawyer. He's acting for Lorenzo over here. His cousin Fabio is Lorenzo's lawyer in Rome. He wanted to write to you – Giulio, I mean – but I said there is no time. It might have taken months and I don't think we have even weeks. What else could I do?'

Off the top of her head, Anna thought she could have phoned or had a letter hand-delivered, if it was so urgent. What kind of lawyer allowed all this to happen? What of her feelings? What kind of family gave an inconvenient child away, then summoned her back when she could serve a purpose? She said all this while Sophia sat with a stricken look on her face, agreeing and nodding. How could she not? Anna thought angrily. It was true.

'I argued against it,' Sophia whispered. 'It was so unfair. They thought only of what they needed. They always have. They thought nothing of my feelings and I am your mother.'

Anna winced. Sophia stretched out her hand. 'Oh, I'm sorry. I didn't mean it to sound that way. You had a wonderful mother . . .'

Anna noted the past tense. 'How do you know about her?'

'Because when we were searching for you we found out these things along the way. I know everything about you, where you lived, went to school. I know about everything. This job – so exciting you must be so clever. And I was so sorry about your . . . mother. And your papa has remarried,' Sophia said, with a small tsk. 'So soon.'

Anna was so much in agreement with this that she overlooked that Sophia, a stranger, had no right to air her opinion or, in view of her own history, to pass moral judgement on anyone else. 'And I don't know whether you will believe this, but I have always, *always* thought of you. Look.' She opened her bag, removed a small leather case and opened it. Anna saw that Sophia's hands were trembling. 'There.' She handed Anna a photograph. 'I keep it with me always.'

Anna gazed down at the picture of a dark-haired baby, only days old, eyes squeezed tightly closed. Then she handed it back.

Sophia hung her head. 'I don't blame you for hating me.'

'I don't hate you,' Anna replied quickly. 'I don't know what I feel. I only met you an hour ago. I've never . . .' She paused, then said in a rush, in case her courage failed her, 'I've never thought about any of you. Not really. Not enough to come looking.'

'I understand. I know what it is to be ignored. That's why I insisted that if anyone saw you it should be me. I had to come myself. It wasn't hard to find you. If it's a medical matter, they tell you where to find children like – you. You have a right to know if it's anything hereditary so they waive all the rules. The papers are in here. Look,' she urged Anna, 'it's all there.'

'What do you mean?' Fear gripped her. 'Medical matter? What's wrong with him?' She pulled the envelope towards her without taking her eyes off Sophia.

Sophia took a deep breath. 'Cirrhosis of the liver,' she said steadily, holding Anna's gaze.

Anna blinked. '*Cirrhosis of the liver,*' she repeated incredulously. 'I'm sorry, is this a joke? Since when has dying of drink been hereditary?'

'It isn't,' Sophia agreed. 'Unless you drink like Lorenzo, no danger at all to you.'

'He drinks?'

54

Sophia's eyes welled with tears again. 'Too much.' Her voice broke. 'And now this.'

'So what's it got to do with me?'

'Giulio said it was the only way we could find you quickly if the doctors said Lorenzo had an inherited disease or condition. You had the right to know so that you could protect yourself, and if you had children, them too.'

'And the adoption agency allowed this?' Anna asked, truly appalled. 'They agreed that drinking was a medical condition that could be passed on?'

Sophia looked down unhappily at her hands. 'I know, I know. But Giulio said your social services here had enough to do without starting any objections to a case like this. If a doctor said it was necessary they would wave it through. And they did. Once, of course, I explained to Lorenzo's doctors. They wrote something not – well, not exactly true.'

The phone rang on Anna's desk. They both looked at it. Anna picked it up. It was Henry, asking irritably if she would be gracing the meeting with her presence. 'Max,' he hissed. 'He's on to Charles. Says this time you'll have to go. For God's sake, who is that woman? What's going on?'

'Sorry,' Anna said, knowing that the head of the station was in Paris and Max wouldn't get far. 'I'll be right there. Five minutes, Henry, just five. Absolutely. Promise.'

She looked at Sophia and got up. 'I'm working. I have to go.'

Sophia rose too, apologizing and saying she understood. 'Anna.' She reached out and grasped Anna's hand. 'I've come all this way and you have no reason to agree to this but I want you to help me – help Lorenzo.'

'How?' Anna gently released her hand.

'Come to Rome. Come and see him. Tell him yourself that you are fine. Just once. And then he will die a happy man. Please?'

Anna took a step back. 'No, I'm sorry, that's not possible. What good would it do? I'm a stranger to him – to both of you. You just tell him instead. Tell him I had the best possible life. I couldn't have been given a better one. Frankly he doesn't need my forgiveness. His family should be asking for his. Now, I really must go.'

'And I cannot see you again?'

Anna paused by the door. She was exhausted. Sophia's face was drawn and Anna could see lines of tiredness around her eyes.

'Dinner,' Sophia said eagerly. 'Dinner. Tonight. I must fly back tomorrow. I cannot leave him for long. Just let me have you for one evening. Please?'

Anna hesitated. She wasn't sure what made her do so. They had given her away but they had to come back to beg. It was a strangely powerful feeling and one, to her shame, that she could not resist. 'It may not be possible,' Anna began. 'I'll call you. Let you know.' She knew she would not be able to refuse. Curiosity was winning over pride. But they had waited over thirty years so they could wait a little longer.

Chapter Six

'If there's nothing else,' Meryl Minstrel looked over her glasses at the Carrigh Parish Council, 'then we are agreed. The second Saturday in August? And we'll ask Morag Fraser to open as usual.'

'Couldn't we get a real celebrity?' Morton Glebe grumbled. 'Morag's a crashing bore and her books are even worse. What about Colin's daughter?' he said. 'Couldn't she ask one of those television people?'

Meryl smiled. 'I think the problem there is the journey,' she said smoothly. 'They're so busy, those television folk. But of course I'll mention it next time I speak to her. Meanwhile, shall we enlist Morag? She has a very strong following, and if by chance someone else crops up we can ask them to share the honours. Now,' she said quickly, before anyone could pursue the subject, 'any other business?'

There was a silence while everyone looked at everyone else and tried to think if there was anything they had forgotten or could add to the planning of the Carrigh summer picnic that couldn't wait for two weeks until the next meeting.

'In which case,' Meryl shuffled pieces of paper into the file in front of her, 'the meeting is adjourned. Lovely. Good. Thank you, everyone.'

As always, Meryl was the last to leave the meeting of the Carrigh Parish Council of which she was chair. Once the seats had been stacked, the door to the small kitchen locked and the windows fastened, she would walk the mile home along a straight road to her sturdy stone-built house, surrounded by an even sturdier rough stone wall, where she had spent the years since Giles died living a lone but busy life. It was said of her that if she could she would organize her own funeral. Meryl had felt her cheeks go a bit pink when Doreen Bishop, her chief lieutenant and secretary to the council, had said this within her hearing, because in fact a letter had been lodged with her solicitors outlining what she thought would be a suitable service when her time came. In it she had asked to be cremated and for her ashes to be buried with Giles's in the rose garden of the small cemetery behind the church where the road left the village. Of course when she had written that she had not been expecting to marry Colin. At some point she planned to broach the subject with her new husband but it seemed a little premature to do so so early in their marriage.

Meryl took a last look round the hall, then stepped outside, hoisting her bag on to her shoulder so that she could close and lock the double doors. Then she slipped the key into her bag and set off down the small path that led round the back of the hall across an asphalt car park. It was a mild day, not hot enough to venture out without a jacket but with the first serious indications that summer was coming. There was already a welcoming smile on her face as she turned the corner, expecting to see Colin waiting in the car. The road was empty. She stopped in surprise and glanced at her watch. It was after one.

She would give him ten minutes, then start to walk towards the house. He was a dear but, if she wasn't with him, he tended to forget the time and Athol would be expecting them. Meryl frowned when she thought of Athol, his very moderate salary and all those children. She had her suspicions that Fenella might be that way again. And that house had really been Fenella's idea. Meryl just hoped they had the money. There was a little from what Giles had left that she could offer them if things got tight, but Sheridan would have to be given the same because that was only fair or Primrose would get that look on her face.

She reached the gate. It was quiet with just an occasional car sweeping along the road towards the village. Meryl reached the entrance to the church, and sat down to wait on a stone bench, tucking the folds of her grey pleated cotton skirt under her. It was warmer now so she took off her navy blazer, folded it carefully on top of her handbag, linked her hands round one crossed leg and waited.

Today it had been a good meeting. The spring and summer ones rarely lasted more than two hours. It was in the winter when they had to brace themselves to venture out with the wind whipping in off the hills that the return journey was delayed. Mostly they sat around and gossiped and had an extra cup of tea, brought by Meryl and Doreen in flasks, just to put off the awful moment.

She glanced at her watch. Nearly a quarter past. Another five minutes and she'd start to walk. In marrying Colin she knew she had taken on a man who needed his life redefined in many ways. The task had been made somewhat easier in that he had no set pattern to his days. In Meryl's view, Barbara had let him drift and her death had simply underlined that he was not fitted to be alone. No one was. But he had had no training to replace, in the empty days and hours, all the things that had been part of his life with her. In that respect, Giles had been a perfect partner, encouraging her to expand and grow in directions that she might not otherwise have explored. In other ways, she had been lonely with him. They had had none of the real togetherness she suspected she would find with Colin. But Giles had left her better equipped to get on without him than Barbara had Colin.

The problem he had was with his daughter, whom he seemed to regard with a mixture of bewilderment and awe. It had not taken Meryl long to see that Anna's upbringing had been left to Barbara and that in all fairness Colin had been content to leave it that way. The result, in her view,

59

was that they still had a lot to learn about each other and she was blowed if she was going to waste whatever years either she or Colin had left waiting for them to do it. Love was in short supply in this world. Unexpected, unlooked-for passion was a gift. Even though she was alone and the only witness at that moment to her private thoughts were an uninterested handful of sheep in the meadow that bounded the opposite side of the road, she glanced round hastily knowing she had blushed. At their age too. So, Anna could continue to baffle her father and in return Meryl would give him much-needed direction. She wouldn't come between father and daughter but neither would she allow Anna to continue to hold him back. The noise of an approaching car coming round the bend in the road made her look up. She gathered up her things and tried to look severe.

'You're late,' she said, climbing into the passenger seat. 'And what in the world are you looking like that for?'

'Sorry, my dear,' he said. He let the brake go, glanced over his shoulder and pulled out again. 'I was held up by Anna.'

Meryl glanced at him. 'Oh?'

'Yes. She's in a bit of a flap. Well, to be honest, so am I.'

'Pull over,' Meryl said sharply. 'What is it, dear? You look ill. Tell me.'

Colin pulled the car off the narrow road on to the grassy verge and turned off the engine.

'It's her mother,' he said bleakly. 'Her real mother. She's turned up.'

Meryl's eyes never left his profile. 'Oh, heavens,' she said, reaching out and laying her hand over one of his where it rested on the steering-wheel. 'How? When? Oh dear, poor Anna. She must be so shocked.'

Colin stared straight ahead. 'No,' he said finally. 'That's just it. She didn't sound shocked.'

'Not shocked?' Meryl tried to look into his face. 'How did she sound?'

A car roared past, causing Colin's car to vibrate in its wake. As it disappeared round a curve in the road, he turned to look at Meryl. His face wore a puzzled look. 'She sounded calm,' he said. 'As though she had been half waiting, half expecting that this might happen. I'm more shocked than she is.'

Anna put down the phone on her father and stared at it, her hand still resting on the receiver. She had waited until the office was reasonably deserted and then, in a hurried call, told her father about Sophia just as he had been on the point of leaving the house to collect Meryl from her committee meeting. They were going straight on to Athol's to collect the children for the weekend while their parents packed ready for the move on Monday morning to the new house with its state-of-the-art waste disposal on the Craighaithan Heights estate.

The last time Anna had been up to see them Meryl had asked Colin to drive past the new house on the way to the airport when they were taking Anna back. She had said all that she could of an estate with matching houses and tried to picture it when the gardens had been stocked and the spindly trees had developed enough to take the bareness away from it. Only the view, Anna thought, saved it from being utterly soulless.

Oddly it was her father who had been most admiring of its situation, pointing out that it was within walking distance of a small village and less than a half-hour's drive from Carrigh. Now his shocked voice asked, 'Why? How did she find you? What does she want?'

Anna could picture him removing the tweed cap he had taken to wearing, taking off his glasses and sitting on the small velvet chair Meryl had placed next to the walnut telephone table. With a wary eye on Henry, who was wandering disconsolately around the office, another assignation with

Melissa having crumbled, she began to speak quietly then stopped. Tessa, sitting close by, pretended to be immersed in a magazine.

'Tess?' Anna put her hand over the receiver and with the other surreptitiously slid that day's copy of the *Guardian* into the top drawer of her desk. 'Be an angel. I need a copy of today's *Guardian*. I think someone's walked off with it.'

A few minutes later, having heard her out in silence, her father asked only if Anna was going to complain to the lawyer who had sanctioned such a blundering entry into her life. She would if Colin wanted her to, she agreed drily. Just to make sure that no other skeletons were ready to fall out of her closet without warning. She tried to laugh, but she couldn't.

'The man needs to be told that that's not how we do things,' her father insisted. 'You have a right to privacy. We all do.'

Anna waited for him to question her, but he didn't. He seemed to have no interest in the woman who had made it possible for him to be a father, what she looked like, how she sounded, her circumstances, nothing.

'Did you know she wasn't what Mum thought?' Anna asked hesitantly.

'In what way?'

'She's not exactly impoverished. She married the man who . . .' she was unable to say 'is my father.' Instead she said, ridiculously, 'The man responsible.'

There was a silence. 'No, I didn't know that,' he said finally. 'We told you what we had been told. We told you all we knew.'

'He's dying. That's why she's here.'

'I'm sorry to hear that,' he said heavily, polite rather than concerned. She began to panic, then guilt flooded her and she didn't know why. She was shocked too. But telling him just how shocked made her feel disloyal. The arrival of Sophia had had a more powerful effect on her than she had ever anticipated.

Anna gripped the phone. She wanted to say, 'Tell me. Tell me what to do,' but he didn't. She tried again. 'She wants me to go to Rome. To meet him.'

'And what have you said?'

'Nothing. I said it wasn't possible. No, actually, in the end I said I'd think about it. But I wanted to talk to you first.'

There was a moment of stillness between the stone cottage in Carrigh and the glaring overhead lights of the Circle Television offices in London. Colin stared through the small porch window, through which he could see the long, paved path that led to the iron gate in the stone wall, clumps of heather and gorse bushes pushing sturdily against a mild wind.

'Dad?' Anna prompted. On one of the screens suspended above her head Julia Somerville and Nick Owen were bringing the lunchtime news to a close. 'All these families,' she joked lamely. 'Taking us over, eh?'

There was a pause. 'Well, something like that. Look, dear, let me talk to you about all this later. Bit of a shock, you see, and Meryl will be waiting.'

'Of course,' she said. Bloody Meryl. Even at this moment. 'I mean there's no rush,' she assured him before she hung up. 'I haven't a clue what to do.'

Absently she began to pull notes together for the meeting. Tessa flapped a copy of the *Guardian* in front of her.

Inevitably, shock had left her feeling limp and wanting to be left alone, but that was impossible. Already she could tell that people were talking. Tessa had excelled herself in reporting on the strange scene in the disused office: it was now being said that the wife of a man with whom Anna had been having a secret affair had turned up to confront her.

Anna's entrance caused covert looks to be exchanged and a small silence descended. 'What?' she asked impatiently, looking around at the silent faces staring back at her. 'Let's go, shall we?'

'Let's go?' Max repeated, his voice almost a squeal. 'Go

where? Just listen to her, will you? Henry? Are you going to allow this? As if we haven't all had our schedules fucked—'

'Sit down, Max,' Henry growled. 'Anna had some urgent personal business to attend to. It's not as if we've never worked through lunch before, is it? It happens. Tess? What's that?' He broke off to peer at the packets of sandwiches piled on his desk. 'Tuna? I hate tuna. I can't bear it. I'll die if I don't at least get the lunch I want.'

Anna threw him a grateful, if surprised, glance.

Max slammed his leather organizer on to the desk. 'That's it, is it, Henry? That's all that you – as this woman's immediate superior – have to say? Well, that remark is going to cost you, believe me.'

'No one else has a problem with me, Max,' Anna butted in. 'Just because I wasn't around at the end of the programme—'

'You think that's the problem? Well, excuse me. The problem is your attitude. Your presence,' he looked around, 'or lack of it, is neither here nor there. You should be begging forgiveness, *begging*.'

Anna put down her files carefully, pushing them into the paper cups and tins of soft drinks that were creating chaos on Henry's already confused desk. Max had a point, a very small one. She was prepared to concede that for an hour, her life had got in the way of theirs, but the thumping pain behind her eyes was getting worse and she would concede no more. 'You mean that I should be deeply and unremittingly sorry that I stopped you making a prat of yourself?' she began, then stopped. Henry threw her an eloquent look of appeal. The rest of the staff had heard it all before. The two researchers were engrossed in *Private Eye* and Tessa was laboriously counting out change before she went in search of something more to Henry's liking in the canteen.

'Okay, Max.' Anna sighed and stood up, resting her hands on the edge of the desk. She dropped her head, then looked up at him. 'I apologize.'

'Far too late,' he shrilled, triumph mixed with dismay.

Having wrung an apology from her, he was at a loss now to know how to proceed. In his mind Max had rehearsed a scene in which his eloquence and dignity had forced Henry to demand a grovelling apology from Anna. Even now Max had a subliminal flash of the woman, contrite, kneeling in front of him as he towered over her . . . So he ranted on in a confused argument, which Aggie privately thought could have done with some heavy editing from the target of his fury.

In a few minutes, Anna knew that Max would have run out of things to say so she stared impassively at him while he boxed himself into a corner of his own making as she wrestled with a far greater conundrum: she who had once believed that knowledge of her real parents would raise in her only mild curiosity now felt an overwhelming desire to know more about the family who had rejected her.

By mid-afternoon Giulio Farrini had phoned twice and twice Anna had mouthed, 'No,' to Tessa. She was waiting for Sophia to phone. The second time she did, Anna spoke to her and said she would see her. Just for dinner. It was the kind of power game Anna despised others for playing, but Sophia was quietly grateful. 'Thank you,' she whispered. 'Thank you.' Anna felt mean.

But in the middle of a frantic office, Anna found it impossible to pursue this line of thought. Aggie reported that the discarded wife of the minister who had lost his seat at the last election was on the brink of agreeing to appear but needed certain reassurances from Anna before she did. Before Anna could call back, the minister's mistress, who had caused his wife grief on a seismic scale, called to say she was thoroughly disenchanted with a man who could do something like that to his wife. The fact that he no longer had a ministerial car at his disposal and that he now had to share the small pied-à-terre at weekends with his two noisy children had no influence on her decision. The point was, she said, in a choice of phrase that betrayed her devotion to the tabloids, that she had decided other women needed to be warned against such a love-rat. She emphasized the last word. Anna could hear the capital letters. Such public-spiritedness deserved its reward: Anna agreed to pay her hotel bill.

At four her father phoned to say that Meryl had reminded him they wouldn't be at home until after nine o'clock, just in case she phoned. Anna closed her eyes against the rush of disappointment. She knew that if she said, 'Please, Dad, I want you to be there,' he would have come, but she couldn't say it. 'Don't worry, Pa. I'm going to meet her for dinner and then she'll go back to Rome and that will be the end of it.' Her voice shook. A thought struck her. 'Pa? You know, don't you, that I would never have gone looking for her? It doesn't matter that my real father's alive. It means nothing to me. You do *know* that, don't you? I mean you and Mum . . .'

'I know, dear.' His voice was not quite steady. 'I know. Ring me later. Please?'

When Giulio Farrini called again, Anna nodded to Tessa that she would speak to him. 'I gather you're the man who thought it was okay to allow a total stranger to barge in on me,' she said coldly. 'Off the top of my head, of course, and I can't be sure, I'm fairly certain several laws have been broken and I'm keeping open my option to inform the Law Society.'

There was a silence. Anna waited.

'I'm naturally sorry you see it that way,' Giulio Farrini said, in accented but perfect English. 'But, of course you must do whatever you think proper.'

'I will,' she promised. Tessa was waving at her that the minister's wife was on another line. 'I'm very busy,' Anna said curtly. 'How can I help you?'

'I've just spoken to Sophia. I've suggested I come along this evening. I wondered if you will be bringing someone with you?'

'Will that be necessary?'

66

'No. But I thought you might prefer it. Maybe your father?'

'No.' She watched the flashing light on the console next to her. 'No one.' She signalled to Tessa to put the caller through, cutting short Sophia's lawyer. 'Mrs Travers? Anna Minstrel,' she said. 'I'm delighted you're going to be on the show. This really sends such a strong message to other women like you. It's going to be terrific. I'm sorry? A friend? Yes, of course you can bring a friend with you. Let me just have his name again . . . And he'll be staying with you at the hotel? Fine. Absolutely fine. Max is longing to meet you.' She grimaced at Henry, who had heard the last part of the conversation: the budget was already tight. 'No problem. I'll get our people to alter the reservation.'

Oliver Manners had had a bad day, and if he wasn't careful it would be followed by a bad evening. He thought of a new client, to whom Rachel had introduced him, a politician whose ambitions stretched beyond his abilities and with whom he had to have dinner. He had taken the man on, against his better judgement, in an effort to make it up to Rachel for all the pain he had caused when he left her for Anna.

Now after a disastrous round of press interviews in the Midlands, they were stuck on the M1 and, rather than talk to him, Oliver had purposefully opened a black-leather organizer. By the time they reached the slip-road heading for the M25, which was solid with traffic, he was seriously considering unloading the man, Rachel or no Rachel. He had been relying on Anna to join them for dinner when they reached London, mostly because he had been thinking of her in a fairly carnal way since they had left Birmingham two hours earlier but also because she understood the dismaying need of quite sensible people to tell journalists the most unfortunate details of their life.

Sitting beside him in the back of the Mercedes, the new head of a left-wing think-tank was snoring off an excellent lunch. Oliver looked at him with loathing. For no apparent reason, his new, and possibly former, client had volunteered to a press briefing that, as a student, he had been no stranger to certain chemical substances. When Oliver's mobile rang, the man gave a grunt, then slid back to sleep.

'You poor baby.' Oliver whistled softly when Anna told him what had happened. 'What a shock. Put it off,' he urged, turning his shoulder in case his client awoke and started to listen. 'Put it off until I get back and we can talk about it.'

But she couldn't. 'She flies back tomorrow. And it's not every day you get to meet the woman who gave birth to you. I'll go this once. Get it over with. Apologize to Tony, won't you? Explain about my long-lost mother.'

'Well, I won't tell him who she is,' Oliver replied.

'Why ever not?' Anna asked. 'I've nothing to hide. I've never denied being adopted.'

'No, of course not,' Oliver said soothingly. 'I simply think you should be discreet. After all, you know nothing about them. They could be anyone.'

'Sicilian bandits,' she suggested lightly. 'Oh, nothing,' she said, when he sounded blank. 'Just because they snap their fingers it doesn't mean I'll go running. It's only dinner. Come over later. Please? I'll need you.'

Oliver switched off the phone and looked out at the crawling line of traffic shuffling along beside them. He was not given to overreacting, but there was something about Anna's mother turning up, just like that, that made him feel outraged. In the end, he decided that being tired and disillusioned with his profession had made him feel a stronger sense of fear than was reasonable.

Beside him the dreadful Tony slumbered on. Oliver couldn't bear it. Carefully he switched on his phone and called Rachel. She got him into this, the least she could do was help him out of it.

'Rach? Hi it's me. Come to dinner? Great. See you at the Ivy. Eight o'clock?'

*

Giulio Farrini was waiting for Anna in the discreet hotel where Sophia was staying. It was the kind of hotel that refused to acknowledge new celebrity and relied, as it had with considerable success and increasing profit for several dozen decades, on rock-solid old money. He was sitting at one of the tables in the small bar adjacent to the dining room, and knew who she was as soon as she paused in the entrance. He rose as she came towards him, almost as tall as he was. He took in the sleeveless coral shift, lightly tanned arms and the way that the seriousness of her face vanished as she smiled and made you want to smile back. She wasn't what he'd expected. She was clearly well educated and intelligent. Nor, according to Sophia, had she dissolved into hysterics or was likely to. For that he was grateful.

Giulio's short-lived marriage to an Englishwoman had been characterized by stormy, tearful scenes reminiscent of his youthful girlfriends in Milan and tempestuous family lunches. Throughout it, he had been reminded constantly of the reasons why he had decided to read law at Oxford instead of in Rome, and why he had put as much distance as he could between him, his suffocating father and his excitable family. He no longer had any interest in marriage. His current affair, however, was also proving difficult in that her excitement value no longer compensated for her expensive tastes.

Anna guessed that Giulio Farrini was probably in his late thirties. He had no way of knowing the time and trouble she had taken over her appearance, the number of times she had reached for the phone to pull out of the meeting, the misgivings that, even as she walked towards him, crowded her mind. He was of medium build and only just taller than she was, with black hair going grey at the sides and receding at the front. He looked more like the brains behind a Mafia cabal than a respected international lawyer, who spent his days protecting the interests of Italian business investments.

As she approached he extended his hand and took hers briefly, waited until she was seated before he sat down. Anna glanced at him while he ordered a drink for her. He had a lean face and his hooded eyes looked bored. He was wearing a heavy signet ring on well-manicured hands. 'Sophia will be here directly,' he explained. 'She was called to the phone.'

'Her husband?' Anna queried.

'No. He's much too weak. Andrea. I understand they missed each other earlier.'

'Oh.' Anna fell silent.

'You look like him,' Giulio ventured into the silence. 'Andrea. You could be twins.'

'Really?' was all she said. All day she had been trying to accept that she had a brother. And there would be cousins too, aunts and uncles. Every one of them able to open a photograph album and see her features in theirs. All of them related to her but— Here Anna crossed the line between curiosity and pride. Not one of them had helped Sophia to keep her. If this new family wanted to know her, *they* would have to make the running. Just as Sophia had. Anna knew now that she would never have gone looking for her mother. It was why she had dressed so carefully this evening: she had seized the chance to show Sophia what she had given away and to regret it. If Sophia and Lorenzo were looking for forgiveness, Anna was looking for regret.

Giulio glanced across at her, noting her stillness, the lack of body language he relied on to guide him with a new client. He tried again. 'I hope you've recovered from what must have been a shock – meeting your mother like that.'

'My mother's dead,' she replied calmly, crossing her legs, resting one arm lightly along the arm of her chair. 'I assume you mean Sophia.'

'Of course,' he replied instantly. 'That was clumsy of me.'

'It seems characteristic of you,' she said, looking idly around.

'Earlier, you mean?' He was unmoved by her criticism. 'Hmm. I can see it must have seemed that way.'

'*Seemed?*' Her eyes widened in disbelief. 'Goodness, you lawyers. "Excuse me, m'lud," she mimicked, "I've just allowed a ten-ton truck to roll through the china department, which *seems* to have had the living daylights knocked out of it."' Instantly she was furious with herself for losing control like that. What price pride when it could slip so easily. She glanced at Giulio but he looked amused instead of cross. 'I wouldn't have likened you to china,' he smiled faintly, 'and I don't think Sophia would appreciate being compared to a ten-ton truck.'

'Look,' she turned on him. 'What possessed you to let her do that? I could have had a heart condition, or even *cirrhosis of the liver*, which apparently is now hereditary.' She pronounced each word with deliberate sarcasm. 'And how the hell did you get such flimsy medical evidence past the adoption agency? I called them, you know. They're horrified it happened. They said the papers they saw clearly said hereditary factors were involved in some other disease – I can't remember what it was – that he doesn't even have.'

Giulio rose to his feet. 'She's coming, so perhaps you'd like to put these questions to her.'

Sophia arrived on a drift of perfume, wearing a navy silk dress that Anna had seen on the pages of an American glossy magazine, so costly the editor had balked at including the price. 'You must forgive me for this morning.' She gave a small, embarrassed smile as she took Anna's hand in hers. 'You are recovered, are you not? I realize after I see you, and see you are so happy, that you must get big shock. But the minute I heard you had been traced I did not wait. I board the first flight for London and just came. In my nerves I did not call Giulio.'

'Why not?' Anna asked.

Sophia twisted the rings on her fingers. 'Because I was impatient,' she said, not taking her eyes off Anna's face. 'I am afraid they won't find you in time. So I get my own detective who contact the – what you call it? – post adoption agency. But they will say nothing. And so *slow*. So what could we do? We were *forced* to try another way.'

Anna's eyes widened in horror. 'Are you telling me he *stole* my records? How? Did he break in? Is that what he did? Oh my God! How did he know what to look for?'

Sophia wrung her hands. 'It is better we do not ask,' she pleaded. 'Please. We leave it there. Yes? Once he had your new name he find you on the electoral role. It was not hard.'

Anna looked quickly at Giulio, who was absorbed in the ceiling.

'You will be forgiving?' Sophia asked anxiously. 'We don't tell anyone, no? What good would it do now? If you wanted to find your child, would you have turned down any chance of doing it?'

Anna paused. She took in the gold bracelet, the ring, the aura of unmistakable wealth and knew that whatever laws lay between this woman and finding her had been demolished; anyone who could be bought off had been. God knows how much money had changed hands to find her. What good *would* it do? The harm, if there was harm, had been done.

'No.' She shook her head. 'I don't suppose I would.'

Sophia gave a sigh of relief and a small laugh that sounded rather like a sob. Anna watched as Sophia lowered herself into the remaining seat, and she settled down to study the woman who had given her away and now so desperately wanted her back.

Chapter Seven

There was an effortless elegance about Sophia, which had as much to do with how she behaved as what she wore. She didn't seem to do anything at all to have the staff quietly on constant alert to her needs. Waiters appeared from nowhere to guide her to their table, another swept out a chair for her, the maître d' arrived, flourishing menus, the moment she sat. It could be said that it was what they had been trained to do, and their courtesy to Anna and Giulio Farrini was no less evident, but the willowy, glistening, middle-aged woman drew them to her, like flowers, thought Anna, leaning towards the sun. She was doing a bit of leaning herself. With a self-conscious start, she sat up straight. There was an imperceptible air about Sophia, Anna realized, that somehow commanded attention. It wasn't hard to see why a besotted Lorenzo had failed to give her up.

She was nothing like the shy, ill-educated, abandoned girl of Anna's imagination. Now that Sophia had stopped crying, Anna could see that, at almost fifty, she could pass for a woman ten years younger. She could not imagine being reared by such a creature. But neither could she help hoping that Sophia would reveal her family to her without Anna having to expose her own need to hear about them.

If confusion was the immediate sensation the day had brought, guilt was now beginning to surface. She felt disloyal to Barbara and Colin, and if she could, she would have pushed back her chair and walked away. Instead she said, too loudly, 'I'm sorry to be a bore, but I won't be able to stay long.'

It was impossible to think of Sophia as her mother, hard to imagine her feeling comfortable with a determinedly active child, as Anna had been. She pictured Barbara pushing her, aged four, on her bike when she was learning to ride a two-wheeler, then years later hauling duvets and suitcases up three flights of stairs the day Anna arrived at university, and later still, her hair tucked under a showercap, routing out years of neglect in the disused chimney at Braverton Street.

Sophia was charming and witty, gently teasing about the close-knit, morally upright Grescobaldis, her composure cracking only when she spoke of Lorenzo. She had devoted her life to him, a man who had branched out on his own from the third generation of a family business in printing, which had made them strangers to anything other than almost incomprehensible wealth. 'Lorenzo is the most successful,' Sophia said simply. 'He could have just inherited, like his brother, who just accepted what he was given, but he worked hard for what he has.'

'Gianni?' Giulio interjected gently, with one eyebrow raised.

Sophia hesitated. Anna thought her shoulders drooped a little. 'Well,' Sophia conceded, 'perhaps I meant Gianni is not inventive. And Lorenzo listens, to me or Roberto – his partner,' she explained. 'Roberto Andreotti, a good, wise man, Lorenzo's right arm.'

'What does he do?' Anna ventured. 'Lorenzo.'

Sophia looked blank. 'Do? Of course, I forget. Well, of course, he was not suited to the family business, running printers. He is more artistic, more creative. Andrea has it in him too.' Anna glanced away and caught Giulio's eye. She looked down. 'When Andrea was very small,' Sophia was explaining, 'Lorenzo's parents agreed he could start a photographic agency. It is called Nuovama. You know this?'

Anna blinked. Who didn't? In a previous job as a lowly researcher, she had used them via their London agent. Heavens, she thought inwardly.

'We start very small,' Sophia explained. 'You understand? But I knew it would be wonderful – and big. And it is. Is it not, Giulio?'

'Very.'

'But it is not me we talk about,' Sophia said turning to Anna. 'Would you . . .' she asked hesitantly . . . 'would you tell me about you? I have no right, I understand that. But I would like so much to know.'

Anna was taken off guard. 'Me? What do you want to know? I'm thirty-something, degree, career, small house – actually,' she corrected herself, in a burst of honesty, 'a very small house – and a man with a fashionable career. You read about women like me every day in the paper.'

'Not all like you,' Sophia insisted. 'Tell me about this man of yours. Your job. And you are not eating.' She looked, dismayed, at the almost untouched food on Anna's plate. 'Something else, yes? A salad is not enough. You worked all day and, poor child, such a day.'

She turned to the waiter, who was only a breath away from her but Anna stopped her. 'No. Really. This is fine.'

'You're sure?' Sophia asked doubtfully. 'No,' she held up her hands in a gesture of surrender as Anna began to insist, 'I won't fuss. Andrea also hates me for fussing. Now,' she gently touched Anna's arm, 'tell me. Please. Everything.'

When Anna had finished there was an odd look on Sophia's face, as though something blindingly obvious had occurred to her. While she said, 'I am so glad. So happy. So relieved,' Anna didn't have to be told that she was looking at what might have been. A triumphant flicker stirred. She could feel it rising to her eyes. She'd done it: she had done enough with her life to merit every expression of regret the entire Grescobaldi family could muster. And she had done it on her own. The inconvenient baby who had represented poverty and embarrassment was doing just fine.

Barbara had been so right. Where you came from didn't matter, it was what you did that counted. She *could* handle this.

'Your grandmother,' Sophia said, 'Lorenzo's mother. She is now too ill to travel from her home but she sent a message to say if you came to Rome maybe you could see her in Bracciano.'

Anna's glass snapped on to the table. 'No,' she said quickly. 'No. I won't – can't. I won't be going to Rome and, besides, I never knew she existed. You see—' She stopped. Her cheeks felt warm. She wasn't interested in meeting a grandmother who had made it impossible for her parents to keep her. Sophia remained silent. 'What would be the point?' Anna said, into the silence. Then she waited. She took a sip of wine and knew that Giulio Farrini was regarding her with curiosity.

'And if I said you would see only Lorenzo and Andrea, and I give you my word that no one else would trouble you? A day, maybe just two, out of your life? It is asking a lot, I know that.'

It was said humbly rather than coaxingly. Anna glanced at her watch. 'Look,' she said gathering up her bag ready to depart, 'I have a very tight schedule. 'I'll think about it,' she said, knowing she didn't need to think. 'But I can't promise.'

Giulio's interest in the proceedings did not seem overwhelming. Indeed he did not appear to have an easy relationship with Sophia, although it was hard for Anna to pinpoint exactly why she thought this because they were perfectly civil to each other – as he was to Anna when he drove her home. She had wanted to be on her own, or with Oliver, but because she was tired and he insisted she accepted his offer.

'Reuniting long-lost families isn't what you do, is it?' she asked, as they drove.

'No. But I aim to please. I like a successful outcome whatever the case.'

'Well,' Anna said carefully, 'I'm sorry to have been your first failure.'

He glanced sideways at her. 'Not my first and you're not a client,' he pointed out.

'Of course not. I couldn't afford you, so I wouldn't be, would I?'

He grunted, and Anna felt foolish at having been so petty. As small-talk did not come easily to either of them, they lapsed into silence.

They went to Bangers in the high street near Carrie's flat because it was Euan's favourite. The lunchtime crowd had overlapped with the Saturday-morning shopping brigade but they found a table for three wedged against a wall. A harassed girl in jeans and T-shirt with a blue striped apron clinging to her hipless frame pushed her way through the tables, holding a chair for Euan above her head. They stood back while she slotted it into place and produced three large plastic menus from a pile on the table behind them.

'Up you go.' Carrie attempted to hoist Euan's sturdy frame into the seat.

'No,' he shrieked, pushing her away. 'No. Me.'

Used to this performance Anna watched patiently while he pulled one knee on to the chair, slipped, banged his chin and set up a roar that made everyone turn expecting to see that a limb had been severed.

'Jesus,' Carrie muttered, hauling him to his feet. 'You're all right,' she insisted, brushing him down. 'Here. Look. It's a special fun-bag just for you. Isn't it, Anna?'

Euan paused in his yells as Carrie ferreted into the bag Anna was holding and produced a plastic bag with a zip into which she had piled enough crayons and books to distract him while they talked. 'There, now,' she said, plonking him into the chair. He tipped the contents on to the table in front of him and began to inspect them. Carrie flopped into the seat next to him. 'Lots of lovely goodies.

Draw Anna a picture. In fact, draw Anna,' she said. She turned to Anna, who was sliding into the seat on the other side of him. 'Want him?'

'No,' Anna replied cheerfully. 'Not right at this moment. For a child who was throwing up yesterday evening he looks disgustingly well. Get any sleep?'

Carrie groaned. 'Oh, yes, at least ten minutes between midnight and one and then again just before it got light. He's fine now.' She regarded her son, who was pressing a crayon heavily on to his drawing pad. 'What a shame they don't do neat gin here. And you look like you got about the same. What's the decision, then?'

Anna sighed and glanced down the menu. 'Margarita,' she said. 'And a Coke.'

'I meant about Rome.' Carrie yawned.

'I know,' Anna replied. 'I just don't know. What do you think?'

'Ten days later, and two phone calls from Sophia, only you can answer that, my precious. What does your father say?'

'Nothing. Well, I haven't asked him again. He just doesn't want to be drawn on it. Except to tell me that Meryl says, "These things are best left to resolve themselves."'

'And Oliver? Still against it?'

Anna leaned down to retrieve the crayon Euan had dropped over the side of his chair. 'Here,' she handed it to him, 'is that supposed to be me?'

He pushed the paper round to show her. 'You,' he announced proudly.

'Wow.' Anna picked it up. 'Amazing. It looks like a pile-up on the M1. Can I keep it?'

Euan thrust it at her. 'Now draw a great big pizza,' she suggested. 'Good enough for me to eat. Really yummy. Oliver is not being entirely helpful.' Anna turned her attention back to Carrie, who had ordered their meal. 'He thinks she's got a cheek and he can't see what good it would do now. But both times she just asked about me. She wasn't pushy at all and . . .' She drew a pattern on the table mat with her fork.

'And what do you think?' Carrie asked.

'Perhaps Oliver's right. I just wish it hadn't all been so rushed, that I could have seen her a day or two later when I'd got used to the idea. As it was, I was still reeling from the shock. And now, of course, I don't know what to do. She can't come here because she can't leave her husband and I don't want to just go because it will look like – well, you know, kind of pathetic.'

'Nonsense.' Carrie sounded impatient. 'Why should doing them a favour be pathetic?' she demanded. 'Ring that lawyer and tell him you'll go but on your terms. Oh, my God, Euan. Give me that. Anna, take it from him. It's going to go everywhere.'

Anna grabbed the beaker of Ribena while Carrie tried to rescue what was left of Euan's pizza.

'Home,' Carrie said. 'And Auntie Anna is going to take you to the park while I go to sleep for an hour. Then she'll be too tired to care if she sounds completely pitiful, let alone pathetic.'

Maybe she should do nothing, Anna thought. Just see what happens. At least it was a decision. But by the time Giulio Farrini called and asked if she was free to see him. Anna was so relieved she almost screamed. 'Yes of course,' she agreed. 'No, not dinner. A drink, perhaps? Yes, anywhere round here would be helpful.'

She hung up and sat very still.

'You all right?' Henry asked, plonking himself on the edge of her desk. 'You look worried.'

Anna shook her head. 'No. Not worried. Just a small family matter.'

'Oh.' He began fiddling with the pens on her desk. 'Anna? You wouldn't do me a favour?'

'Cover up for you with Maggie?' she asked, without looking away from her screen.

Henry looked relieved. 'Yes.'

'No,' she answered, in a chatty voice. 'And, anyway, I've got to go by seven. I'm having a drink with someone.'

Anna clasped her hands around her coffee and said, 'Look, I didn't mean to sound discourteous. It was just . . .'

'Your life is being invaded,' he agreed. 'You're right, take it easy. Sophia just needed to make sure there wasn't anything blocking your decision about going there. You tell me there isn't, so that's what I'll tell her. You haven't changed your mind. Very straightforward.'

'That's right,' she agreed, wishing it was.

'In which case,' Giulio smiled at her, 'we need not pursue it any further.'

They had met in Mancetti's, under the curious gaze of Tessa, two of her girlfriends and a disconsolate Henry, who had five minutes in which to tell Melissa he was required to babysit while his wife went to a keep-fit class. Anna and Giulio ended up eating there too, partly because Bernardo wanted them to eat his famed gnocchi but mostly because despite herself Anna wanted Giulio to tell her about her family.

When they had finished, Giulio drove her home. As they turned into Anna's road they saw immediately that something was wrong. Ahead a police car, its blue light flashing, blocked the road. Little knots of people were peering from their doorways. Giulio pulled the car into a space and Anna leaped out as she saw Dottie standing by her gate.

'It's Mister, dear,' Dottie explained anxiously. 'He won't come in. He ran off when he heard the noise. His ear was all bleeding. He's under that car and he must be in agony, poor blighter. They've broken the windows of that house. What they doing, then?'

'No idea, Dottie.' Anna glanced over her shoulder as Giulio reached them. 'Her cat,' she explained to him. 'He's nearly blind and hurt, and he's dived under that car. Look, you go. I'll try and get him out.'

'In that dress?' Giulio sounded amused. 'Stay here.'

He stripped off his jacket and walked back down the road. Anna craned to see where he'd gone in the mêlée of beer cans and expletives that rose into the warm night air. Then she saw him coming back across the road behind the fracas to rejoin them, the spitting cat bundled into his jacket, his trousers covered in dust and grit. 'A bit of a headache tomorrow and a bloody ear but he's still got a few lives left,' Giulio said reassuringly above the din.

'Oh, thank you, dear,' Dottie said, and shooed her cat into the dark interior of her hallway. 'I'd better put something on him. Are you going to the shops in the morning, dear?' she asked, as Anna tried to brush Giulio's jacket. 'Small tin of sardines, then, and some potatoes,' Dottie went on, as though nothing had happened. 'Don't let him give you them unless they're washed. Pay enough as it is. They need to be called up,' she said, indicating the scene on the other side of the road, now reduced to a vanload of arrests. 'Army. That's what they need.'

As Dottie shuffled away to minister to the battered Mister Anna turned to Giulio. 'That was really kind of you,' she said, still brushing ineffectually at his jacket. 'Oh, hell, look at your hand. That bloody cat. You must come in . . . No, I insist. I'll get you some coffee while you wash all that gunge off.'

'Why did you choose to live here?' he asked, appearing in the kitchen.

'The garden,' she said simply, depressing the cafetière.

He peered through the window at the minute yard behind.

Anna smiled. 'Not there. Here, I'll show you.'

He followed her up the stairs and out on to the small roof. There was a chill in the air but spread out before them were trails of light from distant buildings and the shadowy outline of a jumble of roofs. 'Nice,' he said. 'Can we sit here?'

Anna felt pleased. 'If it gets too cold we can go in, but I like it,' she said, pulling round one of the two chairs for him to sit on. 'I was brought up just round the corner. It's a bit run down but not like King's Cross. How long have you worked for Lorenzo?'

'I don't. Fabio, my cousin, does. His father, my uncle, was a friend of Luigi – your grandfather. I've known them on and off for most of my life.'

'Did Sophia have a bad time of it?' Anna asked. 'It must have been awful being married to an alcoholic.'

'Alcoholic? Lorenzo? Perhaps it would be fairer to say he just drank too much, too unwisely, for too long. He's had his share of problems.'

'Most of us don't have so many toys to cushion the impact of dealing with them, though.'

'Maybe,' Giulio agreed mildly. 'However, the way I heard it, you've led quite a charmed existence yourself. Or did I get that wrong? I mean, great job, pretty house, successful boyfriend, terrific parents. Sounds like you've got it all.'

'What's so unusual about that?' she asked defensively, knowing she had clearly overdone the rosiness of the picture she had painted for them.

'Not unusual,' he said. And then, after a pause, 'Not fair, of course, but not unusual.'

She looked at him for a moment, then began to laugh. She was surprised at how good it made her feel. She hadn't laughed in a long time and it was even longer since someone had made her feel like doing so.

When he finally rose to his feet and said he should go it was past midnight. By then he had told her about coming to England when he was eighteen not because law school in Rome was inferior but because he had to break out of the grip of a doting Italian father. His first turbulent marriage was lightly glossed over, but the reference to a woman in his life was not lost on Anna.

She told him about her father's remarriage and how it had been a bit of a shock. She was tactful about Meryl and glowing about Barbara. He knew about her job but said he hadn't had an opportunity to see the show but now he would make sure he did. Anna gulped. She said Oliver was encouraging her to move on, but she wasn't sure where to.

'Your job or this house?'

'Job – he likes the house.'

Giulio swivelled his head to look at her. 'I'm not surprised. You're obviously a creative person.'

Anna sat very still.

'You saw the potential in this house,' he added smoothly. 'You've done well.' He got up to go.

Behind him Anna said abruptly, 'We haven't got a single thing in common, you know that, don't you? Sophia and me. I mean, what would Grandmama say about Oliver almost living here? We never even *think* of marriage.'

'Silly man.' He turned back smiling, as she followed him out of the house. 'You were saying?'

'I mean, look at the difference in how we live. I'm a working girl, no one supports me. We're poles apart.'

'I'm not sure you're that different,' he answered, surprising her. 'You just do things differently.'

'How long do you think Lorenzo's got?' she asked, as she walked with him to his car.

'Who knows? Certainly not months. Maybe a few weeks. Anna, it could have been very different for you. How much do you mind?'

'Mind? Not a bit,' she replied quickly. But that wasn't quite true. She did mind. But for the moment she couldn't put a name to what it was she minded most. Instead she said, 'You never met my mother. If you had you'd understand. She always said it's not where you come from but where you're going. Not what's behind but what's ahead. I can't find a single thing wrong with that, can you?'

Giulio gave her a long, slow look that disturbed her. She felt he was looking not at her but through her. 'Not a thing,' he said at last. 'She made you practical. Not a dreamer, are you, Miss Minstrel?'

83

She was relieved. Maybe she was not so transparent. 'No. I don't believe in dreams but I'm not without sentiment if, of course, sentiment is required.'

He laughed. 'Don't disappoint me, I was enjoying your Englishness.'

She smiled back. And then, for no reason at all, she said impulsively, 'How much would it mean to them if I agreed to go to Rome?'

'A lot,' he said briefly.

'Okay,' she said. 'I will.'

'Will what?' His thumb was poised to activate the alarm on his car key.

'Go to Rome,' she said, enjoying his surprise. 'One night, two at the most. That's all.'

'Anna . . .' Giulio began to walk back to where she stood on the pavement, hugging her jacket around her shoulders, but whatever else he had planned to say was stopped by the arrival of Oliver's car, which drew up behind them. The lights went out, the door slammed and Oliver strode up to them, tie loosened, pushing his hand through his hair.

When she introduced them Oliver looked as though he was about to say something blunt, but Anna squeezed his hand. Instead he turned briskly to Giulio. 'Thank you for bringing Anna home. She'll be fine now. No need to say what I think of the clumsy way this has been handled.'

'Oliver, please,' Anna said, but he hushed her.

Giulio waved away the admonishment. 'I agree. It must have looked like a ten-ton truck let loose in a china department.' Anna giggled. 'I hope Rome goes okay.' Giulio touched her arm lightly and strode towards his car.

'*Rome?*' Oliver exclaimed, as they watched Giulio's car pull away. 'You're going to Rome? But you don't even know them.'

'I have to. Come inside and I'll tell you everything.' She tried to slip an arm around his waist, but he held her away from him then walked ahead of her into the house.

'I have to go,' she said, when they were alone. 'Why are you so furious? Just a weekend. How can that be a problem?'

'What about your mother?' he demanded, making her catch her breath. 'How would she feel with you just swanning off with the woman who abandoned you? Think how upset you were when your father married Meryl. At least he waited eighteen months. You haven't waited eight minutes. I don't think you've really considered the implications of all this. You're in danger of being sucked in.'

'Sucked in? To what?' she cried. 'I'm thirty-one years old, my life is in place. But surely to God I can be allowed to acknowledge out of sheer bloody compassion a man who made my existence possible? Surely I'm allowed a glimpse of where I came from? Oh, for God's sake, if I'm comfortable with it, why aren't you?'

The look on his face showed he hadn't taken in a word she'd said because her fiery defence had stirred other ideas, which had to be more urgently resolved. He apologized. She accepted and with relief folded herself into bed beside him. No, it had not been a tense meeting, she went on. But it had made her think of Sophia as a person.

'In what way?'

'I don't know,' she began. 'It was the oddest sensation. I felt sorry for her.'

Oliver craned round to look at her face. 'Sorry for her? For God's sake, why? I feel sorry for her because she gave you up, but that's different.'

'I know,' Anna cried. 'I know, I know, *I know*. It doesn't make sense, does it? It's just that I don't think she's happy. She's never been accepted by them and now she's about to be a widow. How can money help that?'

There was no agenda to be resolved. She had never felt bitter. How could she? Her parents had been wonderful. The boot, she said, was on the other foot. Lorenzo and Sophia needed her. It was the other way round. The mention of foot proved too much for Oliver, who liked to start with her toes. It wasn't until he had progressed somewhat further that he lifted his head and asked if her mind was elsewhere.

'No, of course it isn't. I'm not exactly lying here thinking of England.'

'What about Rome, then?'

'Rome? Good heavens, no.' She hoped she sounded duly astounded. She was glad he couldn't see her face in the dark.

She told Henry her godfather was seriously ill in Rome and arranged to leave the following Friday with Tania Prowton as stand-in producer. Everyone loathed Tania: she let Max run circles around her, but Henry swore he would monitor everything Anna had arranged. That, she thought gloomily, was the easy part. Oliver was not being supportive and her father had said nothing at all. When Sophia rang the night before she left to return to Rome, Anna was more brusque with her than she had intended. How easily they could mobilize her guilt.

'Anna?' Sophia asked hesitantly. 'Is this making life difficult for you? Because I have no right to put my needs before anyone else's.'

Anna was taken aback. Only someone perceptive could have sensed her unease. Perhaps there was something in the genes. 'No. It's fine,' she lied. 'My decision. Everyone respects that. I'll see you tomorrow.'

Before she hung up, Sophia advised Anna not to take too much notice of anything Giulio might have said. There was a short pause. 'He is a good lawyer.'

'But not yours. Is that it?' Anna asked.

'Yes,' Sophia said quietly. 'That's exactly it.'

Clearly Colin was not happy, but he remained steadfast that it was her decision. Oliver took comfort in that the Grescobaldis were not penniless and therefore unlikely to embarrass her.

'It wouldn't worry me if they didn't have a penny to their

name,' she pointed out, and wished he would offer to come with her, but he didn't.

The one person she longed to discuss it with was for ever out of her reach: she ached to hear her mother's voice, then felt spasms of guilt so strong that she took to whispering to her as if speaking aloud would produce the answers. But nothing came. Amongst the post the next morning was a letter from the Post Adoption Agency, asking her to get in touch with them. The decision, they said, was entirely hers, but her birth-mother wished to make contact for medical reasons.

Anna read it twice. If only they knew, she thought, what money could do. On the whole she preferred not to. Then she crumpled it into a small ball and threw it into the bin.

Chapter Eight

From the window of his eighth-floor office Giulio Farrini looked out absently over grey roofs struggling to survive amid the glass and steel encroaching on the narrow streets and choked pavements of the City. His hands were dug deep into the pockets of his trousers leaving a crumpled line in his jacket.

Behind him stood a long black marble-topped desk on which someone had straightened the few items that lay beside a dark grey computer screen: a leather diary open at that day's page, a bundle of buff folders, each tied with a red ribbon, and a glass container, square, solid and filled with black marker pens. Only one file was open, which he had been studying for the past hour as he wondered what the hell he had been thinking of to allow Fabio to drag him into invading the life of a girl like Anna Minstrel.

Behind him the door opened and a woman in a neat suit with short, dark, bobbed hair came in quietly. She crossed to the desk and laid on it two more files and a folder of letters to be signed. On the very top she placed an envelope in which was an airline ticket. 'Giulio?'

'Uh-huh?'

'They're waiting.'

'Thanks, Jodie. I'll be right there.'

'Mrs Grescobaldi called.'

'I'm sure she did,' he replied, without much interest.

Jodie Butler looked uncertainly at her watch. 'Shall I say you've been delayed?'

'Five minutes,' he promised.

Through a gap in the towering blocks opposite, the river was visible like a narrow grey ribbon. Down below in the street, tourists forced office workers to step into a stream of slow-moving traffic and tempers to fray.

On the floor above him were his new partners, acquired by a merger that had been tracked with interest in the business press and with unease by their many competitors. From the point of view of Farrini Pasola and Partners it had been their only way forward to compete on a more lucrative footing on the international stage. That was where the real money was, the serious players. And here Giulio knew what he was doing. Here, in this complex, hard-nosed company, his wishes were carried out, his advice taken. His reputation counted, and no one gave a fuck about an overindulged family in Rome who had dragged a young woman into their midst because he had gone out of his way to find her.

Fabio had said they could up the ante if the price wasn't right. 'Give her what she wants,' he had said. 'Just get the girl here.'

'How do you know she'll want money?' Giulio asked. 'Won't being reunited with her mother be enough?'

Fabio grunted. 'Who knows. They might have given her up, but if she's got their genes, I wouldn't bank on it.'

Giulio frowned at the airline ticket lying on the desk. She'd asked for nothing and she was nowhere near as tough as she made out. She was scared shitless by it all, he could tell. And why shouldn't she be? But all that cool indifference, which vanished when she smiled. He thought of her smiling, and shook his head.

His instinct was to reach for the phone and ask Anna seriously to consider what she was doing. But it was none of his business. She was old enough to take care of herself, he reasoned, so why this sudden attack of conscience? He picked up a pen and scrawled his name across a compliments slip.

*

Anna lowered the envelope and looked into the distance. There was no note, just a compliments slip with the name of the firm of lawyers, Farrini Pasola Partnership. There was an address in the City. She briefly studied the heavily scrawled black signature. She held the card away from her. Odd. She had assumed that a man who had sat drinking coffee on your roof late at night might be a little less formal the next day.

She stuffed the card into her bag, along with the ticket. Perhaps sitting so companionably with Sophia's husband's lawyer had been a mistake. But at the time it hadn't seemed that way. She frowned absently at the newspapers lying on her desk. The *Independent* had run a profile on Max, which was not entirely flattering but the kudos of starring in a serious paper had left him almost fainting with pleasure.

Then a thought gripped her. Had she been charmed into going to Rome? Then because it made her feel in control again, she drew glasses on Max's face and blacked out his front teeth. After that she rang Oliver and said why didn't they have dinner in bed.

Fabio Carrini, Giulio's cousin, met Anna as she came through Arrivals shortly after her plane touched down in Rome. She had brought only a weekend case and, in spite of the journey, he thought she looked remarkably cool and uncrumpled. Her dark glasses were pushed back into her hair and her hands were dug into the pockets of her linen trousers. Like his cousin, Fabio had apparently guessed instantly who she was, although Anna looked neither especially English, nor like a tourist. He spoke first. 'Anna?' he said. 'I am Fabio. Welcome to Rome.'

There was a strong family resemblance between Fabio and Giulio, although Fabio was older and if she had been wearing anything other than loafers Anna would have been taller than him. Her nerves made conversation difficult during the forty-minute drive from the airport to Trastevere, where the Grescobaldis lived. When Anna had said for the third time, 'I'm not sure. Let me think,' Fabio looked at her with sympathy and patted her hand. Anna smiled at him gratefully. He was much softer than his cousin, she decided.

When he next spoke it was to tell her that Lorenzo was seriously ill. He was virtually unconscious.

Anna gazed at the speeding traffic. 'How long?'

Fabio shook his head. 'I have no idea. It could be weeks, days, even.'

Eventually, the car swung off the wide boulevard into a narrow road then turned through a high archway that led to a cobbled courtyard. Behind them the huge iron gates closed slowly. The car turned in a narrow arc, before the house, skirted a fountain and pulled up in front of double wooden doors, one of which was open. Sophia was waiting there and this time Anna did not resist her embrace.

'This is so hard to believe,' Sophia said, clutching Anna's hand. 'You are here. I won't thank you again, but you know what is in my heart.'

As she stood in the marble-floored hallway, Anna gazed up at the curved staircase that swept to the upper floor and round into a circular landing. Sophia and Fabio ushered her between them into the nearest salon where light streamed in through half-shuttered windows and the scent of lilies hung heavily on the air. Anna glanced around her and took in the folding white doors that framed casement windows leading out on to the terrace, plump white sofas, loaded with deep blue cushions, stacks of books piled on glass and chrome tables. The priceless contemporary art on the pale coffee walls could not have asked for a finer setting. From far below in the courtyard she could hear water tumbling from the fountain.

A grey-haired housekeeper moved around quietly waiting to show Anna to her room where her luggage was being unpacked. 'Take your time,' Sophia urged. 'I have to attend to some business with Fabio and I must not be away from Lorenzo for too long. Let us meet again in an hour. If there is anything you want, Pilar will be there for you. Pilar?' She turned and spoke to the housekeeper, who nodded, her expression impassive.

Anna watched Sophia curiously during this exchange. Her tone was that of a woman used to dealing with domestic staff; she was giving orders not making requests.

As Pilar moved away, Sophia turned back to Anna. 'She is always cross with me,' she whispered, as she walked with Anna to the foot of the stairs. 'She has to wear canvas shoes like all the others but she thinks that as she is boss, she should be different.'

'Why do they wear canvas shoes?'

'The noise,' Sophia said, tapping her heel on the floor. 'See? It would sound like castanets all day if they wore anything else. But Pilar thinks she is family – which in many ways she is, of course. But what can you do?'

Anna looked uneasily at Pilar, standing by the foot of the stairs. 'Couldn't you make an exception?'

Sophia sighed. 'They'd all walk out. You have no idea what a Mafia they can be. She used to work for my mother-in-law before she came to us. Lorenzo just told me one day that she was coming. So here she is. My mother-in-law makes the rules.'

'What? Even here?' Anna asked.

Sophia nodded. 'Even here.' She gave a quick laugh. 'And it is not so bad. At least it's only rules she imposes. We are used to it.'

Together they mounted the stairs. Anna noticed that Sophia was shaking and that her face under its careful makeup was strained. Her eyes looked haunted. The composure she had shown at dinner in London was gone. Poor, poor woman, she thought.

At the top of the stairs, the house divided into two long corridors stretching to left and right. Overhead an eerie blue light from a vast glass dome above the staircase fell on the landing, filtering the sun's rays. Sophia squeezed Anna's hand. 'I go here.' She pointed. 'Pilar will take you to your room that way.'

Just then the door at the end opened. A white-coated nurse appeared and disappeared into a room next to it. Sophia walked away quickly. The silence that fell over the highly polished floors, the cool marble walls, was like that of a monastery. Anna could feel that someone was dying. It was impossible to think of the man as her father. Her father was living in Scotland with his second wife and a new family.

She realized that the housekeeper, in her navy dress, black hair pinned back neatly, was waiting, a polite smile in place. '*Scusi*,' Anna said, and followed her.

At the end of the gallery that looked down to the centre of the house, they turned into a corridor parallel to the one Sophia had used. At its end Pilar opened a door and stood back to let Anna go through. The suite, which overlooked the courtyard, was serene and cool. Anna walked into the centre and turned around slowly. She was looking at the work of a woman with time on her hands and a need for perfection. For one moment she wished with all her heart that she hadn't said, 'Heavens,' as the door had opened. She hadn't missed Pilar's small smile of satisfaction.

From the matching silk armchairs in the sitting room to the soap in the pink marble bathroom, no detail jarred. Anna wondered if any guest before her had dared to upset the perfect symmetry of the furniture by moving a cushion or one of the books on the glass table. She would not even dare to disturb the round glass bowl filled with a pyramid of peaches and nectarines. Flowers trailed from white cylinder vases, and a day-bed, placed at right angles to the far window, waited, for someone more fashionable, Anna thought, more chic than her to dispose themselves on it. Someone, in fact, like Sophia.

Pilar fussed with the shutters, then indicated a telephone

by which Anna could summon her; then in faltering English, asked if that would be all.

'*Grazie.*' Anna swung round with a smile. The woman looked keenly at her, gave a nod and withdrew.

Anna walked out on to the terrace and stood, with her hands on the stone parapet, gazing across to where Lorenzo drifted in and out of consciousness. Sophia, she decided, had done well for herself by giving up her daughter. She stared across the courtyard, at the uneven terracotta tiles of the roofs, the trailing bougainvillaea cascading from window-boxes and sliding into cracks in the solid stone walls. But if she had kept you, Anna thought, you would never have known the happiness and security that you were given by an irreplaceable woman. 'And that's the bottom line,' she said, almost aloud. But no matter how many times she said it, she couldn't help thinking of what might have been hers if she had stayed with her natural mother.

She turned away from the view and shook herself. She should ring her father. However, it was the answering-machine that greeted her, so she tried Oliver's mobile, which was switched off. She left a message, saying she would call him later. Then she lowered herself tentatively on to the cool cotton surface of the day-bed. Her hands linked behind her head, she settled down to do nothing more energetic than gaze out at the blue sky, feeling the warmth of the sun on her face and listening to the fountain far below. In the distance she could hear the faint murmur of traffic as Trastevere went about its chaotic business.

Shortly before five there was a light tap on the door. Anna glanced at her watch. Pilar was early. 'Come in,' she called, swinging upright and pulling her hair into a slide at the nape of her neck. 'I'm ready.' She groped under the bed for her shoes. 'Come in,' she repeated, as the door remained closed.

'Are you sure?' a man's voice said.

Anna looked up. She sat perfectly still, one hand clutching a shoe, and stared straight into the eyes of a slender young man with carefully groomed thick black hair and a wide, hesitant smile.

'I came myself,' he said, stepping uncertainly a little way into the room. 'To get you. I am Andrea.'

Chapter Nine

At every level Andrea Grescobaldi's world was heaving seismically out of control. Since, only a few weeks before, he had learned of the existence of his sister, he had inspected other areas of his life for deception. He went over and over it, reconstructing, recalling, examining, until he was cocooned in an agony of doubt. There was no longer any question of a discussion with his father, who was beyond anything more than turning his eyes weakly to Andrea and entreating him to understand. However, in a family who had a careless relationship with honesty, Andrea too, was not without fault in this way.

Long ago, protected, smothered, desperate for freedom, when he had insisted on reading for his degree in English in Milan rather than at the university nearest to his home, he had decided that his parents were not equipped to deal with the way he wanted to conduct his life. He wanted to be away from their gaze, not working in the company that was to be his and free to see whom he liked without the constant pressure to bring home a nice girl. He knew too that he could not bring himself to disappoint them or face the questions he would have to answer. Now he struggled with guilt: if he had stayed in Rome, remained as a barrier between them in their antipathy towards each other, he might have prevented the consequences of his father's descent into drink. So much now was clear: the coldness between his mother and his adored *nonna*; his mother's resistance to any overture from Papa's family; their veiled contempt for her. Even so it was hard to know where the truth lay.

All his life Andrea had been instructed to conceal things from his grandparents and even from Uncle Gianni. But who was he to believe? His grandmother, who admitted that she had prevented his parents' marriage but said that she had not known until too late that a child was expected, or his mother, who said they had ignored her letters telling them she was pregnant and sent Papa away so that he could not help her. And Papa had said that he was so young, he had been terrified of what his parents might do and he had never anticipated that Sophia's family would not help her.

Andrea could not bear to watch his father now during the endless hours he sat beside Lorenzo's bed, reading to him or holding his hands. Over and over Andrea told him he understood, forgave him, and promised him that, in spite of his mother's objections, he would make sure that this sister was found and brought to him. And he had. He had gone over Sophia's head and called Fabio.

His mother's horror had been hard to take. 'You don't know what you've done,' she whispered to him, white-faced. And then she had said he was not to interfere any more. Of course he hadn't. The relief was overwhelming that others would take the burden from him. He had been torn between elation and fear when Giulio had found her and at the moment when he knocked on Anna's door, he was gripped by a feeling that his mother might have been right.

Andrea was indeed like her. Giulio had not exaggerated. Anna thought that the family features and the height suited him a great deal better than they did her and ruefully noted that as well as the silver spoon he had been given the looks too.

He came towards her, dark eyes anxiously scanning her face, his hands held out. His English was more than competent, delivered in a charming, fractured accent. Just like

97

Sophia's. 'My God,' he said, staring right into her face. 'My God, what are we supposed to say?' She could see he was trying to keep his emotions in check.

Then they both spoke at once, neither hearing very much, until they suddenly stopped and laughed.

'Sorry,' Anna said. 'You first. No, please. Go ahead.'

'This is so nice, so – emotional for me,' he said. 'I told myself to stay calm, like you. Giulio said you were very calm. But it can't have been easy. For me, it was not.'

'No,' she agreed, pleased that Giulio had failed to see her panic. 'Not for any of us. I'm just so sorry your father is so ill.'

Andrea looked bleakly at her. 'I try not to think, but each day it is worse.' A look of sheer disbelief spread fleetingly across his face.

'I know,' she said gently, touching his arm, feeling only compassion for him. 'I lost my mother just a while ago. It's so hard . . .'

He seemed to give himself a shake. 'Of course. And Mamma said your father has remarried? How are you with that? May I?' He indicated the day-bed.

'Fine,' she said loyally, and they both sat down. Then honesty compelled her to add, 'I don't really know her that well. But Dad seems happy.'

'Good,' he said. 'That's good. You see,' he forced a laugh, 'I'm not making good sense. I don't know where to start. Maybe I should apologize for *them*.' He indicated his absent parents with a nod towards the door.

'Maybe . . .' Anna replied carefully, '. . . maybe it's you who needs the apology. At least I always knew there was the possibility of a brother or sister. You knew nothing.' She looked at him with pity. 'And,' she reminded him, 'in parting with me Sophia gave me to two people who loved me. I had a good life, Andrea. It still is.'

'And you forgive them. For all this?'

'I forgive your mother, of course,' she said, then chose her words carefully. 'I understand the difficulty your father

98

was in. Whether Sophia is prepared to forgive everyone else for not helping her keep me is what matters.'

'Mamma's family were awful,' he agreed. 'They wouldn't help. Papa's were not told until it was too late.'

Anna opened her mouth to object and closed it again. 'Well, that's something for you and your family to sort out. Not for me. Really, I'm here to see your father and then I shall go away again.'

Andrea regarded her with what seemed like envy. 'It is odd,' he sighed, 'I have never quite mastered the Catholic forgiveness. But you have it.'

Anna looked astonished. 'Catholic? Me? Oh heavens, no. Not sure I'm anything, really.'

'Not? But Papa told Nonna that Mamma had insisted—' He stopped. 'Maybe I misunderstood. Nonna told me. These things are important to her so she would have asked. Maybe she misunderstood. She is too ill now, her hips are bad, she does not move. It is so terrible – she wants to see Papa but the journey would kill her. She prays. We just don't tell her, eh?'

'Well,' Anna said briskly, thinking uneasily that maybe Sophia's instructions for a Catholic upbringing had been ignored by Colin and Barbara in their eagerness to have a child, 'I won't be meeting your grandmother so it's up to you what you say.' She paused and smiled. 'Listen. We've just met. I need to know about you.'

Anna watched him as he talked and noted the ease with which he assumed that she would know, without having it explained to her, how they lived. Of course she understood, but from the outside looking in. These were the people Max Warner aspired to, who would impress Oliver's mother. And there was no doubt that Andrea was spoiled, but in an engaging way. At least, she thought, he knew it's and acknowledged it with a shy grin. '*Viziato*.' He pulled a face. 'You know, *rovinato*. Ruined.' His warmth neutralized the vanity inherent in the studied carelessness of his clothes, the thin cotton sweater and narrow trousers, the bare feet

99

pushed into loafers, which might otherwise have been harder to take. It would have annoyed Oliver, though, who had been irritated by Giulio. She sighed. It was not Andrea's fault that he was spoilt.

In the end, of course, he asked her the inevitable question. 'Would you have searched for them? Wondered about who they were? Not knowing must make you feel . . . what is the word I want?'

'Frustrated? No,' she replied honestly. 'I had such a wonderful mother and my father is still alive. Occasionally I was curious, of course. But, then, how would I have known where to begin? There were no clues.'

He seemed surprised. 'None? I thought my mother said there was a note in case you came looking? A letter she left.'

Anna started to say, 'There was nothing in my file,' but that would have been an admission that she had looked. Yet there had been no note. Not then, not all those years ago when she had tentatively inquired one summer on vacation from university. She would have been told. Surely? 'I have no idea,' she said. 'But the important thing now is for me to meet your father. Yes?'

He looked searchingly at her. 'Of course,' he said. 'Let's go and find Mamma.' He held out a hand. She smiled and let him pull her to her feet.

As they went to find Sophia, she kept thinking, This is my brother. My *brother*. She waited for emotion to invest itself in the word, but it didn't.

'And you have a job that is, you know, *affascinante*,' he said admiringly, as they approached the cavernous salon across the marble floor of the hall where Sophia was waiting for them.

Anna laughed. 'If that's what I think it means, glamorous is the last word I'd use for trying not to murder a man who's a pain in the butt. Butt?' She patted her own as he looked puzzled.

'Ah,' he said in delight. 'You mean *deretano*.'

'That's right. Butt,' she said.

They were laughing as they entered the salon.

'Andrea,' Sophia said sharply, a note of anger in her voice. She rose from a sofa, laying aside some papers. 'Please. What is there to laugh about? And Pilar said you had disturbed Anna.' She crossed to where they stood. Anna glanced uncertainly from mother to son. 'I asked you to remember her wishes.'

'They didn't include not seeing me, Mamma,' he replied firmly. 'And you should not listen to Pilar's gossip.'

'Don't use that tone, Andrea.'

'I'll choose my tone, Mamma. And I'll choose what I say to Anna. She might be your daughter but she's my sister. And, by the way, she isn't a Catholic.'

'Andrea,' Sophia's voice rose warningly, 'this is not a subject for now . . .'

'No?' he said, his voice laced with sarcasm. 'When would you like to discuss it, Mamma? In another thirty years?'

'This is not right, Andrea,' Sophia began, faltering, and lapsed into Italian. Andrea looked sullen, drooping against the doorframe, as if he'd heard it all before.

At first Anna thought he was going to retaliate. 'Look, I'll leave you both,' she began, but Andrea stopped her.

'No. I'm going to sit with Papa.'

There was an embarrassed silence as the women watched him stride across the hall and take the stairs two at a time.

'I apologize, Anna,' Sophia said wearily. 'He is finding it hard to forgive me. Everyone is. They never have, of course. I find it hard with them, but Andrea . . . that is more difficult. Now,' she took a deep breath and forced a smile, 'you have everything you need? Your room is comfortable? You like it?'

Anna nodded, feeling sympathy stir for Sophia, and dismay that time hadn't softened Lorenzo's family to what they saw as Sophia's scandalous conduct. She understood Andrea's feelings, but if she could handle it – and she had more to feel bitter about – so could he. Yet having been at the centre of everyone's universe, it must be harder for him to grasp that his parents were not perfect. But see it he must if he was to be fair to his mother. She would tell him that disappointment, adjustment and sadness had visited her too.

'And now,' Sophia asked gently, 'you meet your – Lorenzo,' she corrected herself.

The room was cool and shaded, the shutters standing only inches ajar, but she could see that it was no less magnificent than the others in this house. A dusty shaft of sunlight streamed in to fall on a small table on which was a statue of Our Lady with white roses entwined around her feet, arms open to embrace those who came to kneel before it. A prayer stool with a rich crimson cushion was placed before it. A solitary votive candle flickered in its red holder. Suddenly Anna shivered.

The doctor came forward. 'Are you okay?' he asked, gazing searchingly at her.

'Absolutely,' she said firmly.

He took her by the arm and explained quietly that he had increased the dose of morphine. 'Your father is drifting in and out of consciousness but this will help. At this time he is a little more alert, but very ill. Don't be afraid. Come.' With his hand under her elbow and Sophia's arm protectively around her shoulders they led her forward.

Anna tried to ease herself away from them. 'Please?' she asked, indicating that she would like them to release her. 'Please,' she said again, more insistently, when they seemed reluctant to do so. They exchanged a worried look, and then, by silent consent, stood back.

As she approached the bed Andrea stood up and gestured for her to take his place. Lorenzo's shrunken figure lay already like a corpse in the centre of a small, narrow bed. His eyes were closed, and he breathed in shallow gasps. As she drew nearer she felt the first flicker of fear. The full understanding of the need for haste, the inaccurate documents, Sophia's terror that she might have been turned away, hit her. It was no longer the power game that had seemed necessary when she had been in the restaurant, struggling to conceal her curiosity from the woman who had given her away and a shrewd, lazy-eyed lawyer.

The nurse and Sophia tried to rouse Lorenzo to see her, their voices shockingly loud in such a still room. He opened his eyes, but did not seem to understand who she was. Anna held her breath, her eyes wide, but his lids closed.

It was hopeless. Try as she might, she could summon no feeling for this man, just disbelief that this was happening. But the setting, the sorrow of Sophia and Andrea, touched her more deeply than she had expected. She felt close to tears as she leaned over the gaunt figure and told him gently in faltering Italian, that she was fine, her life had been good. She bore him no grudge. All of this she had arranged with Sophia, who had assured her that it was what Lorenzo wanted to hear. She even placed her hand over the cold, veined one that lay motionless on the white cover clutching a rosary. There was no returning pressure. Nor had she expected there to be. She was too late. Anyone could see that.

She stared down at the exhausted face, the pale yellow skin, and a rush of emotions took her by storm. She was staring at death. The man she had been told was her father was slowly drifting into another life. She listened to his struggle for breath and, more fervently than ever before in her life, she wished she was anywhere but here, where she had no place.

Anna could do nothing but stroke Lorenzo's arm. A leather band, holding an electronic dial that measured the dose he needed to sedate him, was strapped to a wrist that was no more than bone, pumping drugs into a body that had effectively ceased to function, just keeping pain at bay and dignity intact.

'Take his hand,' Sophia whispered. Anna did as she was

told but the only words Lorenzo uttered were incoherent and in Italian.

Anna felt scared and sick. Nothing had prepared her for this and inside her a wave of grief was making its way to her eyes and mouth. She stifled a sob.

Sophia had to lean close to Lorenzo's mouth to hear what he said and, with admirable composure, quietly repeated to Anna that he was happy and grateful that she was here, that she was beautiful and that he wanted his children to know each other better and to support their mother.

'Say, "Papa, it's Anna",' Sophia said urgently.

Without warning Andrea moved forward and began to protest.

Sophia held up a hand to stop him. 'Not now, Andrea,' she said firmly. 'Leave us.'

'Why? More secrets, Mamma?'

'Andrea, please.' Sophia grabbed his wrist.

The nurse threw up her hands, muttered something unintelligible then evidently begged them to remember where they were. Clearly they could not. The doctor moved to restrain Andrea and to soothe Sophia. For a few seconds uproar ensued. Anna looked wildly from one to the other, then back at the man on the bed. His eyes were open, resting on her. Without thinking she leaned as close to him as she could and, under cover of the astonishing yelling around them, gave him the assurance he needed '*Si*,' she said, looking straight into his exhausted eyes. '*Si, si. Prometto, prometto.*'

Only the nurse seemed still aware that Anna was with them. 'Please,' she said, in a low voice, placing both hands on Anna's shoulders, 'please, you go now.'

Anna lowered Lorenzo's hand gently to the bedcover. Then she surprised herself by leaning forward and kissing his forehead. It felt cool and damp. She rose to her feet. Sophia and Andrea both stopped and looked at her.

'And this,' Anna said, faintly incredulous, her eyes on Andrea, 'is what I'm supposed to have missed?'

'*Anna.*' Sophia went to take her arm but Anna brushed her hand aside. Andrea said nothing. Anna walked quickly away and opened the door as a priest was about to enter. He stood aside to let her go past him, then quietly closed the door after her.

Outside she leaned briefly against the wall then turned and made her way to her room. She found some mineral water in the bathroom and drank it, then sat on the edge of the pink marble bath, with its gold taps, pink and white towels piled on marble slabs above it, and waited for the waves of fright to pass.

Chapter Ten

There was no sign of Sophia or Andrea. Pilar was the only person she encountered as she made her way towards the stairs. If she knew of the scene over Lorenzo's bed, she gave no hint of it. Signor Andreotti had just arrived. Heaven only knew where Andrea had gone and at that moment Anna did not want to see him. Or Signor Andreotti – or Monsignor, in his long black robe with purple buttons.

'*La signora*? You want?' Pilar asked.

'No,' Anna whispered sharply. 'No one. I'm going out.' She waved her hand towards the door, as Pilar looked puzzled. 'You know, walk. *Vado via*,' she whispered pointing at herself, fearful that Sophia would come looking for her before Anna could try to unravel the complicated feelings her mother had aroused in her. 'Oh, God, what's the word? *Piedi*,' she said triumphantly. '*Capisce?*'

'*Si*,' Pilar nodded vigorously, understanding. 'You walk, *si*?'

Relieved Anna moved past her towards the stairs. '*Un ora*,' she called back softly, pointing to her watch and holding up one finger. 'That's all. *Ciao*.'

Anna went down to the ground floor, pushed open the heavy wooden door and walked out into the courtyard. It was not quite six but the blast of heat as she stepped on to the cobbles dazzled her. She needed to get away from this oppressive house, sit somewhere and talk to someone where she wouldn't be disturbed. Oliver, Carrie, her father, any of the people she loved most. She wanted to be where she could see people who led normal lives and didn't have skeletons in their closets that could cause this kind of turmoil. People who didn't fly her hundreds of miles to clutch the hand of a dying man while they screamed abuse at each other, in a war of recrimination of which she was the cause. She shouldn't have come, she thought bleakly.

Everything about the shameful scene had offended her. She was shocked by Andrea's behaviour. The very thought of talking to her own mother like that was out of the question. But, then, her mother hadn't lied to her. Yet even if Sophia had prospered, she had also suffered. Why couldn't Andrea see that, understand, have more compassion for a woman who had, after all, given him a good life? Why lay all the blame at Sophia's door and not some of it with Lorenzo?

She knew now that when she had said to Giulio that she would go to Rome, curiosity had been the trigger – but it had also been an impulsive decision to prove something to herself.

She had been walking fast, oblivious to the pandemonium erupting from the streets as Rome roared into the rush-hour. Now she stopped and scrabbled in her bag for her mobile and Giulio's card. She would ring him to ask why he hadn't warned her that Andrea's shock at discovering his parents' secret had triggered such resentment between him and his mother. She should have been told. Giulio should have told her. She had to blame someone.

She got through to his office, spoke to his secretary then heard him say 'Anna?' twice, before she snapped the off button. What was the point?

After that she just walked. Up steep streets and along narrow alleyways, past churches, occasionally peering into dim interiors with sunlight streaming through elaborate stained-glass windows on to stone naves and rows of stiff little chairs with red cushions. It was tempting to go into one, to sit in the shadows and appeal to her dead mother for advice on what to do next.

Eventually she left behind the hilly streets of Trastevere, went into a small leafy park with still glades and found a stone bench to sit on. She would have stayed there longer if the images of Lorenzo's ravaged face had not almost made her cry out. Hastily she got to her feet and retraced her steps. She felt better while she walked.

The sun was still unwelcomely hot and the clothes she was wearing were all wrong. She felt sticky and uncomfortable, and very alone. She was aware only of a raging thirst and that unless she wanted to stoke the hysteria that seemed only a breath away at the sad house she would have to go back. First, though, she called the airline and reserved a seat on the afternoon flight next day.

At the next corner, and without any clear idea where she was heading, she turned into a wide boulevard where lanes of cars and buses roared along. She bought a can of Coke from a street vendor, then rolled the icy cold tin across her forehead and round the back of her neck before pulling the tab to down half the contents in one go. Then she sat on the steps of the nearest church and called Oliver. When she finally caught up with him he was still in a meeting. She felt too tired and confused to say anything other than that she was fine, that she had done what she set out to do and had just booked an earlier flight.

He sounded pleased. 'Where are you?'

She looked around vaguely. 'The Ripetta, I think. Somewhere around there.'

'Listen,' he murmured, 'can't talk now. Client. I'll call you later. Poor baby. What a bugger of a day. Done now. Just keep that in mind. Now you can leave the whole lot of them behind.'

'Physically at least,' she agreed, pressing one hand against her free ear.

'What's that supposed to mean?'

She screwed up her eyes and tried to imagine him sitting in his office and found that she couldn't. The heat, she told herself. 'Well, you don't have to physically see people to think about them,' she shouted, above the screaming of a convoy of Vespas. 'After all, they're a fairly memorable lot.'

She also left a message on Meryl's answering-machine, and was debating how to get back to Trastevere when her phone rang.

'Anna?' came Giulio's voice.

She stood very still and studied the pavement.

'Why did you hang up?'

'I got cut off,' she lied. 'It was nothing. Honestly.'

There was a small silence. 'What's the problem?'

'Problem? Heavens, why should there be a problem? I'm fine. It was just to say – just to say that I've seen Lorenzo and I think now they need to be on their own so I've booked a flight home tomorrow.'

'Have you told Sophia?'

'I will,' she said quickly. 'I'll do that when I get back. Look, thank you for ringing back. And, Giulio, there's no need for you to ring her.'

'Call me when you get back to London.'

'Why? Sorry, that sounded rude, but there won't be any need. My work here is done.'

'Yes?'

'Yes. There's a taxi. Goodbye, Giulio.'

Less than ten minutes later the cab dropped her at the iron gates of the house. She pressed the door-buzzer and heard several pairs of feet rushing to greet her. There was no sign of Andrea, but Sophia hurried towards her as Pilar and a houseboy stood silently by. It was clear that they were bewildered by the commotion, and Anna didn't blame them.

'I was so worried,' Sophia said. 'I'm so sorry. You must forgive us both. Andrea is mortified. Wait, I must tell Fabio you are safe.'

Sophia pulled Anna with her towards the phone, which was being held by a tall man with silver hair, who regarded her curiously. The priest was also there. He smiled and raised his hands in a small gesture of thanksgiving then joined the crowd around her.

'Roberto,' Sophia said eagerly, to the grey-haired man. 'This is Anna. But of course you guessed. We have behaved so badly. I was afraid she had gone to the airport.'

'There is so little I can do now,' Roberto said to Anna, while Sophia saw Monsignor to the door, 'but if I can be of service to you, please, it would give me something to do. One feels so useless. Your father – Lorenzo – he is like a brother to me.'

When he too had left, Sophia came back to Anna. 'I go and sit with Lorenzo for a little while. Till Roberto comes back. Anything you want, just ask Pilar. And, Anna, don't think badly of Andrea. He is still shocked and he loves his papa. Forgive him. Yes?'

'Of course,' Anna said. 'It's been a strain for everyone. I'll be fine. Maybe I could sit with Lorenzo for a little while tomorrow?'

'Oh, yes,' Sophia said eagerly. 'Yes. He would like that. He's so pleased you've come.'

Anna stared after her.

The younger of Gianni Grescobaldi's two daughters, who had recently celebrated her twenty-seventh birthday in some style and with a hundred and fifty of her closest friends in attendance, sat on the edge of his cane chair and draped her arm along the back. The cotton sliver of her dress was short enough to satisfy her own need to show off her bare, tanned legs but long enough not to earn a rebuke from her father, who in Irena's view could be tiresome about these things. 'What if I just turn up? she suggested. 'Pretend I didn't understand. Then I can see her and come back and tell you what she's like.'

Gianni was deeply fond of both his daughters but on occasion he wondered if, even so, he could cope with their need to do exactly as they liked. He looked up at her. 'Irena,' he said, firmly but gently, 'you will assure me that you intend to do no such thing.'

Irena threw her arms in the air and stood up. 'But why? This is so stupid. Andrea is in a terrible state. Lorenzo is practically dead – sorry, Bebbo,' she looked hastily at her father, 'you know what I mean. As usual Sophia is being distant bloody Sophia, and I have a cousin I'm not allowed to see. What's the matter with her? Has she got two heads?'

'Don't be stupid, Irena.' Gianni frowned. He spoke impatiently, but he sympathized. As Lorenzo's only brother he was outraged that Sophia and their unknown daughter had imposed such conditions on her brief visit. 'It was the only way,' he insisted. 'Nonna said it was better than not at all.'

'Nonna would agree to anything where Lorenzo is concerned,' Irena retorted. 'And I tell you this. I have a new view of Nonna. She is very deep. All these years she knew – and, come to that, so did you two. Elena and I feel very badly that we didn't.'

Across the small patio, her mother lifted her head from the magazine she was reading and lowered her sunglasses. 'That is quite enough, Irena. One day you might be asked to be discreet about something and then you will see how very small your choices are.'

'You mean, like Elena?' Irena asked innocently. 'Getting an annulment instead of being divorced.'

'That is quite enough.' Carla raised her voice. 'If Monsignor had not believed Elena that she had had no idea Renato didn't want children he would not have acted. Elena was most upset. You know that. Personally, I think this Anna is good to come at all. How would you feel? Given away, then marched back by your parents because they want the luxury of forgiveness? Exactly.' She returned to her magazine. Like Gianni she would do anything for her children, yet they were more wary of her. And no bad thing either, she thought. Someone has to instil some sense of perspective in anyone with the Grescobaldi genes.

Irena bent over her father and kissed the top of his head. 'I must go,' she announced. 'I love this "discreet". In my newspaper they call it "sex scandal cover-up".'

'Then I suggest,' said Carla reprovingly, 'that you change your newspaper and maybe you will develop some ideas that stretch beyond the Via Condotti.'

Irena pulled a face. 'OK, OK, I'm going.' She began to stroll towards the house. In the doorway she paused. 'Maybe you're right. But I also think that maybe this Anna might be curious and that is also what's got her here. Fabio said she hasn't got much money and lives very modestly.'

'So?' Carla looked up.

'So she might be feeling overawed or something. Fabio said she was very quiet. She doesn't say much.'

'All excellent reasons to leave her alone. To do as she asks. Don't be late for lunch tomorrow. Irena? Are you listening?'

Gianni leaned back in his chair and made sure that his daughter was out of earshot before he spoke. Finally he said, 'It's not right. We know it's not. Do you think I should just phone? No,' he answered for her. 'But, you know what concerns me?'

Carla laid aside her magazine. For weeks now they had been forced to stay in Rome, enduring the heat and the noise instead of the peace and tranquillity of their home by the lake in Bracciano, so that they could be near Lorenzo. She had borne it well, compensated only by the knowledge that she would see more of her daughters and lend some reassurance to her mother-in-law whose access to her dying son was prevented by a combination of her frail health and Sophia's dislike. 'What concerns you?' She asked kindly, knowing what was coming.

Gianni folded his arms and tapped one finger against his elbow. 'When Lorenzo is . . . no longer here,' he said, with some difficulty, 'what about Sophia?'

Carla gritted her teeth. For as long as she had known Gianni, his older brother had been a problem. Mild, un-assuming Lorenzo and his crises had dogged their life. It wasn't so much that Carla disliked him – how could anyone dislike Lorenzo? It was what he brought in his wake. Long ago Carla had ceased saying that Lorenzo would have benefited from a bit more backbone. But the prospect of his rapidly approaching death alarmed her for Gianni's and his mother's sake: it was the uncomfortable thought of Sophia's future that gnawed away at them.

'Sophia will go on as Sophia always has.' Carla spoke calmly but with no conviction. 'The only difference is that she will now have a daughter in her life. And, Gianni?'

'Yes?'

'This girl – Anna? Have you noticed something?'

He nodded. Of course he had. She wanted nothing to do with them either. 'I know.' He sighed. 'But what can anyone do? It's in the genes.'

Andrea was genuinely contrite. He found Anna sitting alone in the courtyard, not quite sure what do with herself as the evening progressed and temporarily forgotten.

'No.' She interrupted his apologies. 'It wasn't easy for anyone. Especially not you two. I shouldn't have spoken as I did. You know that.'

He stubbed out his cigarette. 'Mamma—' he began, but Anna stopped him.

'She's upset and needs support. What she did was not easy, and maybe it was wrong not to tell you, but it happened a long time ago. Let's forget it, shall we? And tell me something, Andrea, did no one try to stop him drinking?'

Andrea lit another cigarette and held out the packet to Anna. She shook her head. 'It was too late when I found out. I went away to university in Milan and when I came back I noticed the rows. I remember when I was a child they rowed but not like this.'

'Why didn't you get help? You have relatives – an uncle, cousins?'

He sighed and flicked ash over the balustrade. 'I did, but what could anyone do? If he wouldn't listen to his wife or his son, who *would* he listen to? All my uncle could do was stop a scandal, not let it affect business. I don't know which was worse, trying to pretend he didn't drink or the drinking itself. Scandal is not what they like in this family.'

'What about me?' she asked. 'Surely bringing me here is going to be an even bigger scandal?'

'Most of the relatives know – they've always known. How could they not? Except me,' he said bitterly. 'You do know,' he went on suddenly, without looking at her, 'that there is no way we can repay the debt. You coming here.'

'You'd have done the same,' she said.

'No.' He ground out his cigarette and turned his face sideways to look at her. 'Never. I could not be like you. I don't think I could forgive.'

'You could,' she said. 'Unless you've been hurt. You can only be hurt by people you love. Believe me,' she said, holding his gaze, 'I'm not the one who's been hurt.'

He slipped his arm around her. 'This Oliver is lucky.'

A glow of pleasure stole through her. 'No, I am,' she insisted. 'It really helped meeting him so soon after my mother died. But you haven't . . . ?' She let the question fall in the air.

'You sound like my mother.' He laughed, sitting back on his hands on the stone parapet. 'And, come to think of it, my grandmother as well. "Find a nice girl, Andrea, make us happy, Andrea,"' he mimicked. 'As if such a girl existed who could please any mother. By the way, Giulio called to speak to you.'

'Did he?' She took a sip of her drink. 'Did he say what he wanted?'

'Just to make sure everything was OK, I think. He said to call if you wanted to talk to him. But I said you were fine. I said I would personally drive you to the airport on Sunday? Is that OK?' he asked anxiously.

'Of course,' she said, placing her glass carefully on the table, and making a mental note to ring the airline again and revert to her original plan.

'I go and see Papa now.' He got up. 'And also to tell my friends I am here for dinner. Not with them.'

'Why?' Anna asked impulsively. 'Why not go? I'll be here. It'll do you good to get out.'

He hesitated, longing to take her up on it. 'Come too,' he said. 'They are my closest friends. An hour?'

But Anna declined: she was exhausted. And she couldn't face the prospect of another eruption.

Besides, she reflected, a short while later, watching him depart with his friends, in her present state the comparison between her and the dazzlingly lovely Chesi was unflatteringly marked – and Oliver would have a fit if she'd gone as far as the door with someone like Stefano.

When Andrea had left, she phoned Oliver, who gave a soft whistle when she described the level of wealth that surrounded the Grescobaldis. 'Every time I turn round someone's expecting me to give them an order,' she whispered. 'Just before I phoned you I asked for a cup of tea so they wouldn't be disappointed. I think they regard me as a bit of a waste of time.'

'How do you feel?' he asked.

'Sorry for them,' she answered, knowing that was not what he meant. 'I know how I felt when my mother was dying.'

'I meant about all that wealth and, well . . .'

'I know what you meant. I could never have been part of it,' she said quickly. 'If Sophia had kept me, she and I would have been cut off. It wasn't her decision. It was Lorenzo's. He was the one who couldn't face another kind of life. It was Lorenzo's mother who forced the issue. That I do know. Oliver? I just can't help wondering how I should feel. I mean, I should feel something, shouldn't I?'

'Why?' She thought he sounded exasperated. 'They gave you up. You don't have to feel anything. What time is your plane tomorrow?'

She took a deep breath. 'Actually it's Sunday now. I

rebooked again. I couldn't tell them I wanted to leave early because there would have been such a fuss. You should have seen them when I came back from a walk. I haven't been as fussed over since I was three and got lost at the zoo and was found hurling Smarties at the chimps.'

She thought he would laugh but he didn't. 'I see.'

'No, I don't think you do,' she said, stung. 'It isn't for me I'm staying on. Honestly. It's for them. Sophia, Andrea and even Roberto . . .'

'Who the hell's he?'

'Lorenzo's business partner. He's coming back later with his wife to have dinner. He was so pleased I'd come. And, to be honest, I think me being here *is* helping. They need me, you see.'

A bath had been run for her; her clothes had been pressed and hung away. Until Sophia appeared, when the night nurse came on duty, she had nothing to do but while away the time inspecting her surroundings. At every turn there was something beautiful to admire, something absorbing to ponder over, some further evidence of a life of surfeit. The few photographs on display were mostly of Andrea. She and her brother were indeed alike. They had been even as toddlers.

For a long while she studied the photograph of Lorenzo, staring down into the laughing eyes, the even white teeth. He was sitting on the end of an upturned boat, looking straight into the camera, a jumper pulled loosely around his shoulders. Thick black hair, lean, like Andrea – like her, too, she supposed. She could see why Sophia had fallen for him. It was silly, she chided herself, but she couldn't help wishing she'd known him then. Not now, not like this, exhausted and skeletal, waiting to die.

She was still holding the photograph as Roberto was ushered in. His wife had been detained in the country, he said, kissing Anna on both cheeks as though they were old friends, but sent her warmest regards to Anna and said how

touched she had been that Anna felt able to overcome . . .
It was as far as he got.

'Truly,' Anna replaced the photograph behind her, and smiled to soften her abrupt intervention, 'I don't need thanks. I feel, as everyone must, just dreadfully sorry for them. I know what it's like to lose a parent. Sophia is under great strain. And Andrea.'

They walked together on to the terrace. 'I can see already you are good for her – when you came back today . . .' He gestured in a way that made clear to Anna the relief Sophia had felt at her reappearance. 'Andrea is, let's say, still quite young here.' He pointed to his head. 'You understand me? Ah, I can see that you do,' he exclaimed, although Anna had said nothing. 'Women, I think, understand more.'

'Well, not all women,' she began. But he was still talking. It was a habit she'd noticed in Andrea. They expressed awe of women, these Italians, but it was of their sex, their femininity, not their views.

'When Lorenzo is gone – and it cannot be much longer and sometimes I pray that it isn't – then what of Sophia?'

'I don't know,' Anna answered frankly. 'I'm not the person to ask.'

He patted her hand. 'I think you have the compassion not to turn away if she asked your advice.'

'Why would she need it?' Anna countered. 'Surely her friends, Lorenzo's family, Andrea, they are who she should be listening to.'

'We will see,' he said. 'Ah, Sophia.'

'Where is Andrea?' Sophia asked. 'Why isn't he here? Pilar, where is Andrea? Anna is here. I said he must stay.'

'His friends came,' Anna said, as Pilar began to explain. 'Chesi, is it? And Stefano. He asked me to join them but I said I would eat with you. Is that all right?'

'You said that?' Sophia's expression softened. 'I am grateful. But Stefano, Chesi, they have no respect for anything but what they want to do. Andrea is a little influenced by them, but he will be back. Now, I've asked Pilar to serve dinner in the small dining room. Roberto? No Sylvana? Never mind, we will be cosy. Just us three.'

Anna was relieved that Roberto managed to coax Sophia into eating a little. She was incredibly thin. Anna, too, ate little and struggled to keep her eyes open. The day began to swamp her. Finally, when her eyelids had drooped for the third time, she had to ask if they would excuse her.

Instantly Sophia and Roberto were on their feet, exclaiming, apologizing and ushering her, like a fragile, favoured child, to the stairs where Sophia embraced her. 'You will never know what this day means to me,' she said huskily. 'All this for Lorenzo. He was overcome by your visit. He said you were beautiful, just as he had imagined you would be.'

Anna said she was pleased but she didn't believe Sophia. Except for one brief moment when she had looked straight into his eyes, Lorenzo, she was sure, was already in a world of his own. Or, at the very least, as Monsignor had sighed, drifting towards his Maker. Sophia was just trying to make her feel that her visit had been worthwhile. Maybe tomorrow he would be more conscious of her. She sank down into the crisp white linen sheets, and slept without stirring until she was woken by Pilar just before dawn. Lorenzo had died.

Chapter Eleven

'Come to us,' Meryl said. She stepped over a packing-case and removed a tea-strainer from Corin's hand. 'Hurt,' she said severely, stopping him from investigating the back of his throat with the handle. 'There,' she went on, as he opened his mouth to roar in protest, 'I'll give it to Grandpa to mind for you. Now, where's Grandpa?

'Colin?' she called from the doorway, above the din of her grandson. 'Stop that Corin. Look what Nanna's got. Lovely sweetie.' For the last few weeks Meryl had had no compunction in bribing her grandchildren into silence with whatever she had once disapproved of and in whatever quantity. She held out the packet she had kept in reserve for just such a moment.

'You can't stay here.' She turned back to look at the heaving figure by the sink. Fenella must be feeling every bit as bad as she looked. She was clinging to the edge of the sink where the new waste disposal had still to be fitted, and plaster fell in a flurry like gentle snowflakes from the ceiling every time the outside door opened or closed.

'Like this with Nonie and Corin,' Fenella gasped. 'Not Fee so much. I'll be fine in a minute.'

Meryl's heart sank. If only Fenella and Athol had accepted Fenella's parents' offer to go and stay with them as a stop-gap while Craighaithan Heights was completed instead of insisting they could manage. But Fenella had said that it was too far to take the children to school, and refused to accept that missing ten days before the end of term would not wreck the education of two under-sevens.

'Don't be silly,' Meryl was saying, as Colin came through the door. 'We'd love to have you. Wouldn't we, Colin?'

Colin encountered a warning look from his wife. 'Of course,' he replied heartily. 'In fact, come now.'

Meryl flashed him a small, grateful smile. Colin felt ashamed. They both knew that his eagerness to oblige was rooted in his desire to show that, in spite of Meryl's refusal to be drawn on Anna, he could be sympathetic when it came to her family. Of course, he hadn't wanted her to be drawn: he just wanted her to tell him what to do and she wouldn't. Now it occurred to Colin how much he had let himself in for with his generous gesture. As he gazed discreetly at the half-finished house he realized that her family might be with them for weeks.

While Meryl pulled a pile of boxes off an armchair and lowered Fenella into it, with a damp towel to her head, Colin grabbed the wailing Corin and pulled him out of the door into the hallway. 'Walk,' he said, firmly shutting the door on the drama around the kitchen sink. 'To the shops to buy Mummy a nice bunch of flowers. What about you two?' he asked, as he passed the foot of the stairs. The duvet from Nonie's bed was draped like a tent from the banister rail. Inside, he knew, Fiona and Nonie were sitting perfectly still and silent. 'Now, where could they be?' Colin said loudly. 'Well, Corin, I'll just have to give you the treats I was going to give them.'

'Yes. Yes,' yelled Corin, tearing his hand from Colin's grasp and flung himself on top of the duvet, which collapsed under his not inconsiderable weight. Immediately there were screams from his sisters, who emerged scarlet-faced and cross.

'We were hiding,' Fiona regarded her baby brother with loathing. 'We don't want to hide with you, Corin. You smell.'

Colin took a deep breath. This was not what he had

envisaged when he asked Meryl to marry him. Two week-ends in a row they'd had the children while Athol and Fenella tried to cope with an unrelenting tide of problems surrounding their new home. He had been thrust into a family whose problems might not be being played out on the international stage like Anna's but were every bit as invasive. He wanted Meryl to himself so that he could tell her how frightened he was to think of Anna on her own in the midst of all those strangers, how they might draw her in. Instead he had this. 'Now, now,' he said, with admirable patience, which he wished Meryl was witnessing. 'You won't need sweaters, it's nice and warm.'

He began to usher all three out of the door as Athol came storming out of the small study where a phone could be seen lying in the middle of a carpetless room. 'Bloody builders,' he panted. 'Tuesday week. *Tuesday*. We'll just have to put up makeshift beds. Colin, could you give me a hand? Just until I can find Sherry?'

'No. No,' shrieked all three children at once. 'Grandpa's taking us to buy sweets.'

Colin looked helplessly at Athol, then back at the children. The noise brought Meryl out into the hallway and behind her Fenella, white-faced, leaning against the door-way. The phone began to ring insistently in the empty room as they all strove to make their feelings and needs plain.

'Colin,' Meryl said, 'just take them out. Away. Go on.'

'You don't understand,' he tried to make her listen. 'The builders. Athol wants me to—'

Angrily Athol snatched up the phone. 'Who? Oh, yes. Of course. Colin?' He thrust it at him. 'It's Anna.'

Anna looked up, dazed, into Pilar's tired face. Sophia and Andrea, she gathered, were with Monsignor. She must come. Andrea was beside himself; he would not be comforted. Without a word Anna pushed back the sheet and ran barefoot to the salon in the cotton vest and drawstring cotton pyjama bottoms she had slept in, arriving just as the doctor was leaving. The shutters were only partially open and the room looked as sombre as it had been dazzling only the day before. It was too early for the sun to have warmed the cold marble floor, which served only to highlight the gloom.

Still in her robe, Sophia was sitting next to Monsignor. In her hands she was clutching a rosary while the priest steadily worked his way through all five Mysteries. It was only later that Anna realized no one had woken her when the end was near, and that she had slept soundly through it all while the doctors, a priest, nurses and a griefstricken wife and son had gathered in Lorenzo's bedroom.

Slowly Sophia's eyes lifted as Anna paused in the doorway. Andrea was slumped in a chair several feet away from his mother. The doctor, whom Anna recognized as the man she had encountered the day before in Lorenzo's bedroom, squeezed his shoulder as he went past. Andrea seemed not to notice.

'Shock.' The doctor spoke in a low voice as Anna halted briefly in front of him. 'Make him understand that he couldn't have helped. He is torturing himself.'

'What do you mean?' Anna whispered.

'He wasn't here.'

'Wha—?' Anna's eyes flew to the doctors. Sophia had been alone. Dear God. 'Not here? Where was he?'

'At a friend's apartment. But it would have made no difference to his father. Lorenzo slipped into unconsciousness. He knew no one, not even Sophia. At a time like this, Andrea and his mother need each other, but Sophia said some things . . .'

'Oh God,' Anna breathed. Not now. Not at this moment.

'Who told him?' Anna kept her eyes on Andrea's slumped form.

'No one. He came back half an hour ago not knowing. Terrible, terrible. But I must go.'

'Of course.' Anna stood aside. He must have been with Chesi and would never quite forgive himself. When Barbara had died, she had been at an interview with a rival TV station and had deliberately not told anyone where she could be found. She nearly hadn't gone. But her mother had said she should, only that very morning. It was the last conversation they shared.

Sometimes she didn't know which was worse: knowing that she had been enjoying flirting with a good-looking man, which compensated for the awfulness of the job on offer, while her mother was already lying dead, or that her father had had to sit alone in that dreary little side ward, in a leather armchair, with a kind but strange policeman, for almost an hour before she got there.

'I'll come back in a while,' the doctor murmured, bringing her back to the present. 'The remains will be taken away later this morning.'

Remains. She shivered. Is that what it came to? A cold, heartless word summing up a life that had spawned such a mixture of intrigue, ambition and, ultimately, calamity. Remains. In her view the remains were in front of her, waiting to be told what to do, what to say, how to go on.

She nodded, her eyes on the pitiful couple. She felt anxious to comfort them. 'Go to them,' the doctor urged. 'They need you.'

'Oh, you poor, poor thing,' Anna whispered, dropping to her knees to hug Andrea.

'Help me,' he said, his eyes shocked and wild. 'Help us. I wasn't there. When he needed me, I wasn't there. She's right.' He began to cry. 'Mamma is right. I am of no use to anyone.'

'No, no,' Anna said. 'She didn't mean it.' His hands were cold and he was shaking fiercely – she could imagine the scene that must have taken place. They both must have been distraught and needing to vent their despair. Andrea must have stayed with Chesi because Sophia was beyond comforting anyone. 'He wouldn't have known who was there.' She pushed his hair out of his eyes. 'You mustn't punish yourself. Sophia needs you, you know she does.'

His whole body shuddered. 'No, she doesn't,' he sobbed. 'Only Papa.'

'Gio?' Anna turned to the houseboy, who was transfixed by the scene in front of him. 'Coffee. Lots of it. *Molto*. And,' she glanced back at Andrea, 'I think, some brandy. Pilar?' She glanced the other way. 'Get a sweater or something for Andrea. Sweater,' she repeated, then mimed wrapping something around her shoulders.

'Ah, *maglione*,' Pilar cried, and rushed away.

Anna turned back to her brother and bent her head to look into his ashen face. 'Andrea? I must go to Sophia,' she said.

'So quick, so quick,' Sophia whispered, as Anna reached her.

There was nothing Anna could do but signal to the priest, who was well into the Sorrowful Mysteries, that Andrea was in greater need of his support than Lorenzo, whose Eternal Fate must surely have already been decided.

'*Si*,' he agreed and, with something like relief, moved away from the new widow.

'I know, I know.' Anna wrapped her arm around Sophia and held her hand. 'I'm here,' she whispered, over and over, because she couldn't think of anything else to say.

For the next hour they sat together. Anna coaxed Sophia to drink some coffee, urging Andrea to do the same, wondering why no one came until it dawned on her that no one had been told of Lorenzo's death. Quietly Anna signalled for Pilar to come to her. The day must begin. There would be visitors and she must prepare for them.

'*Ma*,' Pilar began, gesturing anxiously at Andrea who had stopped weeping but was seemingly beyond comfort, '*cosa dovrei fare*? Andrea ...'

Anna firmly shook her head. 'Andrea will be OK with me.' She pointed first to her brother then to herself and made a hugging movement.

Beside her Sophia gave a wan smile and patted her hand. 'Thank you,' she whispered. 'I cannot.'

'Sophia,' Anna asked as the doors closed behind Pilar, 'I must call someone. Shall I call Fabio?' Fabio would know whom to ring.

Sophia looked silently at her. 'Fabio?' she repeated, and then, in a stronger voice, 'No. Not Fabio.'

'Not Fabio? Then who? I must call someone.'

'Roberto,' Sophia said, surprisingly firmly. 'Roberto will be here. I called him. He will act for me. Fabio is – was – Lorenzo's lawyer, not mine.'

'No,' Andrea cried hoarsely, without moving from his seat. They both turned. 'I want Fabio to be here. He is my father's lawyer. He would have wanted him. He did everything for him.'

For seconds they stared at each other, then Sophia said, 'Please, Andrea, not in front of Anna. Remember, she is a guest here even though she is your sister.'

As Andrea pushed himself to his feet, the coffee Gio had placed near his elbow slid to the floor with a crash, the liquid snaking across the white marble surface. 'I haven't forgotten, Mamma,' he said, as he almost ran from the room. 'I think we all know it was you who did that.'

If she couldn't feel their grief for Lorenzo at least she could feel compassion for these lost people, who were so busy blaming each other it had left them blind to the greater need to help each other. To be fair, Anna thought, dragging a brush through her hair, it was Andrea not Sophia who was doing all the blaming.

It had taken her days to feel like living, let alone dressing, after her mother had died but in mobilizing Sophia upstairs to her room she had an ally in Roberto, who came with his wife, Sylvana. A small blonde woman, Sylvana was as round as Sophia was slender, sharp-featured and distant, not at all the kind of woman she had imagined for the more glamorous Roberto. She greeted Anna politely but without warmth, and in her presence, Roberto seemed more distant than he had the day before. It was then she realized that she was still in a state of undress.

In an effort to meet Sophia and Andrea's differing needs, Anna had phoned Fabio, who arrived soon afterwards. Pilar came bustling to her room to tell her he was waiting. To Anna's surprise he hugged her, which she found comforting, and it wasn't until much later that it occurred to her that Pilar had elevated her to mistress of the house until Sophia could cope with her tragedy. It was Anna who stood with Sophia and Andrea as Monsignor intoned the *de profundis*, walking behind the body of Lorenzo as it was taken from his house, Anna who supported Andrea in his grief and anguished cries of 'Papa' as the black limousine turned out of the square and was swallowed up in the noise and chaos of a Saturday morning in Trastevere.

Sophia had remained white-faced but composed, her eyes shut, tightly leaning on Roberto's arm while Fabio stood respectfully behind.

'*Il medico*?' Pilar asked Anna, as she emerged from checking on Andrea in his room.

'*Grazie*, Pilar,' Anna said. 'But for Andrea. *La signora* is calm.'

All the way down the corridor, Pilar followed her with problems. The guests would be numerous, Signor Lorenzo would be shamed if they did not treat them well. 'Of course,' Anna agreed, tying her hair back into a band and guessing that Pilar was short-staffed, it being Saturday. She turned to Fabio. 'Please would you explain to Pilar that she must phone the two girls who were here yesterday – find someone? Tell her to pay them more money because it is Saturday.' Fabio assented and spoke rapidly to Pilar.

'Sophia is fortunate you were here,' Roberto murmured, one wary eye on his wife's back as the doctor left and Pilar bustled off. He placed his arm round Anna's shoulder.

Anna shrugged. 'I went through it myself. Once their friends and relatives are here they will be a little better.'

And then the house was filled with people. Sophia had emerged wearing a simple black dress and was tenderly escorted to a seat in the salon by Monsignor, who had remained in almost permanent attendance. The shutters were closed as a mark of respect. Anna slipped quietly away. She had no place there.

Once back in her room, she rang Oliver and told him of Lorenzo's death. 'It's so awful for them,' she said. 'And they row all the time. Even this morning.'

'How ghastly,' Oliver said. 'Just as well you're coming home. You don't need all that – and, frankly, darling, they probably don't want you around either, with all those relatives and friends staring at you. There's nothing to keep you now, is there?'

Anna hesitated. 'No. Nothing. I'll talk to Fabio.'

'Fabio? About what?'

Of course, he was quite right: there was nothing to discuss. However, as she stood on the terrace overlooking the courtyard, which was baking in the sun as the fountain arched and cascaded, shimmering with reflected light, into the shallow stone pond that surrounded it, Anna wanted to say, 'Well, rather a lot actually, not because I need to but because I can't just walk away when everything I've ever wanted to know is just feet away.'

'Look,' Oliver said, heavily. She turned away from the view. 'First of all you were told what to do by that Mafia mogul in London. Fellini? Bellini?'

'Farrini,' she said.

'Whatever. Now there's another. Just come home, will you?'

'It's not as easy as that,' she argued. 'I don't want to appear insensitive. Pilar is relying—'

'Who, in God's name, is Pilar?'

'The housekeeper. There's no one to tell her what to do. Sophia's out of it and Andrea—'

'Who has managed his life perfectly well for thirty-odd years – all right twenty-nine – without your input can now resume it. Darling, this is for you. Unless you know something I don't, I assume the house will be packed with all the Grescobaldis you've never wanted to meet. I'm trying to protect you. Heaven knows, you sound like you're in far too deep as it is. I'm just trying to remind you of the deal you struck and you're outnumbered there. I should have gone with you.'

'Why didn't you?' she asked, surprised at the anger in her voice.

'You didn't ask.'

'Why didn't you offer?'

'Anna,' he exploded. 'This is ridiculous. Why are we arguing? If it had been your father – and by that I mean Colin – I would have dropped everything. But for a man you never knew?'

It was not in Anna's nature to confront, so she didn't. She said he was right, that she was tired and it had been a trying morning. She said, striving to sound normal when she doubted she would ever feel normal again, that she would call him later. When they hung up neither felt the other had been entirely fair.

Anna conceded that Oliver was probably right except in one thing. The rest of the family did want to meet her.

'You will see,' Andrea said. 'They want only for you to like them. It is no one's fault except—'

She stopped him. Another tirade against Sophia's motives and behaviour, on a day when she must feel as though her world had ended, was not to be borne.

'Of course,' she said. 'Of course I'll come. Andrea? Would it be easier if I went home today instead of tomorrow?'

'Home?' He looked at her in consternation and tears welled again in his eyes. 'But you come back again, for Papa's funeral? But . . .' he looked at her sadly '. . . I am asking too much and I don't blame you if you refuse. It's just I hoped,' he said humbly and not terribly hopefully, 'that you might be able to spare a few more days.'

Anna hesitated. 'What does Sophia say?'

'She said it was your decision. Everything is your decision.'

Chapter Twelve

Anna was brave but her courage almost failed her when she was confronted by what seemed a sea of faces. In reality there were probably no more than ten, but it was almost her undoing. In her imagination, she had seen herself being composed and indifferent. Now she looked and sounded stiff, stern and disapproving.

It was only because Andrea gave her a gentle tug that she moved forward slightly and scanned the room for Sophia, with whom she planned to take refuge – first, because it seemed the right thing to do and, second, as an act of solidarity. Then they began to take shape. Lorenzo's brother Gianni – who else could have had the same lean face as she had seen in the photograph? – was standing nearest to the door with his wife, Carla, in close conversation with Fabio and his wife, Rosanna.

The unexpectedly noisy conversation faded as the realization of who she was struck them. Sophia was sitting a little apart, with Monsignor standing guard beside her. There was no doubt that she was the centre of everyone's attention, yet Anna could see from the way she sat, stiffly upright, slender legs sheathed in sheer black stockings and suede high heels, crossed gracefully at the ankle, that she was taking no part in the gathering. Her hands gripped the arms of her chair, her shiny red nail varnish at odds with the sombreness of her dress. It was black, with sleeves that reached her elbows. A single gold bangle was clasped to one wrist and a heavy gold cross was suspended from her neck on a thick gold chain. She appeared to have abandoned the rosary Monsignor had pushed into her hands earlier. She looked almost defiant in her composure, when anything from raging grief to cursing would have been more understandable.

Anna took a deep breath and walked in. Andrea escorted her quickly to the centre of the room but with a slight pressure on his hand she moved to sit with Sophia. This was not a party. He'd already told her that his favourite cousins, Gianni's daughters, were in Milan at a wedding. The elder, Elena he said, could be tricky but the younger, Irena, was like a sister to him.

Although everyone tried valiantly to go on with their conversation when she came in with Andrea, their curiosity defeated them. Some kissed her calmly on both cheeks, as though they had met many times before, while exclaiming to each other their first impressions. Others hesitated, then clutched her in a wordless embrace. What a tragedy, they all said, mournfully. It had been expected, of course, but still they were not prepared for it. Anna remembered the day she had met Meryl's family: where they had been quiet and awkward, this group seemed anxious to draw her in. Throughout it all, Sophia just sat with Anna standing behind her chair. If she was listening, she gave no clue to it. If contempt for their effusion after so much rejection was in her heart, there was nothing in her blank expression that said so.

In the midst of it all, Anna, like Sophia, was capable only of staring and listening to the furore. The sight of so many Grescobaldis, so many chic, tailored, expensive people all gathered together, was overpowering. She felt lost. A persistent inner voice kept questioning what she was doing there. She found it easier to dispatch that troublesome voice to the back of her mind, rather than listen to the answers that came to her.

In one peculiar way, however, it was easier to be among the mourners than she had expected: they behaved as though she had not kept in touch rather than having been given away and now tracked down.

'A sad moment, yes? For visit?' asked a woman in careful English, as though the coincidence of Lorenzo's death and Anna's arrival was due to unfortunate planning rather than the months of frantic search and much persuasion.

In this room, she told herself, was her history. She just wanted to absorb it so her answers were brief, polite but restrained. She was mesmerized, not – as she had once thought she might be when faced with this moment – overcome with emotion but overwhelmed with the scale of all she had never known. At last Gianni claimed her attention. He was so like Lorenzo – or how Lorenzo might have been, lean-faced with grey streaks slicing through his carefully groomed hair. For one silly second – of course, it was silly – she imagined what it would have been like to have talked to Lorenzo and if it would have been in just this gentle, concerned way. Gianni concentrated fiercely on her face, his eyes roving from her eyes to her mouth to the set of her chin as he asked after her father and her life in London. Occasionally she thought she could detect a slight shake of his head, as though he were trying to rid himself of a ghost.

'And you are enjoying Rome?' asked a cousin, joining them. Her *cousin*, the eldest son of Lorenzo's only sister Chiara, who would be arriving in Rome from Milan in time for the funeral. Anna hardly heard what he said.

'Go and sit next to your aunt,' Gianni suggested to him. 'She's waiting. Poor woman.'

Anna didn't think Sophia was waiting for anyone, least of all for a nephew who was only a nephew by marriage, and who had no hope of succeeding with her where everyone else had failed. She repelled all attempts to talk to her with a wave of the hand. Only Anna won a small smile from her. 'It was not what I planned,' Sophia whispered, drawing down Anna's head so that she could murmur in her ear. 'All these people. I know what you asked me – I hoped I could protect you – but there, it is done.'

Anna shook her head. 'Sophia, it's OK. It doesn't matter.'

'And you are not cross with me?'

'Of course not,' Anna said, 'as long as it's what you want.'

'Not what I want,' Sophia said wearily. 'What I must do. Lorenzo would have demanded it.' She fell silent again. It dawned on Anna that Sophia was not so much composed as stranded in another time and place. Occasionally she glanced towards the door as though expecting someone to walk in. Anna's heart bled for her.

Shortly before her father told her about Meryl, he had said that for months after her mother's death, he had heard the sounds she made. He would hear her footfall, her cough, and so strong was the sense of her that he would be convinced she was in the next room or find himself looking towards the door waiting for her to come in. Suddenly Anna wanted to talk to him very badly.

As they moved to another room for lunch, Anna slipped away and rang him at Athol's new home where they had all gathered to help with the move. At first she thought she must have dialled a wrong number – she could hear angry shouting.

'Athol? It's Anna.' She raised her voice. 'Is my father there?'

'Who? Oh, yes. Just a moment.' Then she heard him say, quite tersely, 'Colin, it's Anna.' And wished to heaven she hadn't phoned.

A few minutes later she hung up. Call later, he had said, once he'd got the children home. Then they could talk.

She sat with her hand on the phone.

'Anna?'

She turned to see Sophia standing just feet away. 'Is everything all right at home?'

Caught off guard, Anna had no answer ready except a truthful one. 'I think I chose a bad moment,' she managed. 'You know how it is.'

Sophia sat down beside her and took her hand. 'Yes,' she

said. 'I know all about those. We sit here, yes? Just for a minute.'

Anna stared at the beringed and manicured hand clutching hers. So different. They were sitting thus when Gianni came to find them.

She had to ring Henry and tell him she would not be in the office for at least a week. In the background she could hear a small child wailing and Henry's frantic voice before he was able to give her his attention.

'Henry, this is a bad moment, I can tell,' Anna began.

'Anna? No, not bad, try vile,' came Henry's bitter voice. 'You should have seen them earlier. Bridget cut herself on the bread knife while I was tying Rose's shoes and we've just got back from the doctor's – James, this is absolutely your final warning – Sorry, Anna. Where was I? Oh, yes. Blood everywhere. Maggie will have a fit. Mind you, I've just pulled the dressing back and the stitches aren't as ghastly—'

'Henry,' Anna interrupted desperately, 'I'm really sorry about Bridget. You sound up to your eyes but I need to talk to you.'

'Just a minute,' Henry said. 'I thought you were in Rome?'

'I am. That's why I'm ringing. You see my father – my real father – has just died.' Then she remembered, too late, the cover story she had told Henry.

'Died? Good God. Oh, Anna, I'm so sorry. You poor thing. What a shock and your godfather ill too. How – sssh, Bridget, in a minute, sweetheart – did it happen? Now look, Anna, don't worry. You'll be wanting to go straight to Scotland. Will you be all right? Oh, poor Anna. *James.* Stop pulling at that cord.'

'Actually, Henry,' Anna said, taking a deep breath, 'it's not my father, he's fine. You see my godfather isn't my godfather. He was my real father.' She explained the whole sorry story, making it sound as though she had known about the Grescobaldis for years, they just hadn't seen each other very often and she had always thought of Lorenzo as her godfather.

For once Anna was relieved that Henry's domestic arrangements were poised as ever at meltdown so that he was in no position to press her further. He understood, he said, someone would cover – Tania, he added, at random. Friday had been OK and at least Max loved Tania, he added gloomily, even if no one else did. 'It will mean I'll have to go in tomorrow. No way round it. Maggie will understand. I know it's Sunday but, after all,' he said, his voice laced with happiness at such unexpected deliverance from his progeny, 'a death is a death.'

Oliver Manners replaced the receiver, lay back and contemplated his bedroom ceiling. For the first time in ages he had woken up in his own bed on Saturday morning and he was disoriented. In fact he had felt as though the goalposts in his well-ordered life had taken a considerable shift since the arrival of Anna's mother.

He paused. Arrival? Such a tame word for the cataclysmic effect she was having on Anna, which in turn meant him, and it was getting harder and harder to convey that to Anna. Just now she had demanded what he would do in her place, and he could not deny that he would have found it a difficult decision to make.

If he had managed to get Anna's attention in the last ten days it had been by pure chance. And now this. Of course she had to stay, and of course he was being unreasonable in wanting her to get the next plane home. If he were to be truthful, it was the first time since they had met that Oliver had felt Anna was in another world in which he played only a minor role. He was not the central force as he had been for the last two years.

It was eleven o'clock and by now Anna, had she not been whisked off to Rome, would have started the day in just the way Oliver liked. The thought caused a small shiver to ripple through him. It was not, he frowned, just the sex although, God knows, that was a powerful factor – all the more so, he suspected, because Anna had held out until he had ended it with Rachel, with whom he had been genuinely in love and of whom could not think even now, without a wave of guilt at the hurt he had caused her. The need to possess Anna had overwhelmed his feelings for Rachel. In the whole of his life Oliver had never found himself so helplessly torn.

The day stretched before him. He pushed back the covers and swung himself out of bed, rubbed his fingers through his hair and sat for a moment thinking of what to do next. A shower, coffee, then maybe lunch with someone. It wasn't like him to feel the need to talk to anyone, except Anna, of course, but Anna was talking to total strangers in another country. A flash of resentment shot through him. He knew it was stupid but it was more comforting to feel anger than sympathy.

He was not, he knew, a possessive man, but it had taken all his will-power not to order her home. Neither was he a stupid man and he knew that she would have forced him to accept that for the moment her family came first.

In the end he phoned his mother and told her that they would not be coming to lunch next day, after all.

'Good heavens,' Christina Manners exclaimed, when she heard why. 'Come anyway. Come and put your feet up. I feel like spoiling someone and you'll do perfectly. And then you can tell me all about it.'

'Not much to tell,' he said, hoping he sounded unperturbed by the tangled events taking place in his life. 'Poor Anna's bearing the brunt of it.'

'Well, of course, but poor you having to take the fall-out. Now, don't argue. I'll expect you by one.'

It was pathetic, he knew, to feel so cheered, but he couldn't help it.

At midnight on Sunday he drew up outside Anna's house and let himself in with his own key, took in the milk that

Anna had forgotten to cancel and the Sunday papers lying in a solid wedge on the doormat on which Mister, Dottie's cat, was curled up. As Oliver approached, he stirred and arched his back, turned his head away disdainfully as Oliver tried to tickle his ear, hissed and streaked away into the night, heading for Dottie's door. For a cat who was almost blind, Oliver thought staring after him, he had a marvellous sense of direction.

The house was dark and still as Oliver closed the front door behind him. Light from the street-lamp outside threw shadows across the living room. In the kitchen, he plonked the papers on the table and plugged in the kettle. Then he opened the fridge, put the milk inside and took a cup down from the cupboard over the sink. For a brief, panicky moment he wondered what he was doing there, miles from his own flat, miles from Anna in Rome. But he needed to be somewhere they shared, and this was it. This was Anna's house and this was where he wanted to be, at first in her wonderfully cluttered kitchen, then in her bed with its high bank of cushions and pillows under the bedspread her mother had made. He wanted to share his life with Anna. What puzzled him – or, perhaps more accurately, frightened him – was that he couldn't understand why he had never told Anna.

On the side of the fridge there was a clear plastic board and a thick Pentel pen hanging from a piece of string. Anna had written reminders to herself in her scrawling hand: 'Eamonn's bash Fri. Toothpaste, bleach, eggs.'

Smiling to himself, Oliver picked up the pen and added, 'We're out of juice.' He underlined the 'we'.

For a girl used to fending for herself in every way, shopping, working, commuting, cleaning, it was hard to resist being looked after. Anna was not quite sure what to say in the nightly, one-sided conversations she held in her head with Barbara arguing that it was easier now to stay than go, to offer support to Sophia rather than withhold it. In the end she decided that her mother would have approved, at least, of the support she was giving the blameless Andrea and must know – wherever she was – that no one could ever take her place. Even if, in these last few days, it might have seemed that her loyalty to a woman who had devoted her life to her well-being was being usurped, she knew it wasn't. She was being drawn irresistibly to the layers of family life that were now lying ready to be inspected.

The following day Gianni had arranged for all the family to gather at his home on the outskirts of the city, partly, he confided to Anna, because they needed to be together – Lorenzo had been much loved – but mostly to help Andrea with his mother. 'Just for a few hours away from here,' he said. 'Poor boy, he has a hard time ahead of him.'

'Do you think she'll go?' Anna asked doubtfully. Her own father had not stirred from the house until the funeral.

'You talk to her,' Gianni suggested. 'She seems to listen to you. Andrea cannot handle her just now.'

'What a shame,' Anna said carefully. 'They could be such a support to each other. I wonder why that is?'

There was a short pause. 'You would have to ask Andrea,' Gianni said simply. 'Lorenzo told me Andrea had been very shocked but more so because he felt cheated. You understand?'

'A bit,' she conceded. 'I never have,' she added quickly. 'Felt cheated, I mean. Personally – and it's nothing to do with me – I think they both need help, maybe in different ways. But they're both suffering.'

'Sophia resists being helped,' Gianni said.

'Why?'

He shrugged. 'If you dislike someone, for whatever reason, it is hard to let them help you. Families are very complex. But who am I telling?'

'Well,' she said, trying again, 'I feel very sorry for her. Whatever else may have happened, she and Lorenzo were obviously devoted to each other. Look at her. She's utterly lost. I respect that. Everyone makes mistakes.'

Gianni gave her a sidelong look. He appeared about to say something then changed his mind. 'It's hard at this time for everyone,' he said finally. 'I, too, respect Sophia's feelings. And Lorenzo's. I always have tried. Maybe when this week is over Sophia will feel more like talking. We can only try. Ah, here she is.'

It had taken a lot to persuade Anna to go but in the end Sophia had settled it. She was too immersed in shock and grief, she said, to venture out, but she would not hear of Anna staying with her. 'Go,' Sophia said. 'Go, because Lorenzo would want his family to know you and because . . .' she laid a hand on Anna's shoulder '. . . because I think this way they see it is your decision what you do. It will make it a little easier for me. You and I understand this. Yes?'

Anna could only agree.

'And I have my own two or three close friends who will sit quietly with me until you return,' Sophia reassured her.

It was a sombre group who assembled at Gianni's home, but the strong family unit drew her irresistibly in. It was a strange feeling, kindness from strangers, but they didn't feel like strangers. That would have been impossible with everyone so eager, so willing to establish her at the centre of their lives. Family issues that had bypassed her in her own life – sibling rivalry, family feuds, decisions, loyalties and rituals – transfixed her. In turn, the aunts, cousins and uncles trod carefully around what they said about Sophia in Anna's presence, fearing, Anna supposed, how she would react about a woman who in their eyes was still her mother even though she had given her up.

Gianni's pink-washed, sprawling villa was reached from the road along a worn track surrounded by olive groves and fruit-bearing trees, the smell of jasmine and eucalyptus mingling sweetly on the hot afternoon air. Clearly the brothers' taste in living was as different as their taste in wives. Lorenzo's house dazzled the senses, demanding attention, while Gianni's, which was no less impressively large, was instead redolent of family history and a more ordered life. It was filled with heavily carved furniture that looked comfortably, if rather unimaginatively, in place against white walls and open fireplaces.

Carla, slender, practical and clearly scornful of the need to wear clothes that shrieked their price, was undoubtedly the centre of the house. Wherever she went faces turned to her. She was brisk in her movements, stern with Gianni, who meekly acknowledged her role as queen of her kitchen.

Anna was not surprised to see Fabio and his wife there, but Giulio was a bit of a surprise. Half-way through lunch, which after four was still in progress, he strolled in off the afternoon flight from London, his jacket hooked over his shoulder, tie loosened. She was quite pleased to see him, knowing that he, at least, wouldn't be scrutinizing her as she knew the others were. He was greeted with hugs from Fabio and Carla before he made his way over to her. 'Not what you expected?' he said, indicating the crowd of Grescobaldis over his shoulder. She shook her head with a slight smile. He bent and kissed her on both cheeks. 'I was sorry you had to hang up so quickly.'

Anna blushed. 'Sorry,' she said. 'Slight problem.'

'And now resolved?'

She nodded. 'It must have sounded a bit dramatic, but it wasn't meant to be.'

'It didn't sound dramatic at all,' he answered mildly, glancing around the room. 'I think I would have been less restrained in the circumstances. I would have actually got on an earlier plane instead of just thinking about it. You didn't actually book it, did you?' He turned and looked directly at her.

There seemed no point in denying it. 'Yes,' she said. 'But that was before Lorenzo died. And Andrea and Sophia seemed to want me to stay. They, um . . . said they needed me to stay.'

'Did they?' He smiled politely. 'Ah, look, Andrea has

been sent to take you away. And I must pay my respects to the rest of the family.'

'When did they last see him?' Anna whispered to Andrea, watching their effusive welcome of the latest arrival.

'A few weeks ago,' he answered, 'when he came to see us about you. Why?'

'All that kissing and hugging.'

Andrea looked puzzled. 'That's how we do it. And look. Oh, look.' He pulled her to her feet. 'They are here.'

Hastily Anna placed her glass on the nearest surface and turned to look towards the latest arrivals whom Andrea had raced to meet. They could have been her sisters but both had the sleek, smooth hair for which Anna had always longed. They wore black because it suited them, Anna guessed, rather than out of respect for the occasion. The daughters of Lorenzo's brother Gianni who had come hot-foot home, primarily because their uncle had died but mostly, as they admitted in a whispered aside to Anna when they greeted her, because they wanted to meet her.

The elder of the two, Elena, with a skirt moulded to her flat bottom and skinny hips, made a beeline for Giulio, placed her hand on the back of his neck, kissed him, then bore him off, her arm wound into his. It was the younger sister, Irena, whom Anna immediately preferred. She giggled, refused to share her new cousin with anyone, saying they had all stolen a march on her, anyway, by meeting her the previous day, and settled in beside her in a quiet corner of the garden to ask endless questions that were as intimate as they were startling. 'Oh, stop it.' Irena laughed, punching her gently on the arm. 'Why should I not know if Giulio has slept with you? We are cousins. We will not trouble ourselves with all this shock and stupidity, no? Good. So, has he?'

'Good God, no.' Anna was outraged and laughing all at once. 'How could he? I have a boyfriend and, besides, I've only met him twice before.'

'So?' Irena blew out a cloud of smoke from one of her

incessant cigarettes. 'He only knew his wife for an hour when they went to bed.'

'How do you know that?' Anna asked, looking around covertly.

'Elena told me. Just after their affair broke up. Don't ask me why. Elena bores me with her men. Always the big affair, never the one to end it. And she is only behaving herself because she has made such a big fuss of being a divorcée. And I say to her, "You,"' Irena stabbed a finger at Anna to demonstrate how she had made her point to her sister, '"you are hooked on tragedy. Just like this family. Drama, drama."'

'Divorced?' Anna asked.

'Annulled. Renato would not have children. Monsignor interceded so her marriage never happen and there is no messy divorce.'

'Heavens,' Anna said. 'How awful not to know that before you marry someone.'

Her new cousin raised her eyebrows. 'No. It was the *reason* to get the annulment. Not the cause. You understand?'

Anna was entranced by her. As well as imparting the kind of gossip Sophia clearly didn't know about – which Fabio could not repeat since he was paid to protect their reputations, and which Giulio had chosen to ignore – Anna could see that Irena was irredeemably and wonderfully mischievous.

Across the room she caught Giulio looking thoughtfully at them. She started to smile, but decided that if one hour was his personal best, even a small smile might encourage him. So she raised her eyebrows as though querying his interest. He grinned and turned away.

Irena rattled on in a scandalous litany of secrets and cover-ups, constantly glancing towards her parents before imparting the next indiscretion. 'Don't look like that,' she begged, as Anna's eyes widened and her jaw went slack. 'You don't live with them. How else could Elena and I have a good time? They'd stop everything. The convent was bad enough.' She shuddered dramatically. 'And, besides, they can talk.' She tilted her chin in the direction of her parents, who were talking quietly to a group around a wooden table in the paved courtyard, which was shielded from the sun by a roof of vines and mimosa. 'Look at how they kept you quiet.'

Anna could only agree. Poor Sophia. Her crime had been to get found out.

It was Irena, who worked intermitterly in PR and smoked endlessly, leaving vermilion streaks on the butts as she inhaled deeply, who told Anna all about Giulio's first marriage, his current mistress and Elena's intention of getting him into bed. 'They had this big thing – oh, just after his marriage broke up and she left Renato. She was a nice person, his wife, but Giulio is impossible. Elena is only interested in hooking him so she can dump him back. Mad. I wish Issy had been the same.' Irena yawned. 'You know, Isabella, Lorenzo's woman,' Irena explained, with an airy wave of her hand.

'Lorenzo's woman?' Anna asked weakly, hoping fervently that she had misunderstood.

'Oh, hasn't Giulio told you?' Irena clamped a hand over her mouth. 'God, he can be so strait-laced. When you think what he and Elena got up to that summer. Oh,' she looked anxiously at Anna, 'you're not shocked? You mustn't be. Surely your papa had a diversion?'

'Well, actually, no,' Anna replied, feeling more shocked at the very idea than Irena could imagine.

'So,' a voice spoke gently behind her, 'has Irena left anyone's reputation intact?'

Anna gave a startled, guilty jump as Giulio smiled only inches from her face. 'No need to answer,' he said drily. 'It's written all over you.'

Chapter Thirteen

'Can I not speak to my own cousin without everyone listening?' Irena asked crossly. 'Go away, Giulio. Go and seduce someone for half an hour.'

Giulio ignored her and crouched down so that he could talk to Anna, who was still trying to imagine her father with a 'diversion'. It was impossible. Poor Sophia, with infidelity to shoulder as well as the blame.

'I will talk to Andrea,' Irena announced, pushing herself to her feet. She gave a theatrical toss of her head. 'Where is he?'

'I thought I'd find you behaving like Mister,' Giulio said, moving into the vacated place next to Anna as Irena strolled off towards the house.

'Mister?' Anna looked perplexed. 'Dottie's cat? Good God, why?'

'You know, ready to bolt at the first open door.'

'The situation changed.'

'It invariably does.' Giulio stretched his legs and crossed his ankles. 'Still, I'm pleased for your sake. I recall that it was one of your specific conditions that you didn't meet any of your relatives.'

Anna felt uncomfortable. 'When I said that I didn't know Lorenzo was going to die so soon. What would you expect me to do? Storm out and demand that everyone stayed away? And it would have been something else to heap on Sophia's doorstep. Besides, after the funeral I go home. No harm done.'

'Then I apologize,' he said. 'And I'm relieved. You might have sued me for negligence.'

'Don't be silly,' she replied calmly. 'Besides, you're not my lawyer. You're theirs.'

He placed one arm along the back of the garden seat they were sharing. Anna sat forward. 'Actually, I'm not,' he corrected her, studying a crowd of Grescobaldis still sitting under the white canopy at the long table in a small grove where lunch had been served. 'Fabio consulted me because I was in London. That's all. I don't specialize in tracking down lost Grescobaldis.'

'I don't think lost is quite the word,' she pointed out.

'True. And your father? He knows you're staying on?'

Anna nodded.

'He must be a little worried, yes?'

'A little, I suspect,' she agreed. 'He doesn't say a great deal. He's left all of this more or less up to me.'

'I see. And Oliver? Is he going to join you?'

Anna flicked away an imaginary piece of fluff from her skirt. 'There's no need,' she said lightly, repeating Oliver's own explanation as though it were hers. 'If it were my father, it would be different. He rings all the time,' she lied, tapping her bag to indicate her mobile phone. Oliver was not happy about any of this and she couldn't work out why. 'Anyway,' she changed the subject, 'what's happening in Milan that's brought you here so urgently?'

'One of my clients is being inconvenienced by his board.'

'Which one? Client, I mean.'

'Banca Milano Commerciale.'

'Is that one of yours? Goodness. They want the ex-finance minister to take the chair in London and the board don't. Is that it?'

He looked at her surprised. 'Something like that.'

'Actually,' Anna said, leaning over to select an olive from the bowl in front of her, 'on the face of it, I can't understand why they don't just fire the board. It's politics, isn't it?' She looked at him. He was studying her with interest. 'He's got to be worth biting the bullet for. All that inside information he's got – I'd snap him up. Or, at least, if I were an investor I would. So, Mr Lawyer,' she grinned, 'what's the real problem? Or can't you say?'

'The real problem,' he said, 'is that way back, when they were lusting after each other, they thought marriage was the answer so they made all sorts of promises they can't now keep.'

'You mean, you've got to fix the divorce.' She laughed.

'You're a surprising woman.'

The afternoon was very still. Anna shifted in her seat. A lazy kind of heat had descended, sending everyone for the haven of shady canopies or inside where the shutters were closed against the sunlight.

'I'm back in a day or two,' Giulio said, into the silence. 'If you feel like making any more phone calls, this is my mobile number.' He wrote something swiftly on the back of a small white card.

She took it, glanced down, then tucked it into her pocket. She could detect the faint smell of an aftershave she recognized and he looked taller and thinner than he had in London – but then she had been measuring him against Oliver and no one was taller, leaner or better-looking than Oliver. She suddenly longed for Oliver, to feel safe and to be enveloped in familiarity and told what to do. 'I won't,' she said to Giulio, with a greater confidence than she felt, 'but it's kind of you. I'm sure Irena or someone will bail me out if I need help.'

'Irena will relish having someone to bail out,' he retorted. 'She's usually the one who requires it.'

Anna looked straight ahead to where Irena was talking intensely to Elena, who had her eye trained on her new cousin. 'Irena,' she said carefully, 'did not denigrate anyone, rather she balanced things up – you know, helped me see a less one-sided view of things.'

'Well, that's obviously very kind of her,' he said, getting to his feet. 'However, I have no knowledge of her being noted for accuracy. I must go. I have to be in Milan tonight. My schedule has been turned round so I can be at the funeral.'

'I think I should go too,' Anna said. 'I wouldn't want Sophia to be alone after her friends have gone. Roberto said he would stay until Andrea and I got back.'

Irena had seen Giulio prepare to leave, and had come across to join Anna. Now she said, 'Of course you must. Andrea is going too but he's stopping off to see someone, so I'll drive you,' she insisted, 'and we can gossip on the way.'

As they arrived, with incalculable damage to Irena's tyres and Anna's nerves, having experienced Irena's disregard for road signs and speed restrictions, Roberto was just leaving saying that Sophia had felt like talking for a while and had now gone to bed. 'She is sleeping. The pill helped. Pilar is back and I heard you arrive, so I feel safe to go.'

'Where's Sylvana?' Irena demanded. 'Why didn't she stay too?'

Roberto was clearly annoyed at Irena's questions. 'Sylvana was so tired, she went home with the others. And you should too,' he added. 'Anna looks as though she could do with her bed.'

'Will you be all right?' Irena asked Anna.

'Absolutely,' she said, smiling gratefully at Roberto for noticing.

Left alone, Anna went first to look in on Sophia, pushing the door open carefully. It was dark in her room, not because it was late but because the shutters were almost closed. She was lying to the side of a vast bed, strewn with blue and crimson silk cushions, which looked unbelievably tragic with its solitary occupant.

Anna walked quietly to the bed and gently pulled the cotton cover, which had partially slipped off, over Sophia's sleeping form. She didn't stir. For a moment Anna's eyes roved around the immense room, looking for something that would give her the key to this woman. Sophia was lying very still, her mouth slightly open, breathing deeply. On the floor, her robe was lying in a heap. Automatically Anna picked it up and folded it carefully across the end of a scarlet silk armchair next to a small table on which a pair of gold and silver cufflinks were lying and a pair of glasses, tortoiseshell, pale almost orange. Why was it that a discarded pair of spectacles should bring tears to the eyes? They looked vulnerable, lost, never to be worn again. For no reason that made sense she reached out and carefully stroked the rim without disturbing them, then walked back to the bed and looked down on Sophia. Families were so stupid. For thirty years they had dangled a sole teenage mistake in front of her, kept her at the edge of their lives, and now they were exasperated when she wouldn't do as they wanted and allow them to share her private, most intimate sorrow.

A part of Anna knew that Sophia should meet them just a little way, if only for Andrea's sake, but she also knew she couldn't blame her for refusing, preferring a pill to blot it all out rather than talk about it with her beloved Lorenzo's family.

From far below she heard a car door slam. She guessed it was Andrea returning. Sophia didn't stir. Next to the bed there was a small white block of paper and a pen. Hastily she scribbled a note and propped it next to the lamp: 'When you wake come and find me. Whatever the time. Anna.'

Quietly she slipped out and made her way downstairs to find that it had not been Andrea but Roberto. 'I am not happy,' he whispered, looking up through the lofty atrium to the top of the winding staircase, as though Sophia could hear so far away and might wake. He glanced towards Gio's disappearing back. 'I hear from Irena that Andrea is not following. What is he thinking,' he said, taking her arm and leading her into the salon, 'leaving you alone? So I come to keep you company and I am going to phone Carla to say he must come back.'

'Oh, no, please,' Anna exclaimed, touched by his concern. She was relieved, too. At least, in Roberto and his wife, Sophia had support. 'It's so nice of you but I'm fine, and honestly, Roberto, I would prefer it if Andrea stayed where he was. He's gone to a friend. He's so much better away from all this. Truly.'

'Yes?' He looked doubtful. Then his expression cleared. 'You are right of course. Lorenzo, he was a wonderful father, but responsibility?' He shook his head sadly. 'Thank God you are here. And I know she feels you understand. So many of them don't. You're sure you're all right?'

'Absolutely. Hey, I'm a big girl. Sophia is asleep and when I've poured myself a large drink I'm going to go to bed. Really.' He looked so worried that she reached out and squeezed his arm. What a bunch these Italian men were. 'Listen,' she said, feeling quite touched at his solicitude. 'Come and have a drink with me. Please. I'd enjoy that.' They moved on to the terrace.

It was a beautiful night but she would still have preferred her bed. When Roberto had gone, she would ring Oliver and maybe Carrie. They all felt a long way away. However, she could see why Sophia leaned on Roberto now that Lorenzo was gone: he was a charming man, if severely old-fashioned and absurdly extravagant with compliments.

'Roberto,' she chided, when he had exclaimed over her smile, the way Lorenzo's family had taken to her, her exquisite hair – So much more attractive on her than Andrea, he claimed – 'you are a rogue.'

'But a rogue who appreciates beauty,' he said. She looked at him and instantly felt uneasy. She had not realized how close to her he had moved. She gasped and stepped back but he was quicker. In one deft movement Roberto had slipped an arm around her shoulders and before she could stop him, his mouth was clamped to hers, his tongue filled her mouth, his free hand dragged at her skirt and they both fell backwards into a reclining chair. Fury and revulsion flooded her. Her outstretched arm hit a stone urn in the corner of the terrace and brought it crashing down on to the marble floor. She grabbed a hank of Roberto's silver hair and yanked it so hard that he screamed and let her go, clutching his head.

She felt utterly foolish.

'But what is wrong?' he protested, reeling around. 'You were giving me very obvious signals.'

'You were getting no signals at all, you old lech,' she panted. 'How dare you? How could you? At a time like this? Just go.'

'What is this?' he exclaimed. 'You were not expecting this? You laugh and flirt. You are just a tease, is that it?'

'You're a married man,' she hissed, terrified that Sophia would come to investigate the noise. 'And Lorenzo's close friend. What would he think about you hitting on his . . . daughter? Go, just go.'

'I am Italian,' he pronounced stiffly. 'I do not hit or insult a woman for not responding to my overtures.'

Anna couldn't contain herself. 'Overtures? *Overtures?*' She bent down ignoring him and began to collect up the broken plant. 'You sound about as sensible as an Italian opera.' She began to laugh at his absurdity, his pompous explanation, his vanity.

'Well, really.' His colour was considerably heightened. 'There was just a mistake and you are much too seductive for your own good. You smile at me a lot. Why should I not think you mean something else?'

'Roberto,' she warned, glancing up from her task, 'I think you should go. Now. I mean it.'

'Certainly,' he said, wincing as he fingered the area Anna had bruised. He straightened his tie and walked towards the door with as much dignity as the situation allowed, while Anna went on with clearing up the debris. 'By the way' – she looked up, startled, as Roberto reappeared – 'there is no need to mention this misunderstanding to your mother.'

'Roberto,' Anna stood up, fuming, her hands on her hips, 'you should be praying I don't tell Sylvana.'

At almost midnight, Anna could not stay awake any more. There was no sign of Andrea and she guessed that he would probably stay at Chesi's, knowing that she was here if Sophia awoke. And why not? She yawned. The sight of Oliver would have been a comfort to her.

She found Gio in the kitchen, watching football on television. As Anna put her head around the door, he leaped to his feet. She signalled for him to go on watching the programme, and said, 'If Andrea comes back, tell him to wake me if he needs to talk, OK?'

In the privacy of her own sitting room, she tried to call Oliver but the machine answered and his mobile was switched off. She left a message to say she was going to bed and would call tomorrow. 'Love you,' she said softly. 'Miss you.'

Briefly she debated ringing her father but it was after ten and late to call Meryl's house. Even now she could not think of it as her father's. As she dialled Carrie's number, she remembered that her friend had taken Euan to stay with her parents for the weekend and hung up. She felt very lonely. For all their warmth, there was no one in the Grescobaldi family she could ring. She stepped out of her dress, and as she did so, the card Giulio had given her fluttered to the ground. For a while she stared at the mobile number and felt tempted to ring. But to say what? Instead she tucked it back into her pocket.

There was nothing for her to do except sleep. As she emerged from the shower, her hair still damp, it was pleasant to know she could just fall into a bed already turned down, a robe draped neatly across the end. Then she noticed, on the pillow, a small white box. Inside there was a silver and gold brooch, and a note from Sophia saying simply, 'Thank you.'

*

Irena sped her off to buy a black linen dress for the funeral and made it an excuse for lunch as well, pointing out that Andrea and his mother would be locked in for hours with Monsignor organizing the requiem mass to be held on Friday. Anna was pleased to have a legitimate excuse to be out of the house. An early phone call to Oliver on his mobile had been more comforting and left her feeling that she had been unjust to think he was not supporting her. 'Of course I am,' he protested. 'I just think it's very difficult for all of us. Remember, I don't know these people – well, just the Mafia person – so of course I'm concerned.'

'I'm sorry,' she said, leaning back on the pillows. 'It has to be done, and then we can all get on with our lives again.'

'That's my girl,' he said. 'Hey, it's lonely here without you. I miss whole bits of you.'

Anna closed her eyes. 'Not fair,' she said, smiling at the ceiling.

'On me, you mean.' He laughed. 'I'll list them if you like.'

And she would have let him, had she not heard Maria in the outer room, opening the shutters and getting Anna's day under way. 'Raincheck,' she whispered. 'I'll call you later. *Ciao.*'

'*Ciao*?' he repeated. 'Whatever happened to "goodbye, darling"?'

Anna laughed down the phone. 'OK. *Ciao*, darling.'

Meryl said her father had gone to the village on foot and she would get him to call Anna.

'Don't worry,' Anna said. 'I'll call him later from my mobile. I'm going to be out all morning and possibly this afternoon. Will you tell him I'm fine, Meryl? And give him my love, won't you?'

'Of course I will, and don't worry about him. I expect you've got a lot to do. It's chaos here. All the children are with us. I'll tell him to expect to hear from you when you can.' Anna took a deep breath. 'Actually, no, Meryl. I said

I'll call him later today and I will. Dad and I always call when we say we will.' She hung up, wishing her step-mother would be content with having most but not all of her new husband's life under her control.

Irena made her laugh and talked to her about Lorenzo. She praised the photographic library he had built up, which she had no compunction about plundering to add kudos to her occasional foray as a PR into glossy magazines, where access to exclusive pictures opened doors. It was evident that neither she nor Elena needed to work, but Carla had insisted they did something and what better, Irena giggled, than to turn her life into her work? 'I'll say this for Sophia,' Irena remarked, waving a fork to make her point, 'she kept the agency in the news – you know, diary pictures of them at everything. Oh, galleries, restaurants. Andrea said Lorenzo hated it. He went because Sophia said it was good for business.'

'Poor Andrea,' Anna said. 'Is that really his problem? Why he is so angry with Sophia? Not just me?'

Irena shook her head. 'It didn't help. You know, maybe I shouldn't say this, but Sophia has always wanted things for him that he didn't want. He wanted to live in New York for a while like Antonio – you met him, Chiara's son, yes? But she said he should learn to take over the business. So he stayed. Then there was a big commotion when he wanted to go to Paris to university to study art history and she said he needed business studies. The fuss. Oh, my God, the rows when for once he put his foot down and said if he did it would be in Milan. And he has never quite forgiven himself because he says if he was here maybe he would have seen Lorenzo starting to drink. But Elena and I tell him nothing could stop that. Lorenzo had other things to worry about.'

'Like?'

'Please?' Irena looked disbelieving. 'You, for a start. Isn't that enough? On the other hand, the relief that you look like you do must have made them all happy. Imagine the

Grescobaldis with an ugly duckling in the middle. Or the Carrinis,' she added, as an afterthought.

'Are looks important to you all?'

Irena wrinkled her nose and lit a cigarette. 'That's a very English remark,' she said reprovingly. 'Of course not. But you make being concerned with how you look seem shameful. It is a celebration,' she cried extravagantly. 'You should revel in knowing anyone can be beautiful – with a little effort. You know, Elena and I used to talk about it and be relieved we had the money to look good.'

'All the makeup in the world—' Anna began.

'Oh, makeup.' Irena dismissed it with an impatient wave. 'I mean things like Elena's boobs.'

'She's had them done?' Anna asked.

'Of course. And her stomach. And,' she added, 'my teeth.' She was so remarkably frank that Anna couldn't help but laugh.

'So you mean Sophia only made it on looks?' Anna asked.

Irena dragged on her cigarette and screwed up her eyes against the smoke. 'Sophia made it on her wits,' she began, then stopped. 'I mean, to deal with a secret like you all this time, to turn your back on your family. You need more than a pretty face to survive. Although she had the nose job, of course.'

Irena picked up her spoon and plunged it into the *panna cotta* lying untouched in front of Anna, who pushed it towards her. 'Irena, Sophia only did what everyone else made her do. She didn't lie, or sneak off and have an abortion even if she could have done. Lorenzo must have loved her a lot to have refused to give her up a second time.'

Irena dabbed at her mouth with her napkin, leaving a scarlet trace on it. 'Of course. Don't take any notice of me. Anyway, they bore me with their silly petty little lives. Oh, not that you're petty, I mean the hypocrisy of it all. Don't say I said any of this. I can see we are going to be friends. I like having an English cousin. And, besides,' she added, more frankly, 'I can't afford to be cast out just at the moment. I have just bought the most divine flat. And I've got a new lover, so I need it. It won't last, though.' She lit another cigarette.

'Why ever not?' Anna asked.

'He's married, of course,' Irena said flatly. 'You must have guessed?'

Anna blinked. Surely not Giulio again. Irena rolled her eyes and gave a peal of laughter. 'God, no. I'm not stupid. Roberto, of course.'

Chapter Fourteen

'*Roberto*?' Anna could not disguise her shock. 'Irena, you're not serious?'

Irena paused as she was about to light a cigarette and looked sharply at her. 'Did he make a pass at you?'

'Certainly not,' Anna lied. She was getting good at this.

'Sorry. I can't help it.' Irena sighed gloomily. 'I imagine him with everyone. Even in bed. Even when he is giving me so much pleasure, even then . . .' She closed her eyes, inhaling deeply on her cigarette. A rapturous look spread over her face and with one hand she massaged her bare shoulder. Anna swallowed hard and took a quick glance around. 'And I can't help it, even then,' Irena was saying, with a reminiscent shiver. 'Even then, I ask him who else there is . . .'

'Irena,' Anna gulped, 'stop it. I get the picture. Honestly. Of course I'm not embarrassed. Well, yes, a bit. Everyone's watching. I suppose you know what you're doing?'

Irena sniffed and slumped down in her chair. 'Of course not. That is why it is *ah-gony*.' She dragged out the word, emphasizing her anguish. 'It's why I feel so sorry for Issy. Knowing Lorenzo would never have left Sophia, of course. It is the same with Roberto. I'm sure he'll never leave that sour old cat Sylvana.' She groaned and ground out her half-finished cigarette. 'He is so . . .'

'I'm sure he's wonderful,' Anna broke in, before Irena could go off again.

'My mother says she's definitely going to be at the funeral.'

'Sylvana? What's wrong with that?'

Irena raised an eyebrow impatiently. 'Not Sylvana. Issy.'

Anna's fork clattered to her plate. 'Lorenzo's mistress? Are you sure? Good God. Does Sophia know?'

'No.' Irena looked pointedly at Anna over the lighter she had just snapped into life. 'And she won't unless you tell her.'

For two evenings in a row, Anna dined with Sophia and Andrea. Not that they dined: Sophia refused all food, wore black and twisted her rings constantly. Most of the time it was only Anna who caught her attention. It was probably, Anna told Andrea, when he pointed this out, because she did not remind Sophia so much of happier times. He agreed that she was probably right. But Anna did begin to wonder if she was overstepping her role.

Andrea's distress was easier to deal with. He was open, tearful and bitter in his loss. Sophia's dry-eyed composure, the emptiness in her eyes were so much harder. Whenever it looked as though the uneasy truce she and Andrea adopted when Anna was present was about to break, Anna would silently signal to Andrea to leave them. Each time he would mouth, 'Are you sure?' and she would nod reassuringly. It was so much easier to keep them apart.

During the day there was little for Anna to do. She had never seen a house run so smoothly while enveloped in such sorrow. When her mother had died her home had been filled with friends who wanted to help. Her aunt Sarah had stayed the entire week, ferrying tea and sandwiches, which invariably lay uneaten, to her father and anyone else who dropped by. Routine halted; their lives came to a standstill. But here, even Lorenzo's death had not disrupted the business of how they lived, except that Sophia issued orders more sharply – for which everyone forgave her – and

Lorenzo's suite now stood empty and bleak. And this worried Anna because routine and normality had obliterated the need for someone close to be constantly with Sophia.

'And your friends, Sophia?' Anna asked at six one morning, finding her already up after another sleepless night. 'Wouldn't you like to see them?'

Sophia hesitated. 'Yes, of course. Maybe when all this is over, maybe then I will pick up the pieces,' she said. Death, Sophia had told Anna with a wan smile, was the strongest motive for people to make themselves scarce. 'It is so hard. But not yet, yes?'

'Of course.' Anna nodded sympathetically. 'When you're ready.'

All Anna could do was wait until Friday, the day of the funeral, and then a flight home. By Wednesday, and after an unsatisfactory conversation with her father, she decided to give herself up to being spoilt – or as spoilt as a house in mourning would allow. And, in Anna's view, this was very spoilt indeed.

Earlier that day she had came close to accusing Colin of letting her down.

'Dear,' he had said, 'I'm sure you will make all the decisions that are right for you. Meryl says—'

'I'm not sure that's possible.' Anna cut across him, not able to bear for one more minute hearing what Meryl thought on any subject. 'I'm not sure anyone ever makes the *right* decisions. They make what appears to be the *best* ones at the time. That's all I'm doing.'

It was strange talking to him and looking out over a trickling fountain instead of over a dingy alleyway at the side of her office in central London, or from her kitchen in Braverton Street where she would invariably be interrupted by Dottie banging on the wall or Eamonn arriving to raid her coffee or milk supply. Even odder that instead of signalling to Tessa to negotiate a sandwich and coffee next time she was heading for the canteen, she had only to pick up the slim white house phone next to her, press a button and ask Constanza or Gio for whatever she wanted.

'In fact, I think I'm just going with whatever happens next,' she told her father frankly.

'Are they kind to you?' he asked. 'I mean, understanding what all this means?'

'Kind to me? Oh, yes. They're amazingly kind, even though they're all suffering. It's as though they've known me all my life.'

There was a small pause. 'Well,' he said, 'that's good, dear. Why don't you ring me when you get back? And, Anna?'

'Yes?' she said eagerly, wishing the careful note would go from his voice, willing him to say he loved her and was thinking of her and whatever she was doing made no difference, that he understood.

'I was going to wait until you came back to tell you, but I know you'd like to know. Fenella is pregnant.'

Anna kept her eyes fixed on the fountain. 'Heavens,' she managed. 'Well, do say congratulations for me.'

Each evening, while Andrea sought comfort with his friends, Anna sat with Sophia. They were drifting increasingly easily into discovering each other's lives. Anna tried to get her to talk about Lorenzo but Sophia wanted only to talk about Anna. So they did. Bit by bit Anna found herself confiding in her, perhaps more than she should but Sophia made it so easy. So she talked first about Oliver, and then about her father, Meryl, the ghastly Athol and Fenella, the wedding, at which she had felt like a stranger. Sophia said that brought back memories of herself when she first knew she was to be allowed to marry Lorenzo. 'A guest in their house,' she explained. 'Nothing I could claim as my own . . . And now it will be the same again.'

Anna said, 'But, you have all this now. All these wonderful things.'

Sophia glanced round. 'Not mine, my dear. Andrea's. It never was mine. Loretta, my mother-in-law, wouldn't hear of it.'

Anna looked warily at her. 'Nonsense. This is your home.'

'I live here,' Sophia said bluntly, 'but it is not my home. Now, come, we mustn't be gloomy. Lorenzo would be cross. He's listening to all of this. So, tell me more about Oliver. I hope some time I can meet him.'

Anna showed her a photograph, taken one weekend when they had been visiting his parents, of Oliver lounging in a wicker chair on the lawn, when the long evening shadows were creeping over the grass.

'And his parents like you – how could they not? You like them?'

Anna nodded and yawned. 'Yes. I think they find me a bit hard to accept – because I work, because they had Oliver all lined up for Rachel, his ex-girlfriend. Their fathers were at Oxford together, then in the diplomatic service. Bit hard to be landed with a schoolteacher's daughter from Clapham.' She smiled.

'But now you have your own house, a wonderful job,' Sophia cried in amazement. 'You have done so well. Silly people. Just tell them you now have an apartment in Rome and a villa in Bracciano you can use anytime.'

Anna was embarrassed. 'Oh, that won't be nec— Sophia? What is it?'

'Oh, Anna.' Sophia wrapped her arms around herself and rocked to and fro. Her eyes were almost black, her face gaunt. 'I look at you, I listen and all I can hear in my head is, what did they make me do?'

The odd thing about Sophia was that while she looked grey and haunted, she hadn't cried since Lorenzo died and didn't seem to have a best friend to fall back on. Andrea explained that she had always relied heavily on Lorenzo, his friends, his relations, his business associates. She had devoted her life to him. Now Anna could see that she needed someone who could talk to her about Lorenzo and about things that mattered to her in a way Anna herself couldn't as they had no shared history.

In the end she talked to Giulio. He phoned from his car on Wednesday afternoon, on his way back from Milan, as she was about to embark on a walk, and suggested dinner. 'I can't,' she said, annoyed with herself for being disappointed. 'It's so kind of you, but I can't leave Sophia. Giulio? Did you know, no one comes to see her? Who can I ask to help?'

'Leave it to me,' he said, 'and I'll pick you up in an hour. Why not? You're going for a walk and I've been sitting behind this wheel since Milan. Unless, of course, you prefer to walk alone?'

'No, of course not,' she admitted. 'I'd appreciate your company.'

By the time he arrived Fabio had called and Gianni immediately after. A rota of relatives, they said, would be organized to take it in turns to sit with Sophia. Discreetly, of course. And, no, they would not let Sophia know that Anna had arranged it. Anna was surprised but grateful at Giulio's intervention.

'It wasn't a problem for me,' she assured him. 'I just know I can't be everything to Sophia.'

'You shouldn't have to be,' he said, kissing her cheek and sounding so like Oliver she almost laughed. 'You've done enough. Gianni is grateful to you just for being here. Now, let's go because that woman climbing out of the car down there is your great aunt Isabella and she is one of the few Grescobaldis who can silence all the others.'

They drove as far as the Piazza d'Espagna where Giulio's company had offices and began to walk companionably towards the Villa Borghese. The heat was not conducive to anything more than easy exchanges, and without the trappings of a suit, Giulio looked younger, less tired or, perhaps, less bored. She couldn't tell which because his eyes were hidden behind dark glasses.

The stone steps at the foot of the grounds that surrounded the Villa Borghese wound up in a steep incline from the road, which made Anna, who was already hot and unprepared for the gradient, gasp for breath. 'Here.' Giulio reached back and took her hand. 'You showbiz people are so unfit.'

'I am neither unfit,' she panted, grateful for the assistance but glaring at him, 'nor in anything remotely like showbiz. It must be ninety degrees.' She pulled her cotton vest from the waistband of her skirt in an effort to feel cooler.

'Actually,' he said apologetically, as she flapped it like a fan, 'I think you'll find it's only about seventy. You should come back in August.'

'In August,' she said, getting a second wind and moving after him, 'I hope I will have more sense than to be in Rome. Thank you.' She let go of his hand as they reached the top.

The grass and trees were heaven after the chaos of Rome in mid-afternoon but after a while Anna began to regret that she had ever thought of the park. Did Italians think of nothing but sex? Everywhere she looked couples were entwined on benches or balancing precariously on stone parapets. How they managed to look so erotic while remaining fully clothed was one of life's greater mysteries.

Giulio did not appear to notice them or again the next day when he took her off for lunch, with Sophia's guarded blessing and Irena's giggled warning in her ears.

'Come with us,' Anna urged, to square her conscience about Oliver.

'Giulio? Agree to that?' Irena gurgled.

'He's just being kind,' Anna protested. 'And if you were any sort of cousin, you would have asked first,' she added severely.

'Pooh,' said Irena. 'I am coming to stay with you in London. Think how chic that will sound to all my

162

friends. I won't have to stay with Giulio. I can stay with *my cousin*.'

'I'd better warn you,' Anna said, wondering what Dottie would make of Irena, 'I don't live on anything like the scale you lot do. I'm a working girl.'

She met Giulio at a small restaurant in a square near the Vatican. He rose to kiss her as she arrived, and she waited for him to compliment her on her dress or her perfume, but he asked instead if she was happy with the restaurant or would prefer somewhere else.

The thing about Giulio, she decided, was that in spite of his reputation and his toughness he made her feel relaxed – and, even more flattering, he laughed at her stories. In fact, he threw his head back and roared when she described Henry's miserable attempts at starting his fantasy of an extra-marital affair and Max's more successful but tackier triumphs. She could even joke about Roberto. The waiters had cleared the table, refilled their coffee cups three times, and still they sat there.

'And do you think Roberto is going to have his way with his best friend's daughter?' he asked abruptly.

She gave him a startled look. Daughter sounded so odd. But Giulio missed nothing. She laughed. 'He's just a serial seducer. But the answer is, "Dream on, Roberto."'

'I'm glad to hear it,' he said. 'For Irena's sake, naturally.'

'Oh, my God. You know? Poor Irena.'

'They're not terribly discreet. You like your new family, then?'

'They're certainly unconventional,' she admitted.

'I've always thought they were slaves to morality,' he said, signalling for the bill.

'You know they're not,' she said, reprovingly and reluctantly. 'It's just a shame that grief frightens so many people. They seem afraid to talk to Sophia for fear she'll break down or that, having treated her as an outsider for so long, they don't know how to deal with her. It's different for me. I can handle her.'

'Can you?' He gave her an odd look.

'Of course. It was like this when my mother died, only Dad had me to talk to. Andrea has no one, and no one to help him with Sophia because they've all been so po-faced about her for years. And all she did was get caught. The rest manage to cover up everything they do, or go into denial. I'm beginning to feel very sorry for her.'

'I can see that,' Giulio agreed. 'But, then, so am I. She missed out on an exceptional daughter.'

She looked sideways at him. He had removed his sunglasses and his eyes were resting on her mouth. For a brief moment she knew she only half regretted that this was as far as the moment would go. She looked away quickly. And to think she had been shocked at Irena. It must be because she had been thrust into his company for nearly a week. Italians – even those who had lived in London for twenty years – were instinctive seducers. Look at Lorenzo. Look at Roberto. Don't look at Giulio like that.

'What's the matter?' he asked, sliding his sunglasses on so that she could no longer see his eyes.

'Just the heat,' she said, with a calmness she was far from feeling. 'Maybe we should get back.'

Giulio glanced at his watch. She knew he had a meeting at five so they left and, with a cheery wave, she strolled off along the Corso towards Trastevere. The matter, indeed. He knew precisely what he was doing. Slaves to morality? Anna almost laughed out loud.

It was late afternoon when she arrived back. The walk had taken much longer than she had imagined. The apartment was silent. Pilar went off duty each day at three and returned in the early evening and Roberto had persuaded Sophia to lunch at his home with Sylvana and one or two other business friends of Lorenzo's. Anna slipped off her shoes and made her way, yawning, along the corridor to her room. As she drew level with Andrea's, she heard what she thought was a stifled sob coming from inside. 'Oh, God, poor

Andrea,' she muttered. She tapped lightly on the door and pushed it open.

Her hand flew to her mouth. Andrea was lying naked and face down on the bed. Stefano was sprawled on top of him. Andrea lifted his head, his companion swivelled his. Stunned, the three stared at each other in shocked silence. Then she heard a torrent of outraged Italian. 'Sorry,' she gasped, and pulling the door shut behind her, she fled. No wonder there wasn't a girl he could bring home to Mamma. Or Nonna.

Chapter Fifteen

There was a light tap on her door. Half an hour had passed in which Anna had had time to reflect on why it had never occurred to her that her brother was gay, and to wonder if there was anything left in this family that would not satisfy all the criteria required to make it on to *Max Meets*.

'It's open,' she called.

'Can I come in?' Andrea asked, peering round the door. He looked nervous, uncertain of his welcome.

'Of course.' She walked away from the terrace and positioned herself behind one of the armchairs as Andrea came into the room. Carefully he closed the door behind him and leaned against it, shutting his eyes, not ready to see anyone but knowing he had to.

'Look,' Anna began, with a rueful smile, 'I'm so dreadfully sorry. I thought everyone was out and that you were upset. I shouldn't have barged in like that. Honestly, I had no right.'

He waved a hand to stop her and lit a cigarette, ducking his head over the flame from the silver lighter. He didn't move from the door. She noticed that his hand was shaking. 'It doesn't matter,' he said, pushing the lighter into his pocket and inhaling deeply. 'I can see you're very shocked.'

'No, of course not. Just I feel, you know—'

'No, it's my fault, I should have thought—'

They both stopped.

'You,' he invited. 'Go ahead, please.'

She took a deep breath, and chose her words with deliberation. 'Look, Andrea,' she said, arms wrapped around her waist, studying her feet, 'as moments go, it's not right up there with a gentle stroll in the park. Of course I was shocked. No. That's not right. Embarrassed. Wouldn't you be? It would have been the same if I'd barged in on anyone who was – was . . .' She trailed off lamely as he looked questioningly at her. 'I suppose that's why you weren't here when Lorenzo died, yes?'

Andrea slumped down in the chair opposite to her and pushed his fingers through his hair. He looked haunted. 'I'm glad you know.' He suddenly seemed immature and defiant. 'I wanted to tell someone. But what could I say? But it's a relief. I've been living here for a month, not daring to leave her.' He jerked his head as though Sophia were behind them. 'Stupid of me. Papa dying has just made me feel . . .' he gave a helpless gesture '. . . so desperate and lost. Anna, you must believe me, the night Papa died will haunt me for the rest of my life. It was a punishment. God was punishing me for rowing with Mamma in front of him. Do you realize, it's probably the last thing he heard us do? Oh, God, I can't bear it.' He pressed the ball of his hand against his eyes wiping away the tears that were, by now, a familiar but no less wretched sight to Anna.

'I doubt God's got anything to do with this.' She sighed. 'And you're doing the punishing, not Him.'

'And Stefano has been so patient,' he said brokenly, not really listening. 'It just happened. He came to find me and I was very upset by rowing with my mother in front of you and he was so . . . you know.' He looked up, appealing to her to understand. 'You know when you just want to blot something out, and this afternoon was the first time since then.'

'It's your home,' she said, 'not mine. You have every right to do as you like here.' She moved around to sit in front of him. 'Does Sophia know?'

He shook his head.

'What would happen if you told her?'

He sliced a finger across his throat. 'I promise you,' he gave a small laugh as she protested, 'she would never speak to me again.'

'I don't believe that,' Anna said flatly. 'After all she's been through, she would never do that to her own child. I'm sure you've got that wrong.'

'You don't get it, do you?' He looked curiously at her. 'She loathes Papa's family so much that she would not want them to think she hasn't been the perfect mother. I couldn't tell her because then she would not be able to say truthfully that she was faultless where I was concerned.'

'But that's ridiculous,' Anna cried. 'Archaic. How could they believe that Sophia could influence the way you are?'

'I don't think they would. But she thinks they would pity her. Believe me, you don't know Mamma. All my life we have to keep things from Nonna, from Gianni. "Don't tell them, Andrea," she always said. "Keep it between us."'

'Like what?' Anna asked.

'Oh, like everything. Who their friends are, where they go, the business. *Anything.* Even Roberto was a secret for a long while.'

'Roberto?' Anna looked at him in amazement. 'How do you keep him a secret? And why?'

'Because Mamma said they would make Papa have someone they chose, not someone he wanted. I forget now what happened but I think they waited until Roberto was already in place. But then there was a row because Nonna found out before they could say anything and Mamma said it was Pilar who told.'

'And was it?'

'But of course.' He looked surprised. 'And what did it matter? He couldn't be kept a secret for ever. So stupid. Games. That's all it is. For a small child it was easy just to do as they asked – you think it's normal. But later you know it's ridiculous and by then it's too late. And serious – *really* serious – problems are left for us to deal with in secret.

168

Like Papa's drinking. She could have asked for help. But, oh, no, no one must know. They would blame her, she said.'

'Maybe they would,' Anna pointed out, more sharply than she intended. 'I mean, she has good cause to suspect they might. They don't seem to have dealt with the problem of me very well.'

'But that's just it. Don't you see?' he cried eagerly. 'If she had gone to Nonna, tried to be friends, but she wouldn't. And she would not speak to Papa when he asked her to try. So he stopped asking.' He stood up and went across to the window.

'You know, Andrea,' Anna got up and joined him, 'it's none of my business but I wonder if Sophia's point of view has ever truly been considered.'

'How can you say that?' he demanded, wheeling round. 'I'm considering her now. Don't you see that? This is not my choice to be silent. It's hers.'

Anna looked helplessly at his miserable face. How could she undo years of conditioning? How could she make him see that, after all the rejection, a woman as proud as Sophia could never have gone cap in hand asking to be accepted? She could see it so plainly. Instead, she reached out her hand and squeezed his arm.

'Nothing is ever that simple, is it? Did Lorenzo know?'

'Maybe. No. I don't know,' he said distractedly. 'I never said anything and he didn't ask. We were both very good at secrets in the end. And you didn't know, did you? But Irena knows, and Elena. No one else. Not in the family. You do understand? You won't say anything?'

Next to her the phone emitted a low buzz. They both looked at it. Andrea reached for it. 'Promise me?' Andrea held his hand over the receiver before handing it to her.

'Of course.' Anna took it from him. Another secret from Sophia.

'Signorina Anna?' came Gio's voice. '*Una telefonata urgente*. Signor Spidding.'

Henry was in a state. While Anna was talking to him, Andrea slipped out with a wave.

'Henry.' Anna had to shout over him to make him listen. 'Calm down. What is it? Max has done what?'

'Got himself made executive producer, the bastard. He's calling the shots.'

'Good heavens, Henry, how? And, more interestingly, why?'

'Because Tania, stupid cow, got conned into letting some jokers come on claiming they were married but the husband said he was having a sex change and wanted a baby, and this dodgy doctor came on and said he was going to do it – but the whole thing was a set-up and they said so right on camera and all their mates invaded the stage and—'

Anna started to laugh, holding her hand over the mouth-piece so that Henry would not be driven right over the edge.

'So Max got in first with Charles and said *his* fucking reputation had suffered most and unless he had control over the programme that was it and Charles said . . .'

She listened until he ran out of steam. She sympathized with Henry but felt no anger or dismay for herself. What did it matter if Max wanted to invest himself with responsi-bility for a show that was universally regarded as his? If Henry would just calm down, she would tell him that, in an odd kind of way, it would be better. Only Max could now be responsible every time something went wrong – and it would. Max was going to make a mess of it and, in the greater scheme of things, did it really matter what he called himself when she was hundreds of miles away, sorting out her own dysfunctional family? It mattered so little to Anna that she was quite shocked.

On Friday, Lorenzo was buried with all the pomp and cere-mony that Sophia could demand, not just socially but of her faith. A requiem mass at Santa Maria dei Rosario, in the centre of Rome at the height of the evening rush-hour, had been Sophia's choice. It was the church where they had married and, later, where Monsignor presided. Afterwards, Lorenzo's body would be driven directly to Bracciano for burial in the family plot. Anna had quietly made it clear to Sophia that she would not be going with them.

'I don't blame you.' Sophia kept her voice low. 'And maybe it's for the best. I'll tell Loretta you had to fly back to England.'

Anna was about to say, 'Tell her the truth.' But what was the point? It was Sophia and Andrea who had to live with it, not her. And, besides, whatever Loretta's crimes against Sophia and Anna, the woman was a mother and grief-stricken and this was not the moment to make a further, final point about what had happened so long ago.

Battling to get to the service against a tide of snarling traffic was nothing compared to the belligerence needed to elbow through the crowds, who paused to watch the line of black limousines circling the square in front of the church, before depositing their cargo of mourners at the steps.

Anna stole a glance around. Over the severely cut Armanis, the exquisite Valentinos, the discreet elegance of Gucci, the women uniformly wore black veils and fanned themselves with their stiff white service sheets. Inside these were listed the names of all those invited to speak for a man who had been loved as much for his gentle nature as his generosity.

Anna wore a veil too. Sophia had brought it to her as she waited in the salon for the moment when she and Giulio along with Fabio and his wife, would leave for the church. It seemed to Anna that only the real mourners, for whom Lorenzo's passing had irrevocably altered their lives, could possibly need such a screen for their grief. But Sophia, her face white, the faint smell of brandy on her breath, had said, 'Please?' and Anna had instantly agreed. Appearances, that's what it was. Even now.

Apart from those of the family she had come to know

over the last few days, she recognized only a handful of the people around her but many more appeared to find her of interest. Anna studied her service sheet and ignored their stares. It had been her choice not to sit with Sophia and Andrea or walk in procession with them behind the coffin of a man she had never known. For an obscure reason, she felt that such a demonstration would be misconstrued. This was her only chance to show that she, too, was on the edge of this family and that she understood the woman who had given her up.

The church blazed with candles; the scent of incense hung over the dim interior; the perfume from hundreds of white lilies and peonies clung to the air. The choir softly sang a psalm that made tears prick the back of Anna's eyes. Their voices soared gently up into the cavernous dome of the church and if until now Anna had never thought much about faith, at that moment she could understand its powerful pull.

Suddenly the unmistakable sound of activity drifted in from the back of the church and everyone stood as Lorenzo's coffin was brought in slowly by the pallbearers and laid on a waiting bier. It was covered in white roses. As they came to a halt Anna turned. Andrea and Sophia walked immediately behind it. After them came Gianni with his family, Irena, Elena, and then a procession of nephews and nieces.

The congregation on both sides of the packed church turned to watch until they had all filed into place in two pews either side of the ornate altar. Anna caught Stefano's eye. He gave her an apologetic shrug and she half-smiled in return. My brother's lover, she thought. She could not imagine telling Oliver that she had caught her brother in bed with another man. Certainly not her father – and as for Meryl. The idea almost made her gasp aloud.

Irena gave her a discreet wave and rolled her eyes towards Roberto, who was sitting next to his wife whose attention was focused on a late arrival. Several pairs of eyes turned, including Anna's, to watch as the birdlike figure slipped into a seat at the back accompanied by two women friends. One whispered in her ear and her head turned towards Anna. For a brief moment the woman lifted her veil and stared hard at her before sinking to her knees. Anna glanced fearfully at Sophia, but if she had noticed, she gave no indication of it, her gaze on the flower-strewn coffin a few feet from where she sat. Anna breathed out.

'Are you all right?' Giulio whispered, following her gaze.

'Fine,' she said hurriedly. 'I'm just not good at being a Catholic.'

And all Sophia had been guilty of was not lying, Anna thought, as she sat, knelt or stood in response to whatever the service demanded.

When the congregation filed up to the altar for communion, Anna had had enough and decided to slip away. Outside in the warmth of the late-afternoon sun, with the now familiar clamour and fuss of Rome going home, she sat on a bench and waited for the family to emerge. Giulio was first, with the woman who had stared so keenly at Anna, and stood talking to her for a few minutes before kissing her on both cheeks. He was followed by Fabio, then three people she recognized as Lorenzo's friends. Elena and Irena hurried over, too, to hug the woman. She saw Elena indicate where she was sitting on the bench almost as Giulio reached her. The woman raised her hand to Anna. Anna turned away. It was too much.

'Who was that?' Anna asked indifferently, making room for Giulio on the bench as the woman walked away into the crowd accompanied by her friends.

'You know perfectly well,' he answered, loosening his tie.

'I don't get this,' Anna cried. 'Or you. Do none of you care about Sophia's feelings? God Almighty, Giulio, she's just been widowed. Her son is no use to her he's so . . . so upset. And there you are, all of you, kissing the mistress.'

'Saying goodbye to her,' he corrected. 'She's not a bad

woman, Anna. She just fell in love with the wrong man. It happens. Stop being so judgemental.'

'Me?' she protested. 'Look, I might be judgemental but I know where my loyalty lies. And of all of you I have the best reason not to have an ounce of it. Look at you all. You have all the charm in the world yet Sophia hasn't got a real ally in there, except Andrea and he's mixed up over her. Because of me, of course. And everything else as well,' she added, taking his silence for agreement. 'I expect you think I should know better than to take sides, but they really are behaving disgracefully to her. This is meant to be a funeral. Frankly, it's the most scandalous performance I've ever seen.'

'Is it?' he asked politely. 'But, then, there's a lot you can't be expected to understand.'

'You mean the way you all hug and kiss each other but have no idea how to treat people's feelings?' she fumed.

'Meaning that I think you shouldn't worry if you don't get to know everything about these people or make decisions about them in just a few days.'

'I probably won't see them again after tomorrow,' she replied.

'Even better reason,' he said.

She didn't bother to reply. He was right. Why get involved? She removed the cotton jacket she had worn in church over the hastily bought black linen dress. She moved so that her arm was not pressed against his.

'Stop it, Anna,' he suggested mildly.

'Stop what?' she asked, feeling cross and miserable.

'Stop making me wish we were not in such a public place.'

'I'm amazed you have such scruples after that little exhibition.' She flicked an imaginary speck of dust from her shoulder. 'And, in case it's slipped your mind you're at a funeral.'

'Is that what it is? I thought you said it was a scandalous performance.'

He turned and smiled at her until she had to smile back. And the thought of returning home was not as attractive as it had been only a week ago. She wanted to go on sitting in the warmth of the Roman afternoon, feeling wanted and possibly wanton, although she preferred not to examine the latter too closely. She wanted to go and sit on the terrace at Trastevere and sort out why it was she felt repelled and fascinated in equal measures by this family. She had nothing in common with them just as she had nothing in common with Meryl's family. They were used to luxury; she lived in Braverton Street next to Dottie. Her upbringing had been in a small terraced house where she walked to the local comprehensive and her parents had saved to go on holiday to a self-catering cottage in Devon; Andrea and Irena had gone to exclusive schools and spent their summers in a lakeside villa at Bracciano.

She thought of Carrie and the days at university when they would get into bed and eat Pot Noodles to save money and heat and travelled home on the cheapest tickets they could find. Andrea had been given his own car to commute between Rome and Milan. In this setting, what had seemed comfortable, fun and normal became shrouded in dullness. She felt as though she had never truly lived.

Anna watched as Lorenzo's coffin was placed in the back of the hearse for the long drive to Bracciano. Andrea and Sophia were waiting for their car to pull round into the square.

'She's pushing herself too hard,' Anna muttered to Giulio. 'I mean, even today she looks immaculate.'

'Is that what grief looks like?' Giulio took in the exquisitely cut crêpe suit, the cream silk shirt. 'I never knew before.'

'Don't be so cynical,' she reproved.

'Said the idealist to the realist,' he said.

Anna ignored him. 'She's doing it because Lorenzo would have expected her to.' And with that she went over to Irena, who had clearly managed to have a row with Roberto.

'He is a pig,' Irena hissed, taking Anna's arm. 'Why do I always want pigs?'

When he heard that she had no intention of going to Bracciano, Giulio suggested they met for dinner at a restaurant in Piazza Navona since Sophia and Andrea would not be returning until very late.

'Won't you be missed?' she asked.

'I'm not one of them,' he pointed out. 'I'm not a Grescobaldi.'

The square was warm and bustling. Anna arrived first having changed out of the black funeral clothes and into cotton trousers and a vest. If only, she thought, she could eat out like this every night, she would never complain again, and after a day that had been tragic and intriguing in equal measures, she wanted space to think why, in the midst of all that had happened, she felt an odd sense of elation.

Oliver had left a message on her mobile to say that he was going out to dinner but could she call him with the time of her flight next day. She took a swift sip of water, then slipped off her shoes, and her earrings, which she placed beside her glass with her sunglasses.

She had planned to phone to tell him she was having dinner with Giulio. But he was out so she couldn't. She consoled herself that at least she had tried. And that was a relief. Seeing Oliver was the best possible reason to go back to London in a list that was getting shorter as each hour passed.

'So tomorrow,' Giulio said, when they had ordered, 'you go back?'

She nodded.

'And pick up where you left off?'

She nodded again, but this time with less certainty. 'Of course,' she said. 'There've been some changes at the office. I'll have to see how that's working out.'

'Tell me about your mother,' he said suddenly, refilling her glass and his own.

'What about her?'

'What was she like? What did she do? Was she funny, solemn, argumentative?'

'My mother?'

'Yes.'

'Really?'

'Yes, really,' he mimicked.

Anna stared sideways into the square. Where did you begin with such a creature as her mother? 'She was smaller than me,' she began, looking at him, 'and academically I could outstrip her. But she was so smart I could never fool her. She never told jokes, but she was witty. Shrewd, too. Her hair was once red, but by the time she died it had started to go grey and she just let it. She was the least vain woman I ever knew. I could ask her anything and felt totally guilty if I kept anything from her.'

'Like?' he asked, watching her face.

'Like taking a job in an awful boozy pub – Carrie did too. We wanted to backpack around Thailand and needed the money.'

'And she would have stopped you?'

Anna gave a comical groan. 'No. Worse. She would have found the money from somewhere for me and I knew it would be their holiday fund or the new car that would go out the window. And that *would* have made me feel even more guilty. But she could never see that. It drove me mad.'

'And when she died?'

'Suddenly.' Anna heard her voice begin to go. 'Without warning and sometimes even now I can feel her, as real as this.' She reached over and touched his arm, trying to make him understand. He looked at her hand. 'And you have no idea what it's like not being able to hear her.' She half expected him to say something sympathetic but he didn't.

'And your father?' he said. 'What's he like? Were they happy?'

'Dad?' She sat back, letting her hand slide away from his arm. 'Quiet, bookish. Rather more easy-going than Mum. Yes, they were happy. They rarely argued.'

'Is that the same thing? The key to happiness. No rows?'

'It helps,' she said, beginning to feel uncertain. 'Yes. Heavens. What am I saying? Of course they were happy. I would have known.'

She watched him pick up her earrings and jangle them from hand to hand.

'And you are close to him? Like with your mother?'

'In a different way. He let me and Mum just get on with things, and we both looked after him. Especially after Mum died, I did. He's fine now. He'd known Meryl for a long time – long before Mum died. He was her first husband's best friend at university. He's happy.'

'You like Meryl?'

'Pass.'

'That bad? Why?'

'Because she's taken him over, and because he's so anxious to do the right thing by her that he does the wrong thing by me. It's almost as though I've lost him as well as Mum. Still, Dad seems to have fitted in well with her family so I suppose that's all that matters. Isn't it? And,' she smiled brightly at him, 'he likes playing at being a grandfather. Well, a step-grandfather at any rate. Me having not yet honoured my obligations to him in that department.' She pulled her mouth down in an exaggerated grimace.

'You don't want children?'

'Oh, yes. At some point. Did you and Victoria not want them?'

'Of course. Good job we didn't. Anyway, she's pregnant – she told me last week.'

'You still see her? You're still friends?'

He looked amused. 'With Victoria? Impossible. She wanted to tell me herself she would be getting married. Presumably,' he added drily, 'in case I heard it from else-where and decided to kill myself in the ensuing grief.' He took a sip of wine and looked at her over the rim. 'Do I look devastated?'

Anna had to agree that he didn't. She would have quite liked him to have been as forthcoming about his on-off relationship with the art-dealer he had told her about.

'And Oliver?' He looked away briefly. 'You must have missed him this week.'

'Absolutely,' she said, sitting very still. 'And if you're about to suggest brandy, yes, I'd love one. And while I enjoy it, you can tell me what *your* mother is like.'

He signalled for the waiter. 'I hope I never have to live in the same house as her ever again, but I love her to death. Fortunately my father does too. And in Oliver you have found what you are looking for?'

One of the things she had noticed about Giulio was that he was difficult to deflect. She pushed a spoon around the white cloth in an abstract pattern. 'I have found something in Oliver that is very special. And I know,' she went on carefully, 'that he would hate it if I discussed him with any-one.'

'You're assuming I want to discuss him. My question was about you.' He took her hand and removed the spoon from it. 'Are you trying to tunnel your way out?' He smiled.

Anna swallowed hard and stared fixedly at the lean, tanned hand holding her own. Then she pulled away and placed hers in her lap. 'Sorry.' She grabbed her drink. 'Wasn't thinking.'

'Would you like to have this brandy at my apartment?' he asked matter-of-factly.

'No,' Anna said quickly. Too quickly. 'I mean, thank you, another time. I'm very tired. It's been quite a day. Well, actually, quite a week. I have to phone Oliver and pack.'

'Hmm,' he said thoughtfully, studying her face. 'In which case,' he signalled to the waiter, 'we should go at once.'

He dropped her at the entrance to the house and made no attempt to see her upstairs. 'What time is your flight?' he asked, as she went inside.

'Five,' she said, not quite knowing where to look. 'Sophia asked me to get the later one.'

'Pity.' He smiled down at her. 'I'm catching the early-morning one. We could have travelled back together.'

An inexplicable flicker of panic fluttered through her. All week she had unconsciously come to depend on knowing he was there, a strange ally in an odd, exhausting world and now she would be on her own. She tried to thank him.

'On the contrary, I should be thanking you,' he teased her. 'You've restored my faith in the Grescobaldis.'

'But I'm not really one of them,' she pointed out. 'And I'm English, remember.'

'Even better,' he said, pushing her hair out of her face. 'I was having trouble with them too.'

For a moment she thought he was going to kiss her. His face was only inches from hers. Instead he took her by the shoulders and kissed her lightly on both cheeks. '*Ciao*, Anna,' he said. And then he was gone.

'I should have told him sooner.' Sophia sighed quietly as they walked next morning, through the leafy glades of a nearby park, avoiding the frisbee throwers and the roller-bladers. Small knots of schoolchildren were being ushered in a group under a tree where a young nun was dispensing pencils and paper. The sun filtered through the trees. It was one of the most peaceful days Anna had spent since she arrived. Only the thought of what was waiting for her in London made her anxious to be on the plane.

'How could I tell him such awful things when he loved his father – and who was to say Lorenzo might have given up the drink? Even when he was in a rage, when he hurt me—' Sophia stopped.

'Hurt you?' Anna halted. 'Do you mean he hit you?'

Sophia turned back and patted her hand. 'Once or twice. Nothing I couldn't deal with. He was a good man until the drink took over. But he made his peace with me and his Maker. And you. Most of all, you.'

Anna was horrified. If she had known what kind of man it was who wanted her forgiveness she would never have come. It was bad enough that he had had a mistress and a drink problem. 'Does Andrea know?' she exclaimed. 'He should,' she said angrily. 'He should know how his mother was treated. He's a man, Sophia, not a child. Does anyone know?'

Sophia shrugged. 'What for? they would never have believed me. They prefer to think of him as a gentle, sweet-natured man. And he was, he was. But now I don't care. What good would come of it now, telling Andrea? He has a lot to deal with.'

Anna said nothing.

Sophia didn't seem to notice. 'I just want now to secure my own future. Roberto has promised to help me – he has been very supportive and he thinks you are wonderful.'

'Does he?' she said drily.

'Maybe I can persuade Fabio to let me have enough money to buy an apartment. Away from all the memories.'

'Sophia,' Anna began firmly, 'I know they have been monsters but I seriously doubt Andrea or anyone would wish you to move unless you really wanted to.'

'Of course not,' Sophia agreed. 'I just want Andrea now to be happy and settled. Maybe now he has to lead a more organized life he will find a girl.'

Anna reached up and pulled a leaf from a tree as she passed under it. She had no right to tell Sophia what she knew. And she knew she couldn't tell Andrea the truth about his father. It wasn't her place to do so. Nor could she put Sophia right about Roberto. She had almost asked Sophia if Lorenzo had also hit Issy, then remembered she wasn't meant to know about Issy either. For a brief moment she considered just telling Andrea but it would be like throwing a Molotov cocktail through the window of their lives then running for cover, back to her own life.

After all, as Giulio had pointed out, she didn't know

them. They had over three decades of a shared history. She had barely three weeks.

'I have no right,' Sophia said quietly, as Anna was leaving to go to the airport with Andrea, 'to expect to be part of your life. But is that the same as just wanting to know if you're all right, what you're doing?'

'No, of course not,' Anna said. 'And I'd like to hear from all of you.'

'Come back, won't you?' Sophia said. 'Come back often.'

Chapter Sixteen

Sitting on the plane, as Rome fell away below, Anna closed her eyes and reviewed the life she had left behind her and the one waiting for her. She was shocked to find she felt happy. For the first time in almost two years she felt released. It had taken a death to force her into a cul-de-sac and another to show her how to resume where she had left off. Now she knew where she had come from, who she was. She had a family to which she had a right to belong rather than just a half-hearted invitation to join in someone else's.

The marvel of seeing herself so vividly mirrored in Andrea was matched only by the thrill of seeing in Irena and Elena her dark looks and lean limbs. Sometimes even in Gianni she thought she could detect an expression that was hers. And he was so like Lorenzo.

'There you are, dear,' Dottie had called, from her usual stance at the gate as Anna stepped from the cab well after nine on Saturday night. 'Nice holiday? Those dustmen have left a trail of litter right up my path. Eamonn said he'd ring and tell them to come back, but they won't, mark my words, they won't.'

Anna put down her case and fished in her bag for her key. 'Don't worry, Dottie. First thing in the morning I'll clear it up. How's your hip?'

'Don't go mad,' Oliver cautioned next day, watching her pile armfuls of clothes into bin liners. He felt alarmed by

183

all this activity. 'They wore you out over there. You've been yawning ever since you got back.'

'Have I?' She examined a jacket and held it up against herself. 'I'll never wear this again,' she said, and rammed it on top of the last of three bulging black plastic sacks.

Oliver lay back on her bed and said, with more hope than conviction, 'I suppose you wouldn't like to um . . . relax for a minute?'

'I'd love to, but if I do I won't get this finished,' she replied, 'so don't distract me.'

'As if I could,' he grumbled. 'And now I expect you'll disappear for hours getting rid of that lot.' He craned his neck to watch her pull the yellow drawstring around the top of each sack.

'No, I won't.' She grinned. 'You will.'

'Me? Oh, my God. *An-na*. It's our first day together for nearly ten days.'

Ten days? Was that all? She took his hands and pulled him off the bed. 'My hero,' she teased, giving him a gentle push in the back. 'Charity shop. High street. Corner by the video shop. Can't miss it.'

'There'd better be something in this for me,' he growled.

'Uh-huh.' She nodded. 'I'll be right here.' She kissed his cheek. 'When you get back.'

While he was gone she returned Sophia's phone call.

Her house, with its charming clutter, was next to fall victim to her new mood. Out went the mountain of bright, cheerful cushions, and in came perfectly matched ones in white and blue, so severely cut that Eamonn, arriving at the end of the day to unload his usual catalogue of complaints about an uncaring social order and urban blight, blinked and said he could sharpen knives on them. Anna ignored him, and instead of the instant coffee he was used to offered him an exotic brew from an awesome-looking glass percolator.

'Grief,' he muttered, watching her pour into two mugs what was an undoubtedly superior blend to anything sold at the corner shop. 'That's much too grand for these old things,' he said, tapping the side of his. 'What on earth made you buy it?'

'I didn't,' she said, with what she hoped was a careless voice. 'Irena – my cousin – sent it.'

'Did she?' Eamonn said. 'Now, there's a thing.'

Photographs that had crowded every available space were ruthlessly pruned until only five survived. These she arranged in a straight line on the wall in plain glass frames bought from a demanding design shop in Covent Garden. The first was the one of her mother sitting in the garden reading, strands of hair escaping from a top-knot, rammed into place with huge, tortoiseshell slides. The others were of Oliver, of course, smiling confidently, his hands dug into his pockets, a wineglass in his hand, at some reception or other shortly after they first met, of Carrie and Euan, both wearing woolly hats and mittens clutching snowballs, her parents at her graduation, wearing formal clothes bought for the occasion, Anna between them clutching her degree. It had been her mother's favourite. The last was one Anna had taken of her parents when she was fifteen. Apart from her graduation photograph it was the only one of them together that she could find. She stood back and gave herself a shake.

Flowers were no longer grabbed from the supermarket checkout because they looked warm and cheerful, but carefully chosen and in a single colour. The inspiration had been Sophia's extravagant box of orchids in different shades of blue, which had arrived when she heard Anna was redecorating. They cried out for something more stylish than the mismatch of vases whose provenance could be traced to a Paris flea-market or a Tunisian souk. Perfectly cut glass ones replaced them. The books were packed into boxes and stored in the loft, leaving on display only the glossy, elegant ones that Oliver had given her and one from Andrea on Titian's women, which Anna had mentioned she liked. Inside he inscribed it from 'Tuo fratello, Andrea.'

'Touching,' Oliver said heavily, snapping it shut.

'And thoughtful,' she replied firmly.

Swathes of voile replaced the heavy cotton curtains, thrown artlessly over a wooden pole. The carpet came up, the floors were sanded.

'Wow,' Carrie said, taking in the results of Anna's feverish activity. 'How very – different.'

'What's wrong with it?' Anna asked.

'Nothing. I just can't bear the thought of Euan in here.'

Anna followed her gaze. 'Oh, well,' she said. 'Andrea was brought up in practically a glass palace and he said he never broke a thing.'

'Didn't he?' Carrie said. 'I must tell Euan.'

The following Sunday, Carrie looked thoughtfully at Anna watching Oliver arguing with the friend Eamonn had brought with him about the benefits system as applied to those with no fixed address, and could see no visible difference in the girl who had shared penniless student days with her or supported her during the ghastliness when Gregg had left her pregnant and unemployed. Right at this moment the difference in her friend was rooted elsewhere. That's it, Carrie realized, she isn't listening. Of that she was certain. Anna hadn't been listening to anyone for some time. But then, she sighed, glancing at her son who was almost asleep on Eamonn's lap, Anna wasn't so much not listening but waiting to hear something. Someone, Carrie thought, had better say whatever it was she wanted to hear and soon.

Within a month Anna had resigned from *Max Meets*. Henry was distraught. The only bright light on his dismal, shrinking career horizon had been knowing that Anna would be back to stand alongside him in the relentless tyranny exercised over them by the new executive producer.

'And I bet you'll take Aggie,' he said mournfully. 'But if you even think of employing that bitch troll,' he hissed, looking furtively around, 'Melissa bloody Bowden, my suicide note will name you first. I can't bear it. They'll be vile to you. And, you know, no one lasts more than two weeks there without therapy.'

'Oh, stop it, Henry.' Anna felt scared enough without Henry adding to it. 'You'll be fine. I can't stay here for ever. Anyway, how do you know Max won't be better once I'm gone? It's me he loathes. Tania will be fine. Where is she, by the way?'

'Off sick,' he said. 'And I hope it's nothing trivial. This is all her fault.'

'Any calls?' she asked Tessa, who had been hovering attentively around her, plying her with unasked-for cups of coffee ever since she had heard Anna was leaving. There was a good chance she might take her with her.

Tessa reeled off a list. '. . . and Oliver said he would be in meetings until four,' she finished.

'Anyone else?' Anna asked casually.

'Don't think so.' Tessa anxiously checked the list again. 'That's about it. Are you expecting someone?'

'No,' Anna said quickly. 'Not really.'

Oddly enough, Max was as aghast as Henry when he heard that she was going to Marksman Television to become editor on a new live weekday programme called *Newsbeat*, which was to be aired first in London and then, if the ratings proved strong enough, taken up nationally. In one move she had deprived him of the chief pleasure of his newly created title, that of finally, blissfully, putting her in her place. He was also quite scared. In her new role Anna could bestow credibility, save reputations or destroy them. More than ever Max knew she was exactly the person he needed to cultivate and the one person he would rather shave his head than nurture. More worryingly, it was also perfectly possible she would discover the number of approaches his own agent had been ordered to make to the head of Marksman with ideas for Max himself to move on.

Surprisingly Oliver, too, had reacted badly about her swift change of job.

'You were the one who told me to move,' Anna reminded

him as they flopped out after her leaving party. 'You said no more trailer-park trash.'

He was flicking through the channels on the television. 'I know,' he said. 'But I had no idea you were going to move quite so soon.'

'But you did,' she protested, stung by his lack of enthusiasm. 'I did what you've been nagging me to do.'

'I think nagging's a bit extreme,' he said evenly, pausing to watch the cricket results. 'I thought I was encouraging you.'

'All right, what you encouraged me to do. And I've done it, haven't I?'

He wouldn't look at her. 'I would have appreciated knowing you were talking to them.'

'I'm sorry.' Anna sounded contrite. She had wanted to show him that she was capable of much more than producing an area of television that had always made her feel acutely uncomfortable. 'I should have told you,' she conceded. 'I just wanted to surprise you.'

'Well, you've certainly done that,' he said, with emphasis.

'Look,' she said, smoothing the lock of hair back from his forehead. 'Let's just wait and see, eh? Who knows?' she teased. 'I might actually be good at it.'

'I never said you wouldn't be good at it,' Oliver said, clearly determined not to let her off the hook. 'That's not the point.'

'Let's not talk about it,' she said abruptly. 'Let's just not talk about anything.'

Oliver turned up the volume on the television. 'As you wish,' he said stiffly. 'By the way your – Sophia called.'

'Did she?' Anna said. And then, quite casually, 'Anyone else?'

'Oh, yes. Carrie. Wants to know if she can leave Euan overnight tomorrow.'

At the weekend Oliver went to Paris then straight to Manchester for a couple of days. In his absence Anna tried to do something that she knew would please him.

The roof garden. That's what she would do. Once, it had made her feel warm and secure. Now it seemed conventional and over-eager, and Oliver had never liked it. This, at least, was his decision and one she now agreed with. Eamonn was dragged protesting from his bed on Saturday morning to find himself helping Anna to paint the pink walls white, the railings glossy black and to replace the chairs with canvas-backed folding ones.

'Well, I hope you bloody like it,' Eamonn said, with feeling. 'My arms will never be the same again.'

'Like what?' asked Oliver, keeping a wary eye on Eamonn's companion, who stood silently behind his protector and regarded Oliver with blatant misgivings.

It was just after eight and the drive from Manchester had been torture. Any hope that Anna might, for once, be there before him had been abandoned as he turned the key in the lock of a darkened house. Eamonn had practically followed him up the path, towing the latest victim of homelessness in his wake.

'The roof, man,' Eamonn roared. 'Haven't you seen my artistic endeavours on the roof? Oh, Christ. I expect it was meant to be a surprise. Say nothing, my man, and after I have helped myself to a pint of milk – and a bit of cheese and maybe an egg or two,' he went on, exploring the contents of Anna's fridge, 'I'll leave you to be surprised.'

'Does Anna know you're taking all that?' Oliver inquired. It was not a big deal, but Oliver was not feeling reasonable. He was feeling troubled. And the trouble was definitely Anna. Resentment welled in him now at anyone who felt they could command what little time she had from that job or help themselves to something that belonged to her. Even cheese. He knew he was being pathetic but he was too angry and too tired and the M1 should never have been built and he wanted Anna very badly.

He was still glaring at Eamonn. 'No,' said Eamonn, closing the fridge door with his foot, 'but she won't mind. She understands that sometimes I have the odd emergency. As she does. Now, come along, Gary, we'll leave this gentleman to practise his Oscar-winning performance at saying how he loves the new roof garden. *Ciao*, as Anna would say.'

Oliver was standing in the kitchen leaning against the sink and flicking through a paper when Anna let herself in an hour later.

'Hey,' she said dropping her bag and reaching up to kiss his cheek. 'Did you watch?'

'No,' he said, barely lowering the paper.

'Never mind,' she said, her heart sinking. She kicked off her shoes and scooped up some of Euan's toys and his pyjamas. 'I've got a video. Anything the matter?' She pushed the pyjamas into the washing-machine and the space-fighters into a cupboard. Then she unloaded the shopping she had picked up from the delicatessen on her way from the tube.

Oliver went on reading. 'Matter? Not unless you count the fact that you're so busy I had to hear about more changes from Eamonn,' he said carefully, not looking up.

Anna paused and looked up. 'Eamonn?' she said blankly.

'Yes,' Oliver said, reaching behind him for a glass of wine. He took a careful sip, then returned to his paper. 'He came round with one of those weirdos he carts around after him and asked me what I thought of the roof. And I had to say,' he said, scanning the paper as though searching for something specific, 'that I had no idea you'd changed it.'

'But you've always wanted me to change the roof. Oliver,' she tugged the paper, 'listen to me. Please?'

'I am listening.' He lowered the paper, looking over the top at her, but not all the way in case he needed it to establish the point that he was refusing to be drawn into her new, frantic world. 'I never said *change* the garden. It was just a *suggestion*. And he helped himself to stuff in the fridge. What are you doing? Supporting the whole street?'

Anna's shoulders sagged. 'Oliver,' she said slowly, 'Eamonn knows I don't mind. And without asking for so much as a cup of coffee he gave up an entire Saturday to help me surprise you.'

Oliver rustled the paper.

'Are you telling me,' Anna asked quietly, when he didn't answer, 'that I have to ask your permission for everything I do? Because if you are then we have a very big discussion ahead of us.'

'Don't be childish,' he snapped. 'You can do what you like. I thought the idea of being together is that we had no secrets.'

Anna gasped. 'You call a surprise a secret? I'm sorry. I can't deal with this.'

She slammed the kitchen door and went for a walk. She skirted the park and the derelict garages, which were boarded up waiting for developers, and walked without thinking of where she was heading until, with a start, she saw that she was at the end of Granton Street. It was after nine but not yet dark. She began to walk along the road, passing the video store, the betting shop and then Mr Viraswami's shop, with its heavy grille pulled across the door and padlocked for the night.

She walked on until she was opposite her parents' house. She stopped and stared, as though just being near where her mother had once been waiting for her she would know what it was she wanted and what she had to do, and why now everything that had once seemed easy was becoming like an uphill struggle. The elation had slipped away.

But nothing, she thought forlornly, gazing in dismay at the once-familiar house, was sacred. The window-frames had been painted navy blue and the rust-coloured Victorian brickwork buried under a thick coat of pale blue paint. A porch had been added, inside which Anna glimpsed a folded pushchair beneath a plastic spray of flowers pinned to the wall in a startling slash of colour. There was a satellite dish clinging to the front just above what had been Anna's bedroom window. Austrian blinds, half pulled down, crowded the upper windows.

'I thought it was you,' a voice said behind her. Anna wheeled round.

'Goodness,' she gasped, at the beaming man standing behind her. 'You gave me a start.'

'I am sorry,' he said. 'You remember me? Viraswami. Mr Viraswami. From the shop.'

'Yes,' she said, awkwardly. 'Of course I remember you. How are you? I was just visiting an old friend, on the off-chance,' she said hurriedly. 'They're out,' she added, as he continued to smile and nod. 'I should have phoned first. I was just going back. Different.' She tried to smile, indicating her old home.

'My son's house now,' he sighed, 'although it doesn't make him any earlier for work. I'm just going to see my grandson. And also to fetch my wife. Since they move over here, she is never home.'

For a brief moment they contemplated the awfulness of the house. Mr Viraswami folded his arms. He sounded apologetic. 'It is not what I would have done with it,' he began. '"Try new pointing," I said. Something in keeping. But there you are.' He spread his hands helplessly at the garish façade, which would have made Barbara groan with disbelief. 'And they like to make their own personality on it,' Mr Viraswami was saying. 'I expect,' he added hopefully, recalling that Colin Minstrel had seemed unaffected by the ways of the young, 'you think it's an improvement. You young people do your own thing. That's what your father said to me,' and he laughed heartily. 'Give him my regards, and his new wife,' he said, as she prepared to move on, and crossed the street to the house that had once been hers.

She watched him as the door opened and he bent down to pick up a small child. Then the door closed, leaving her alone on the pavement. She looked around, surprised that she wasn't moved to tears or felt any closer to her mother. In a way she was glad. It was gone. All of it. What was important was in her head. It's where you're going, not where you started, what was possible, not what might have been.

A fleeting picture of the person she had become in Rome rose up before her, of Anna basking in being powerful and admired, effortlessly commanding attention. She shut her eyes and groaned. She had skirted so close to a meaningless fling with a man she hardly knew, like some stupid holiday romance, she berated herself. It was so different here at home, no sun or lazy afternoons to while away the time. Those lingering walks, the lunch and dinner made her blush. To think what she might have risked. She was suddenly anxious to be home where she knew the safety of familiarity. At the end of the street she flagged down a taxi.

When she got back, Oliver was sitting on the sofa watching a video recording of her programme.

'Sorry,' she said, coming up behind him and slipping her arms around him. 'Just the new job. Ignore me.'

'I'll try,' he said, sounding better. 'Just let me in on what you plan to do before you do it. And incidentally,' he pulled her round and down beside him, indicating the presenter of *Newsbeat*, 'the other guy should have handled this item. She's not strong enough.'

'You're right.' Anna didn't argue: there'd been enough of that. To her annoyance she could hear Giulio saying, 'And is not arguing the sign of happiness?'

'Absolutely right.' She curled up against Oliver and shut her eyes. 'Anything else?'

The two regular presenters of *Newsbeat* were nice but tricky. It would have helped if they had been blessed with a streak of humour in their unrelenting ambition to unseat each other, but after Max nothing was impossible. In fact, faced now with serious issues and razor-sharp minds, she marvelled at how the old Anna had put up with him. Tania Prowton was welcome to him. And never again would the dilemma of having to rake the country for serial womanizers or chronic shoppers, exes bent on revenge or unrepentant sexual deviants trouble her.

The pleasure of discarding so much of what she had always regarded as dross did not blind her to what lay ahead. No budget and high expectations was the agenda by which Marksman hired and fired. Within a week of being plunged in, she arrived in her office each morning to a mountain of phone messages and faxes from what seemed to be half the House of Commons offering themselves for interview, but never from the MPs she really wanted. Royal stories jostled with crime, fashion with sport. *Max Meets* seemed light years away.

Oliver, of course, had to be thought of and led gently to the realization that she could no longer be exactly as he wanted her to be. He had liked Anna as she was, home when he arrived, ready to go where he wanted and to rely on him, the Anna who waited patiently while his mobile rang incessantly when they were out.

'God, we sound like the percussion section of an orchestra.' She giggled as both their mobiles rang in unison. This new Anna was likely to be home at midnight – on a good day.

'But, Oliver,' she protested, as he ostentatiously read the business section of the *Financial Times*. He was in bed and it was very late. The dinner she had attended had been too long, too dreary, too necessary and had left her too weary to argue. 'I couldn't get out of it. It's my job. I don't complain when you have to do the same.'

If Oliver objected to the way her job had sliced into her life, others were thrilled for her. Andrea and Sophia had sent flowers to wish her luck. She stuck their note on her screen. Irena sent a very rude card, which she grinned at before pushing it into the back of her diary. Even Carla had written saying how glad they were that she had been there for Sophia and Andrea, that they hoped to see more of her and that if she needed a break from her job, they would be so happy to see her and, of course, Oliver in Rome.

Oliver was not as thrilled by this invitation as she had

hoped, but she felt a surge of happiness and knew it was the feeling of being accepted that gave her the confidence to take her father's new family out to dinner. A week after she had started her new job, she paid a flying visit to Scotland to see him.

For once he came to meet her alone. She saw him immediately as she came through Arrivals and thought he had put on a little weight. He was wearing a tweed jacket she had never seen before and he looked different. 'Hey,' she said, holding him away from her. 'Where are your glasses?'

He grinned. 'Contacts,' he said bashfully. 'I thought I was too old for it all, but Meryl said that was nonsense and she was right, bless her. And you, dear?' he said, taking her case. 'Are you all right? Was it all OK?'

'Fine,' she said. 'I'm glad I've got you to myself. I'll tell you on the drive.'

'Good idea. We're picking Meryl up on the way. She had to do some errands in town.'

'Lovely,' Anna lied.

On the short drive into the city centre, he listened quietly to what Anna had to say about Sophia and the manner of Lorenzo's death, but he didn't ask how she felt and Anna didn't volunteer to tell him. Besides, there wasn't time. Meryl was already waiting for them when they reached the Caledonian hotel where she was having morning coffee.

'I've asked Athol and Fenella over,' Meryl said, offering her cheek for Anna to kiss. 'I thought she'd escape all the morning sickness, this being their fourth, but the poor girl doesn't seem to be coping too well. And Primmie's given me a wonderful recipe for lamb.'

'I've got a better idea,' Anna broke in, smiling brightly. 'Why don't I take you all out to dinner? Yes, really, I insist. It will do Fenella good to get out of the house for a bit. And you too, Meryl. Dad? Great. I'll book.'

Sheridan and Primrose had not been able to make it, but that didn't matter. This time she was there on her own terms; this time, she could talk about her brother – which she did, casually – and her cousins, even what her uncle had said. She inquired kindly after the progress of Athol and Fenella's home in Craigaithan Heights, which she gathered they had moved into although it wasn't quite ready.

Meryl looked thoughtfully at her, and was more silent than usual. Her father said he was glad she was on good form. He had been worried.

Sitting on the plane bringing her into Heathrow, Anna tried to fathom out why the visit had not given her as much pleasure as she had thought it would. She decided it was the effect Athol and Fenella had on her. Why couldn't they be as welcoming as Andrea, as wickedly mischievous as Irena, warm like Gianni and Carla? Even Giulio had played his part. She frowned down at her unread newspaper. Even Giulio.

By the time she had let herself in and run through her messages, she assumed it was just tiredness that had made her burst into unaccustomed tears. Sophia had called, then two friends inviting her and Oliver to dinner, then Andrea, who had clearly not known that Sophia had already phoned, Carrie to remind her about supper the following week, and Oliver asking her to ring as soon as she returned. No one else.

After she had made herself some coffee, forgetting her new machine and spooning instant into one of the mugs she had still not replaced, she climbed the stairs. Her reflection in the bathroom mirror told her nothing. She placed her hands on the sink and gazed and gazed. Nothing had changed. But it had. All of it. Which is, of course, what she had wanted. So when she cried again, she put it down to exhaustion.

She was lying in the bath, her coffee mug balanced on her stomach, when Oliver came in.

'Hey,' Oliver said, seeing her red eyes, 'what's all this?'

'Take no notice.' She struggled to smile. 'Just a long weekend and not enough sleep. You know what it's like in Meryl's spare room. The pipes creak all night and you think the roof's going to fall in or the floor collapse. Give me traffic any day. That I can deal with. Here, take this,' she handed him her cup, 'I'll be down in a minute.'

He was waiting for her in the kitchen. 'OK?'

'Sure. Fancy an omelette?' She moved to the fridge, took out eggs and began to crack them into a bowl. 'How was your meeting?' she asked, reaching up for a pan.

'Fine. Anna?'

'Uh-huh,' she said, pouring the mixture into the pan. 'Want cheese with yours?'

'Er . . . whatever. Anna? Could you just listen to me?'

Since her return, Oliver had been alternately distant and sexually demanding. Anna sighed. 'Just give me a minute.' She tossed the omelettes on to two plates and, with a flourish, set one before him. 'There, Signore, *frittata*. Hey,' she said, as he pushed away his plate, 'I don't crack eggs for everyone. What's wrong?'

'Anna,' he said, reaching out and taking her hand, 'I think we should get married. I think it's where we should go next. I was going to mention it before you went to Rome but I didn't want something so special to be overshadowed by anything else. And you are a difficult girl to pin down, these days. But I really do think we should be married. Apart from anything else,' he grinned, 'it's what people who love each other do.'

Anna thought she must have been walking round in a daze for weeks. She had no inkling that Oliver had been planning marriage. What they had worked so well, gave them satisfaction, and Oliver was her future. No one else. They were so right in every way. They knew each other's friends, her new job would be useful to him for his clients – everyone wanted to be on *Newsbeat*. And there was no reason at all that she could think of for saying no. Or, at least, none that had made its presence felt since she got back from Rome.

'Well, say something,' he said. 'You're unnerving me.'

'Yes,' she said, smiling at him. 'Yes. I can't think of a single reason why that isn't a wonderful idea.'

197

Chapter Seventeen

Anna rang her aunt Sarah in Cumbria, told her the news and said she would bring Oliver for a weekend just as soon as she could. Sarah was thrilled and full of praise for Oliver – whom she had met once and liked. 'What a shame your mother never met him,' she said. 'She would have approved. Well done, darling. I must ring my brats and tell them. How's Colin?'

'Fine,' Anna said. 'He's coming down later to meet Oliver's parents.'

'Well, say hello, won't you? And to Meryl, too, of course.'

'Of course,' Anna laughed. Sarah understood.

Almost immediately Sophia rang to say that Lorenzo's will had not made provision for Anna, but she wasn't to think that meant he hadn't thought of her. 'When he made the will it was before he was ill,' Sophia said, 'before he knew you would be found. I know if he had been capable of changing it he would have done so. But I don't under-stand why Fabio did nothing when there was time. So many things he could have done.'

Anna was shocked. She had expected and wanted nothing, and clearly the Grescobaldis had ensured that she would get nothing. It had never occurred to her that anyone would think she might. In fact, she had been so unsettled by the sight of the early wedding present that had already arrived from Sophia that it was still sitting in its wrapping paper, waiting for Anna to find somewhere safe to store the dozen crystal and gold goblets that had made her gasp and Oliver momentarily forget his unexplained antipathy to the Grescobaldis.

Sophia sounded as though the effort of speaking was exhausting her. Anna wasn't surprised. It would take a long time.

'I'm sorry,' Sophia said, as Euan shrieked with laughter suddenly. 'I can hear you are busy.'

To her horror Anna heard Sophia's voice break. She waited. It was Saturday morning and the sun was streaming through the window of her kitchen. Dottie was sitting at the table, one hand resting on her walking-frame, the other nursing a mug of tea with which Anna had just presented her. Euan, who had stayed the night while Carrie went on a rare date, was picking bits of raisin out of his cereal and dropping them with bombing noises into the little pool of spilt milk by his bowl.

'When I was a little girl,' Dottie said severely, 'they would have been a treat. We were grateful.'

'Here you are,' he said kindly. Carefully he removed a soggy offering from the pond next to him. He held it out to Dottie. 'You eat it all up.'

'Generous, I'm sure.' Dottie cackled with delight.

Oliver had retreated to the roof, which he now rather liked, with the papers, saying that he could take Euan and Dottie but not both together. Later he and Anna were going to Wiltshire to stay with his parents. Her father and Meryl had been invited for the weekend to celebrate their engagement. Just a family party, Christina had said happily.

Anna turned slightly away. 'Take it easy,' she said quietly into the phone. 'I'll wait. I'm here. Sophia?' she said after a pause. 'Who's with you?'

'With me?' Sophia cleared her throat. 'Why, no one. Did you think there was? Who would there be?' she added wearily. 'Andrea is away. He must look after the business. And no one likes a widow. Too much grief. Too much sadness. Just listen to me,' she said, more valiantly. 'I'm being stupid and spoiling your day. You must send my congratulations to Oliver's parents. They're very lucky.'

It was obvious whom she should phone. Giulio had sent only a note when her engagement appeared in *The Times*. Anna read the short paragraph several times then threw it away. History was a good word. That route to Anna was now closed. Instead she rang Fabio and made it clear to him, as the family lawyer, that any suggestion that she should inherit or had expected to was very wide of the mark. He was pleased to hear from her, surprised she had not heard from Giulio.

She thought she would scream. 'We're both busy,' she said, injecting cheerfulness into her voice. 'I'm sure he'll call when he has time. I just want to make it clear that what I did was a favour to – to a desperate woman.'

'I don't think anyone ever thought you had any other motive than to be generous and compassionate,' Fabio said soothingly. 'But it's entirely up to Sophia what she leaves you or gives you.'

She heard him hesitate.

'And, of course, although Sophia is not my client. I still act for Andrea.'

Of course, she thought. Andrea had inherited his father's company, the house in Trastevere and the villa in Bracciano, the paintings and Lorenzo's collection of first editions. He was now an even wealthier young man.

'I have no idea yet who Sophia wants to look after her affairs,' Fabio went on. 'Andrea is very cross with her for being so independent.'

A letter arrived shortly afterwards from Fabio saying that Andrea had insisted that Anna be given one of the paintings as a wedding present and that it would have to be brought to England by special carrier. She gasped. So did Oliver. It was worth a small fortune. Her first reaction was to refuse it, but Andrea was adamant.

She settled for leaving it in Rome until such a time as they could argue about it again or when she and Oliver had decided where they would live after their marriage and if they could afford a place grand enough for crystal and gold goblets and valuable paintings.

There were, of course, other compensations in having this new family: her relations with Oliver's mother eased. Her adoptive status – or, rather, as Anna more fairly suspected, her own lack of interest in her history – had always stood between them, no matter how much it was not discussed. The news that the Grescobaldis, affluent and respected, were her family and not Sicilian bandits meant that Christina Manners was delighted at the prospect of having Anna in the family. Rachel appeared to be history. 'As a matter of fact,' she confided at dinner that evening, 'my own parents were strongly drawn to Italy. That's why they called me Christina.'

Last time Anna had been at a family gathering it had been at Gianni's home in Rome, with loud chatter, scurrilous gossip, and a man with lazy, bored eyes keeping a watchful eye on her being regaled with family scandals. Her brother had been secretly arranging to spend the night with his handsome lover, safe in the knowledge that his mother would have his new sister for company and not ask where he was. And the knowledge that her father's mistress was limbering up to outrage her mother by coming to the funeral had hung nervously in the air.

This party was so different. This one was her life. Nice people, gentle laughter, her father so proud and happy. Anna stole a look at Meryl. She, too, was altered from the last time they had met in Scotland. Then she had been reserved; now she was animated, fussing over Oliver, as near, Anna thought, to being relaxed as she'd ever seen her. Doubtless because her step-daughter was soon to be someone else's problem. Anna could afford to be generous: she had Oliver now and a whole family they knew nothing about, and another one that was at the heart of what *she* was about. It was just right for her: all of them finding out about each other but not, like Irena, going too far. No one was sleeping with anyone they shouldn't be, no one was trying to seduce anyone.

Oliver's older sister, Kate, married to her rather nice solicitor, was being pleasant to Colin. The rather nice solicitor, sitting two places away, was being nice to Meryl. Oliver's younger brother, Jasper, the only one regretting Anna's departure from *Max Meets*, was suitably bored by the whole occasion. She glanced around the table and caught Oliver's eye. Silently he raised his glass to her. She smiled back and mouthed a kiss at him. He really was so nice. She had made the right decision.

'You're sure?' Irena demanded. 'Blonde, small, nose-job?'

'Irena,' Anna protested, but laughing, 'he said, "This is Julia." Yes, she was blonde and quite small, but I really didn't notice much about her.'

Nor had she. The encounter had been accidental. She and Oliver, with friends from Oliver's company, and Giulio, with another group, had chosen the same restaurant on the same night. Anna had seen him first: he was helping a woman Anna guessed was Julia, his on-off affair, to be seated.

He kissed Anna on both cheeks and shook hands with Oliver. Introductions were made, her ring admired. Vague arrangements for dinner were mooted and not followed up. There was nothing, she thought listening to Irena, in the Grescobaldi family that went unnoticed, even when it happened in London.

At her end of the line, Anna felt a sudden terrible tug of longing to be back in a restaurant with Irena. Carrie – with her job and Euan to care for – never had time for that kind of lunch any more. Then she remembered that her job meant she didn't either. And she was feeling hammered after three business dinners on three consecutive nights. That must be why she was feeling less elated than a soon-to-be bride should be.

'Elena said it couldn't have been Victoria because she is

with this man who paints – I forget his name. Awful paint-ings. Well, who would have thought it? And I think Giulio deliberately took Julia to Milan and then New York so that Victoria would get jealous.'

'Why would he do that?' Anna asked, tracing a pattern on the floor with her toe.

'Because he's such a – what you call it?' Irena giggled. 'A tom-cat. He likes having options.' She thought this was hilarious. Anna thought it monstrous.

'Anyway, how did she find out?' she asked, not strong enough to suppress her curiosity when she had vowed she would. 'His ex-wife, I mean.'

'Oh, I expect Elena made sure she did,' Irena confided. 'No love lost there. And you, you sly thing, I am coming there to relieve you of Oliver. Does he sleep with his mother?'

'Irena,' Anna screamed. 'What an awful thing to say.'

Irena gave a snort. 'Get it out of the way and everything after that is a bonus,' she explained calmly.

In the end it was Andrea who Anna saw first. *En route* to New York, he stopped off in London and was delighted when she asked if he would like to stay overnight with her. He called in at the studio and watched *Newsbeat* transmitted before going out to dinner with her, Carrie and Eamonn. She wanted him to meet her friends. He, however, had assumed that she would have dinner with him and Giulio, and in the end the entire group went together, including Oliver who hadn't intended to be there but changed his mind when he heard who else would be.

Anna's mood lifted – because Andrea was there, of course. She liked having a brother and knowing that her friends had liked him, in spite of his impossible glamour. Even Eamonn warmed to him when Andrea spoke quite sensibly about Juventus, and good-naturedly took the camera Andrea had brought with him to photograph Anna and her friends. Seated on the other side of Giulio, Carrie drew some interesting conclusions about him. She told Anna later that when he heard she had a law degree going to waste he had said he would arrange for her to see a colleague to talk about a more satisfying, better-paid job, and that, for an Italian, he was amazingly feminist.

Oliver said he was a typical bloody lawyer – the way he quietly observed them all and then took over. And Anna had really not found him *that* funny, had she? Unwisely Anna leaped to Giulio's defence, listing his kindnesses to her in Rome and describing the walks and meals they'd had together, which served only to infuriate Oliver even more. The arrival of Dottie in search of Mister, which coincided with Andrea making a leisurely entrance to breakfast just as Oliver was leaving to play squash, was the final straw.

'Anna,' Oliver shouted irritably, 'Dottie wants her cat.'

'This beautiful creature is yours?' Andrea crooned to a transfixed Dottie as he scooped Mister into his arms. 'You are most lucky,' he told the wriggling cat, 'to be cared for by this wonderful person. You are just like my *nonna*,' he said, as he helped Dottie down the path. He was wrapped in a white towelling robe, his tanned feet slipped into mules, Mister was still tucked under his arm and his hair was gleaming and slicked back straight from the shower. Anna could not stop laughing. He looked so exotic and divorced from reality in Braverton Road on a Saturday morning.

'Your what?' Dottie asked rudely, because she was flustered. 'Speak English.'

Andrea was delighted. 'How you say? My granny,' he explained. 'She is, of course, not so young-looking as you.'

'Get out of it.' Dottie aimed her walking-frame at his ankles. She was pink with pleasure.

'Next time *I* bring you shopping,' he promised, flirting shamelessly. 'Not my sister.'

'Your sister? Anna's your sister?' Dottie looked utterly bewildered. 'But you're foreign.'

'I'll explain, Dottie,' Anna called hastily.

She wasn't sure how it happened, but Andrea's visit had left Oliver even more anti-Giulio – although he grudgingly admitted that Andrea was nice enough in spite of being unbelievably vain. Anna was learning to ignore his barbed comments. Oliver seemed unnecessarily insecure about her family. She thought he was being silly, but privately she agreed that Andrea was rarely out of range of a mirror.

Before he left for New York, Andrea confessed that Stefano was going with him but that Sophia didn't know. It was becoming difficult for them because she clearly couldn't be left on her own and he had decided that he would tell her the truth, but had never found the right moment. 'She is in no state for any more shocks,' he explained sadly. 'She sees only me and Roberto. All business. Sometimes Monsignor. Not even Sylvana sees her now. All she wants is for me to be there – but, Anna, I can't. The business will suffer. Roberto is already anxious. I am in despair.'

'Look,' she said giving him a hug, 'I'll call her for you. I can't do anything else, like go there, but at least I can talk to her.'

Andrea looked at her hopefully. 'Would you, Anna? That would be a relief.' It had been four months since Lorenzo's death. No time at all, Anna thought, for someone even to begin the recovery process. She just wished Sophia would let someone get close enough to help her.

'And,' Carrie said excitedly, 'he's arranged for me to see a contact of his and we're going to have dinner. That *is* OK, isn't it?'

'Heavens, yes. I'm really pleased for you,' Anna said, peeling a banana for Euan. 'When did all this happen?'

Carrie took a gulp of tea. 'Well, just now but you'd already left to come here when I rang you. I thought he was just being polite, that he would forget. But he doesn't forget anything, does he?'

'I don't know him that well,' Anna said.

Carrie hugged herself. 'Just think, if it comes off, more money, better hours ... And you must have got to know him quite well. I rather got the impression he wouldn't be averse to a little *flingetto*.' Carrie rolled her eyes suggestively.

'Oh, I'm sure he would. You looked stunning the other night.' Anna pretended she had misunderstood.

'Hmm.' Carrie helped herself to a biscuit. 'You're a dreadful liar. Wouldn't blame you if you did. Not that I don't think Oliver's wonderful, but I rather fancy old Giulio. And I'll even offer to make an honest man of him, if this job comes off,'

Less than a week later, as she was preparing to leave for a weekend in the country with Oliver, she got a phone call from Sophia saying she was coming to London – just to get away. 'I hoped you would come and visit, but you are so busy,' she said. 'And I thought we could have just the odd lunch and maybe dinner. I wouldn't invade your life – not like last time.' She gave a rueful laugh.

For Anna, Rome was a constant reminder of things she preferred to push to the back of her mind. It was why she had resisted all Sophia's and Andrea's invitations to go back, even if her new job had allowed such a luxury. Not seeing Rome helped her get over what had been a very silly episode. A man like Giulio was dangerously easy to feel drawn to: it was his job, it was him. She congratulated herself on knowing that she had no illusions about him, recognized that he would not be averse to a *flingetto*, as Carrie had called it, and that she had come through it unscathed with no damage done. Thank God, she told herself with relief, that she had not said anything to anyone of the absurd, adolescent angst that had so clouded her first days home after Rome.

Oliver was so easy to read, so easy to be with. He didn't mobilize subliminal images of them doing unspeakably wanton things – writhing in a field of long cool grass or moulded together on white hot sand – the minute she thought about him.

'I'll let you know where I will be staying,' Sophia now

told her. 'I'm a widow now so it must be something a little more modest. Maybe near you.'

'Stay here,' Anna said impulsively.

'With you? But won't I be in the way? And I'm not very good company.'

'I'm sure you are,' Anna replied warmly. 'And, anyway, I'd like you to.'

When Andrea heard, he was delighted. It would make the rest of his trip much easier to bear, he said, from the hotel in Chicago, if he thought his mother was not alone. He sent love to Oliver and especially to Carrie and Eamonn. He asked after Dottie, who had never met anyone so exotic as Andrea and had already asked Anna when he was coming back.

Anna told him of the impression he had made on her friends. He made no secret of his pleasure. 'No one ever told me how wonderful it would be to have a sister.' He laughed. 'Stefano said that in another life you'd be my only competition. And I believe him. I hate you.'

She managed a creditable display of indifference to his inquiries about Giulio. Did she see much of him? 'Nothing at all,' she answered truthfully. 'He's been very kind and recommended Carrie for a rather good job – not in his company, with a friend of his. They specialize in employment wrangles, which is right up her street. But I don't see him at all. There's really no reason to, unless any of you are here.'

And there wasn't, she thought, and slammed two or three doors quite unnecessarily as she left the house.

Anna began to feel excited about showing Sophia what nice people she had in her life. She was pleased that she could help Andrea and perhaps send Sophia back to Rome a little stronger and more ready to let people into her life.

As the weekend approached, though, the doubts Anna had so readily swept aside when she suggested that Sophia come to her crept back. The weather, of course, was no help – in early October London did not enjoy the still warm days of Rome – Braverton Street was not Trastevere, and a walk in the recreation ground could hardly match one at the Villa Borghese. All of this she mentioned; all of it Sophia dismissed. 'It is who you are with, not where,' she said, sounding so like Anna's own mother that a small shock went through her.

'Well,' Anna said, rallying, 'I always think so.'

Oliver said that of course he would be delighted to help entertain Sophia.

Before she could mention Sophia's impending visit to her father, Colin telephoned to say that Fenella and Athol would be in London and it would be nice if Anna could see them, perhaps invite them for a meal. She groaned. Of all the times to choose. But, of course, she said yes, because it was for her father, and anyway, since her engagement to Oliver, their relationship had regained much of its former footing. Even Meryl had relaxed and kept Anna talking for a minute or two when she phoned Carrigh.

'Sophia will be here,' she mentioned it as casually as she could to her father, 'but they won't mind that, will they?'

'Sophia?' Colin said, and immediately Anna heard his voice stiffen. 'In London?'

'Well, yes. With me. She's staying here for a few days.'

'I see.'

'I'm doing this for Andrea, Dad,' she insisted, resenting having to explain a charitable act. 'It isn't his fault that any of this happened. He has no one to turn to. He's an only child too. Even if I can't love her like I loved Mum, surely it can't be wrong to have some compassion for her? She didn't want to give me away, you know. She had no option. It's really scarred her. Even I can see that.'

'Can you?' he said heavily. 'You don't think this is all going too fast? A little breathing space . . .'

'Four months,' Anna said. 'I haven't seen her for four months and she's in pain. Is that so wrong?'

'Your mother would have counselled caution,' he said.

'No, she wouldn't, Dad.' Anna was almost crying. The

first real opinion he had expressed since Sophia's arrival in her life was to chip away at her decisions. 'She would have said it was where you were going that mattered. I've always kept her in mind. Sophia could never take Mum's place, ever. How could anyone think that? This is so different. I mean, you said it yourself when you were marrying Meryl. You said it would never affect how you felt about Mum. I never said to you to take it slowly, you're rushing things. What's the difference?'

She was still wondering how she would find time for all these people and her demanding job when Giulio phoned and asked to see her. The sound of his voice made Anna jump.

'Andrea tells me Sophia's going to be in town, staying with you.'

She stood up, clutching the phone, looking furtively around her office. 'Yes.' She felt ridiculous and promptly sat down.

'He said you might need some support.'

'No.' She almost screamed it. 'No. Thank you. I can manage. It's just a few days. A break,' she added. 'And there's Oliver. I've got Oliver.'

'Of course you have,' he agreed affably. 'Which is why I have only suggested dinner.'

She told Oliver and managed to make it sound a real bore. 'It's Sophia,' she explained. She felt a complete hypocrite. 'Andrea's got into a panic about her.' She yawned elaborately and flicked through the pages of a magazine as she spoke. 'I've told Giulio I haven't got a clue what time I'll finish, so he'll just have to expect me when he sees me. God, what a day. I'm whacked.'

Later, she peered at her eyes in the small handglass propped up against her screen. 'A Grescobaldi, in fact,' she told her reflection with brutal frankness. 'You look terrible, which you deserve, because you're going to be punished and you don't even believe in confession.'

Chapter Eighteen

'I agree it's odd,' Carla said, with a resigned sigh. 'And so soon. However – and don't look like that – I just wish you'd be consistent. Before Lorenzo died you were complaining that you didn't know what would happen to Sophia. Now you do and you're still complaining.'

Gianni slapped down his paper and angrily pushed back his chair. 'I did not complain,' he said indignantly. 'I merely said—'

Carla rolled her eyes. 'I know what you said. We've finished, Maria.' She broke off to smile at the maid, who had come in to clear away the breakfast. '*Il signore* has indigestion, that's all. And the miracle is,' she muttered under her breath, 'that I haven't got it too.'

They waited until the maid disappeared. For the first time in many months, Carla had driven to the lake free of the burden of her brother-in-law's widow. It was the first week in October and still very warm. From the upper terrace of the whitewashed villa that had been their country retreat for as long as she had been married to Gianni, she could see out across the water that stretched endlessly in either direction, westerly towards the medieval castle on the edge of the little town of Bracciano and south where it melted into open country. Small waves tossed across the surface of the shimmering water as a persistent breeze blew lazily around the shore, lined with waist-high reeds and rocky inlets.

Every once in a while a small white sailboat swayed and

tacked across the choppy bay or a lone skier swept across her vision. It should have been perfect: Elena, for once, was behaving herself and Irena . . . Carla paused. Well, these little affairs of hers rarely lasted more than a few weeks.

But now this. It was less than a day since she had left Rome and it was still Sophia. Thirty years on it was, once again, as it always had been, and she despaired that it would ever be anything else. Sophia. If only they had handled things better thirty years ago they wouldn't be paying for it now.

'What is the matter with you?' she hissed to her husband, as Maria left them. 'Isn't this what you've always wanted? For Sophia to be solved? And now you have your solution. Anna has invited her to stay with her.'

'But what does it look like?' Gianni lowered his voice. 'That we've got rid of her? Foisted her on to Anna?'

'You forget. Anna invited her.'

'Did she?' Gianni asked sceptically. 'I wonder. I told Giulio that. And he's right.'

'About what?'

'Anna. All that reserve, not talking about herself. You can see she's as vulnerable as Lorenzo ever was.'

'Well, we'll soon find out,' Carla said comfortably, closing her eyes and turning her face to the sun. 'If she can't manage, she'll let someone know. Hopefully Andrea or the wretched Roberto. Even better,' she pulled a visor down over her eyes, 'Giulio.'

'I wonder,' Gianni said. 'Lorenzo never told anyone. Not until it was too late.'

Giulio's house was in Notting Hill and overlooked a garden square. The venue had been decided on not because it was more convenient but because Anna had put up endless obstacles in the way of a meeting. Finally she had settled on his house because she had no other option that wasn't screaming, 'Excuse'.

It was not that she was afraid of how to deal with a meeting or with him – she had long ago settled it in her mind that Giulio had been part of Rome and the extraordinary events that had temporarily tilted her judgement. She winced at the memory. It was now a matter of importance to her that Giulio recognized that she had not so much moved on as returned to where she belonged. Possibly renewed, and certainly invigorated, but definitely to the right place.

'I don't know what time I'll finish,' she had told him. 'It could be any time. It drives Oliver mad.' This was true but she had mentioned Oliver's name to show that they were a couple, that between them there was an affectionate exasperation that bounced off their solid relationship.

'Then, meet me here,' he said. 'It won't matter how delayed you are. Unless,' there was a pause, 'you'd rather not.'

'Oh, it's not that,' she lied. 'It's just that I might have to rush off too.'

'Well, let's look on the bright side.' She thought he was trying not to laugh. 'Let's just regard it as a bonus if you get here at all.'

'Remind me of your address,' she said politely.

'I suppose,' she observed to no one when she hung up, 'you know what you're doing?'

The drawing room was on the first floor and as unlike the carefully designed Grescobaldi mansion in Rome as it could have been. Giulio was clearly not a poor man but neither did he enjoy anything like the wealth of the Grescobaldis. There were deep, comfortable sofas, a couple of nineteenth-century wing chairs, pale blue walls, subdued lighting and the warm glow of a fire. In the corner stood a pile of textbooks, and behind the sofa, on a straw and wood marquetry table, lay a chessboard with carved wooden pieces suspended in mid-play.

Anna looked at it. 'Queen four to Knight?' she suggested, looking up at him.

He walked up behind her and glanced over her shoulder. 'Then what do I do with the Bishop?'

'That,' she said, 'is for your opponent to decide.'

'I am my opponent.'

She laughed. 'Then you will win, whatever you do. What a powerful position to be in.'

'Only in theory. Drink?'

It was not a particularly masculine house, which was what Anna had expected. Rather, there were traces of another existence. The needlepoint cushions and the rather over-dressed swagged curtains sat at variance with what she knew of Giulio's dislike of the ornate. Of course, she realized, this was where he had lived when he was married to Victoria.

'You look tired,' he said, as he handed her a drink.

'What a gentleman.' She mustered a smile. 'You're meant to say, *"Ravissimo"*, or whatever it is you say to your women.'

'You should stop reading trashy novels,' he said mildly. 'And I'm flattered you regard yourself as one of my women.'

'Where are we going for dinner?' She didn't feel safe.

'Nearby,' he said easily. 'How are you?'

'Fine.'

He shook his head sadly. 'Terrible word. Only the English find it adequate.'

'OK.' She laughed. She couldn't help it. 'I had a bloody gruelling day, if you want the truth.'

'Much better,' he approved, sitting at the other end of the sofa. 'Go on.'

She began to count on her fingers. 'Well, the Home Secretary pulled out at five o'clock and would only issue a tedious and unoriginal statement on immigration. I spent forty minutes sucking up to his spin-doctor to get the prisons minister on instead, and when I thought nothing else could go wrong Bea Blackman – supermodel? – well, the guy she was dating called her on her mobile while she was in Makeup and dumped her so I had to pour champagne down her and tell her this was a defining moment in her life and to go on and smile if it killed her and say she had done the dumping because she'd met someone else.'

'So that's what that was about,' he said. 'She looked murderous.'

'She was.' Anna sipped her wine, pleased that he'd watched. 'But nothing like the guy from the tabloid who'd bought her ex's story for tomorrow. Shouldn't gloat, should I? But it was a vile thing to do to her. They hoped she'd break down on camera. They must have put him up to it. So,' she smiled and raised her glass to him, 'is that better?'

'Er . . . exhausting,' he said. 'Wouldn't it have been stronger for you if she'd cried?'

'Probably.' Anna sighed and dropped her head back on the cushion. 'But I've had enough of relying on people to burst into tears to get an audience. Max Warner would have held her hand and turned her into a victim.'

'What did you do?' he asked curiously.

'Gave her dignity,' she said bluntly.

'Impressive.'

'Not really.' She suppressed a yawn. 'I have a whole team scouring the streets for my daily fix of Valium. So, that's me. How about your day?'

'The kind of day that gets better when you know you have a pleasant evening to look forward to.'

'Yes,' she said, and glanced at her watch. 'Shouldn't we be going?'

'We should,' he said, removing her glass, 'but you look done in. We could eat here, if you like. I'll cook. It'll be quicker and then if you want to rush off you can.'

'You? Cook?'

'Yes, me,' he said, watching her cautiously. 'And I said eat. Nothing else. Stop looking so edgy.'

'I'm not,' she said briskly. 'Just hungry. And you're right, I do have a very early start. Er . . . *can* you cook?'

'Sure,' he said. 'Let me tell you, my marriage only lasted

as long as it did because I could. Otherwise I would have added starvation as a reason for our divorce.'

Anna followed him down into the kitchen, which stretched the length of the basement and had a small dining area at one end. She watched, amused, as he expertly tossed onions, tomatoes and herbs into a pan. She was impressed.

'What's the matter?' he asked, glancing up from sprinkling liberal dollops of Parmesan on to the pasta. 'It runs in the family. We're not all lawyers. A lot of my cousins are chefs.'

'How many do you have?'

He moved her out of the way to open a drawer behind her. 'Well, on the Catholic side, there are more. Obviously. The Jewish side can't keep up.'

'Which are you?'

'The jury's still out. At school I said Catholic because on holy days of obligation we got the day off. But the Jewish side were more practical – you should see me run up a shirt.'

'You're making it up.' She laughed, taking the glass of red wine he had poured for her.

'No, I'm not.' He grinned, touching her glass with his. 'My uncle and four of my cousins are bespoke tailors. How do you think I afford these suits?'

They ate in the kitchen and she tried to thank him for helping Carrie, but he said he never recommended anyone for anything unless he thought they could do it. 'And she really understands the job. I knew they'd like her.'

'Well, thanks anyway,' she said. 'She's transformed.'

Later they took the remains of the wine upstairs and sat at either end of the big sofa. She didn't think they had paused for breath. She gave her a head a slight shake. Here she was with a divorced, nearly forty-year-old lawyer, with receding hair, who was only an inch or two taller than her, who made her laugh, not politely but creased-up, bent double with tears running down her face. It was so unusual for her to let go, like losing control with a skilful but trusted lover who understood everything about her. And when he stayed where he was, right next to her, after he had refilled her glass and kissed her mouth, his fingers tangled in her hair as she was still laughing, she kissed him back and felt like someone who had known all along that she hadn't been wrong, just afraid to let go and just as afraid of losing everything altogether. So she pushed him away.

'What?' he asked, searching her face. 'Look at me.'

She shook her head. 'Oliver, of course.'

'Bollocks,' he said, making her eyes fly wide open.

'I beg your pardon,' she croaked. 'Of course Oliver. What else could it be? You're meant to be a friend.'

'Try a grown-up reason,' he snapped. 'Friends don't kiss like that. I don't play games. You know what's going on here. What's been going on since Rome. Why didn't you just say you didn't want to see me?'

'Because Andrea wanted me to,' she said wildly.

'He didn't say you also had to do this.'

She couldn't move. She stared helplessly at him. 'It was just a kiss,' she whispered. 'It wasn't meant to happen. You don't change your whole life because someone kisses you. You haven't bothered before to call – or anything.'

'You sound ridiculous,' he snapped, then dropped his head to stare at the floor. 'You could have called me,' he said steadily, looking sideways at her. 'You're not sixteen. You're the one with the boyfriend. I don't break up relationships. Stop asking for proof all the time. Proof that you're needed, proof you're wanted.'

'I came here,' she said angrily, groping for her shoes and for a dignified reason that would cope with the crushing guilt she felt about Oliver, the awful hypocrisy she knew she would have to face every time she looked in the mirror, 'because my – because it would make Andrea happy. He's feeling low and wants me to help with Sophia. The rest wasn't meant to happen.'

'Oh, yes, it was. And help Sophia?' He laughed at her. 'Why would she need your help? Do you want my opinion?'

'No,' she said, beginning to get up.

He pulled her down and round to face him. 'You're going to get it anyway. There is nothing wrong with Sophia that standing on her own two feet wouldn't cure,' he countered grimly. 'This isn't about Sophia, is it? It's about you and Oliver and your father and God knows what other stuff you've thrown in, and most of all it's about me and you, and you know it.'

Anna flushed. 'I don't know anything. This is childish.' She stood up, pulling her skirt straight. 'I don't think anything of the sort. I'm engaged to Oliver. And incidentally,' she said, knowing that he was perfectly within his rights to have pointed out to her that it was a shame she hadn't thought of Oliver sooner, 'Oliver would never say anything as insensitive as that about a woman who's just lost her husband.'

'He might if he knew her. Sophia's an emotional blackmailer,' Giulio said bluntly. 'A control freak. No one hates Sophia, no one's ever made her feel like an outsider. She's done it herself. She got pregnant and she's never forgiven Lorenzo's family for – quite rightly, given the time and the kind of family they were – being horrified. Her *own* family were. It's not like it is now. And she knows it. But will she let them make amends? The hell she will.'

He got up and leaned both hands against the fireplace and gazed down fiercely into the flames. He turned his head and looked to where she was standing, gripping the back of a winged chair, her coat slung around her shoulders, her eyes black and wide staring out from a furious white face. 'Don't you get it?' he demanded. 'Mobilizing guilt in Lorenzo – and, believe me, that wasn't hard – until he couldn't take it any more and found Issy?'

'Did he? Did he?' she said softly. 'Now, you listen for a change. God knows, someone has to.' It was out before she could stop herself, a confidence betrayed but her moral values had crumbled disastrously in the last couple of hours.

'He used to hit her,' she said. 'Oh, yes. The saintly Lorenzo,' she said. 'When she tried to stop him drinking.'

Giulio said slowly, 'What?'

Anna nodded. 'She told me. Have you taken that on board? No. I can see you haven't. So much easier to keep the clients happy, isn't it, than rescue a woman who tried to make a man of him?'

'You don't know what you're talking about,' he said, in an odd voice.

'Really? I know what it's like in here.' She tapped her chest fiercely. 'Andrea can't talk to her. He's too close to it. I know what it is to lose someone. I've been where she is.'

'No, you haven't,' he interrupted. 'You've been where you and your father found yourselves. And why can't Andrea talk to her? Of course he's gay but how does that stop him sympathizing with her?'

'He does,' she shouted angrily. 'Of course he does.' She paused, startled. 'You know that he's gay?'

'Of course. And Lorenzo hit Sophia? Oh, stop it. Fantasy, pure fantasy. Frankly, the miracle is that he didn't. Look,' he ran his fingers distractedly through his hair, 'Anna, stop this. You don't understand . . .'

She pulled her coat around her, hugged her bag to her chest. 'Not understand? What would any of you know about what went on in their marriage? How do you know he didn't hit her?' She wheeled round and headed for the door. 'Give her some credit,' she shouted as she pulled it open. He didn't try to stop her. 'Stop thinking of her as a waitress from Napoli on the make, like they all did and still do, and bear in mind that if it hadn't been for them, I might have grown up with my real family. Lorenzo could have stood up to them – he could have stood by her. But he didn't, and she was blamed for giving me away. Not him.'

'Anna . . .'

For a dreadful moment she thought she was going to cry. But it wasn't for Lorenzo, or Sophia or her father. It was for herself, because she was in such a muddle and she was so tired. Tiredness got in the way of the common sense that tried to tell her to stop. But any link with sense had fled. So she went on catastrophically. 'Oh, no,' she said bitterly. 'Not him. When he betrayed her he couldn't live with the guilt and took to drink then blamed her for that, too. But he mustn't be blamed for any of it, must he? Oh, no. So much easier to paper over their own shortcomings, pay people to do their dirty work . . .'

'Dirty work?'

'Yes,' she shouted. 'Medical certificates forged to get to me. Keeping it from Sophia that he had a mistress. Even Elena's divorce was fixed.'

'Anna.' He strode towards her and tried to grab her. She shrank back. 'Stop this,' he begged. 'You're forgetting, I've known Lorenzo's family for a long time—'

'You know only one side of them. Until I came along, Sophia was pushed to the edge of their lives. I know what that's like. At least I listen to her. At least I can't do her any damage.'

He stood silently until she'd finished. 'Listen to me,' he said urgently. 'You *must* listen to me.'

Rather childishly Anna covered her ears with her hands. 'No. I don't want to listen. Not any more. I do not want to hear another word against her.'

'Why are you doing this?' he asked quietly. 'Why *really*?'

'Because . . .' She looked squarely at him, and because her pride wouldn't let her say, 'Because I know what it's like to be shoved to the edge of everyone's life,' she blurted out, 'Because I promised Lorenzo I would.'

'*Promised Lorenzo?*' Incredulity spread over his face. But she was gone.

From that disastrous evening until Sophia's arrival Anna plunged herself into getting the house ready so that she didn't have time to think.

Furious and miserable, she often had to stop what she

was doing and take deep gulps of air to steady herself. She should never have gone to see him. Carrie had asked her why she was going and she had said – quite dishonestly, she knew that now – that it was because they were old friends when they had never been friends. Giulio didn't make friends with women.

The photographs of Barbara, sitting with Anna in a park when she was about seven, and of Anna at her graduation teasingly holding her mortar-board above her mother's head, were in her bedroom, still in the same wooden frames Barbara had bought. Now Anna picked one up and touched her mother's face with her fingertips. 'Oh, Mum,' she whispered. 'What shall I do? She's got no one. And if it hadn't been for me, she wouldn't be in this mess. But I was so very lucky to get you.' And she struggled with the realization that she might have made another mistake – no, she *knew* she had made a terrible mistake. She put a pillow over her face and crushed her arms around it.

The small house seemed even smaller when Sophia appeared, and it had nothing to do with her luggage, which spilled over into the tiny box room. Looking at the pile of suitcases and matching hand luggage waiting to be unpacked, Anna suspected that if Sophia turned up at Windsor Castle it would be filled with her presence. Sophia looked startled as she took in Anna's living room and the view from the windows of the skip on the other side of the street. Clearly unprepared for the size of Anna's house, she summoned a dazzling smile. 'Darling, it's so – so sweet,' she proclaimed at last. 'So – how you say? You know, when you fit everything in?'

'Squashed' came to mind but instead Anna said hopefully, 'Compact?'

'Of course. *E ben comoda e intima*,' she said, with a mischievous smile. '*Bellissima*.'

Anna wondered fleetingly if she should have booked her into a hotel. Sophia was cross at the very idea. She wanted to be in Anna's home. Here, she said, spreading her arms, she felt welcome. Here she already felt at home.

The plans Anna outlined for Sophia for the next couple of weeks, which she had tried to make as varied as possible and within the bounds of her working life, were greeted with almost tearful appreciation. It was going to be hard, Anna knew, but it could be done. And, as she had told her father, Oliver and Giulio – her stomach churned – it wasn't for ever.

'You're a dear girl,' Sophia smiled, 'but naughty. Seeing you, and being part of your life for just a little while, is enough. I'm not good with people at the moment,' she said. 'I don't expect to be entertained.'

'Oh, I haven't forgotten,' Anna assured her anxiously. 'I know how you must be feeling. Look, you don't have to do any of this.'

But Sophia wouldn't hear of that either. 'After all the trouble you've taken? Nonsense. It will do me good and you'll be there to help me through it.'

Anna was relieved. It was a start. At least she wasn't refusing to go anywhere – not like her father, whose first venture had been to Scotland to stay with Meryl. It was different for men, Sophia said. 'They are taken up, cosseted, fussed over. Women like me? *Phut*,' she said dismissively. 'They are a nuisance.'

'Well, not here they're not,' Anna said warmly. She was enjoying herself. She showed Sophia everything, from the newly painted roof garden to the rapidly cleared kitchen, which doubled as a dining room. Sophia had exclaimed over everything, admired, touched, inspected.

'May I?' she asked, looking at the photographs on the wall. She studied the one of Colin and Barbara, and the one of Barbara in the garden. Anna watched carefully.

'Lovely,' Sophia said softly, turning to smile at her.

Anna smiled back. 'Yes, it was her favourite place. Now, tonight we're having dinner with Oliver, just us because you've had a tiring journey and Oliver is travelling back from Bristol specially to meet you.' Sophia clasped her hands in delight. 'And tomorrow we thought you might like to drive down to Henley and have lunch on the river.'

'Which days are you at the office?' Sophia asked, as Anna poured her a drink.

'Every day,' Anna said, puzzled. ''Fraid I have to leave quite early, but I'll make sure you have the papers. And if you want to go shopping, just call these people.' She handed her a card with the car company phone number. 'I have an account with them.'

Sophia looked at the card, a small frown on her face. 'But when will you be here?' she asked.

'Well, in the evenings, of course,' Anna said. 'And at the weekend.'

'But *I'm* here.' Sophia's voice was raised a fraction in surprise. 'Surely your office can do without you for a day or two?'

Anna looked aghast. Sophia had misunderstood. 'Oh, Sophia, I'm so sorry but I can't,' she said.

'But what will I do here on my own?' Sophia looked in alarm at the small house.

'Well, you can have a lie-in, go shopping, meet me from work, maybe, if you're not too tired. Or even . . .' Anna was knitting it as she went along, trying to eradicate the stricken look from Sophia's face '. . . come and watch the programme go out. I was hoping you would.'

'Well,' Sophia said uncertainly, 'of course. I don't want to be in the way.'

'In the way? Absolutely not. It's just that I thought you understood. Sophia,' Anna held up both hands in a gesture of submission, 'it's my fault, I should have thought. But I've made lots of plans. You won't be bored. Promise. In fact, you'll probably need to rest during the day to get over them.'

Sophia gave her head a shake. 'Darling, of course. The flight. It's been a long journey and I was afraid for a moment I would see nothing of you. And please remember I am not worried about boredom. It is just that I find it easier if I can take my mind off Lorenzo.'

Anna pulled out a chair on the other side of the kitchen table. 'Sophia,' she said treading carefully, 'if you want to talk about Lorenzo, cry, scream, shout, do it. I so understand where you are, and I'd like to talk to you about it.'

'No,' Sophia said sharply. 'No. It is better that I don't talk. I can't deal with the memories. We don't talk.'

'No. No, of course not,' Anna agreed instantly. 'But if you change your mind, you know I'm here.'

Within hours Anna could see something different about Sophia. She was edgy. When Anna handed her a drink her hands were shaking. By the time she had persuaded her to have a nap, Anna was glad she had suggested Sophia arrived on a Saturday so that she could be at the airport to meet her. She was very fragile. A weekend, that's what she needed, to get her used to the house and Anna's friends before Anna hit the office again on Monday.

Everyone was charmed by her. Anna breathed out. The tricky start was forgotten. Sophia was so used to Irena and Elena working only when it suited them, and she herself had never been constrained by a job, that she simply hadn't been prepared for the reality of Anna not having that luxury. In Rome Anna had been there for her.

When Oliver arrived from Bristol, Sophia embraced him as an old friend. Anna could see he was rather thrown by it. He was so English and Sophia so Italian. She smiled, pleased that they were getting on famously and that he was obviously delighted that Sophia was thrilled with his choice of restaurant. She was the easiest-to-please person Anna had ever come across, she thought. Considering how she had been entertained, and by whom, in Rome, it only went to show that the more you had the less you wanted.

She had made sure that Sophia was entertained on the two or three evenings she couldn't be home early, and on the others they went to a movie, to dinner, the ballet. When Anna had to duck out of a dinner with Oliver and two of his clients who were rising political stars, she urged him to take Sophia instead. Their names meant nothing to Sophia but this did not appear to have marred the evening: as Oliver told Anna, after he had returned Sophia home and she had gone to bed, she was a born charmer and had made his clients feel that their fame extended beyond Westminster.

Sophia was thrilled that she had been able to help, and Oliver thanked her, however, without the same effusion. All the things that made Oliver so attractive, his patience and courtesy, his Englishness, were all the things that clashed with Sophia's overwhelming presence. Anyone witnessing the cordial relationship between them would not have guessed at the effort Anna had made to ensure that they were comfortable with each other. And when she saw the heroic effort Oliver made with Sophia, often after a long, exhausting day at work, her conscience nearly slayed her. The memory of that evening at Giulio's house filled her with remorse.

Perhaps it was that which prevented her from seeing just how agitated Sophia was: she jumped at the slightest noise, hardly ate, and appeared to have an endless capacity for sleep when she got round to it, which wasn't surprising since she took sleeping pills. And therein lay a further dilemma. Anna was certain that if Sophia could just try and sleep without the pills, her mind would become more capable of dealing with the hours when she was awake but when she suggested it, Sophia panicked. 'I have to blot out the night,' she insisted. 'I can't bear the dawn. Lorenzo died at dawn.'

And she was untidy. Obviously unused to doing anything for herself, cups, glasses clothes were left strewn around. Anna spent a lot of time tidying up when she arrived home from work.

Chapter Nineteen

Towards the end of Sophia's first week, Anna came to two conclusions. The first was that Euan might be a great deal easier to care for than a recently widowed woman, unused to London, who had for too long relied on an army of servants to see to her every need. The second was that since her new job demanded so much of her, it had been a huge mistake to invite Sophia, in her fragile and jumpy state, to stay for two or three weeks. Anna hoped guiltily that two would be sufficient to restore Sophia's confidence enough to return to Rome and begin to pick up the threads of her life.

Before she left the office on Friday evening, Anna rang Oliver and said she just couldn't face another restaurant meal. 'Could you bear to leave me and Sophia out? I'm so whacked.'

Oliver harumphed. 'With all due respect I can bear to leave Sophia out. It's you I miss.'

'Miss me? I see you every day. Well, almost.'

There was a pause.

'Well, in truth,' Oliver said, 'I miss just being me and you and not having to include anyone else in our plans. And I miss knowing what kind of mood you're going to be in.'

'Oliver,' she protested. 'You make me sound neurotic. I'm not.'

He sighed. 'No. Never that. Maybe since Rome, since the new job, now taking another hard-luck case on board . . .'

'You can hardly call Sophia hard luck,' she pointed out.

'True. But she behaves like it.'

Nothing that standing on her own two feet couldn't cure, as Giulio had said. Anna was so tired that it was tempting just to chuck in the job and be there when he came home. But even as she thought it, she knew it would lead nowhere at all that she fancied being. Not any more.

'She's recently widowed,' she said carefully. 'Don't you like her?'

'She's too charming for that. But it's hard going. And – oh, bugger it, Anna – it's bloody tough on you. And me.'

'I'll make it up to you,' she promised. 'Just as soon as she goes home. Maybe only another week. Two tops.'

Then she rang Sophia to say that she had cancelled dinner and they would be having a relaxing evening, just the two of them. 'Of course, darling,' Sophia said. 'Maybe I meet you somewhere and we see a movie.'

Inwardly Anna groaned. 'I'm so tired. It's been a pretty piggish day. Would you mind if we just crashed out at home?'

'Here? Just me and you? But of course. Whatever you say.'

Sophia ate almost nothing of the meal Anna pulled together as soon as she got home. Sophia poured a glass of wine for each of them and said that Anna should not work so hard.

'Nonsense.' Anna yawned. 'Sophia, would you like me to get you something else? You're not eating.'

'It's wonderful, darling,' Sophia assured her, sipping her wine. 'I should have said I rarely eat smoked salmon and I'm sure the eggs are delicious but I will just eat this salad and take myself out of your way.'

'Sophia, you must eat more than that. I bet you haven't eaten all day.'

'Of course I did,' Sophia speared a lettuce leaf. 'I had some toast this morning at the hairdresser's.'

Anna was surprised. 'Where did you go?'

'I go to Alessandro, of course, in Knightsbridge. Naturally, it isn't like my own dear Luigi in Via Condotti but it will do. I direct him and he learn. And this,' she indicated the salad, 'will be good for me. I eat a lot since I came here. And you, look at you, you are not touching your food either. I have a good mind to telephone that producer and say he is working you much too hard. You have no life at all.'

Anna ate her dinner so that Sophia would not suspect the depth of her exhaustion. At least she was beginning to find her way around. She almost smiled – and, of course, it would have been to a hairdresser.

'And you have phone call from someone wanting to put extra windows in your house and I say to him you have plenty windows and you are not poverty-stricken. If you want windows you only have to ask and I, your mother, will pay.'

Anna gaped at her. 'Sophia,' she said, 'that happens all the time. Everyone gets calls like that.'

'And someone banged on your wall,' Sophia added. 'So rude. At first I think it is because I am watching television, but I turned it down and a little while later it started again.'

'About seven, was it?' Anna asked, looking up. 'It was Dottie. I used to get in at that time and she probably thought I'd forgotten her shopping.'

Sophia looked puzzled. 'Why you shop for her? You have enough to do.'

'Because she's alone and very old, and she doesn't move around very well. Honestly, Sophia,' she tried to reassure her, 'it's no big deal. I pick up my stuff so what's the odd loaf or potatoes for her?'

Sophia put down her wineglass and folded her hands. She looked shocked. 'You didn't tell me you look after old lady. No wonder you are tired. This must stop.'

Anna laughed at her outraged face. 'No. No. It mustn't stop. There is no one else and I don't mind. Sophia, stop it. You're getting worked up for nothing.'

'I'm sorry,' Sophia said stiffly. 'I'm very near the surface, these days. But where is her family?'

Anna smiled weakly feeling more than a little close to the surface herself. 'She has a dreadful son.' She took a gulp of wine. 'I think I'm family to her.'

Sophia wrinkled her brows. 'You? Family?'

'Not really. I just check on her. In one way she hates it but she knows it's keeping her independent. She hates anyone knowing anything about her.'

'And just adding to your problems,' Sophia said sternly. 'And now you have me. You should have said when you invite me that you have all this. I would never have imposed.'

'Sophia, this is ridiculous. I'm just tired this evening.'

'Then I will go to bed. No,' Sophia held up a hand, 'I am very tired and I think I am in the way.'

'Sophia,' Anna exclaimed. 'You've just misunderstood. I've just had a dreadful day—'

Alone, Anna slumped forward and let her head fall to the table. From the darkness of the circle of her arms, she heard Sophia slowly mount the stairs. Then her door closed, not with a slam but loud enough for Anna to hear. For a long while she stayed where she was because for the first time all day – in fact, for several days – no one was speaking to her or asking her to do something, or demanding her attention. Then, without meaning to, she fell into a doze, which turned into a deep sleep.

Much later she woke with a start. Her neck and arms were stiff and cold. The heat had gone off long before. Ahead of her, almost at eye-level, the remains of the abandoned supper she had prepared lay in congealed testimony to the couple of hours that must have passed since she placed it there. Carefully she lifted her head until she could focus on the clock. It was eleven. Her mouth felt like sandpaper. She groaned, began to gather up the plates and tried to decide what to do. Sophia had to be appeased, reassured, Oliver to be phoned.

Before she could pick up the receiver the phone shrilled. Shame it hadn't done that two hours earlier, she grumbled inwardly. It occurred to her that it was odd for the phone not to have rung at all.

'Who have you been talking to?' came Oliver's voice as she answered it. 'It's been busy all evening.' Anna rubbed the back of her neck and tested it.

'It can't have been.' She stifled a yawn. 'I fell asleep and Sophia went to bed over two hours ago. Come over,' she suggested.

'Can't,' he said. He sounded as though he was keeping his voice down. 'I'm feeling a bit whacked. I'll stay here. That's all I wanted to say. I'll call you tomorrow.'

Anna hung up. Automatically, she began to switch off the lamps, checked the doors and went upstairs. There was a narrow shaft of light under Sophia's door and Anna went in to say goodnight.

She found Sophia sitting up in bed and on the phone apparently feeling much better. 'Wait,' she mouthed, indicating that her call was still to be wound up. No wonder the phone had been engaged.

Anna sat on the bed and began to collect up the endless glossy magazines that were strewn haphazardly over the covers. An array of nail polish, creams in glass pots and phials of oil, which Sophia never closed her eyes without applying to some part of her face or hands, covered the small bedside table.

Anna longed for bed.

'*Tutto a posta*,' Sophia was saying soothingly. '*Devo andare. Ciao. A domani, si, si. Ciao.*' 'I'm sorry.' She sighed, watching Anna. 'I was just feeling lonely and cross because you looked tired and all these people were slicing you into little bits and I am not here for long. That was all.'

'Nonsense,' Anna said, yawning and feeling guilty. 'Maybe I've organized too much. Perhaps an early night or two will do us both good.'

'Ah,' Sophia said, with a huge smile, 'but you don't

understand. That was Roberto. He is coming to London tomorrow. Quite unexpectedly. He said he'd adore to see you. Isn't that wonderful?'

Anna tried to sound sincere when she said, 'What can I say? In fact, I think my cup is almost in danger of running over.'

'What?' Sophia said. 'Are you telling me a joke? I say to Roberto you would be thrilled.' She leaned back on her pillows. 'I will persuade him to escort me now that he is here for a little while. Relieve you of your burden. No,' she held up a hand as Anna started to protest, 'you must be longing for me to go.'

As there was a modicum of truth in this, and it had been so directly put, Anna stuttered an untruthful reply. 'Of course I'm not.' She made a space on the small chest of drawers and stacked the magazines neatly on it. 'I just think you've been through an awful time and that's enough to make anyone feel on edge. I do understand. Promise.'

Sophia gave her a long, hard look. Then she patted the bed. 'Sit here,' she said. 'Look at me.' Anna thought wistfully of her bed but she did as Sophia asked.

Sophia stretched out a hand and lifted Anna's chin. 'These few days have been a relief for me. That is all that I asked. It is so much better here than in Rome. I will like to see Roberto too, because he has been so good to me. And after that, who knows? He is going to New York and I will go with him to see Andrea. I am better with a little company.' She gave a rueful laugh. 'But I do not wish to become a burden.'

'Well,' Anna said, and got up. She pulled the cover straight and glanced around. Sophia's clothes were piled on a chair, silk shirts mangled with crêpe skirts, shoes discarded in the corner. In Rome, it must drive Pilar mad. 'You might find you need a rest rather than New York once Roberto has gone.' She began a half-hearted attempt at hanging up the tangled heap of clothes. 'I must get some hangers tomorrow.' She rescued a suede shirt from the pile and shook it. Sophia didn't appear to notice. Anna tried to smooth out the creases: it looked now like a well-worn chamois duster rather than the delicate artistry of an Italian couturier. You couldn't treat such a delicate suede so brutally and expect it to survive.

'By the way,' she said from the doorway. 'My step-brother and -sister-in-law are in London for the weekend. I'm afraid I have to include them for dinner tomorrow night. I've asked Carrie as well. And Eamonn.'

'You do far too much.' Sophia paused, about to pull the mask over her eyes. 'No wonder you are always tired. But with Carrie, I myself feel for her. She is someone I understand – *how* I understand – and needs friends. She is so lucky. What a difference it would have made if I had had someone like you when I was on my own.'

'You were in another country. Besides, it was a different time. It wouldn't happen now. There are too many other problems, like Eamonn's cases.'

Sophia shrugged. 'Eamonn is not the same. He is very nice. But, my darling, you won't mind if I say I find the friends of Eamonn *molto strani*? You understand?'

'Odd?' Anna asked. 'Well, they're homeless, which makes it difficult for them to be normal. If they're really desperate Eamonn gives them a bed for a day or two and the most he ever asks of me is to raid the fridge if he can't feed them. He earns so little.'

'I know.' Sophia sighed. 'It is just that he was here last night and Oliver was cross. I think you must put Oliver's feelings first, maybe?'

'Maybe. Night, Sophia.' She started to close the door.

'Just a minute,' Sophia called. She half sat up, realizing suddenly what Anna had said. 'Your step-brother? You mean the one who make you feel outsider? Why do you ask these people? You don't need them in your life.'

Anna felt a twinge of guilt that, in a moment of thoughtlessness, she had described Athol and Fenella to Sophia, who had a particularly retentive memory. As though reading her thoughts, Sophia said, 'I will ask Roberto. And he will be nice to these people who do not deserve it, but I can see you have no choice. Leave it to me.'

Breaking the news to Oliver the following morning was a little harder. 'I can't help it,' she whispered, with one eye on the kitchen door in case Sophia came in. 'He's already here. Yes, here. In London. He's been good to her and, besides, you have no idea how heavy-going Athol can be when he gets started. And bloody Fenella with her recipes and waste-disposals and – the whole wretched family bit.'

'Family? Christ, Anna.' Oliver glared at her. 'If anyone's dumping families on anyone, it's you. Who else are you going to drum up?'

'No one,' she mumbled. She felt herself in no position to say that none of these families had been her choice and just prayed that Irena, who had phoned that morning to announce *her* arrival in London, would be too tired to join them. No wonder Roberto was here. Irena had elected to stay with Giulio, which, she said, was a relief to her parents. 'So, ridiculous,' Irena scoffed. 'As if Giulio could stop me seeing Roberto at his hotel. And, in his present mood, I am unlikely to get much of his attention, so what reassurance they get from it I have no idea.'

'Mood? What do you mean?'

'Oh, God knows.' Irena sounded bored. 'Fabio said he thinks one of his women is giving him a hard time. Serves him right. And you are not very cross with me? Not really? Did he mention me?'

'Giulio?' Anna asked.

'No. *Roberto.*'

'Oh, him. I haven't seen him yet. He's coming here tomorrow evening.'

'And seeing me afterwards.' Irena giggled.

Sophia rose early to go to the hairdresser. Her hair –

which looked immaculate – was not, she said, good enough for *la madre di* Anna to meet her relatives. Anna was relieved that she had one less thing to worry about and ordered a car. At midday, when Sophia returned clutching a bag from Harvey Nichols, she announced that she had a terrible headache, due to the stupidity of the hairdresser who had pulled at her hair, and would lie down for a while.

'Hung over,' Oliver muttered, unloading shopping and stacking wine in the fridge.

Anna stopped chopping a mountain of spinach and dashed a hand across her brow. 'She hardly touches the stuff,' she said, stirring the leaves into a saucepan. 'She was out with Roberto last night and, in my opinion, that's enough to give anyone a migraine. Do you think there'll be enough?' She peered dubiously into the brown earthenware dish that contained chicken Florentine.

'Unless you're planning to invite anyone else,' Oliver said, giving it only a cursory glance.

'Like who?' she asked, returning to her task.

'Well, it wouldn't surprise me to hear you'd invited the rest of the Mafia, like that bloody lawyer.'

She knew he was looking at her. She went on carefully stirring the spinach. Lately she had been pleading almost as many headaches as Sophia. 'Why on earth would I do that?' she asked lightly. 'Darling, pass me that lid. I think this is as good as it's going to get.'

Into the seventh month of her fourth pregnancy, Fenella looked uncomfortably heavy but instantly dismissed Anna's concern: when Anna had had as many pregnancies as she, Fenella, had gone through, she said, she would treat it as no more demanding than a trip to the supermarket. 'But just mineral water,' Fenella said, 'if you don't mind. Athol? You're driving.'

Their arrival coincided with Roberto's. He was carrying a jar of caviare that he said he had spent half an hour selecting at Fortnum and Mason. 'Because,' he whispered, as he kissed Anna, 'you have made Sophia so welcome and we forget our own little troubles, *si?*'

Anna smiled and wondered what Irena saw in him. She felt a genuine wave of sympathy for Sylvana. 'Of course,' she said. 'Sophia will be down in a moment.'

It was a little more than a moment. Twenty minutes passed during which time Eamonn and Carrie turned up and Oliver had twice whispered to Anna that it was a bit much being late in the house she was staying in.

Anna worried that Sophia might be making a point and would not turn up at all – her sense of loyalty was admirable but unnerving. However, the wait was worth it. Sophia's entrance was charmingly apologetic, her black trousers and cream silk shirt immaculate – God knows how she's managed it, Anna thought, dreading the mess she knew was waiting upstairs. Even so, she felt a flicker of unexpected satisfaction at Athol and Fenella's obvious surprise at the picture of warmth and ease Sophia presented.

Sophia was an undoubted hit. She greeted Carrie like an old friend and even Eamonn got a playful tap on the wrist. Anna could see that Athol was mesmerized and Fenella's expression was gathering hostility until Sophia had taken her hand in both hers, sat her down on the sofa and asked her how when she was so pregnant she managed to look so well. 'You must have a secret,' she said, her head on one side. 'And you should share it.'

Over dinner, the charm offensive continued. Sophia paid almost slavish attention to Athol, and was apparently enraptured by Fenella's choice of hobbies for her children, curtains and holiday plans. Throughout the pre-dinner drinks and then the chicken Florentine, which Sophia said was perfection, Sophia encouraged the Carltons to talk about themselves.

By the time Anna rose to make coffee, there was little about the workings of a small but perfectly run school in a remote Scottish town that had not been thoroughly explored by Sophia. Life on Craighaithan Heights had prompted a lot of 'fascinating' and 'how interesting', and Sophia marvelled at Fenella's organizational skills. And all without help, she exclaimed. Ingenious. Fenella shot an uneasy look at her, but Sophia's attention was already on Athol.

Oliver was right, Anna thought, Sophia *was* a born hostess.

She caught Oliver's eye and he smiled. She smiled back. Carrie and Eamonn were arguing a point of law in a case Carrie was working on and were clearly of much less interest to Athol and Fenella than Anna's exotic Italian guests.

I have earned the right to relax, Anna told herself. In another half-hour Athol will begin to take his leave and Roberto will be anxious to get to Irena. She wouldn't think about that or worry about Sylvana who, bound by the laws of her faith, would not think of divorce, to which Anna would have resorted years before, had she been married to such a philanderer.

If Sophia was a born hostess, then Roberto was out to be the perfect guest. He couldn't help himself, Anna could see. His arm was lying across the back of Fenella's chair, and Fenella was agreeing that it was bitterly cold in Scotland. 'Then you need to be warm.' He smiled. 'A woman like you needs to be basking in sunlight.'

'Well,' Fenella looked flustered but not displeased, 'I don't know about basking . . .'

'Anna,' Sophia broke in, 'I have an idea. Why don't you invite Athol and Fenella to come to Rome?' She threw Anna a huge, affectionate smile, then said confidingly, 'Anna is wonderful the way she organize the staff. They do everything for her. If she say her relations must be looked after,' Sophia snapped her fingers, 'they fall over themselves.'

Anna dragged her eyes away from Roberto to Sophia. Please stop, she prayed. But Sophia was on a roll.

She clapped her hands together in mock dismay. 'But what am I thinking of? Of course. Our summer-house in Bracciano. With all those children, it's about time someone gave you a little help. We have plenty of staff there to take them off your hands. Yes, the more I think about it, I think it would be better, don't you, Anna? You won't be any trouble in the guest villa,' she said, with enormous kindness to the transfixed pair. 'It's miles away from the main house.' And in one gracious sentence paid off a couple of scores on Anna's behalf. A palatial apartment with staff to do her bidding. A villa rather than a guest suite. And a family of her own, instead of being permitted occasionally to glimpse theirs. Dear God. The look of humiliation mingled with outrage that passed between Athol and Fenella told Anna everything she needed to know.

'I'll get some coffee,' Anna said hastily.

It was as she turned to carry it to the table that Fenella yelped.

Conversation halted as all faces turned in her direction. 'We have to go.' Fenella sounded as though she was choking. Her face was flushed.

Anna put down the pot. 'Fenella? Are you all right?' she asked anxiously.

'Now, Athol,' Fenella almost screamed, ignoring her. She heaved herself to her feet.

Athol paused, unsure what to do. Help his wife or interrupt Sophia? He looked helplessly at Anna. 'Well, of course,' he said, dabbing his mouth with his napkin and pushing his chair back. 'Are you all right? Nothing happening, is there?'

'Of course not,' Fenella snapped, taking deep breaths.

A dreadful suspicion flickered through Anna's head. She darted a quick glance at Roberto, who was regarding Fenella with a blank expression.

'You have to go?' Sophia sounded dismayed. 'So soon? Then *arrivederci* until you let us know when you want to come to Roma.'

'Let me get your coats,' Oliver said calmly, into the silence. 'Athol, you must let me organize a game of squash next time you're down. No, don't get up, Roberto.'

Anna couldn't bear to look at Oliver. His voice was perfectly polite. 'Why don't you pour the coffee,' he said evenly to Anna, 'while I see Athol and Fenella out?'

Chapter Twenty

'I know, I know,' Anna whispered, afraid that Sophia, in the next room, might hear. 'She meant to side with me. Oliver, please listen to me. I know what it sounded like. She didn't mean it. It's my fault, I should never have told her how awful they were in Carrigh. It never occurred to me she felt so strongly about it. If you'd been where she's been forced to be, part of a family who never really accepted her—'

'And are we surprised?' Oliver hissed back. He stretched out his hand and snapped out the lamp on his side of the bed. 'And Roberto?' he asked acidly. 'You'll be saying next he groped Fenella because he was bullied at school.'

'We don't know that he did. Not for sure.'

'Anna. Please.' He sounded weary.

She leaned over him. 'What?'

There was a silence.

'Nothing,' he said finally. 'Just go to sleep. OK?'

You would have thought that nothing had happened, Anna mused next day, as she listened to Oliver point out places of interest to Sophia, who sat in the front while Anna, trying to stay awake, sat gratefully in the back. Soon, she comforted herself, Sophia would be gone and all this would be forgotten. It was a bright, sharp day, almost November. Banks of white cloud drifted across a brilliantly blue sky and the sun shone down, but without warmth, on carpets of golden leaves piled into gutters, whipping along pavements.

Eventually, the suburbs gave way to a ribbon of motorway that wound through Hampshire and Wiltshire and, as it neared midday, Somerset.

With each passing mile Anna tried to put distance between the disastrous events of the night before and to concentrate on the day ahead. Earlier Oliver had found her in the kitchen removing all traces of the previous nightmarish evening. He had quietly gathered her to him and hugged her. 'Forget it.' He kissed her. Anna was so relieved that she kissed him back with fervour and gratitude. 'I'll keep you to that,' he murmured into her neck. 'Just as soon as we get back.'

Sometime after they joined the motorway Anna gave up the battle against sleep and dozed fitfully until they turned off the motorway, five miles before they reached the village where Oliver's parents still lived and where he had grown up. She opened her eyes to find that they were in the midst of the countryside, making their way through lanes bounded on both sides by fields, interrupted by the occasional farmhouse or a sleepy hamlet. Few people failed to be charmed by it and Sophia exclaimed with pleasure as they turned into the driveway of the stone-built Georgian house on the edge of the village. A giant oak tree towered over one end of the garden and sent graceful shadows across a well-trimmed lawn.

A gravel path circled the house and led to a tennis court and a swimming-pool, installed by Oliver's grandfather. The present incumbent had decided this spoiled the view from the terrace of rolling fields and open country and had planted a series of fir trees to distract the eye to something more pleasing.

In spite of his claims to have been bored witless through long school holidays and adolescent years before he left for university, Oliver clearly, if rather sheepishly, adored his old home and was not immune to hearing it so extravagantly admired. One day he hoped to live there with Anna. Kate and Greg wouldn't want it and Jasper would prefer to be bought out so that he could live permanently in Camden Town. He glanced sideways at his prospective mother-in-law and tried, but failed, to imagine her, in a Barbour and green wellingtons, spending weekends with them.

Meryl, though, with her countrywoman pursuits and fearless walking across moors and glens in the highlands, would be quite at home. Of Barbara, he had the impression that she would have preferred to raid his father's library than join them in striding across the fields.

He tried to imagine his own mother in the black leather skirt, so supple it looked like silk, and the black polo-neck sweater Sophia wore, and failed. A coat that perfectly matched the skirt was languishing in the back with Anna who had absently used the silver fox collar as a pillow while she dozed. The one thing in her favour, he conceded in a rapidly growing unease with Anna's mother, was that she had amazingly good legs. Anna's legs. He wondered what his mother would say to bringing such a sexy-looking woman to lunch in such dangerously high-heeled shoes and black stockings.

'I hope,' Sophia smiled at Oliver as he helped her from the car, 'that you intend to invite me here when you and Anna live here.'

Oliver, who was attached to his parents and hoped that day would be some way off, simply said, 'But of course.'

'Mum,' Jasper Manners complained, from the top of the stairs, 'do I really have to be at this lunch? I went to the last one.' He leaned over perilously in an effort to make his mother hear. 'Anna won't mind and Ollie couldn't give a toss. You know he couldn't.'

Christina was hurrying across the hall with a vase of flowers from the garden. She craned her neck upwards. 'But *I* mind. And please wear a decent sweater and none of your jokes. Jasper, are you listening?'

'I can't do anything else, the way you're shouting,' he grumbled loudly, disappearing back down the corridor to his room. At twenty-three and living in some squalor with three friends in Camden Town, he was fed up that his brother, who was ten years his senior and, in his view, a total prat, had demanded a bit too much attention of late. 'Anyone would think it was the Royal bloody Family coming. If I'd known, I wouldn't have bothered coming home this weekend. You might have warned me.'

There was the sound of a door slamming then silence. Christina grimaced and carried on. Several years' experience as a chairman's wife, and a seasoned campaigner at hosting corporate dinners, had made dealing with the most demanding or dull guest second nature to her, so it wasn't the thought of meeting yet another strand of Anna's life that was making her feel unusually unsettled. Indeed, if she were truthful, Christina Manners said to her husband, she was intrigued by the idea of Sophia.

'Well, I'm not,' Martin retorted. He'd had quite enough of Anna's complex life over the last few months. 'Surely it's Anna's concern.' Like Jasper, he thought Oliver was taking up too much of their time. In his heart of hearts, which Martin tended to leave untapped because it might be tiresome to have to address an issue once you'd acknowledged it, Oliver had been easier to understand when he was with Rachel Stourton. Rachel was a good sort of girl, who presented a less complicated view of life than Anna. Certainly she hadn't presented him and Christina with a string of mothers to consider.

'Well, that's just it,' Christina said. 'Oliver has to be considered and I get the feeling he's not even in the equation. He's on the side rather than at the centre of Anna's life. Don't you get that feeling?'

'Oh, nonsense,' Martin exclaimed. 'You've seen them together. She listens to everything he says. And,' he added grimly, 'that's often absolute codswallop.'

'I think that's what it is,' Christina said, ignoring him. 'It's making him quieter.'

'Calmer, if you ask me,' Martin said irritably. He adored

his elder son but this endless analysing of Oliver's moods served only to make Martin wish he'd just buck up and get married and stop being a source of concern. After all he was thirty-three, for God's sake.

'No. It isn't that. It's Sophia,' Christina said. 'It's the strain of being nice to someone who gave Anna away and has just swanned back into her life again. There's a value at stake here and I have to say that Oliver, to his credit, believes in some old-fashioned ones. Like loyalty and sticking by people.'

Her husband groaned inwardly. Better hear her out.

'I must say, I find that a bit off, too,' Christina went on, 'but Oliver said Anna feels sorry for her and thinks she's had a raw deal in life. She feels somehow responsible for redressing the balance.'

'In which case,' Martin said, making another attempt to bring the conversation to a close, 'it's Anna's concern. Anyway, it seemed to me it was the Scottish one she couldn't stand.'

'Anna never said that,' Christina pointed out.

'Didn't have to. I know Anna. She comes over all polite and listens carefully as though she's taking what you're saying seriously and all the time you know she's longing to say, "Oh, bugger off."'

'Anna doesn't swear,' she said. 'But I think you might be right. She might be *listening* to Oliver but I don't think she's taking a blind bit of notice of him and he knows it. If you're going upstairs, could you tell Jasper to get a move on? They'll be here in a minute and so will all the others.'

Of course, it was a relief that Anna appeared to have accepted Sophia more readily than the step-mother who, in Christina's view, had all the traits of a woman used to managing her own life and finding it hard to absorb not just her new husband but his grown-up daughter into a settled and marked-out existence. But Martin was right. It was so hard to tell with Anna what she was really thinking. No matter how gently or firmly one pushed her to confide about her family and her mother, she deflected it all with a laugh and a teasing rejoinder that her life was so ordinary she would undoubtedly end up in the *Guinness Book of Records* for the most uneventful family in history. Even her adoption apparently held little interest for her. But it interested Christina, for Oliver's sake.

Unfailingly polite, that's what Anna was. Thank God she'd given up that ghastly job. Christina stepped back and gave the table a last-minute check. Perfect.

At least the widow of Lorenzo Grescobaldi had peerless social standing and there was no reason to blush, Christina decided, as she heard Jasper open the door to the first of her guests, when introducing her as Oliver's future mother-in-law. It was such a shame that he didn't seem to relish it.

To Anna it sounded quite wrong to introduce Sophia in this way but, in the strictest sense, it was perfectly true.

The Manners' friends – from the vicar to the head of the parish council – were, like Oliver, too courteous to make direct reference to the fact that Oliver Manners' fiancée's background had absorbed them for days. Of the half-dozen people present, not one would have turned down the chance to meet this extraordinary woman who had burst back into Anna's life – or to get better acquainted with the girl who had ousted the highly acceptable Rachel Stourton from Oliver's.

Anna was glad when they had gone to their own homes, with a long, lazy, somnolent Sunday ahead of them to discuss the little they had gleaned from the encounter, leaving Christina and Martin to continue entertaining their future daughter-in-law's charming Italian mother. Her warmth and friendliness stretched, it seemed, to everyone she met. Christina breathed a sigh of relief.

'Now we can just be us,' she said, as the last guest disappeared and she led the way into lunch. 'I hope there weren't too many faces for you to get to know, Sophia, but they are all old friends and watched Oliver grow up. They so rarely see him, these days.'

'Just being here is enough.' Sophia smiled. 'Anna worries so much. She is wonderful. And not so many strangers either.'

'No?' Christina halted in surprise.

'Such a small world. Who is the diplomatic person who lives here? Your friend Mr Wentworth mention him. Now, what was his name?'

'Stourton.' Christina shot an alarmed look at Oliver.

'Ah, that was it.' Sophia sounded delighted. 'Boring man. Boring family. Some embassy party or other that my poor late husband was always having to go to. We meet him. But I end it there because of the rumours. So many rumours . . . Christina.' On seeing the table she stopped. 'It all looks so inviting. Really it is a shame to eat – one should frame it. *Bellissimo.*'

'Rumours?' Martin asked casually, glancing at his wife over Sophia's head. He held out a chair for Sophia to sit down.

'I forget,' Sophia waved a hand. 'And one is discreet. But let us just say I would not let Andrea go near the family. Just in case. You really can't be too careful – so many awful people around. But I adore – absolutely *adore* this room. Anna said you had exquisite taste and she is right.'

Christina turned to Anna. 'Thank you, my dear. Now will you sit here, next to Martin? Greg,' she turned to her son-in-law, 'perhaps you'd like to sit on Sophia's left.'

And so it began. Looking back, Anna could not imagine why she thought Sophia would have forgotten that Oliver's parents had been horrified when he parted from Rachel Stourton, having fallen giddily in love with the more enigmatic Anna.

Oliver's face was like glass. Anna thought she was going to be sick. Without even having to be told, she knew, beyond a doubt, that Sophia had never met John Stourton. She had just recalled the name, the slight this family had inflicted on Anna by preferring someone because they had clear evidence that no skeletons would be waiting to fall out of a family closet.

Sophia went blithely on. She flirted gently with Oliver's father. Normally the most reserved of men, he became uncomfortably jovial. Oliver's brother-in-law, the unassuming solicitor who had married his younger sister, Kate, was pressed into joining in the rather boisterous section of the table where Sophia exclaimed at the successes he had racked up in settling land disputes. Even Jasper, who had wrung a promise from his mother that he would be able to slide away at dead on three o'clock, was still in his place at half past, hugely entertained by Sophia's flirtatious seduction of his brother-in-law – and astonished at his father being flirted with at all.

Anna glanced uneasily at her prospective mother-in-law. Christina was pressing on with her questions about Anna's new job and Anna just prayed that the odd snatch of conversation, which now seemed to imply that Anna had inherited several valuable paintings, would not reach her.

It was too much to hope that Christina's careful, over-strained English reserve would triumph over Sophia's determination to be heard.

'Christina,' Sophia interrupted them, 'I was just saying to Martin that when these two delightful young people have settled on a house we must get my curator to advise on the hangings.'.

'Hangings?' repeated Christina blankly.

'Why, yes. Of course Anna particularly liked the Olitski, which is magical, but Oliver's taste might be more classical. So,' Sophia gave a lilting, delighted laugh, 'we await Anna's instructions. But, then, she might prefer to hang them here. Oh, not yet, of course,' she stretched out her hand and clasped Christina's reassuringly, 'we hope not for many years. Is that not so, Oliver?'

Oliver put down his knife and fork and took a sip of wine. 'If ever,' he said quite deliberately, then went on with his meal. It wasn't true. Just one painting and she'd given that back. It was too embarrassing. Anna smiled uneasily at Oliver, who looked away, and then she turned, with a look of pleading, to Sophia.

Any hope that the assembled group gathered around the table might have missed the broad, conspiratorial wink Sophia gave her was a forlorn one.

'Would you like to take Sophia into the garden?' Christina addressed her husband. She rose to her feet. 'I think we could do with a breath of fresh air.'

Sophia had gone to bed, yawning, replete, saying she wanted to have a long, long lie-in. Anna should just slip off to work and not waken her.

They both watched her go. Oliver, who had driven back in near silence, turned to Anna. 'She,' he said, in a voice of dangerous calm, 'is outrageous.'

'Of course she is,' Anna argued feebly. 'She's Italian.'

'No.' He paused by the door, fury etched in every line of his face. 'In any language, make no mistake, Anna, she's absolutely vulgar.'

She ran into Henry, lunching with Max and Tania Prowton, purely by chance. Well, perhaps not so much chance – it was more surprising that it hadn't happened before. The restaurant was chosen by most of the television people who frequented it for almost the sole purpose of networking and dropping a word here and there. Deals were never closed there, but seeds were planted, and words of warning, wrapped in velvet assurances of value being recognized, were issued.

'Anna,' Henry cried, leaping to his feet as he spotted her, 'you haven't returned any of my calls and I'm not calling you again. Well,' he whispered, kissing her, 'not any more today at any rate.'

Out of the corner of her eye, as she hugged him, she saw Max beginning to rise from his seat. Tania sat where she was.

'Just so busy, Henry,' she said, as Max bore down on her.

'Anna,' he smiled, holding her at arm's length before he kissed her, 'my congratulations. The programme looks marvellous. And so, of course, do you.'

He was good, she marvelled. 'Thank you, Max. Henry, I'll definitely call you,' she promised. 'I've got my – my Italian mother with me. But she's going at the end of the week and I'll be back to normal. Must dash, quick lunch with Gilbert and he's just arrived. *Ciao.*'

'She looks dreadful,' Max said, watching Anna thread her way to the table where Gilbert Cochran was already seated. 'I never rated her. Mark my words, she's in over her head.'

'Honestly, Max,' Henry protested, 'that's hardly fair. She's getting very good names on screen and, frankly, what does it matter what any of us looks like? It's what's on screen that matters. Anyway, we're all bloody wrecks,' he muttered gloomily. 'That's what this fucking business does, drains every ounce of talent to the great god of money and schedules and wankering management.'

Max looked at him pityingly. 'For God's sake, Henry, speak for yourself,' he snapped. 'And mark my words, you'll see. The word is that Gilbert is not thrilled to bits with her.'

'Well, in that case you know Charles would have her back tomorrow,' Henry said. 'I don't like those ratings and neither does he.'

Tania looked furiously at Henry then at Max. Under the table Max moved his thigh closer to hers and very gently pressed it. 'A temporary blip,' he snarled. 'A pity more people can't get out there and come up with some ideas. Bloody Anna Minstrel wouldn't have found time for that. Oh, no, much too grand. Tania and I are not going to New York for a holiday, you know. Our schedule is very full.'

Tania suppressed a smile and slipped her hand under the table. Max guided it helpfully to where it would most usefully be employed.

'On the other hand, I think we can achieve a lot,' Tania

said. 'Even in just two days.' Max's eyes began to glaze over. 'Oh, Henry.' Tania gave a little gasp of dismay. 'I forgot to mention. You had a call from Melissa. She said it was urgent. Clean forgot. Look, use the phone here. We'll wait.'

From her seat on the other side of the room, Anna saw Henry shoving his way slightly frantically through the diners and decided that whatever it was that Gilbert had to say it could not be worse than the prospect of lunching with Max. Absence had not improved him. Nor, as it turned out, had her job prospects. Sophia's intrusion into her working life, not least her constant phone calls distracting Anna, had been noticed.

'Nothing wrong, is there, sweetheart?' Gilbert asked mildly, studying the menu. 'Just thought a little one-to-one might be the answer. Don't want to lose you. Just say if we're pushing you too hard.'

'Hard?' Anna forced a laugh and lowered the menu to look at him. Her stomach lurched. 'Heavens, no. Sometimes I don't feel stretched enough. Um, just a salad for me. Which reminds me. I was thinking, Gil,' she placed the menu on the edge of the table and frowned, 'the headline round-up needs to be punchier. What do you think of tracking the headlines every five minutes across the bottom of the screen, give them more urgency? I think the pace is too slow at the moment and we can use that time to get viewers' e-mail reactions. It means a bit more pressure but I think we can pull it off.'

But *she* couldn't. Not a lunch like that, never again. And she knew she would not be given the chance. They left the restaurant talking animatedly. Anna made sure that, in full view of Max, she timed a wicked observation on one of their rivals so that Gilbert threw his head back and was laughing delightedly as they disappeared back to the studio.

As the third, and in Anna's view final, week of Sophia's visit drew to a close, Anna knew Gilbert had cause for concern. She was exhausted, and without Roberto, who had left almost on Irena's heels for Rome and not New York, she had had to cope with a woman who seemed incapable of doing anything on her own.

Newsbeat was more demanding than *Max Meets* had ever been but it would all have been well within her grasp if she hadn't had Sophia to contend with. Sophia, who failed to understand Anna's demanding job or why Anna was so angry with her for protecting her. 'But why do you let them walk over you?' Sophia cried, partly in English and mostly in Italian, which was difficult for Anna to follow. 'It was different for me. I had no choice. I yearned,' Sophia beat her breast, 'for someone to be there for me. Why do you tell me these things if they're not true?' Huge tears welled in her eyes. 'I did it for you,' she went on, pressing the side of her hand against her mouth. 'Just for you.'

Anna gave in and said rather more gently, 'Well, they are true – or, rather, were true, and possibly might still be true.' She placed her hands on the edge of the table and dropped her head. Sophia sat on the other side, arms crossed, looking bewildered. 'But,' Anna went on, emphasizing each word so that Sophia might just be able to understand, 'there are some things best left unsaid. It's how we do things. I was just letting off steam to you, that's all.'

'I see,' Sophia said, her eyes wide. 'You want me to say nothing, then I say nothing. Giulio was right. He said you were hard to help.'

Anna lifted her head sharply. 'I am not hard to help if I need help, but I don't. Not from anyone. Now, I'm going to have a bath and when I've done that I'll organize supper.'

Sophia stood up. 'Not for me. I am going to bed.'

Conscience rather than inclination made her ring Oliver to suggest that he came over for dinner. He was out. Anna hung up. She had failed to call him back when he had rung at four and then at five so he had quite obviously – and for the third night in a row – made separate plans. But how could she have phoned him? Gilbert was on her back, the programme was in danger of overrunning by two minutes when news came in that a major football star was holed up in his mock-Tudor house in Hertfordshire holding his agent hostage and to blame for the downturn in his career. Live coverage was hastily pressed into operation, witnesses rounded up, heroes found and a psychologist brought in to explain all about stress. 'Drop the phoney Santas,' she ordered, running an eye over the schedule. There was four minutes to air. 'And we'll do voice-over on the libel case if we have to.'

'Police say they might be able to talk him out,' a young researcher reported. 'Suppose they do that while we're on air? And your mother called. She said it was urgent.'

'Then you get on the phone instead of talking to me. Call the press office of that soft-drinks company who've just signed him up for their ads and that other lot,' she was already jamming her headphones on, 'the trendy trainers. We want lots of deep reservations about their deal with him – and keep the Santas on standby. We might need them. How're we doing?'

The producer was holding up five fingers as Anna slid into her seat beside him. 'Four, three, stand by, studio. Two, one.'

'Tonight *Newsbeat* are bringing live pictures . . .' The presenter began to read his autocue. What the hell was so urgent, Anna thought, that Sophia couldn't wait until the programme was over? She scribbled a note to her PA. 'Call my home. Find out what's urgent.'

Five minutes later her PA slid a note in front of her. On screen the psychologist was saying that when someone reached breaking point, it often had nothing to do with the job. Usually something quite trivial triggered it – a car breaking down, a flight delayed . . . cancelling a weekend visit to see her father. Again. Or, Anna thought, glancing at the note, Sophia. She wanted to know what time Anna would be home.

Oliver was right, damn him – and oh, God damn him, so too was Giulio. Sophia was not helpless, just horribly, frustratingly and selfishly dependent on everyone around her. Why she hadn't noticed it in Rome she couldn't imagine. But in Rome Sophia had been a different person. There, they were all more excitable, passions ran higher, honour was quickly defended and Sophia herself had been in shock. No wonder her behaviour had seemed more cautious, more restrained than that of the rest of the Grescobaldis.

Over and over again she berated herself for having indulged in such indiscreet revelations to Sophia. So harmless at the time, so horrendously embarrassing now. And all the things she had said seemeed pitiful and small, not worthy of her, but – like Pandora's box – the lid was off and she couldn't push anything back in.

'I don't think she can make it,' Colin Minstrel told Meryl. He walked through from the hall to where she was valiantly attempting to read one of the six books Morag Fraser had sent her. Moreton was right, they *were* simply dreadful, but Morag had invited them to join her table at a charity dinner for some heritage preservation society she belonged to and it was only right that Meryl should know something of her hostess's life.

'Who, dear?' Meryl removed her glasses and looked up.

'Anna,' he said, standing with his back to her and staring out of the window into the gathering gloom. He jingled some change in his pockets. 'Sophia,' he glanced round to where Meryl was sitting quietly just listening, 'of course.'

Meryl put aside her book, folded her glasses and got up. 'Now, listen,' she said tucking her arm into his, 'Anna is grown-up and can decide on her own life. And she has Oliver, remember. She'll come another weekend, when Sophia has gone home.'

'I haven't seen her since the engagement,' he reminded her. The thing is, Meryl,' he looked down into her face, 'Barbara would have done something. I don't think she would be at all happy with any of this.'

'Like what?' Meryl asked.

'Like stopping it before it began.'

'You couldn't,' she said sharply. 'How could you? Anna made all the decisions. Anna agreed to go. She's not a child, Colin. Stop treating her like one.'

'That's just it.' He turned away forlornly. 'I don't think I ever did. I always thought of her as grown-up and that, I think, has been my mistake. I should have gone that day.'

Meryl stiffened. Then she walked back to where she had been sitting, picked up her book and placed it on top of all the other sentimentally titled books that Morag had shipped over. *Highland Love*, said one. *Romance in the Glen*, said another. Dreadful. All absolutely dreadful. And, if Fenella and Athol were correct, so was Anna's mother. There was little charity in Meryl's heart for anyone who had cruelly humiliated her son – and it spoke volumes for what Anna must have been saying about them. 'Then I'm sorry I spoke,' she said. 'I didn't mean to interfere. You asked me and I told you. Anna is thirty-one, Colin. Not thirteen.'

Colin went on staring out of the window. 'I know. But that doesn't make her any less my child, does it? I think —' He stopped and corrected himself. 'I think *we* should remember that, don't you?'

'Certainly, as long as we both remember the welcome given to my son and his wife by your daughter.'

He heard the door click behind him. He'd never before had more than a mild cross word with Meryl and he'd never felt so torn or that it had been so inevitable.

Anna tried to picture Sophia sitting in Carrie's minuscule kitchen with Euan refusing to go to bed. In three days she would be gone. Anna had seen the tickets, checked the flight and the result was that she had begun to feel more tolerant of her, even more kindly disposed towards her. It was strange how generous you could be when the end was near.

'I think,' she said to Carrie, who had offered to entertain Sophia while Anna went to dinner, 'she's easier out than in. But thanks. I'll think of something.'

'Ask Giulio,' Carrie suggested. 'I had lunch with him today.'

'Did you? How?'

'Actually, it's happened a couple of times, although today was a bit of an accident, I think. He was lunching with William – one of the partners I work with, they do stuff for him from time to time. Anyway, apparently Giulio asked how I was getting on and William thought it would be useful for me to sit in.'

'Did he mention Sophia?' Anna asked. What she meant was, 'Did he ask about me?' A wave of jealousy had crept over her. She switched the phone to her other hand.

'No,' Carrie said. 'I did. I said she was proving a handful.'

'You didn't?' Anna almost screamed. 'Oh God, why did you say that?'

Carrie sounded very calm. 'Because it's true. And what's wrong with that? Giulio didn't seem at all surprised. And if I were you, my girl, I'd get this Giulio thing out of the way. It's eating you up, I can see it.'

'I know,' Anna said. 'But I won't. Oliver's worth more than that.'

At breakfast the next morning Sophia told Anna she had decided to stay on for a bit. Anna looked blankly at her.

'A bit?' she said. 'What do you mean, a bit?' She'd been on the point of leaving for work – late, of course. 'Why?'

'I thought of looking for a flat in London.' Sophia yawned. 'It's wonderful here. And I can be near you.'

'Near me? Sophia, what about Andrea? What about the business?' She spoke calmly but inside a small explosion of shock, mingled with dismay, was doing irreparable damage to her nervous system. She didn't think Sophia was listening: her attention had been captured by a flaw that only she could see in a nail. 'Sophia,' Anna repeated, trying to steady her voice, 'when did you decide this? Why didn't you say?'

Sophia stretched and yawned. 'I didn't decide until last

night and you were asleep so I'm telling you now. I phoned Pilar for messages and that kind of thing and she said Roberto had asked me to ring. He said he would be back in a week and help me look for somewhere. Oh, and I am not telling Andrea. He would try to stop me and be very jealous that it is you I want to be with.'

Somewhere behind Anna there was a chair. She groped for it and sat down.

Chapter Twenty-one

But she did tell Andrea. At the very first opportunity that presented itself, she got through to him. It was about six in Chicago and not quite midday by the studio clock. She could hear the familiar single low burr of a phone thousands of miles away in the apartment he had rented with Stefano, overlooking the water at Highland Lake. Sitting at her desk, a stone's throw from Euston, with rain cascading down the windows, Anna tucked the phone under her chin and glanced around carefully to locate Gilbert. She kept him in her sights while she got through.

The grey screen perched on the edge of her desk was swimming with myriad luridly coloured goldfish. It had been for the past hour. She pressed the return button and a menu appeared. Links edit. Time out. Subject closed. Reactivate? it inquired.

Seconds before, Oliver had phoned. 'I'll call you,' she said frantically. 'I've got to ring Andrea urgently.'

Anna ran the mouse up and down the list with a look of studied concentration. Not one word registered. Watching her from the other side of the room, Gilbert grunted to himself and turned away.

The phone was answered by the machine.

Anna cursed under her breath. 'Andrea,' she spoke in a low voice, 'it's me, Anna. Andrea, *please* pick up. It's urgent.'

There was a clatter as someone dragged the phone from its cradle and a small pause. Then, finally, a voice, hoarse and bleary from sleep: 'Anna? What is it? What time is it? Are you ill? Mamma?'

'No,' she whispered hurriedly, glancing around the crowded room for signs of Gilbert. 'Nothing like that. No, I can't speak up. I'm in the office. I haven't got much time. I'm needed in the studio. Andrea, *please* don't go back to sleep. I need your help.'

She could hear Stefano stirring beside him, and a small charge of envy at the thought of being curled around a warm body, letting another day drift lazily in, which had not happened for some time, caught her by surprise. She glanced up at the studio clock. In five minutes she had to be at a meeting and, while it might have suited Andrea for her to ring later, she had borne alone the prospect of a permanent Sophia for more than four hours with no one to tell and that, in her view, was more than enough. Andrea was Sophia's son. Someone, and that someone could only be him, had to share this with her, take the responsibility away from her and take Sophia back to Rome.

The first shock was that Andrea didn't appear to view it as seriously as she did. 'If she wants to buy an apartment let her.' He sounded bewildered. 'What is the problem?'

'The problem is,' Anna said, with mounting impatience, 'she wants a flat here and I'm not supposed to tell you.'

'Not tell me?' He seemed genuinely astonished. 'Anna, wait. Let me take this in the other room. Stefano can't sleep.'

'He was gone. Sod Stefano, she thought savagely. Can't sleep? *Can't sleep?* Is that all he had to trouble him? Her hand clenched the mouse on its rubber mat. It slid under the pressure in jerky little tugs sending the cursor in wild circles across the screen. 'C'mon, *c'mon,*' she breathed.

'I'm here,' Andrea said at last. 'Now. *Un attimo. Bene.* I switch on coffee and it's not plugged in. My brain is not into gear.' He laughed. She almost screamed. 'Now,' he said, and she could hear the yawn, 'all is well. So why mustn't I know? And why didn't you say when I rang last night?'

'Because I didn't know until this morning,' Anna said. 'And I'm telling you, Andrea, I don't think what she's doing is sensible. What will she do all day? Andrea? Are you listening?'

There was a short pause.

'Yes, yes. I listen. I pour coffee but I still listen. I agree. It is very odd. Just a moment, Stefano is coming. The noise wake him. We had a very late night. Poor angel, he's feeling—'

'Andrea,' she tried to remain calm, 'I am very sorry for Stefano, but his hangover will eventually go. My problem might not. Andrea, tell Stefano later.' She could hear him murmuring to Stefano. She gave the keyboard a savage stab. A streak of Rs raced across the screen.

'Anna? Here is the thing. Stefano thinks like me. We think she might be happy there. In Rome she was *very* alone.'

'But she'll be alone here,' Anna protested. 'She has no friends. I'll be at work all day. And frankly, Andrea, she is hopeless, utterly hopeless, at being on her own.'

'But she won't be on her own, will she?' he said. 'You're there. Evenings, weekends, And, Anna, she adores you and just wants to make up for all the time you were apart. Would her being in London be so bad? For just a little while? In a year—'

Anna yelped. 'A year? My God, *a whole year*?'

'Maybe not a year, maybe just a few months,' he amended hastily. 'She gets bored, the novelty will wear off.'

Anna had the strangest feeling that somewhere along the line it was not Andrea but she who had missed the point. At some crucial moment she had slipped from being in control, dictating her terms, to being at their mercy. It was not going to happen.

'She wants to be near me,' she said slowly, 'because she feels lonely and isolated in Rome and she can't deal with being in a place where Lorenzo was her only support. Your family have backed away from her.'

'That isn't true,' he riposted. 'Please, Anna,' he said, hurt. 'She is your family too.'

'Yours first.' She sounded childish, and she knew it.

'Very well. But my family have always tried to help her, but she wouldn't be helped.'

'You don't understand,' she said wearily. 'You were shielded from so much.'

'Like what?' She could hear the wariness.

'Like . . .' she tested the water '. . . like Issy.'

He sounded relieved. 'Oh, Issy. That was not important.'

'So you did know?'

'Of course. But it was not my business and, Anna, really, it's six in the morning and what has this to do with Mamma buying an apartment in London?'

'Don't you see?' She tried to keep her voice down, tried to stop the exasperation and despair from drowning the rational point she had to make. 'That *is* the point. You and Stefano, your father and Issy. Both of you keeping so much of your lives from her. And everyone from Gianni to Great-aunt Isabella all knowing – well, at least about Issy and accepting her. To be honest with you, I was shocked. I don't mind telling you, Andrea, I was shocked at the funeral to find everyone hugging and kissing her and Sophia grieving only yards away.'

'But they all know her,' he began feebly. 'You can't just pretend.'

'But you did,' she said, 'didn't you? One rule for the Grescobaldis, one for outsiders. And that's what she's always been. No wonder she's a mess. Are you surprised that, in her head, I'm the best thing that's happened to her? And she gave me up. Can you imagine what that's doing to her? The one person she was forced to abandon is now the only person she feels she can turn to. And she's causing chaos.'

There was a silence.

On the other side of the room, looking pointedly towards

her desk, she could see Gilbert. With the phone still tucked under her chin she rose purposefully and held up her hand, her fingers spread, to tell him she would be there in five minutes.

'Anna,' Andrea said, 'this is a big surprise. You were very willing to help her and you came to Rome and wouldn't meet Nonna because you felt so strongly for her. You have created this. Not me.'

'Me?' she gasped. 'I did what anyone with an ounce of compassion and,' she drew a deep breath, 'sense of honour would have done. I listened and I tried to understand and, believe me, it wasn't hard for any of you to have made the jump from your side of the fence to see it from hers. No wonder she wanted to get away.'

'You invited her,' he cried. 'What were we all supposed to think? And now you don't want her.'

'No. It's not that I don't *want* her, but my life here is not geared to dealing with her on a permanent basis. And, yes, she's driving me insane. But the next person to come along who just walks away will really hurt her and I don't want to be that person. Do you understand?'

'If you understand her so well, what is so bad about her staying near you?' he said sulkily.

'Andrea,' she answered, her voice dangerously quiet, 'I'm not sure that it matters *who* understands her. But I do know she is not going to solve her problems here. She doesn't know me well enough, how I live, my friends. She likes it because I've made sure she had plenty to do and lots of people to meet. But I can't keep it up. None of it. Now, if you won't help, get Roberto to come back here and talk to her. She'll listen to him.'

Giulio phoned – some hours later, and just as Anna was on the point of returning Oliver's call. It was a shock. She almost failed to recognize his voice because it had been weeks since she had heard it. He sounded bored. Impatient, even.

'Andrea thinks you might need some help,' he began, without preamble.

Anna looked at the ceiling – concealed lights behind frosted panels that were meant to reduce the strain of screens and tension and managed neither. She closed her eyes.

'He's got that wrong,' she replied quietly. 'I'm not the one who needs help. He does.'

There was a small pause. 'In what way?'

'Because his mother needs to be helped to pick up the threads of her life, whatever life that is. She needs to go home. I can see that. He must be the one to make it happen.'

'And you think he'll try?'

It was what she feared. 'Yes,' she said firmly. 'Because, underneath it all, I'm sure he loves her and they need to start putting Lorenzo's death behind them.'

'And that can be done, can it? Less than six months later?'

Anna swallowed. 'Yes. No. What I mean is, they can start. Not complete it. But they have to start.'

'And they do that how?'

She took a deep breath. 'By not fighting each other, blaming each other.'

'Oh, for God's sake,' he exploded, 'you sound like Max Warner on a bad day. You're turning her into a victim.'

'I have done no such thing,' she retorted furiously. 'The Grescobaldis did that. And now they want me to pick up the pieces. Well, I won't.'

'You said you could handle her,' he pointed out. 'You said, if I recall, "I promised Lorenzo". You invited her, you—'

Anna slammed down the phone. She hadn't forgotten what she had said that night, any of it. Her hand was still resting on the receiver. She stared at it, trying to picture his face, furious at being cut off, recognizing that she was not to be trifled with, and waited for the wave of satisfaction to hit her. When it didn't, she closed her eyes and dropped her head. Then she punched in Oliver's number.

'I'm sorry, Anna, he's left,' said his PA. 'I know he tried a couple of times to get you.'

'OK, Linda,' Anna said. 'Don't worry. I'll try his mobile.'

It was switched off. She left a message and another at his flat. She knew he wouldn't go to Braverton Street, not while Sophia was there. He'll ring later, she comforted herself, pushing her way down the escalator to the tube. Besides, it'll be easier for me to talk from there.

Oliver sat in a small wine bar in Soho and waited. 'Ready to order, sir?'

He glanced at the menu and laid it aside. She certainly wouldn't want to eat here and he didn't want them to either. It was too intimate, it smacked of the clandestine, and he couldn't bear to be reduced to that. It had been just the first place he could think of when she said, 'Let's meet.'

'Wine. White wine,' he said. 'I'm waiting for someone. We'll decide then.'

There was a copy of the *Standard* beside him. It lay unopened and unread. He was a patient man, but he had a life too. He had hoped, still did, that his life was also going to be bound up with Anna's. It was what they both wanted, where they both wanted to be. If he was honest with himself, which was what Oliver was unwillingly beginning to acknowledge he must be, he knew that he had pushed through their engagement to make her focus on their life. For a brief moment it had worked.

Now, though, he knew that until the question of Sophia was resolved, he could not be sure of what Anna really wanted. And he missed her. Not just the sex, although that was the most miserable of the lot, he missed the seriousness of her commitment, the teasing self-deprecation, the admiration she had for his job, the interest she took in his clients. When was the last time she had asked him what had happened in his job?

If there was a moment that Oliver could have changed – and it had been there for him to seize but he had let it slip from his grasp – it was when he had let Anna go alone to meet her mother for the first time. Instead he had gone out to dinner, with a client. Then he could have guided her, instead of allowing Giulio Farrini to influence her, a man with a vested interest in getting her to Rome. She had been left alone to deal with a troubled past and now an uncertain future. They needed to talk, away from everyone, just the two of them. And at this moment he needed to talk very badly.

'Hello,' a soft voice said. 'Am I late?'

He glanced up and looked blankly at the young woman sliding into the seat opposite. Then he smiled. It was a weary smile but relieved too. He leaned across the table and kissed her cheek. 'Hi, Rachel,' he said. 'Thanks for coming.'

It was hard to work out who in the end had called Roberto – Giulio or Andrea – but all that mattered was that he had promised to be in London within a few days to talk to Sophia. 'Although,' he said, with a note of censure in his voice, 'I am surprised at you, Anna. I thought you had become fond of her and wanted to help her. It was what Lorenzo wanted.'

'Well, of course I want to help her,' she said, wondering if she should have it stamped on her head, 'and the way to help her is to make her see all the disadvantages of her plan. And don't bring Lorenzo into this. He didn't care twopence for her.'

'That is not true,' Roberto said.

'Oh, stop it. He had a mistress. I know that, Andrea knows that. And don't tell me you didn't.'

'Why would she listen to me?' he asked. 'I have no influence with her.'

'You do,' Anna said, 'you know you do. She says it all the time. "Roberto will tell me what to do. Roberto will advise Andrea." So, Roberto, *please*? Just come.'

But Roberto's trip was delayed by a week. When she was

facing the second week with no clear evidence that he was going to be in London, Anna phoned his office to find that he was in New York. She knew that Irena had been there too for at least some of the time, and felt that action was called for but she couldn't work out what it should be. She could hardly order Roberto to dump Irena and come to London.

Patience, my girl, she scolded herself. Just hang on in there. Even Roberto has to go home at some point. All around her the world seemed to be conspiring to keep Sophia in London and Anna from a life she could hardly call her own. Each day she headed for her office and barely noticed that Christmas trees had sprung up in shop windows. Her father had asked her to come to Scotland for the holiday, and Oliver had said his mother was anxious for a decision.

No one mentioned Sophia because no one knew they had to. It was almost December. Another week, and the serious business of Christmas would have to be considered. It was then that Oliver had insisted she come to the flat and leave Sophia where she was, but she could not face the conversation he had planned. 'Darling,' she said, 'not now. When all this is over we'll talk as much as you want. Right now I just need a drink.'

'Is that all?' he asked, looking down at her. He bent over her, leaning his arms either side of hers and searched her eyes. 'Is that really all? Just a drink?'

Anna opened one eye. 'Well,' she stretched out a hand and slid it around the back of his neck, 'to start with,' she said, and tried to smile.

Several times during the following week, Anna asked nervously how the flat-hunting was going, but Sophia was dismissive of all that had been laid before her by what appeared to be an army of eager young estate agents. Anna grew used to hearing that Roger from Prideaux and Sternham had called, or Simon from Excelsior Properties. Rupert, who represented Bayswater Homes, was by far the most persist-ent, even eclipsing Joshua from Knightsbridge Apartments, who had taken Sophia off for an entire day and failed to impress her with anything on his books. Anna was relieved. Roberto would be here soon, and Sophia was nowhere near buying a property, which would save endless complications once he had persuaded her that the decision was the wrong one.

But other changes had to take place to deal with the evidence of Sophia in residence. Anna, who had never had a cleaner in her life, leafed through the *Yellow Pages*, found a company called KleneUp and put herself on their books. Two days later a cheerful yellow van pulled up outside and from out of the back stepped a trio of uniformed women, armed with dustpans, Hoovers and buckets. Anna practi-cally wept with relief. 'Three of us,' said the one in charge. 'That way you get it all done in an hour and a half. Top and bottom. Anything special?'

'God, no,' Anna exclaimed. 'I have a visitor who's still in bed, but I'll warn her you're here. Look, here's my number at my office.' She scribbled it on a piece of paper. 'Call if you need anything and the money's in that envelope.'

For once she walked down Braverton Street without dreading the day ahead. Whatever they did, good or bad, it had to be better than her doing it.

At midday the forewoman phoned Anna to say that they were sorry but they had not been able to clean upstairs because her visitor had refused to get up and the noise of the Hoover was disturbing her, which meant they couldn't do the other rooms either. 'Not quite sure what was the problem,' the woman said. 'Italian, is she? Thought as much. Not our fault, Miss Minstrel,' she apologized. 'I'm afraid we can't give you a refund because we weren't given access, you see. No access is counted as cancellation in less than twenty-four hours. And there'll be a slight charge for the repair of the Hoover.'

'Repair of the Hoover?' Anna yelped. 'Why?'

'Your guest. She kicked it and now the socket's all bent. Jean was only hoovering the landing and out she comes, shouting her head off. I suppose she must have been saying, "Turn it off", but how was Jean to know? She comes from Stockwell, not bleedin' Sorrento.'

'Pilar would never have spoken to me like that,' Sophia said. 'I ask not to be disturbed. I tell her, "*Ho mal di testa.*" I tap my head, so, but still she goes on.' She straightened up. 'You see, you are not used to servants, Anna. They have to be told what to do. And if they don't,' she clicked her fingers, 'they know what will happen.'

Anna surveyed the kitchen, which at least was clean, the living room too. The windows gleamed back at her. There was nothing to be gained from a discussion with Sophia about domestic staff. Sophia's occupied a palatial apartment and seemed happy to be treated akin to serfs, but this morning's three women couldn't have given a monkey's for Sophia's tantrum. If they were given the elbow so what? There was always more work somewhere else.

Sophia appeared not to notice that Anna resumed cleaning the house herself. Each morning she sailed off in a car supplied by Anna and arrived home with armfuls of brochures, including those of some fashionable interior designers.

'Maybe you're looking for something that you would find only in Rome?' Anna suggested diffidently. The pile of catalogues on the table, small wads of fabric samples lay with them, colour charts and little square tufts of carpet on cards. 'London apartments are nowhere near as stylish as the ones in Italy.'

'But, darling, I don't want one like in Rome.' Sophia stretched out on the sofa. 'I want one that is near you and where I can take a little walk to the shops.' She yawned. 'I wait until Roberto advise me. And when I have one I like I take you first to see it. Now, Riccardo – or maybe it was the other one, the one who does the colour – he said there

265

was a restaurant in Covent Garden that we simply must try. Let's go there tonight.'

'Riccardo?' Anna asked. 'Who's he?'

'My hairdresser.' Sophia tilted her head to one side to show Anna the quite superb new cut.

'I thought you went to Alessandro's?'

Sophia wrinkled her nose. 'Oh, darling, did you not see what he did with the cut? No, no, no. I ring Luigi. I say you send me to the wrong person. Very bad. And he say, "You will adore Riccardo." And I do. Now, shall we go? No? You surely don't want to cook?'

Anna no longer cared if Sophia had to eat alone at the house and, oddly enough, she herself seemed not to mind. Her taste in television ran to soaps and talk-shows. On days when she stayed home, she watched *Ricki Lake* or *Jerry Springer* and was astonished that Anna should have given up *Max Meets* for something as dry as *Newsbeat*. All of this, to her shame, Anna encouraged. It took Sophia's mind off Anna's absence.

'It won't be long,' she assured Oliver, as they parted in Covent Garden, Anna to take a cab home to Braverton Street, Oliver to a reception that she had promised to go to with him until a phone call from Sophia had changed all that.

'Anna.' He held her shoulders and looked skywards. 'You said that last week and the week before. Unless you put an end to it, you've got her for life.'

'Don't say that,' she begged. 'I can't bear it. I don't know what to do. But she will go. It's funny, two weeks ago I couldn't bear the thought of Roberto being here and now I can't wait for him to come back. I'm so sorry about the reception. Will you mind going on your own?'

Oliver looked down at her. 'No. And anyway I think Rachel will be there. I'll talk to her.'

Anna paused, about to get into the cab. 'Yes, of course,' she said. 'Oliver?'

'Yes?'

'Nothing. I'll call you later.'

*

'Where is he?' Anna fumed on the phone to Andrea. 'I've called his office and they said they would tell him to ring me, but he hasn't.'

'Oh dear. Can't you manage just for a day or two more?'

'Andrea, it's been almost two weeks. I don't care what you say or do, but get Roberto back here to organize a flat or get her back to Rome. I no longer care which. Unless you do,' she took a deep breath and lied, 'she's talking about going to Chicago to see you and I have no way of stopping her.'

'Here?' he screamed. 'Oh, my God, no, she mustn't. Stefano is here. She must go back to Rome. Home. She must go home. Leave it to me. I'll call Roberto. Call Giulio – he'll know what to do.'

'No,' she said quickly, 'not Giulio. Just Roberto.'

Two days later Roberto arrived. Anna greeted him warmly and decided it was his business what he told his wife. 'I tell her New York because she has silly ideas about who she imagines I might be with in London.' He smiled serenely. 'And it's only a day or two.'

'Won't she phone you?' Anna asked. 'Won't she wonder where you are if she needs to speak to you?'

Roberto looked indignant. 'What do you take me for? I do not neglect my wife. I ring her three times a day so she is never in need of finding me.'

They all lied, to each other, about each other. If he wanted to tell his wife he was in New York when he was in London, that was his own affair. All Anna cared about was that now, at last, Sophia would go.

Sylvana Andreotti was every bit as suspicious of her husband as he believed her not to be. Anna knew instantly that she must have irrefutable proof of his philandering when she telephoned the day after Roberto's arrival. It was a Saturday and Sophia had left early to show Roberto where she thought she might live.

'Where is he?' Sylvana demanded. 'Where is my

husband? No,' she went on, before Anna could speak, 'do not lie to me. You are nothing but a tart. A heartless little whore.'

Anna gasped and tried to stop her. 'Sylvana, you don't know what you're saying.' But Sylvana was not to be stopped.

'Ever since poor Lorenzo's funeral all I hear from the Grescobaldis is Anna this and Anna that and now, *now*, you have reached out for Roberto. Is no one safe from your greed?'

'Sylvana, it's not true,' Anna protested, her heart hammering against her ribs. 'Who told you this?'

'Told me,' Sylvana jeered, and collapsed into a torrent of Italian, most of which left Anna bewildered and some of which led her to understand that, by mistake, the hotel had phoned Roberto's office in Rome to query a credit-card number. His secretary had phoned Sylvana for clarification, and Sylvana had erupted.

'Sylvana,' she pleaded. *'Piu piano. Non capisco.'*

'You think I am stupid. Well, you will see how stupid I am. Stay away from him. I thought it was Giulio Farrini you were playing around with,' Sylvana said bitterly. 'And to think all along it was my husband. You are a bitch and a marriage-wrecker. I want my husband left alone. I will tell everyone. You will lose your job, your friends. You wait.'

'Sylvana,' Anna shouted to make herself heard, 'I have not been with Roberto anywhere. And if I had, how do you suppose I could force a grown man to get on a plane and come here? Don't you think he had some say in this?'

But Sylvana had hung up.

Roberto went pale with fright when Anna told him. He licked his lips and begged Anna not to mention it to Sophia or that he had been seeing Irena.

Anna banged her head with the heel of her hand. 'Oh, yes. I'm really going to tell her that her niece is having an affair with you. Roberto, you are having an affair with my cousin. You tell your wife you are in New York when you are in London. You don't want Sophia to know. Your wife is distraught. I am being blamed. What is wrong with this picture?'

All the next day Anna felt sick with nerves – and with good cause. Sylvana did not issue idle threats and by mid-morning she had penetrated the layers of secretaries and researchers to get to the man who counted. Gilbert. It had absolutely nothing to do with him and at least he pointed that out to the enraged woman. But it made Anna look tacky.

'An-na,' Gilbert drawled, 'a word in your shell-like. Keep the old love life out of here, eh? Amusing for the staff. Not good for us when we're about to ask a cabinet minister why he isn't suing *The Times* for mentioning his adulterous behaviour. Pots and kettles, dear heart. Only needs *Private Eye* to get hold of it.'

And, of course, it did. Roberto had caught the first plane home on Sunday morning, insisting to Sylvana that he had been there at Anna's request to try to help Sophia, who was in a very depressed state. He therefore missed the damning and gleeful paragraph that appeared the following Wednesday, but almost everyone Anna knew appeared to have seen it. She thought she would die of shame. With Roberto, of all people. Oliver was aghast. Only Sophia gave her any support.

'Anna, my dear,' she asked, in a hurt voice, 'why didn't you tell me? I would have protected you. I phoned Giulio to see if you could sue. But he said, "Least said", or something like that. I feel for Sylvana, of course. And I have phoned her to say there has been a stupid mistake. But she said I would defend you as your mother, so she expected nothing less. She is a vulgar woman. And Roberto *is* an attractive man.'

Anna gasped. 'Sophia, it's not true. That's why I didn't tell you. Roberto was not in London to see me. You didn't have to phone anyone. Oh, God, what did he say?'

'Giulio? Nothing. What could he say? He said, "Anna knows where to find me. It's up to her." But then he would not be helpful. I am surprised; I thought he would be. It is just being away from them, I forget how they all distance themselves from me. But I am here for you. You must never doubt that.'

It was not that Anna any longer had doubts on that score. She was certain of it. And with Roberto back in Rome, any real hope of persuading Sophia to leave had gone. All she could do now was hope that she would find an apartment. Then, at least, they wouldn't be under the same roof.

'I am very worried, Anna,' Sophia said later, wandering into Anna's bedroom. 'Sylvana will never have him back. We must be good to him, as he has been good to me, and give him a home until he is back on his feet. I feel very responsible. You are, after all, my daughter.'

'Yes, she will.' Anna punched the pillow into a more satisfying shape and found it therapeutic. She punched it again. 'Andrea called and said there is no question of Sylvana divorcing him. He's glued to her side, contrite and making amends to the tune of several small, expensive items from Cartier. I'd be amazed if he sets foot in England again.'

'Glued to her side?' Sophia said, in an odd little voice. She sat down and stared at Anna. 'But what about my apartment?' she said. 'What about me?'

Chapter Twenty-two

'Giulio,' Carrie exclaimed. 'What are *you* doing here?'

He turned to see who was plucking at his sleeve.

'Being taken to see a play.' He grimaced and kissed her on both cheeks. 'A play I am told the whole of London wants to see, with a group of people whom I would rather not be with.'

'Business?'

He nodded, took her arm and guided her out of the crowd to stand near the wall of the foyer.

'Poor you. Escape at the interval, why don't you? Come and join me and William.'

'William?' He raised his eyebrows and scanned the crowd for Carrie's boss. 'Is he here?'

Carrie suddenly found it necessary to fiddle with the strap on her bag. 'Why, yes,' she said, looking vaguely around. 'He had a couple of tickets and knew I hadn't seen it, so he suggested I came with him. That's all. Nothing else. I mean, what could there be?'

'Two nice people having a night out together?' he suggested mildly. 'How's Euan?'

'Anna's got him for the night,' she said. She was pleased that he hadn't teased her about dating her boss, over which she had agonized. She had only agreed to go after a robust push from Anna . . .

'I can't get a babysitter,' Carrie had said.

'Yes, you can.' Anna had refused to let her off the hook. 'I'll do it.'

271

'You can't leave Sophia.'

'I don't have to. I'll have Euan here. And it might do Sophia good to see I have a life – and that includes Euan.'

'What about Oliver?' Carrie asked. 'He might object. You know what Euan's like. He'll expect to sleep in your bed.'

Anna winced. 'Oliver doesn't sleep here any more. I go to his flat and trail home again like a bloody teenager so that Sophia doesn't feel alarmed at being in the house on her own. Believe me, the only male in my bed on Friday night will be Euan. Now, go for it, you twit. He sounds terrific.'

Carrie groaned. 'I'm afraid he is,' she said. 'That's the problem.'

'I wish I had your problems,' Anna said. 'For heaven's sake, he's asked you to see a play, not get married. And I'll be very disappointed if I see you here before Saturday afternoon . . .'

As a doting mother Carrie was delighted when anyone asked after her son and, now, it had given her the chance to mention Anna. 'I expect he'll keep her awake half the night,' she said ruefully, when Giulio grunted. 'On the other hand there is the possibility, a very strong one, in fact, that he might succeed where everyone else has failed to drive Sophia back to Rome.'

'Still hanging on, is she?'

Carrie rolled her eyes. 'Tell me about it. Anna suggested she went back to Rome and then in the spring she'd go over to see her and help her find something smaller there.'

'Why can't Andrea?'

'No idea. Sophia said it was something about him not understanding and then she said setting up the Chicago office was taking longer than they all thought, then she started crying, so Anna said they'd talk about it another time. Frankly, Giulio, Anna could do with some ingenious ideas.'

He gave a faint smile. 'Don't tell her you told me that.'

'Why not? It's true. Someone's got to help.'

'Ah, there's William.' He turned and smiled as his friend's beanpole figure pushed its way through the crowd. 'And you're right. Someone's got to, but it can't be me.'

'Don't be silly. Why ever not? You know the whole Grescobaldi set-up better than anyone.'

He turned and gave her a wry smile. 'Because I know Anna too. I'm the last person she'll take help from over this. William,' he held out his hand as William joined them, clutching two programmes, 'you take too many risks. I would not leave someone like this alone with someone like me. Just be grateful I'm fond of you.'

'You really do overrate your charms,' William said. He gave Giulio a withering look. 'And I'm not going to suggest you join us for dinner because it's been a hell of a day – hasn't it, Carrie? – and you might just try to prove me wrong.'

All three moved towards the stairs that led down to the stalls, making vague plans to have dinner another time. As William greeted a couple he recognized, Giulio touched Carrie's arm. 'Tell me, why doesn't Oliver help her?'

Carrie groaned. 'Poor Oliver. He's so nice but unfortunately he loathes Sophia and all his suggestions seem utterly heartless to Anna.'

'Like what?'

'Like pack her bags, change the locks, move while she's out. Shoot her. Want me to go on?'

He laughed. 'Carrie, this is an odd question, but what was Anna's mother like? Her adoptive mother?'

'Barbara?' Carrie looked at him. 'Anna adored her.'

'That's not really what I asked,' he said. 'That's what Anna thought of her. What about you?'

Carrie frowned. 'Me? Well, I liked her. Yes,' she nodded, having never given it much thought. 'I did. She didn't say much when she came up to see Anna when we were at university. It wasn't often, maybe just once a term. She was friendly but quite shy, I think. Anna always said they never stopped talking once they were on their own. I suppose, like the students we were, we had no social graces and Barbara wasn't one to intrude unasked. Not like my mother.' Carrie gave a mock shiver. 'She plonked herself down in our disgusting kitchen and *inquired*.' She gave the word a great deal of stress. 'But Barbara seemed quite content just to go off for lunch with Anna and then she'd get the train home.'

'What about her father?'

'Never saw him during term-time – but, then, I never saw my father at all, or only when his latest marriage or girlfriend left him room to remember he had a daughter,' she said drily. 'I only met Colin when I went to stay with Anna during vacations.'

Giulio looked thoughtful. 'And what about him?'

'I got to know him better after Barbara died. He came to Anna's a lot. Not that he wanted to be there all the time, you could tell. It was just Anna. She couldn't bear to think of him on his own. I think that's why she was so shocked when he married so soon after Barbara died. She thought it was sheer loneliness and that somehow, because she was so griefstricken herself, she'd neglected him. But they were a nice family,' Carrie said, giving Giulio a level look. 'Look, Giulio, if you're trying to imply Anna's looking for a mother figure, you couldn't be more wrong. She's thirty-one, for God's sake.'

'I've never thought that. Or,' he said, as she began to interrupt, 'a father figure or any other kind of figure. In fact, you've been very helpful. I mustn't keep you.' He nodded to where William was already at the door of the stalls looking around for her.

'Well,' Carrie looked doubtfully at him, 'I can't think how. But I'll tell you this, Barbara made Anna what she is, not a set of dodgy genes from the bloody Grescobaldis.'

'I can see that,' he said. 'Here,' he pulled her to him and whispered in her ear, 'look at William's face. Tell him I was trying to run off with you. I like to keep him on his toes.'

'I will.' She laughed back. But to herself she decided she had a more interesting position in mind for William than on his toes but she didn't know Giulio nearly well enough to let him in on it. She waved and took the hand William was holding out.

As Anna tried not to be swallowed up by her mother's demands, there was no avoiding the fact that the once charming requests were now sounding like complaints. Her phone at the office rang constantly, with Sophia needing more and more attention. For several days in a row Anna was late for work because her mother claimed she couldn't work the remote control or the microwave. Seeing Anna standing in the kitchen, downing a cup of coffee, coat on, one eye on the news was no deterrent to her catalogue of woes. Even the language, Sophia announced, was baffling. 'How you can live here for so long?' she exclaimed. 'How do you know what they're saying? They do not speak like this in Harrods. Is it English? That woman at that dreadful little shop you say have magazines – and they don't – does not understand a word I say.'

Anna plonked her bag on the table, crossed her arms and leaned on the edge. 'Sophia,' she said, lifting her head, 'Mrs Singh speaks perfect English. In fact, considering her natural language is Punjabi, she is quite brilliant in her native tongue of Urdu, and Bengali, and for all I know she's a dab hand at Sindhi too, which are all languages that are used in this area. There isn't a huge call for Italian. Could it be that in her presence, for some reason, your English becomes – how shall I say this? – less fluent? And she does sell magazines. The ones people around here would buy. Sad to relate,' she picked up her bag and set off for the door, 'that tends not to include Italian *Vogue*. Now, can I get you anything else before I go?'

Tears rolled down Sophia's face. Anna's shoulders sagged. 'Sophia, look . . .' she began.

Sophia held up a restraining hand and lowered herself

into a chair. 'No. No,' she said. 'You must go. I just feel so unwell and last night I dream of Lorenzo and that always upsets me.'

Anna closed her eyes in despair. It was what they were all forgetting, that Sophia had been widowed a very short time. Grief was a terrible thing. 'Sophia, I'm sorry,' she said, coming back into the kitchen. 'I shouldn't have spoken like that. I didn't get much sleep last night either. Look,' she bent down and squeezed Sophia's hands, 'I'll get you a cup of coffee and I'll call you later from the office. Maybe tonight, if I'm not too late, we can go over to Mancetti's for a quick supper.'

Sophia blew her nose. 'Maybe. I will let you know but I cannot eat now after eight. It keeps me awake.'

Anna didn't mention that getting back before eight was almost impossible – she dreaded the heavy air of sorrow that greeted any such pronouncement. Neither did she add that there was a greater dread in her life, which was Gilbert.

While *Newsbeat* made it on to the air on time and the items reflected the news and even anticipated it, her work was undoubtedly suffering. She began to cut corners. Twice she had to rely on packages regarded for emergency use only, when nothing could warrant their inclusion except that the programme's editor was hopelessly distracted by her domestic confusion.

'Keeping you up, are we?' Gilbert asked, amiably enough, at the morning conference. The youngest researcher, who had high hopes of a job on Anna's team and couldn't bear the gleeful looks being exchanged by the presenters, who only felt secure when blame was being laid squarely at some-one else's door, nudged her.

'What?' Anna jumped. All eyes were on her.

'The German Chancellor,' muttered the researcher, her head well down.

'I know,' Anna lied gratefully. 'I was just trying to, er,' she swallowed hard, 'decide if we couldn't get someone to shadow his wife while he's here. She's certainly very glamorous. Lighten up the end slot. And you, Bridget,' she stared out the presenter who didn't much like her and had smirked at Gilbert when she thought Anna was for it, 'I wonder if you would feel more comfortable with leaving the political stuff to Sean.'

It was a cheap shot but she didn't feel generous. Bridget, round-eyed with indignation, started to protest.

'Good idea,' Gilbert agreed. He waved Bridget aside. He was as relieved as Anna that she had rescued him from his need to rethink her. 'Bridget, that's not sexist at all,' he went on. 'But I'm sure Anna will be happy to consider giving Sean the interview with Joe Fiennes if you think that's sexist too. No? Good.'

Anna studied her notes, automatically running through the schedule for that night. By the skin of your wits, my girl, she told herself, as they filed out. And a very thin skin it's becoming.

'How's Oliver?' Gilbert asked, throwing an arm casually around her shoulders as they walked back up the corridor. 'Must be up to his eyes in it. Getting the CBI account. Clever lad. Congratulate him for me, won't you?'

'Of course,' she said, turning into her own office. Congratulate him? It was the first she'd heard of it.

By the time her father rang to ask if she was ever going to visit again, Anna had failed three times to reach Oliver and had just put down the phone on Sophia.

'I thought you might have forgotten you were going to let us know about Christmas.'

Of course she had. Nor had it escaped Anna's notice that her father had taken to ringing her at work.

'I was going to ring you tonight,' she lied. 'I don't know yet, Dad. I've got to fix for Sophia to get home, and work and stuff. Is it urgent I let you know? And why don't you and Meryl come down here?' She could hear her voice rising.

'Well, that's certainly an idea for next year. But you know Fenella's almost due and we can't be too far away.'

'Why not?' she cried. 'She's got a family of her own, hasn't she? Oh, for God's sake, Dad,' she shouted, 'can't you get away from them all and just come to London to see me? Why does it always have to be me going there? Why do I have to do all the running?'

Sophia's encounter with Dottie would have been comical if they could only have understood each other and if Anna had been less tired. Anna arrived home to find Dottie standing bewildered outside her gate while Sophia's voice could be heard screaming in furious Italian from somewhere inside.

'What's wrong?' Anna cried, dropping her bag and pushing past Dottie.

'I don't know, dear,' Dottie said unhappily. 'I was looking for Mister. He hasn't been home and I've got a nice piece of whiting for him – with the head off because he won't eat the head and it's such a waste. But, like I always do on Tuesday – it is Tuesday, isn't it, dear? – I got some and that lady staying with you just started screaming. Like she is now. Just listen. I bet you can hear her clear across the high street.'

'Sophia,' Anna shouted, colliding with her mother in the hallway. She tried to grab her arms to get her attention. 'What's the matter? It's only Dottie looking for her cat. What *is* it?'

'Cat? What cat? She say I have her husband in here.' Sophia's breath was coming in furious little gasps. 'I tell her to look for her Mr Whatever-his-name-is wherever she likes. And I tell her in Italian too because she is clearly very stupid and very mean. Me? *Una vedova*, and I who know no one here. To suggest such a thing. You,' she snapped at the shaken Dottie. 'Search my bedroom. You will see. I have nothing to hide. *Niente.*'

'Wait, Dottie, just wait,' Anna called over her shoulder. 'Sit down, Sophia. Sit down at once. She's looking for her cat. Her *cat*, Sophia. His name is Mister. Do you under-

278

stand? There's been a mistake, that's all. Poor Dottie would never think such a thing, let alone accuse you of it. OK?'

'You take her side?' Sophia cried, appalled. 'Against me? She should be in a home. She is crazy.' She flicked the back of her fingers against her forehead. 'That is what I think of her.'

'She's not crazy,' Anna retorted, forcing Sophia into a chair. 'Stay there. I'll be back in a minute.'

An interested little knot of people had now gathered behind Dottie, drawn by the noise and the possibility of witnessing a fight. Mister was in his usual place tucked under Dottie's arm.

'All over now, Dottie.' Anna spoke cheerfully, guiding her to the gate. 'Did you want to see me, Mrs Mulvaney?' Anna directed her question at the nearest face in the six-strong group of neighbours. 'No? Gosh, you must be cold with just those slippers on and the pavement so damp. Now, Dottie, let's have you.'

'Who is she, dear?' Dottie asked, as the disappointed audience melted away. 'She kept going on and on about her son suing me. She won't do that, will she, dear?'

'What? Andrea? Your biggest fan?'

Dottie stopped and stared at Anna perplexed. 'What? That nice boy? That's his mother? But you said he's your brother. What's she to you, then?'

'My mother. But it's a long story.'

'But you had a lovely mum, dear,' Dottie said, visibly confused. 'And you've got that lady in Scotland – and now this one too.'

Anna closed her eyes. 'Don't worry, Dottie, I don't collect them. It's like this . . .'

'Who would have thought it?' Dottie exclaimed, as Anna rose to go, having made her a cup of tea and stayed until she was calm and her world of small routines had been restored.

'Got a right temper she has, dear. I couldn't get up your

279

stairs even if I wanted to, although Gawd knows what Mister would be doing up there. He only ever goes into your hallway. Is she a bit,' Dottie tapped her head, 'a bit, you know?'

'Don't worry, Dottie. Her husband died in the summer. She's not coping terribly well.'

Dottie looked at her doubtfully, and said, 'Well, if it's all right with you, dear, I'll wait until she's gone and then I'll pop round. When's she going?'

'Soon, Dottie. I'll let you know. Just knock, like you always do, if you want anything.'

Frazzled already from a day that had not gone well, Anna had to raise her voice to get Sophia's attention, but Sophia was too upset at what she had thought was an attack on her virtue to see the joke.

'Sophia. Dottie is old and infirm,' Anna tried, one last time. 'She could not have got up those stairs. And Mister's blind.'

'Not so blind he can't find his way in here, and she gets up the stairs in her own house,' Sophia pointed out angrily.

Anna looked at the clock. It was nine and she had not stopped since seven that morning. 'Who knows what Dottie can manage any more? Now, let's think about supper.'

Alone with Anna, and hearing that nothing was planned, Sophia said she would go to bed. Dottie had exhausted her. Anna felt guilty but when she had relayed the whole story to Eamonn who had dropped by and couldn't stop laughing when he heard what the commotion had been about, she started to feel better. In fact so much so that she was imagining Oliver's face and his delight in the account when Irena phoned to say that her affair with Roberto was *finita* on account of Sylvana's close attention to his whereabouts. She, too, thought it was hilarious.

'I must tell Giulio. He's here. And we are all at the same dinner tonight. Very boring. Didn't he tell you he was

280

coming over? No wonder he gets nowhere with you if he can't even remember to tell you he's left the country.'

Sophia left Anna to organize everything and stayed longer and longer in bed. Sometimes when Anna arrived home she hadn't even got out of her dressing-gown. Her conversation centred on the people she had met when Lorenzo was alive and the places they went, yet none of these people seemed to be in contact with her any more than they had when Anna was in Trastevere. Anna was in despair. Andrea was being pitifully useless. He would, he said, at the very least, collect her to take her back to Rome by Christmas. Two weeks away. 'But don't mention an actual date,' he warned her. 'She hates it if she thinks I am organizing her.'

'I can't believe that,' Anna said. 'She absolutely insists that I arrange everything.'

'But you're different,' he said. 'You're her daughter. It's what daughters do.'

Anna gasped. 'I am not that kind of daughter. If it were my real mother, you might be right. But, then, my mother never needed organizing. If anything,' she said bleakly, 'she was the one who organized me.'

It was Carrie who said what Anna had been guiltily thinking: 'She's not your problem.' A week later, they were sitting on a bench in the play area of the local park in a temperature that had kept all but the most desperate indoors. Around them a handful of yawning parents, bent on keeping their offspring distracted, sat hunched on the other benches or stamped their feet on the hard concrete in the uninspiring surroundings.

Carrie, too, was fed up with Anna. She glanced sideways at her friend, slumped beside her. The wind was pushing her hair in every direction as she dug her chin into the warm folds of a shawl wrapped round her neck.

In front of them, bundled into a blue bomber jacket, on which the words *Space Hero* were emblazoned in red, and a pair of sturdy corduroy jeans, Euan crouched in the sandpit, piling as much sand into a plastic carton as his chubby hands could manage. 'Euan, no.' Carrie started up from the bench. Euan hastily poured the fistful he had earmarked for his pocket into another tub and turned his back. Carrie sat down again.

'This suits Andrea,' she said, picking up where she had left off. 'He can have a life with Stefano without Mamma finding out. Tell him, why don't you? Tell him the date you want him here, not the one that suits him. For heaven's sake, Anna, he's copped the lot – the money, the business, freedom.'

'But I don't want any money,' she began.

'One day,' Carrie said threateningly, 'your limbs will be found in three counties and no jury would ever indict me. Stop being such a bloody doormat. You don't want Sophia either but you've got her. You owe her nothing. You've done your bit. Look, Anna, if you don't, I'm going to tell Giulio to ring Andrea. Oh, shut up. I don't care what the scene is between you two but this is not helping anyone. Least of all you and Oliver.'

'OK, OK,' Anna cried, pressing her hands over her ears. 'I'll call Andrea. And I'll make it up to Oliver. But promise me you won't tell Giulio? Anyone but him.'

Carrie rolled her eyes heavenwards. 'Oh, for God's sake,' she muttered. 'He says you won't accept any help from him and you—'

'When did he say that?' Anna demanded, turning towards her. 'When?'

'I see him a lot,' Carrie reminded her. 'I don't remember. At the theatre, I think. What does it matter when he said it? And there's no one better to do it. But you just snarl "over my dead body". Well, if you want my view, I think Sophia needs help. Hasn't it ever occurred to you that she might be unhinged?'

'Yes,' Anna said. 'It has. But that's what grief does to some people. I'm afraid if she goes back to Rome she *will* go mad. At least I'm stopping her falling apart completely.'

'And,' Carrie stood up, preparing to go, 'as a matter of interest, who's stopping you from doing just that?'

Chapter Twenty-three

When he had sneezed for the fifth time and his voice had almost gone, Giulio gave in and went home. Jodie fussed around him, urging him not to appear the next day for fear that his virus might turn into full-scale flu. Jodie liked Giulio as a boss but it had to be said that her concern on this occasion was for herself. So near Christmas too. 'It's going around,' she said, locking his briefcase, 'and I don't want to get it. The whole of Accounts are down with it and I wouldn't be surprised if you're off for the rest of the week. Now, leave those.' She eased a pile of documents from his arms and put them firmly back on the desk. 'You won't feel like doing anything. Maggie?' She called through the communicating doors to the outer office, bringing her assistant in. 'Take this down to the lobby and tell Joe to have someone bring Giulio's car round,' she said, handing her the briefcase. 'And call these people. Cancel the first two meetings and tell this lot I'll rearrange in the morning. Now, let me see if there's anything else.'

It said volumes for his state of health that Giulio gave in meekly. He grinned sheepishly at Maggie, who went pink. She wished he wouldn't do it, because she had quite strong fantasies about him and sometimes it worried her that he might in some quite mysterious way discover this and take advantage. She rather wished he would, but he was boringly strict about that kind of thing in the office. 'Maybe you're right,' he agreed. 'I'll call you in the morning. And, Jodie?'

'Yes?' She looked up from tidying his desk.

'A favour? Are you Christmas shopping tomorrow? Might as well if I'm not here. Would you get me this? I had to write it down or I wouldn't have remembered.' He reached into his wallet and extracted a slip of paper.

Jodie took it and read it aloud. 'Intergalactic space invader with retractable wings.' She looked up. 'Sorry? Who's this for?'

'Euan Hunt, a young friend of mine. Well, since last Saturday, he's been my best friend and assures me that this will guarantee his mother has a lie-in on Saturday mornings.'

'Really?' Jodie said. 'How kind you are.'

'Not at all.' He smiled back. 'His mother has been very useful and very kind to me too.'

I bet she has, Jodie thought, as he disappeared towards the lifts. She crossed to the long sash-window of his office and peered down, waiting to see him emerge into the street and disappear in the gathering gloom of the afternoon, towards the black Jaguar that had pulled up outside.

After a couple of minutes she watched as Joe got out of the driver's seat and Giulio slipped behind the wheel. The tail-lights winked and she saw him move into the stream of traffic.

Jodie was loyal and, after ten years, she had demonstrated her loyalty in many ways. She prided herself on knowing who stood where with Giulio Farrini. On this occasion, he had stumped her. After Victoria, his girlfriends and affairs had been short-lived and unaccompanied by domestic arrangements for children.

'Well.' Maggie reappeared, with all the suppressed excitement of one with the power that comes only from knowing a worthy piece of gossip.

'Well, what?'

'Carrie Hunt,' Maggie squealed. 'That's who it is.'

'Who is what?' Jodie carried on flicking through a report she was compiling.

'Over at William Morgan's,' she said impatiently. 'That girl he got the job for. Of course it is.'

'And if it is,' Jodie said, looking over her glasses, 'it is none of our business. Now, have you made those phone calls?'

It would be all over the building by the morning, Jodie sighed. And to think she had speculated so pointlessly about Anna Minstrel. He'd gone to Rome for her. It just went to show, she thought.

By the time he reached home, Giulio was well on the way to flu. His limbs ached, his head felt like cotton wool, all of it compounded by the angry frustration that had gripped him by what was happening in Anna Minstrel's life. Carrie was right. On Saturday he had phoned Carrie, gone to see her and missed Anna by minutes. He wasn't sure now why he'd gone because they hadn't solved anything. He just wanted to talk to someone who knew her well and Carrie was that person. Of course, Oliver Manners should have been his quarry but even Carrie agreed with him that Oliver knew an Anna who suited him, not the real one.

'I'll ring her,' he said, as he left. 'I will. You're right. She's living with a maniac.'

And he *would* ring her. He had intended to that day, but a man with a streaming cold, raging sore throat, craving a whole bottle of brandy was in no shape to deal with anyone, let alone a crazed woman who had nearly destroyed one family and was close to doing the same with her misguided, frustratingly obstinate daughter, who had haunted him for months.

Anna came home late on Thursday evening. Sophia or no Sophia, she had Christmas cards and presents to buy, and there was only a week to go. Why, she thought savagely, walking along the wet pavement from the tube to Braverton Street, laden with carrier-bags, does everyone have to have a decision about Christmas Day? Why does Oliver have to tell his mother right now? What difference would it make to Dad and Meryl if I'm there or not? As long as bloody

Athol and bloody Fenella and the kids are creating havoc, isn't that enough for them? I just want to be left alone. And then she paused, causing a mini-jam on the pavement, because it hit her quite forcefully right there, outside a row of shops, their windows glistening with Christmas lights and messages wishing their customers seasons greetings, that she would be alone at Christmas with Sophia: no one would have her if it meant Sophia being there too.

Dear God. She would call Andrea. She would insist. She couldn't let it go on. Panic hit her and she began to run, scanning the crawling traffic for a taxi.

There was none to be had, so she half ran, half walked until she rounded the corner of her street and saw Eamonn waiting on the pavement.

'Your bloody mother, or whatever she calls herself,' he roared, advancing towards her, 'I've got to see my area manager first thing in the morning because someone tipped them off that I give shelter to some poor sods who can't help themselves.'

'Oh, my God, Eamonn. How do you know it was her? How would she know who to ring?'

'For Christ's sake, who else round here would care? And – and this is the worst bit.'

'Dear God.' Anna's bags slid to the ground. 'Not more?'

'I'll say there's bloody more,' Eamonn fumed. 'She phoned social services and told them Dottie was unable to look after herself. She must have done it days ago – just because Dottie banged on the wall to see if you were in. They were round here asking her all sorts of questions and suggesting a home. She's in a right old state. They've even contacted that awful son of hers who can't wait to get his hands on the house. He's apparently backing their move to get her into a home. She's a bloody disgrace. Oh, don't look like that, you know she is.'

And she did.

Inside the house, Sophia was sitting in front of the television. She looked round with a huge smile as Anna came in. 'Darling,' she extended a hand, 'where have you been? So quiet without you.'

Anna pushed her bags into the kitchen and removed her coat. 'Sophia,' she began, not caring that Eamonn had walked in after her, 'I have to talk to you. Please turn the television off and listen to me.'

When Anna had finished, Sophia burst into tears. It was Anna's fault, she said. Anna had upset her so much with the idea of Dottie having no one and relying on Anna. Everyone was so heartless to lonely people. And as for Eamonn, he deserved to be found out. How could she live next door to so many dreadful people?

Eamonn began to shout back. He even took a few steps towards her, his fury spilling over at the prospect of no job. Of course he had broken the rules and in Braverton Street no one had ever got even that close – he held up a finger and thumb – to splitting on him until *she* came there. It was too much for Sophia who shrieked back, thankfully in Italian, that he was a disgusting pervert, just as Oliver arrived from a meeting that had not gone particularly well.

'She's your mother,' he said coldly, as Anna tried to make him stay. 'And don't we all know it.'

Twice the next day Anna was called from meetings to deal with Sophia's problems. Gilbert asked to speak to her. It was blunt, hurtful, but Anna knew she deserved it. He didn't want to let her go but the programme was suffering, morale was low and people were talking.

Anna nodded silently. 'I know,' she said. She couldn't argue. 'I'll sort it out. Promise.'

'Anna? Please just listen. You look like shit. Sorry, but someone's got to tell you.'

'And feel it,' she muttered, closing the door. She rang Sophia and said she wasn't to call her at work. At the very most she could leave a message but she must not insist that Anna was dragged from a meeting.

'Meetings, meetings.' Sophia gave a brittle laugh. 'You

sound just like your father. He was always too busy to speak to me. No one has time for me. No one. They never did. And why? I tell you—'

'Sophia,' Anna broke in desperately, 'please let me call you later.'

The receiver crashed into the cradle at Braverton Street.

That Sophia needed counselling was no longer an issue. A suspicion that had taken root began to flourish in Anna, not least because Sophia's greatest complaint against Lorenzo was that he would not take work seriously. If it hadn't been for her and Roberto, she claimed, the business would have been only a fraction the success it was today. Sophia's mood swings frightened Anna. There was something so chaotic about them that even the explanation of grief was hard to attach to the euphoric highs followed by plunges into immeasurable gloom laced with vitriol. It was as though Sophia was venting her rage on someone far away. If Anna was terminally exhausted, Sophia was permanently enraged. Even when she was smiling.

'Well, you know,' John Rinker explained, when Anna phoned him covertly, during the lunch break, 'anger is a sign of grief. Try not to worry too much. Take her out a bit more. Get people in. Listen to her.'

Anna wondered why she bothered. John Rinker was her tame psychologist, the one she brought in when she needed the credibility of science to lend weight to discussions on the peculiar behaviour of public figures caught doing something they shouldn't. Clearly he needed the benefit of cameras and sound to trigger reality into his soundbite psychology.

She felt someone watching her. Bridget Corman, clutching a polythene bag which held her on-screen jackets, was staring at her as she passed by her desk.

Anna discovered her fist was clenched. She stretched her fingers. 'Cramp,' she mouthed. 'Sorry, John, you were saying?'

'I'll willingly see her,' he said, suddenly remembering

who was responsible for his continuing fame. 'Thing is, Anna, she has to be willing too. And how do you get someone to come and see me if they don't want to? How about your GP? Start there. You know, it might just be a case of some anti-depressants.'

Who for? Anna asked inwardly. Aloud she said, 'Thanks, John. I'll give it a try.' She couldn't remember when she had last braved the local surgery, couldn't see Sophia there either. Someone would have to come to her.

She called Oliver and asked him if his private doctor could be drafted in to help. 'I know, I know,' she almost pleaded. 'But if I can get her to a doctor he might persuade her to see a shrink. Oliver, I swear she just needs someone to talk to.'

'Yes,' he said bluntly. 'Andrea. Get the little bastard here and get her out. I tell you, Anna, I've had enough.'

'Sorry, Oliver,' she said wearily. 'Sorry, sorry, sorry. I shouldn't have asked. I'll call you later.'

'Anna,' he began. 'Anna, don't – Anna?'

But she was gone.

Next morning, Sophia was up before Anna left for work, full of apologies and begging her forgiveness. Too weary for another scene, Anna said they would talk about it when she got home. Sophia looked blankly at her. 'About what?'

'About all of this,' Anna said. 'We must sort you out, Sophia. You're very depressed still, and no wonder, so I thought maybe it might help if you talked to my doctor. He can perhaps move things on a bit.'

'Yes.' Sophia smiled, holding out both her hands. 'That's what we will do. We will sell this little house and buy something bigger. Move on. I knew you would realize that's what we must do. And I,' she clasped her hands to her chest, 'am not one to impose. But this is exactly what we must do. And then I can stay with you in London. A new start and I won't need anybody.'

Anna put down her case. 'No, Sophia, I didn't mean that. I meant for you to get help for your perfectly understandable depression and then go back to Rome. It's where you belong.'

Sophia paused, and the smile started to leave her face. 'Rome?' she said blankly. 'Why Rome? I don't belong there. They all hate me.'

Anna pulled out a chair and sat down. 'They don't, Sophia. And there are other people there besides the Grescobaldis. You must go back where you belong, where you will feel more at home. You are not at home here, I can see that. And I have no way – no means – to make it different. I have to work. You need company.'

Sophia had not taken her eyes from Anna's face. 'What you mean,' she said, in a perfectly ordinary voice, 'is that you don't want me with you either.'

'No.' Anna shook her head. 'I meant it's really nice having you to stay but you need to be more settled. You need to be near Andrea, all the people you know best. Come and visit any time but we can't live together and this visit must end some time. Besides, what about Oliver? We'll be getting married soon so I would be living with him.'

'Married?' Sophia said, in a strange voice. 'To a man who talks to you that way? Like he did the other night. About me? Your father would turn in his grave at the thought.'

Anna stood very still. 'Sophia,' she began, striving for calm, 'that isn't the point. Look at my father. No, not Lorenzo, Sophia. *My* father. *He* started again, and you're a very beautiful woman.'

'So?' Sophia asked, as though there could be no doubt of that.

'And you might meet someone else,' Anna finished carefully.

Sophia gave a shrill laugh and picked up her makeup bag. 'Your father?' She rummaged in the bag and produced a lipstick. 'What do you know of him? Leaving me to creep off to that slut.' She drew the lipstick over her mouth, sucked hard and inspected herself in the small compact.

Against the light from the television screen, on which a team of fat women were being taken through an exercise routine by an ageing actress with a video to promote, Sophia's face looked ghostly. The livid red streak against her white face looked unreal. 'It will be many years before I learn to live without him. Go,' she flapped her hand at Anna, 'leave me. I will decide. I thought you, of all people, would understand about rejection. About a need to belong.'

Anna glanced at the clock. She could not risk being late again. She put down her case and went to the phone. The local surgery said that one of the doctors would see her at six, with or without Sophia. When she got back Sophia seemed much calmer and said she was going to make some plans. Anna was relieved. 'Oh, good. Do some shopping . . .'

'Shopping?' There was an odd smile on Sophia's face. 'That's what you think I am good for, is it? It's what your father used to say. "Go shopping, Sophia. Buy something, Sophia." Anything to stop me asking too many questions. Andrea doesn't want me. He never wanted me. He just wants that disgusting little faggot Stefano.' To Anna's horror, she spat on the floor.

'Sophia, please,' she begged. 'Andrea didn't want to upset you . . .'

'And Roberto. He made so many promises . . . so many and . . .' She brushed an angry hand across her face.

'Sophia?' Anna asked sharply. 'What about Roberto? What about him?'

'He's nothing. Like all the rest.'

Anna couldn't get her attention.

'None of it was true, was it?' Sophia turned, her voice soft and accusing. 'You have always resented me. Is this the way you wanted to get your revenge? I thought you had forgiven me. You're all the same. Blame, blame, blame. Lorenzo blamed me for being pregnant. Loretta blamed me for not keeping you. You. All this because I did not have you aborted. All this because I had to carry you inside me and now it comes to this. But yours is the worst revenge because I believed you. I believed I had found someone who would care for me. Someone who came from the gutter as I did.'

As she said it she pointed to some imaginary gutter, her hand sweeping in a savage arc sending the chair behind her flying. Anna reached out instinctively to grab it but Sophia was there before her, wrenching it from her hand. She glared at it then smacked it down on the floor and then looked at Anna. Anna sat down, unable to take her eyes off Sophia, who was standing with one hand on her hip, the other twisting and pulling her hair off her face. 'But look at us,' she said. 'Look at what I achieved. Look at this.' She wrenched the huge square solitaire off her hand and held it out.

They both gazed at it.

'Sophia,' Anna's mouth was dry, 'please sit down. Let me get you some coffee.'

To her relief Sophia did as she was told, temporarily distracted by the glinting diamond she was carefully polishing on her sleeve. Slowly, Anna moved around her and grabbed the coffee jug. 'Here,' she said, 'drink this. And then I think you should go and lie down for a bit.'

Sophia looked at her as though she was seeing her for the first time. 'Yes,' she said, in a surprisingly normal tone. 'Yes. I was shouting, wasn't I? I would like to sleep. I need to be alone. I need to think.'

Anna didn't want to leave her, but she knew another missed meeting would mean the end of her job.

She left Sophia in bed, already drifting off to sleep. 'I'll call you from the office. I'll come home early,' she said desperately. 'I won't be long.'

Just the meeting, Anna thought feverishly, as she ran from the house. I can get back to check on her and then be back in time for the run-through. It wasn't good, but it was better than leaving Sophia all day to feed such misery.

After the meeting she rang home. Sophia sounded distant but normal. Then Anna rang Andrea. He was in a meeting.

Anna whispered fiercely down the phone to a secretary that she was too. He must ring her urgently. Before she left the office she was told that Sophia had phoned an hour earlier but, mindful of Anna's recent instructions, they had not interrupted her meeting.

Anna groaned. 'Ring her for me. Tell her I'll be there in about forty minutes. I'm out of the door now. Anyone can get me on my mobile. Gilbert,' she collided with him, 'I'm so sorry. I promise this is not going to go on. I'll be back before you know it.'

As soon as she put her key in the lock Anna knew that something was wrong. There was no blaring television. The house was tidy, just as she'd left it. She walked into the kitchen and found a note on the table from Sophia. She read it briefly, already mounting the stairs as she went. She let it drop to the floor as she reached the top. 'Sophia,' she called. 'Sophia? Where are you?'

The bedroom door was half open and she glanced in as she raced past. It was empty. She ran through the spare room to the doors that led to the roof.

'Dear God, no,' she prayed. 'Not that.'

They were open, swinging slowly on their hinges as the wind pushed them backwards, giving a dull crack each time they hit the wall behind and swung out again.

Chapter Twenty-four

'Has she said anything?' The young doctor walked to the entrance of the intensive care unit with Sister Caldwell, who had been its custodian for the past five years at South West General. 'She does know, I take it?' He nodded towards a seat at the end of the corridor where Anna was sitting, just staring straight ahead. Sister Caldwell followed his gaze. 'She's been told.' She glanced at Anna's rigid form. 'It may not have sunk in. Said her mother was depressed but . . .'

'. . . never expected this,' he finished with her. 'Do I need to see her?'

Sister Caldwell frowned. 'Maybe a quick word as you go past. I just wish someone would get here. The police said they'd wait to talk to her then.'

The doctor glanced at his watch. 'I'll try. Christ, is that the time? I was hoping to be away by eight. Could have done without a suicide. Dinner,' he explained. 'Girlfriend's birthday. I'll be lucky if I make it for breakfast.'

Sister Caldwell rolled her eyes. 'Oh, all right,' she grumbled. 'I'll see to her. I, of course, am not allowed a social life.'

The corridor in which Anna was sitting was punctuated with side rooms along its length until it ended in double doors with porthole windows leading to the strictly out-of-bounds intensive care unit. It was here that Sophia had been brought after the nightmare race to get her into Re-sus, who had done what they could for the damage twenty-four sleeping pills had done to her. Everyone knew it was pointless.

Sister Caldwell bent over Anna, her hand on her shoulder. 'Would you like someone to get you another cup?'

Anna peered up at her out of the collar of her coat, which was turned up in a shield around her face.

'Tea,' Sister Caldwell repeated, touching the styrofoam cup clutched in Anna's grasp. 'A nice cup of tea? That one looks cold to me.'

It was said gently enough, kindly, even, but she was already signalling with one hand to a more junior nurse that she would be with her in seconds.

At the other end of the corridor Anna could see the two policemen and the WPC who had brought her in talking to a nurse, leaning across the counter of a glass-fronted office, holding their helmets under their arms. They looked away as Anna glanced in their direction. 'No,' Anna said, turning back to Sister Caldwell. 'No, thank you. You're busy. I'm fine. Someone will be here soon.'

Sister Caldwell hesitated. She crouched down so that she was level with Anna's shocked eyes and closed her hand over Anna's, which was screwed up into a tight fist.

'There's no change, is there?' Anna was looking away from her. It was more a statement than a question but, nevertheless, Sister Caldwell detected that she was still clinging to hope.

There was a brief pause. Anna turned and looked directly at her. 'There isn't going to be, is there?' Her tone was blunt, demanding no false hope. 'No.' She turned away, answering her own question. 'No, of course there isn't. I'm sorry. I don't know what I'm saying. How long?'

Poor cow, thought Sister Caldwell. No matter how convinced you were they knew the score, they always went on thinking they might have misheard.

'I'm so sorry,' she said. 'Any time. Maybe a few hours. The damage to her liver is too great. Look, at least come and sit somewhere that's comfortable,' she coaxed. 'As soon as anyone arrives we'll let you know.'

Anna followed her gaze to the other end of the corridor past a muddle of equipment and trolleys, where an elderly man was being pushed in a wheelchair back to his ward, clutching a set of X-rays to his chest. All around him visitors, armed with flowers and magazines, on their way to other wards, stared idly as he went past.

At the far end, Anna knew, was the door to the small room to which Sister Caldwell wanted to take her.

'No.' Anna spoke quickly. 'No, not there.' In there, she knew, there were two green-leather armchairs pushed either side of a small table and nothing to look at except cream walls, nothing to protect her from her own memories. She knew that room. It was where they put shocked people, those who had lost loved ones, or those who waited in terror for someone to tell them there was hope when in their hearts they knew there was none. It was where they had put her father, in that very room, just off this very corridor, while he waited for her to get there. Anna did not want to sit in there with a cup of tea, untouched and cold, on the table in front of her and listen to an awful silence that she knew would rise up, engulf her and solve nothing. Being alone was not what she wanted. At least here, in this care-worn corridor, on the stiff little plastic chair, she was safe and there were signs of a kind of life, which was better than being where Sophia was, drifting towards no life at all. In a moment, when she was feeling stronger, she would go and sit with her. They had said she could. But first she wanted some of the fear to subside. Soon, surely, someone would come? Someone who could think for her.

'No,' she pulled the words from somewhere. 'No, I'm fine. I'd rather not. I don't want to be on my own.'

Sister Caldwell straightened up. 'No,' she said, wondering why, in all her years as a nurse, she had never got over the discomfort of being in the presence of grief. 'No, of course not. Now, look. I'm just here,' she said, pointing to the nurses' station behind her. 'I'll be along every five minutes and if you want me just come over.'

Anna looked around for somewhere to place the cup she was clutching.

'Here,' said Sister Caldwell, taking it from her. 'Let me. Heavens.' She looked at Anna's hands. 'Hasn't anyone done anything about all that? Don't worry, I'll send someone along just as soon as I can.'

Her hands? Anna gazed down at them as Sister Caldwell patted her arm and disappeared. Long streaks of red paint smeared the backs. Anna turned them over and studied her palms. On both large red stains were ingrained in her flesh. On her skirt there was a ghastly sticky patch as though someone's head had been resting there. She stifled a small cry and turned her face towards the wall.

Sophia's final savage act: red paint, sent spinning in a thick, sticky spray across the stone floor of the roof garden. Pieces of jagged glass lay among it and, staring up at her, the face of her mother, Barbara, with the surprised look Anna had captured in the photograph.

'This won't take a minute,' a young nurse said. 'Come in here and I'll get as much off as I can.'

Anna rose unsteadily to her feet and followed her into a side room. She sat down on a wooden chair next to a trolley full of cotton wool and kidney-shaped steel bowls and long-stemmed instruments with round flat shiny discs on the end that could see down throats and up noses. Tweezers, rolls of disposable dressings and boxes of tissues were stacked on the shelf below.

Her hands, she thought, as the nurse rubbed at them, were like Sophia's had been when Anna found her, slumped against the left-hand wall of the roof. A trail of paint had marked a hideous stain down the once-white walls of the roof garden. Her head was slack against her chest, the palms of her hands turned upwards, her legs sticking straight out. Her lipstick was smeared and her eyes were closed.

Anna remembered the nausea that had risen in her

throat as she felt for Sophia's pulse and detected the faintest flutter. And then she had tried to wrap a duvet around Sophia to protect her from the indignity of being found like that.

It was dreadfully cold, up there on the roof that she had once laughingly – so dangerously – described to Sophia as her own special private place where she would go to think about her mother. Jealous. That's what she'd been. Torn with rage that she couldn't get inside Anna's life. Or anyone else's.

Everything else was a blur: phoning Giulio's office and begging Jodie Butler to find him and Andrea and tell him to come, then Oliver, who was in Manchester and said he would leave immediately, and her father. Oh, God, her poor father, who tried to calm her, not knowing that the sound of his familiar voice was making her worse. The police had arrived, and the ambulance men, who had gone to work on Sophia. A policewoman guided Anna into the back of the squad car, although Anna had thought her place was in the ambulance. 'It's better this way,' the young WPC insisted. 'You'd just be in the way.' The last thing Anna had heard before they set off down Braverton Street after the ambulance, sirens wailing, was Dottie standing at her gate calling, 'What's happened, dear? What's happened?' And Mrs Mulvaney in her slippers, arms folded firmly across her chest, telling anyone who would listen that she had said all along that something odd was going on in there.

It was too much to bear on her own. Yet who else could she ask to bear it with her? Everyone had been kept at arm's length until only she and her mother had been left to deal, so clumsily, with each other.

The nurse had finished, and Anna buried her face in her hands.

Of the three people she had called, Giulio got there first, two hours after Sophia had been admitted, and an hour after Eamonn had appeared. He had been alerted by several conflicting stories from neighbours and, more accurately, by the lone policeman standing guard while forensic experts crawled around on Anna's roof.

Eamonn slid an arm around her.

She gave him a watery smile.

'Talk when you feel like it,' he said, taking her hand.

That was how Giulio first glimpsed them as he came through the doors. Downstairs in the car park his driver was waiting to take him or Anna home: Giulio was in no state to drive. Andrea was on his way from Chicago just as soon as he could get a flight and he had called Fabio too. He just hoped that the brandy he'd slugged down would keep him going.

'It's Giulio.' Eamonn nudged her.

Slowly she eased herself up, watched the familiar figure pause in the doorway. Something told her she should move but she didn't want to.

Anna had tried to keep the letter Sophia had left. Would Andrea really want to read that his mother's last thoughts had been a vitriolic and abusive tirade about Anna and Roberto, blaming them for failing her, ordering Andrea to erase Anna from his life then dementedly accusing him of cutting Sophia out of it? After that there had been a rambling litany of accusations against her family in Naples and a shattering denouncement of Lorenzo. The handwriting had deteriorated in relation to the level of abuse. When the police asked Anna to verify that it was Sophia's, she had nodded. 'She must have been writing it all day,' she whispered. 'And I left her.' She handed back the letter. 'I left her,' she repeated. 'I walked away.'

She felt rather than saw Giulio stop beside them. 'I'll get some coffee,' Eamonn offered. He had never seen Giulio so drawn and gaunt. 'Here, sit down.'

Giulio glanced at Eamonn. 'Thanks, Eamonn. Give me a few minutes with Anna?' he asked quietly.

Eamonn looked at her, then back at Giulio. 'I'll make some calls,' he said to her. 'I'll ring Carrie. Anyone else?'

Anna looked up. 'Oliver,' she said. 'Can you ring his mobile? See where he is?'

'They did their best,' Giulio said, as Eamonn departed.

Without looking up she nodded. 'It's all my fault,' she whispered. He made no attempt to touch her as he slumped on to the chair next to her. 'I thought I could handle her. I couldn't. Oh, God, what have I done?'

'Nothing,' he said bluntly. A man in more robust health might have been more considerate. Anna winced. 'It's what she did to herself. Sophia always wanted something she couldn't have. Lorenzo to give her a good life and Roberto, who was married, to take his place.'

'It was in her note,' she said. 'Surely to God she never thought he'd leave Sylvana for her?'

'Why not? It's how it always worked for her. She always got what she went after.'

'Don't say that,' Anna pleaded. 'Not yet. It's not fair. It's not right.'

There was a silence. 'Sorry,' he said.

'It wasn't a great love affair with Lorenzo, was it?' Anna asked, in a small voice. 'He was just besotted with her.'

Giulio leaned forward, his elbows on his knees. He pressed his fingers against his eyes and dragged them down his face. Anna glanced at him – he looked dreadful, as though he had been up all night. 'At first,' he said. 'For a while. And then disillusion set in. Fabio said she was already having an affair with Roberto before Lorenzo died and she expected him to take over where Lorenzo had left off. And then there was you.'

'Me? How could I have given her something better than she already had?'

'You couldn't, not while Lorenzo was alive. But once he died it was different. She thought Roberto might leave Sylvana if they lived far away from gossip. You became the screen, the reason for her to announce she was going to live in London.' He glanced at her stricken face. 'What do you want me to say?'

301

'The truth.' She leaned her head back against the wall. 'Ten-ton truck time.'

He smiled faintly. Sister Caldwell rushed past, giving Anna a fleeting glance, relieved that someone was with her. On the return journey she gave Giulio a slightly harder look. I hope he doesn't intend visiting anyone, she thought. Not with flu.

'Roberto's terrified,' Giulio said. 'Fabio phoned him about an hour ago. He never told her, you know, that he wouldn't live with her. He let her find out through you. He was scared of her towards the end. All the things Lorenzo had been saying started to sound true – obsessive, hysterical, vengeful. To be honest, I don't think he even wanted a mistress, just a diversion. Sophia turned out to be very hard work.'

'And whose fault was that?' Anna cried bitterly. 'She wanted to feel loved and needed and to know she belonged. That's been her problem all along and no one could see it. If just one person had shown her some compassion she wouldn't be lying where she is now.'

Giulio turned and pulled her face roughly towards him. 'You cannot believe that any of that is true?' he said.

Anna dropped her eyes. 'No,' she replied dully. 'No. Not for a long time now. Giulio?'

'Yes?' He was still holding her chin.

'It's none of my business,' she said, without removing his hand, 'but are you drunk?'

On the plane bringing him from Perth on the first flight available to London the following morning, Colin Minstrel thought about his wife. Not the wife who had driven him in stony silence along still dark roads to the airport but the wife who had shared Anna with him. Except shared was the wrong word.

Looking back he could not pinpoint the precise moment when he realized that Barbara had been the emissary between him and Anna. He and Barbara discussed Anna;

Barbara and Anna talked about him. From time to time all three went out together. There must have been moments when he and Anna had been together, just the two of them, but they were insignificant in relation to the overall pattern of their life. When she was very small, he had taken Anna for walks or to ride her bike but, if he was honest – and honesty, since the furious row with Meryl the night before, was no longer to be avoided – Barbara had done all the work for him. Colin shifted uneasily in his seat. Barbara had made it unnecessary for him make any effort with his only child. And Meryl was right. He didn't know Anna.

'I love Anna,' he had insisted to Meryl.

'I'm sure you do,' she cried angrily. 'But you don't *know* her. And, from what I've seen of her, she hasn't a clue about you. All that "Dad isn't like that" and that ghastly politeness to the boys, looking at you as though you'd committed murder by marrying me.'

Colin took a deep breath. 'That is absolutely ridiculous. She was surprised, that's all. And she was the stranger here, not bloody Athol and Sheridan.'

Meryl leaned both hands on the back of a chair and glared furiously at him. 'That's it,' she said. 'You said it. A stranger. And whose bloody fault is that?'

'How can it be mine? This is your house. They're your family. I gave up my home so that you wouldn't have to leave yours.'

Meryl rounded on him. 'You've done nothing you didn't want to do. It was your suggestion. Do you think I chose for all this to happen to me? You said I was imagining things when I tried to tell you Anna was unhappy with what we were doing. But would you listen? Oh, no. Because it didn't suit you. And now look what's happened. She's screaming down the phone—'

'Anna does not scream,' he interrupted.

'Yes, she does,' Meryl shouted. 'In her head she does. If I can see it, why can't you? And,' she went on, without

303

waiting for an answer, 'I'll tell you why. Because you're waiting for me to do something. Well, I'll tell you this, Colin Minstrel, you'll wait a very long time. She's your daughter, not mine.'

He slammed his glass down on the table next to his armchair. Meryl was standing by the fireplace, her coat still on from the drive back from Athol's where she had spent the day. For the second time in a week they had thought Fenella had gone into labour but again it had been a false alarm. Still, Meryl had rushed off in the car with her overnight bag, just in case, and the day had been long. And she had walked into this. Without being told, she had known it was Anna. Again and again and again.

'I do listen,' Colin said angrily. 'I can tell you how Anna votes, I know she loves Oliver, I know she's finding her new job hard going, and I know who her friends are.'

Meryl gave him a withering look. 'All very useful,' she retorted. 'And what about Sophia? How did she feel about her?'

He turned away from her.

'There,' Meryl said. 'There. You see? You haven't a clue. Because you've never asked. And why not?' She moved across the room and turned him round to face her. 'Because you're frightened, aren't you? Scared stiff that this crazy woman was a replacement – not for Barbara but for you. And,' she pulled him back as he tried to move away, 'she made you wake up and see you've failed Anna. You wouldn't even offer to meet her.'

'I haven't failed Anna.' His voice was raised to cover his nerves. 'She never *asked* me to meet her.'

'She was waiting for you to suggest it.'

'You told me to stand back,' he began, knowing his defence was shoddy. 'You said, "What does Anna want?" I remember exactly.'

Meryl dropped her hands from his shoulders. 'That's not the same thing at all. I told you I would stand back, not that you should. It was your decision. I've told you endlessly that I can't come between you and Anna. And, no matter how much you want me to, I can't be Barbara.'

They stared helplessly at each other.

'I never wanted you to be.'

'Then tell Anna. Stop her thinking I boss you around. Do you know which bit I resent most?'

Colin shook his head.

'No. I'm sure you don't. Well, I'll tell you. It's that she believes you've no say in this. That you've been railroaded into this marriage.'

'That's not true.'

'Then tell Anna, not me . . .'

Colin stared out of the window of the plane as it bumped its way through grey banks of cloud. Not like the truth, he thought sadly. 'The more 'tis shook, the more it shines.' He couldn't even remember who'd said it.

'Tea, sir? Coffee?'

He shook his head at the stewardess.

'Paper?'

'No. Sorry. Slight headache,' he added, in case he had been too brusque.

'Poor you. I think we might have some aspirin. Would you like some?'

'No, thank you.' He gave a slight smile. 'No. Nothing getting home won't cure.'

Before she picked up the phone, Rachel Stourton checked the identi-call on her display screen. Oliver's mobile.

'Rach?'

She tucked the phone under her chin and walked round her desk to close the door. 'Hi. Still in Manchester?'

'No. On the motorway. Look, Rach, something's happened. I can't get to your meeting. It's Sophia.'

'Sophia?'

'I've got to get to Anna. She found her. Overdose.'

'Oh my God.'

Rachel sat down heavily on the edge of the desk.

'I know. I know. It's all very confused at the moment. I think Sophia's on life support but I don't know for sure and the hospital won't tell me over the phone and Anna's mobile is off.'

'My God. Why did she do it? Was it an accident?'

'I've no idea. Anna was absolutely distraught. I've never heard her like it before. I just have to go.'

It seemed to Rachel that Oliver sounded more weary than upset.

'She was obviously crazier than I thought.'

Rachel took a deep breath. She tried to feel sorry for someone in such a mess but she could only feel sorry for Oliver. So sorry that, in spite of the hurt and the anger, she could not turn him away. Not ever, really. And he clearly needed a friend. Rachel had turned herself into that friend and because she was a friend she had asked him if he would act as adviser on a new account she'd just picked up. It was what friends did.

'Anything I can do?'

There was a pause. 'No. Thank you, but no. Rach?'

'Yes?'

'I'll call you. Maybe we could have dinner and I can make up for not being at the meeting.'

Rachel took a deep breath. 'Oliver, you don't have to make up for anything, you know that. Take care. Stay in touch.'

She put the phone down before he could answer. Anna. Always bloody Anna.

Andrea had agreed to his mother's life-support machine being switched off. He and Anna wept together as they sat either side of her bed until it was over.

Colin had arrived about an hour before Andrea and just held Anna while she buried her face in his shoulder.

'I couldn't love her, Dad.' Hot tears fell on her hands and her eyes were swollen from crying. Colin was shocked at the sight of her. Dear heaven, how had they all let her stray so far?

'I never even thought to try,' Anna was saying, 'and that was the problem. We simply didn't know each other, let alone love each other. I just felt so sorry for her. All alone, despised by them all because she had got pregnant. I saw it the way she saw it. But I don't think it can have been like that. Giulio told me it wasn't.'

He handed her a hanky. Anna blew her nose and took a deep, steadying gulp of air. 'Giulio said no one had made her give me up. They couldn't have, because they didn't even know she was pregnant. She just took off for London then came back when it was all over and blamed Loretta – that's Lorenzo's mother,' she reminded him.

Colin nodded. 'I know,' he said, and in a very gentle voice. 'In spite of what you might think, I do listen to you, you know.'

'Oh, Dad,' she said, in a small voice. 'Thank you for coming. I really needed you.'

Oliver was standing with his back to them, staring out over the dreary roofline of the hospital. Lack of sleep had left him looking little better than Anna. Of course he was shocked but even while he was dealing with the impact of Anna's phone call, a rush of relief had swept through him. He felt ashamed that while he told Anna of his horror, inside he felt that the weight and the intrusion of Sophia had miraculously been lifted. There was a God, after all, he told himself, fiercely and even jubilantly. Perhaps not one who approved of his present stance, but one who would surely understand.

He glanced to where Anna and Colin were waiting for Andrea. She felt his eyes on her and gave him a rather wobbly smile, then reached out and touched his hand. But he turned away, pretending he hadn't noticed.

Somewhere south of Luton, before the turn-off to the M25, the horror that had precipitated Oliver's headlong dash to London underwent a change, but at whom the anger was directed was unclear. They were all part of it. Anna, who had shut him out and had not understood how displaced he had felt; her father, who had handled her so badly; Giulio Farrini, who appeared to have handled her too well; and then, of course, Sophia.

He had found Anna sitting with Giulio Farrini.

After he had hugged her and Giulio had gone home, she told him, 'Giulio said Sophia couldn't come to terms with any of it. Losing Lorenzo was like losing her whole life. Not because she loved him, because Giulio doesn't think she did in the end. She was having an affair with Roberto. I thought it was just Irena.'

'You surprise me,' he said bitterly.

Anna looked up at him in amazement. 'Did you guess?'

Oliver hesitated. 'Well,' he lied, hating himself, but he couldn't help it, 'I had my suspicions but you weren't really prepared to listen to me, were you?'

Anna winced. 'Everyone keeps saying she had so much but, Oliver, she didn't. In the end she had nothing. The house wasn't hers, and Giulio said she hated it because it was full of stuff from Lorenzo's family and they were always determined she would have nothing. They just thought she was flaky and had used Lorenzo.'

'Maybe she did,' Oliver said. 'Darling, I don't want to be unkind, but left to Sophia she would probably have filled it with designer trash. She had no values.'

Anna put her hands over her ears. Oliver had seen beyond the clothes, the charm. Straight away he'd seen it. 'Don't,' she pleaded. 'Not now. Giulio said it's what Gianni and Loretta have always said, that they could see straight away that this beautiful girl from Naples would be Lorenzo's ruin.'

'And they were right,' Oliver said.

'Maybe.' Anna sighed. 'Perhaps they didn't handle it very well. They sent him away to get away from her, but they swear they never knew she was pregnant. That's what they can't forgive, that they weren't given the chance to bring me up. But what else *would* they say? She wasn't all to blame. No one person ever is. Someone had to stick up for her.'

'You did. What difference did it make?'

He knew he was being cruel and he couldn't stop it. He wanted to go home. He wanted to take Anna and get away from this oppressive corridor. Away from the tubes and trolleys and the impersonal business of it all. Every time a door opened, she half rose out of her seat only to sink back again when a kind but overworked nurse shook her head. If a phone rang, she stiffened. But Anna wouldn't hear of going. 'It's all I can do now. Oh, God, I don't blame them all for deserting her – but they were as much to blame. They were all weak and irresponsible, just like Lorenzo. All she ever had was youth and beauty and when that started to go it was harder to put up with her. She was so demanding – and Giulio is right. How could anyone, even the Grescobaldis, go on loving and forgiving when there was nothing coming back, just more and more anger when things didn't go her way?'

Now he stared fixedly through the window at the dreary cluster of buildings below him. The largest share of anger he knew he had reserved for himself. He was not proud of how he felt, ashamed that he had not stood between Anna and her mother. And what was the point now of telling her?

'C'mon.' Oliver took her gently by the shoulders while Stefano supported Andrea.

'Would you than' Giulio for me?' Anna whispered, as she and Andrea hugged each other goodbye. 'He came straight away. And he stayed until Oliver arrived. He was very kind. And he's not at all well. He's got flu and he looked dreadful. You will make sure he's all right?'

Beside her Oliver remained silent.

'Of course,' Andrea said. 'He said he'd do everything that

309

needed to be done. Anna? I didn't understand, not really.
I thought she was just being Mamma.'

Anna took his hand. 'She was. That's the terrible
tragedy.'

Chapter Twenty-five

Before she left for Rome and Sophia's funeral, her father had phoned Mr Viraswami and asked if his son Aftab, the interior designer, could put Anna's home to rights. In spite of the weight that had descended on all of them, which made Christmas alone with Oliver the most subdued Anna could recall, she could not help laughing. 'Dad,' she exclaimed. 'Aftab Viraswami isn't a painter and decorator, he's an interior designer. A very posh one too. He's much too grand for Braverton Street.'

'Good,' Colin said calmly. 'In which case he can do the whole lot. No, I insist. It's a present from me. And it's not what your mother would have expected of me, it's what I want to do. My decision. And, besides,' he cut her off when she started to protest, 'it's part of your life until you and Oliver decide where you want to live. How is he?'

'Poor Oliver.' She sighed. 'He's ready to kill, and I don't blame him. He's been so patient with me. I'll make it up to him, Dad, when all this is over.'

'What about work?' he asked. 'How are they taking all this?'

Anna groaned. 'Not good. I've got sick leave until after the funeral. I'll deal with that when I get back.'

In fact, they were taking it very badly. Gilbert had just looked at her and said politely, 'Well, of course I'm very sorry, Anna. You must be very shocked – yes, of course you are. I can see that. But I do have to think of the programme. Can you give me some idea of how long you'll be gone?'

'Three days,' she said quickly. 'That's all. Maybe two. No, seriously. I think we'd better say three. To be on the safe side.'

Gilbert pushed himself off his chair and grunted. 'OK, my angel. Three it is. But you can do the programme on Tuesday night?'

Anna looked at him in horror. 'Well, I can get it ready then leave around three to get to Heathrow.'

Gilbert sighed. He ushered her ahead of him out of the door. 'Let's say four days, then, shall we? Ah, Bridget.' He left her abruptly to greet the presenter who had just emerged from the newsroom. 'A word in your shell-like. Was it you,' Anna heard him say, 'who told me that girl – what's her name?, the one who sent me that amazingly long CV – Tania Prowton was looking to move on?'

Anna couldn't loathe him. He was right. In six months she had hardly established a reputation for reliability. On the other hand, it was as well to know what kind of ammunition was trained on her. She rang Henry, who'd left anxious messages for her to ring. 'I've had better times,' she told him, when he came on the line. 'Don't let's talk about it. We'll get together when all this is over. How are things?'

As she knew he would, he poured out a catalogue of complaints about Max Warner, the treachery of Melissa and the fact that Aggie had been poached to another programme. And as for Tania bloody Prowton. A moan came down the line. Anna wondered if Henry had ever experimented with a wider range of emotions than despair or total despair.

He dropped his voice. 'Fallen out with Max, she has. Big bust-up a couple of weeks back. Blaming each other for the ratings. Plunge is not the word. Try suicide mission.' There was a horrified gasp. 'Sorry, oh, God, sorry.'

'That's okay,' Anna said. 'Anyway,' she moved on, swiftly, 'I saw the reports. So Tania's looking for an out?'

'Not sure. Tessa said she heard she's firing off letters

everywhere. But who'd have the silly cow? She keeps saying it's her or him. Ha,' he said scornfully. 'As if they'd get rid of him. If I could I'd get out. Unfortunately, Maggie's going through the great socialist cave-in and wants them all to be paid for. The kids. My children,' he said, when Anna sounded blank. 'You know, schools. Actually I was going to ask you, but I didn't like to with all this going on. But Tania keeps saying you're having a rough time with Bridget.'

Anna wondered why she bothered. It was all so petty. But she needed a job and, in this business, she needed to know whose star was in the ascendant. Certainly it wasn't her own. 'Nothing new there,' she assured him. And it was true. 'She wants heavyweight interviews but she's not up to it. I'm not here to develop her career and she thinks I am. Dinner, Henry? You and Maggie when I get back, yes? I'll deal with everything then.'

Mr Viraswami came ahead of Aftab to meet Anna at Braverton Street, anxious to dispel any ideas about his cherished but confusing son. 'His mother always said he was artistic,' he explained doubtfully. 'And she was right. He will make a lovely job. A *lovely* job. You wait.'

'I'm sure he will,' Anna agreed gratefully. 'When you think of his usual commissions, this is a real favour. All due to you.'

'Not at all.' He waved aside her thanks. 'I am very fond of your father. He's a good man. And, Anna?' Mr Viraswami had taken to calling them Anna and Colin. 'It will not be like Veejay's house. I'm afraid his brother's house causes Aftab physical pain.' He put his head on one side and gave her a meaningful look. They smiled at each other. Every family had its flaws.

As it turned out Aftab, who had brought with him a very beautiful young assistant who stood respectfully by his side ready to take notes, instantly saw what needed to be done. First he inspected the roof without comment, then he made his way downstairs and stood in the centre of Anna's living room. He took in the white walls and the sanded floors, the draped cloud of voile falling from a metal rod above the square window, through which the starkness of the frame could be seen and made the room, on a cold, raw January day, seem even colder. 'Hmm,' he said. He wrapped one arm around his waist, the elbow of the other resting on it, and lightly tapped his forefinger against his lips.

His assistant waited, pen poised over a pad. Anna and Mr Viraswami glanced silently at each other.

'Colour,' Aftab finally pronounced, bending only his wrist and pointing just one finger at the general area of the room. He spun round on the spot, lifting both arms to embrace it in its entirety. 'This house needs warming up. Simon?' He swung to face his assistant. 'Write this down. Yellow,' he said. 'Warm and vibrant. Maybe . . .' He screwed up his eyes and studied the windows his head on one side. 'Maybe a hint, just a hint, you understand, of azure. You,' he turned to Anna with an airy wave, 'must stay away. Go and live with a friend. And when you come back, I will have made it look like the sun is trapped in these walls.'

Anna blinked. It could have been her mother's voice.

Andrea had entrusted Giulio with everything, for which Anna was both grateful and embarrassed. Bad enough the job of packing up all Sophia's possessions to dispatch to Rome, to which bleak task Carrie had lent her assistance. Knowing that the mess she had helped to create was being resolved by the person who had tried so hard to stop her was humiliating. There had been few meetings with Giulio and none on her own. She had always been in the company of Oliver or her father. Anxious not to try Oliver's patience even further, she had encouraged her father to keep Giulio occupied with the vagaries of the education system, life in Carrigh and the very few things, apart from Anna, that he missed about Granton Street.

It was only later that it occurred to her that her father

had hardly mentioned Meryl, and Athol and Sheridan not at all. And that Giulio had looked dreadful.

On Christmas Eve, her father caught the early flight home. Fenella had finally gone into labour. Anna and Oliver had insisted that they would be fine in London on their own. On the same day, Giulio had flown to Rome to be with his family. There was nothing else he could do in London. Early in January an inquest determined that Sophia had taken her own life: her note and Anna's evidence had left no possibility of foul play. The body had been released for burial.

Yet even though Anna might not have wanted to be alone with him, she had made sure Giulio was recovering from flu. She had even phoned Jodie Butler after she and Oliver had had dinner with him and her father, and said, 'He really is much worse than he's letting on. Please try and persuade him to stay at home.'

'I'll try,' Jodie had promised, 'but if you can't make him, I'm not sure what I can do.'

'Me?' Anna exclaimed. 'Heavens, I can't do anything. It's just that Andrea has gone back to Rome and asked Giulio to act for him – both of us – that's all. I don't want him to feel pressured. I know he's got this Banca Milano case on, which must be giving him sleepless nights.'

'Giulio?' Jodie laughed. 'He's lapping it up.'

Anna paused. 'Well,' she said, failing to keep the indignation from her voice, 'that's good. No. No message. Have a nice Christmas.'

Jodie put down the phone and tapped her pen thoughtfully on her desk. Carrie Hunt, indeed. She wasn't sure what to do. Sometimes people left messages with her or said things to her, hoping they would be passed on to Giulio in an oblique way that would be helpful to them. Testing the water, assessing his mood, avoiding a direct refusal, letting him know they were not quite happy. In this case she was quite sure that hadn't been the intention. In fact, she was quite sure it was the reverse but you could never tell and it had been too long and too fraught a day to analyse it deeply.

It was already well after seven. She rang through to the boardroom and asked if the meeting was likely to go on much longer. Possibly until dawn, she was told. At home, Jodie's husband would be waiting, and ten hours in her book was sufficient as evidence of her commitment to Giulio. It was about time she left.

Through the glass partition she could see the rest of the office beginning to wind down for the night. Maggie had gone promptly at five thirty and the more ambitious young lawyers, who usually hung around in the hope of impressing Giulio with their dedication, started to drift off, realizing that since he was unlikely to be back for hours it was a wasted gesture.

First she carried through letters that Maggie had typed for his signature, picked up some stray files and stacked them precisely together. Then she opened his diary at the next day's page and checked it against her own. After that she opened his briefcase and dropped in the two Opinions biked round from Desmond Connelly's office, the QC Giulio had retained on the Banca Milano débâcle. He would need to read both tonight before the court reconvened the following day. The list of messages she had typed for him was usually deposited in a small pocket at the back. Jodie pulled it open and saw a photograph tucked inside. Curiously she took it out. It wasn't a terribly good picture, of a girl, with a young man she recognized as Andrea Grescobaldi. It was hard to say where they were, but it was clearly a restaurant. There were other people with them. Jodie looked closer. She didn't know any of them. A fair-haired girl looking away from the camera was talking to someone across the table whose back was to the camera. Giulio. On the other side, a serious-looking, handsome man was leaning back with his hand on a girl's shoulder. She had thick dark hair and looked very like Andrea. She was smiling. And spoken for, by the looks of things.

Jodie replaced the picture and sighed. 'Dear, oh dear, oh dear,' she muttered to herself. Carrie Hunt, indeed. Then she retrieved the list of messages and wrote on the bottom, 'Anna Minstrel called. No message', which seemed a satisfactory way of dealing with what had happened.

It was a different church from the one where they had held the requiem mass for Lorenzo. Andrea told her that, under the circumstances, Monsignor had thought something simple more appropriate. Anna doubted such a church existed in Rome, and although this one was certainly smaller it was no less grand. Its cavernous dome stretched up into the darkness and cold flagstones sent the smallest sound whispering around the walls. Flowers filled every space and banks of candles cast a flickering, ghostly light into shadowy recesses.

Only Monsignor would give a reading. The funeral rite for a suicide was a matter of discretion to priests, some of whom still held sternly to the view that it was such a grievous offence against all they believed sacred and holy that there was no service they could render without seeming to collude with the transgression that had taken place. Monsignor had chosen to believe that in her last moments, too late to save herself but not her soul, Sophia would have regretted her actions and atoned.

A vision of her garden rose up before Anna. She found it hard to accept this. However, like the rest of the Grescobaldis she wanted to believe it. It was now a matter of importance to her that Sophia was buried with the recognition that she was now at peace with herself.

The strange thing was, Anna thought, walking hand in hand with Andrea, behind Sophia's coffin, followed by the rest of the Grescobaldis and Oliver, it had never occurred to Sophia that if she had wanted less, schemed less, she would have got almost everything to which she believed she was entitled. Her charm alone would have ensured that.

317

Instead, she had allowed it to be obliterated in a frenzy of fury and contempt for those around her.

The most dreadful thing, though, Anna mused, as Monsignor, flanked by a dozen altar boys, walked to the lectern to begin reading, was that there was no one to speak for her. Her own family had almost disappeared – Fabio had been able to contact only one brother, who had listened in silence to all he had to say and simply said, 'Naples is a long way from Rome.'

'Do you want his address?' he asked Anna, when they met at the apartment in Trastevere where she and Oliver were staying with Andrea. 'Would you like to meet him?'

Anna hesitated. She took the piece of paper he held out to her and looked at it. 'Gabriele Perugiamo,' it said. 'Via Santa Maria Lanza, Naples.' There was also a telephone number. 'Does Andrea?' she asked.

'No,' he said. 'He said if his mother hadn't wanted to know them, then neither does he.'

Anna gave back the slip of paper. 'Then I don't either,' she said. 'It would not be what Sophia wanted. Thank you, but no.'

She glanced at Andrea, now sitting beside her, shoulders hunched, his hands twisting in agitation. She reached out and took them.

He turned and smiled at her. There were fewer people than there had been at Lorenzo's funeral, too few to deaden the echo of Monsignor's voice reverberating around the church. Those Grescobaldis who had come for Lorenzo had come for Sophia, and behind her, on the other side of the church, Anna could see Pilar with her brother and sister, and behind her Gio and Constanza, heads together, whispering quietly. There was a sprinkling of people she vaguely recognized and a few strangers, who might have dropped in to light a candle then stayed to watch the service.

Anna turned back and gazed ahead sadly. There were no more tears, just a strong desire to let Lorenzo's family see that while she never knew him, she knew, as a daughter, what he would have wanted for Sophia. 'Take care of her,' he had said, even if he had ceased to love her.

'I'm not sure he ever did,' Gianni had admitted the night before. 'He was fascinated by her, seduced by her, but I think in the end she just made him feel so guilty about you that he married her.'

'Then why did he get her pregnant a second time?' she asked sharply. 'I can see she wasn't perfect – I know as well as you that she wasn't. But Lorenzo was not blameless. I wish you could all see that.'

Gianni lifted his hands in a helpless gesture. 'I wish you'd known him,' he replied. 'He was a dear man, but very weak, not as bright as you imagine, and easily flattered. And this, Anna, you must believe. While we didn't think Sophia could ever make Lorenzo happy, my mother and father could see he would never be enough for her. He just wanted a simple life. And they were right.'

Anna shivered.

'All right?' Irena leaned forward from her seat behind her and whispered anxiously in her ear.

Oliver glanced at her and laid a reassuring hand on her arm. Somewhere Giulio was sitting with Fabio. There was no sign of Roberto or Sylvana. 'They'll be all right,' Gianni had said. 'They'll find a way. Don't worry.'

'I'm not,' Anna said. 'I'm no longer a part of any of that.'

Afterwards, as Sophia's coffin was carefully placed in the back of a black hearse ready for the long drive to Bracciano, where she was to be cremated and her ashes scattered with Lorenzo's, Anna and Andrea waited together at the door of the church. They thanked each person for coming. Then Anna saw Fabio bending down to talk to a couple who had sat at the back. After a few minutes he beckoned Giulio to join him.

It was Giulio who edged his way towards Oliver and spoke briefly to him. They both looked towards her. Afterwards Anna said she knew at that moment who the man was. Why he looked so familiar.

'It's Sophia's brother,' Oliver whispered, drawing her away from Andrea. 'He wants to talk to you. Not to Andrea, just you.'

'Is there somewhere we could talk?' Gabriele spoke in Italian. Giulio glanced at Anna to make sure she understood. She nodded at him to say that she did. 'This is my wife, Marta,' Gabriele was saying, drawing her forward. 'Marta said we must come.'

It was a very strong look that the Perugiamos had. She knew she looked like him, that she and Andrea had taken after Sophia's family. They both had his hair and Gabriele's nose. He wore a scarf wound around a thick, cheap coat and he held a serviceable pair of leather gloves. His wife glanced nervously between them. She looked cold and tired. They were much older than Sophia, well into their sixties and unremarkable in every way. There was a dignified manner about them, which suggested a hard life but a respectable one. So different from the wealthy Grescobaldis. Conscience, Anna supposed, had made them get up and leave Naples before dawn to be here on time. For that, at least, she was prepared to be courteous.

'I don't want anything,' Gabriele assured her. His handshake had been brief, impatient. 'It was Marta. She said we should be here when I told her about Sophia finding you for – for Lorenzo's sake.'

'That was kind of you,' Anna said, taking Marta's hand. 'It's not the best time. Andrea and I are leaving almost immediately for Bracciano. Unless, of course, you're coming there too.'

Giulio interrupted. 'I think they need to talk to you now,' he said gently. 'They can't be away from Naples for too long. Gabriele has a business to run. He's a baker, you see. I think you must hear what he has to say.'

Anna glanced around at Oliver, who nodded. 'I'll tell Andrea you'll be a few minutes,' he whispered, and slipped away.

Very quietly and hesitantly, with three sets of eyes on

him, Gabriele explained that Lorenzo was not Anna's father.

'My God,' she whispered. 'Then who is?'

It seemed that he could have been almost anyone. It just wasn't Lorenzo.

Someone had left the shutters open. On a tray placed on top of a small console table, cups and a teapot lay used and abandoned. An air of neglect clung to the cushions that sagged on the pristine white sofas and flowers past their best had been left in their perfectly sculpted vases. She knew that if she looked closely there would be a film of dust on the stacks of glossy books that lay around. Uncharacteristic wrath swelled in Anna.

She turned sharply away from the windows and strode over to the door. 'Pilar,' she shouted. 'Gio.'

The small group gathered in the salon stared silently at her as she paced around the marble hallway. Pilar came running down the stairs and Gio, with Constanza at his heels wiping her hands on a cloth, emerged from the kitchen.

'Si, Signorina, si?' Pilar asked.

'Look.' Anna took her by the elbow and pointed at the wilting flowers, the discarded tea tray, the shutters wide open after dark. 'What is going on here? Signora Grescobaldi would be outraged.'

'But, Signorina,' Pilar protested, 'she is not here. No one is here.'

'But I am,' Anna said, more quietly, 'and I expect *la signora*'s standards to be maintained. Have I made myself perfectly clear?'

If her disjointed Italian was not entirely correct it was clear enough for the alarmed trio, who dispersed in various directions to restore the house to the pristine state Sophia had demanded.

Only Giulio remained unmoved by her outburst, staring down into the gathering gloom of the evening from his place by the window.

'Anna,' Oliver protested, 'does it matter?'

Everyone sat down, looking uneasily at each other.

'Yes,' she whispered back. 'It matters because it mattered to Sophia. There can't be much left now about her that hasn't been demolished. But at least the way she ran this place wasn't fake. It looked brilliant. And it can stay brilliant. I'm sorry.' She turned to Gabriele, who had not followed the conversation in English. 'So who was he? The man who deserted her?'

'I don't know.' Gabriele clearly hated his task. 'There were a few. Always with money but no one inquired where they got it from. She met them at the restaurant where she worked. They gave her presents. A bangle,' he indicated his wrist with a disdainful flick, 'silk scarves. Always telling her they would give her a new life in a big city but she was day-dreaming. Always dreaming.'

'How do you know it wasn't Lorenzo?'

Gabriele exchanged a look with Marta. 'Because,' he said, 'she was already pregnant when she met him.'

Anna closed her eyes. Andrea turned away.

'The minute she knew, she tried to get an abortion – some waiter or other she worked with said he could get it for her but it would cost money and she didn't have any. I found out because we know everyone in Napoli and a friend told me my little sister was in trouble and getting into worse trouble. So she decided that she would tell Lorenzo, who had money, that he was responsible and he must marry her. Marta said to her – didn't you, Marta? – that she wouldn't get away with it, but she just shouted and said she would say you were premature. She said—' He stopped and glanced uneasily at Andrea. 'Forgive me. But she said Lorenzo would believe it because he was an idiot. But, of course, it did not occur to her that his family weren't. And,' he added contritely, seeing in Andrea's eyes a mixture of fury and grief, 'your father was very young. I'm sure he grew into a very intelligent person.'

Apparently he hadn't. He had been loved for his gentle

warmth and simplicity, for the way he dealt kindly with the mundane not the extraordinary. With no ability to see through people or to run a business, he lacked the strength and courage that would have halted Sophia's ceaseless demands and emotional blackmail.

And then Issy had come along. She had let him be all of those things Sophia had not, but still he went on paying the price for something he had not done. Who could blame Sophia's family for what *they* had done? Certainly Anna couldn't. Maybe, one day, she would deal more competently with the ache that she had truly not been wanted and that the lifeline thrown to Sophia to keep her had been hurled back.

'She refused everything,' Gabriele said. 'We had an aunt in Catania who said Sophia could live there with the baby – with you. We would say her husband had been killed. Anything.'

'So why didn't she?'

Gabriele spread his hands. 'I don't know,' he said. 'She just screamed and said if she couldn't have an abortion it was to be adoption. So we let her have her way.'

Oliver put an arm around Anna's shoulders.

'And then, after I had been adopted, she followed Lorenzo to Rome, cutting you all off? That's right, isn't it?' Anna finished for him. 'And when Lorenzo wanted to see me, she couldn't risk Fabio contacting you and finding out the truth, so she came and got me herself. Is that it?'

Gabriele looked sadly into his drink. 'Even when my mother died, she did not want to know. And we knew she was marrying money. We should have said something, but how were we to know? It wasn't as though you would be here assuming Lorenzo was your father, or that he thought of you as a daughter. It seemed best not to say anything. You were gone. We thought it had all been forgotten. But, as Marta said, you can't do that with the truth. It's out there somewhere, waiting to trip us up, just holding on until we take it for granted just one too many times.'

Chapter Twenty-six

Anna stared down into the courtyard waiting for Gabriele and Marta to appear through the door below and noticed that the fountain had been turned off – no musical trickle of water, no pinpricks of light bouncing off the steady flow into the pool below. Poor fountain, she thought, its magic lost, just another statue in a town that seemed to have invented them. Somewhere, way upstairs, Andrea was with Stefano, trying to absorb the shock of yet another layer of his mother's life being peeled away. Oliver was on the phone in their room. All the relations were gone. Or, rather, her step-relations, because that's as much now as they could ever be. Except Andrea, who was still her brother, a half-brother, but sharing a mother transcended the smallness of such a word. And wasn't that the only important thing?

In a minute she would turn back into the room, now as polished and organized as Pilar had always kept it, and start to try to unravel what was real and what was something she and Sophia had both, in their own ways, wanted. And she had known the truth. Somewhere, on another level, she had known something was wrong when she had looked down at Lorenzo, at his bewildered, dying eyes searching her face for something they knew wasn't there.

All that shouting, and in the panic she had promised a total stranger to look after his wife. Anna pulled her coat closer around her. But had he ever asked? Only Sophia had said so, and Andrea had tried to stop her putting words into his father's mouth, not because he didn't believe them but because he had wanted peace for him.

Down below she saw Fabio shaking hands with Gabriele, helping Marta to slide into the back seat, exchanging a word with the driver who, Andrea had insisted, was to take them all the way back to Naples. At the last minute, Gabriele looked up and raised his hand in farewell. Anna waved back. They hadn't wanted the car. Like Anna, they had come to Rome wanting nothing but to leave as they had arrived. But Anna's gentle insistence, added to Andrea's, had persuaded them.

'It is what Mamma would have expected of me,' Andrea said, from behind her. 'After all, he is my uncle too. Anna? You can see why Mamma did it, can't you? Can you really imagine her with that family? She was so much bigger and extravagant, so desperate to live. You don't believe she would have been better off with them? And you. You would not have had such a good life, no?'

Anna didn't hesitate. 'No,' she replied. 'Not for a single moment. They couldn't contain her but why should they have done more? They had *their* lives to think of. You know, Andrea, there is a moment when you have to do that.'

'I know that now,' he said quietly, his voice breaking. 'You have to stand back, stop being sucked into someone else's fantasy, someone else's plans for you, or you have only their life to lead. And then what?'

She looked over her shoulder at him. 'I couldn't do that,' she said. 'And neither could you, could you? Don't let us deceive each other, not me and you. Neither of us – no one – could be what Sophia wanted. Not in the end.'

He moved forward to stand alongside her, and lit a cigarette. 'No,' he said, finally and sadly. 'No. I thought you were my escape. You seemed to be able to help her. I shouldn't have done that, left her to you. It all suddenly seemed desperately necessary. You see, I had never known freedom from her. But oh, God, I didn't want this kind of freedom. Just enough to breathe. It's odd to think that she knew about me. All that time I hid it and had a half-life. And she would have let me go on, wouldn't she?'

They watched in silence as the car circled the fountain, then moved through the narrow gap that led out through the black gates into the tree-lined avenue. With Gabriele and Marta had gone the spirit Anna thought she had found to make her whole. It was an odd feeling, but she knew the will to care any more where she had come from had gone too. She knew enough. And if for Sophia too much had not been enough, for Anna it was more than she had ever asked.

Before they left, Gianni came to find her. 'I am afraid,' he said, 'that you will go away and not come back and that is not right. How can I in here,' he pressed his hand to his chest, 'think of you as my brother's child and up here,' he tapped his head, 'know that you are not?'

As he spoke he reached out and pulled her to him. He wrapped his arms around her and rocked her gently to and fro. 'I think,' he said, standing back a little so that he could see her, 'Carla is right. We will forget the head and go with the heart, yes?'

'I don't care.' Irena grabbed her and hugged her. 'You are my cousin. What is this "step" anyway?'

Even Elena forgot temporarily that she was cool and distant, and slightly wary of Anna, possibly, as Irena murmured, because she was having an amazing affair and too busy screwing to care, but she said that Anna was family and that was that. 'What,' she asked, pressing her cheek against Anna's as they parted, 'is all this fuss about? Like the Grescobaldis never had skeletons in their closets?'

'Elena,' Gianni slid behind the wheel of his car as the girls got into the back, 'all the skeletons, so far, appear to be in yours. Take care.'

'And that,' Elena retorted, 'is what makes me interesting. Long after I am gone I will be remembered for what I was, not what I look like. Although,' she added, 'in my case, that too.'

The window rolled down, and Irena blew Anna a kiss as they disappeared in the direction of their own lives. After they'd all gone, Anna pulled up the collar of her coat around her neck and turned away from the house. In a while she would have to go back. Not yet.

There were few people about at that time of night, but Anna needed to walk. After tonight she had a lot of decisions to make. Stripped of its warmth, with endless empty tables outside cafés, no lovers entwined in the street, Rome had also been stripped of its charm. She turned in the direction of the city, needing noise around her and people with a sense of purpose.

For a short while she had thought she was one of the Grescobaldis, finding in them expressions, family character-istics that could never be hers. It just showed, she thought sadly, how powerful was the need to belong. And now this. God knew who her father was, and she no longer cared. Her real father, the one who had made her what she was, was where he had always been. It may not quite have been Sicilian bandits and a mother on the game, as she had once claimed Oliver's mother most feared, but it wasn't far from it.

In the end Gabriele and Marta had gone with them to Bracciano then returned with them to Trastevere to talk to both Anna and Andrea, but particularly Anna. They had left, taking with them a promise that Anna would stay in touch with them. Gabriele was all that was left in Italy of Sophia's family, the five children who had dealt with life in such different ways. There was a brother in America, who hadn't been home in forty years; another, a car mechanic, had been killed ironically in a road accident; one sister had become a nun and the other had committed suicide.

It was almost ten before she turned into the courtyard and crossed to the front door. Oliver would be worried.

'Did that solve anything?' A voice from somewhere by the fountain made her jump as she approached. She peered into the gloom and saw Giulio sitting on the edge of the stone parapet. He was holding a glass in his hand and his coat was slung loosely around his shoulders.

'Probably not,' she said carefully, walking slowly over to where he remained sitting. She tried to joke. 'Just how many families can a girl have? And why are you sitting there? You've just had flu. You'll get pneumonia.'

He lifted the glass. 'Not with this.'

'She knew,' she told Giulio, leaning against the cold stone next to him. 'She knew about Andrea and Stefano. About Issy. She knew everything. You're right. While she pretended she didn't know, she could control them all. It was emotional blackmail to get them to do whatever she wanted.'

She looked sideways at him and gave an embarrassed laugh. 'Funny, isn't it? I convinced myself I looked like them. Did Lorenzo really want to see me?' she asked painfully. 'Was any of it real?'

He was leaning forward, his arms resting along his knees, his hands clasped around the glass rolling it slowly between his fingers. She stared at his hands, at the pale gold signet ring he wore, and dug her own deeply into her pockets.

'Yes and no,' he said, not looking up. 'Issy told me he thought his unhappy marriage was a punishment for encouraging Sophia to have you adopted. He wanted forgiveness but he truly wanted to make sure you were all right. That bit was very true. He was a good man, Anna.'

'Yes.' She looked up into the night sky. 'You always said he was. A good person, you said. He never hit her, did he? No. It's OK. I seem to have a list here of assumptions and you should see the one I've got for conjecture and misplaced notions.'

'Hang on,' he smiled reluctantly, 'don't go mad. I never said he was bright. I'll say one thing for Sophia. She got that business under way. She knew that unless Roberto came on board it wasn't going to work left to Lorenzo. At least she did that. At least she gave Andrea something to do.' He stood up and handed her the glass. 'Go on,' he said, when she tried to refuse it. 'You look done in. And frozen.'

Obediently she took a sip. 'OK,' she said, handing it back to him. 'I was wrong. I didn't listen to you. Happy?'

He looked away. 'Of course not. Why should something so stupid as someone not taking my advice be a triumph? I'm used to it. I'm a lawyer.'

'Ah.' She smiled – she couldn't help it. 'But they pay you. I just cause aggravation. I should have listened.'

'You didn't want to hear. You'd fallen in love with the idea that you and Sophia were both pushed to the edge of other people's lives. Just because your mother died and your father remarried. That was it, wasn't it?'

'Nonsense,' she lied crisply.

He gave her an exasperated look. 'You had a great mother, I can see that. You and your father were the centre of her life. But all he did was get married again and you plunged off into all this. It was almost as though you were saying, "I can get a family too."'

When she didn't answer, he put the brandy on the ledge next to him and gripped her shoulders. He gave her a slight shake. Her eyes flew to his. 'I once said to you that you were not unlike Sophia, Anna, and I meant it. You both wanted a better life. The difference is that she wanted someone else to pay for it. You didn't. You'd die rather than ask for anything. She asked for too much and you ask for too little.'

She pushed away his hands. 'For goodness' sake, I'm not a victim.'

'No,' he said, anger in his voice, 'but you're a coward. You wouldn't risk asking me to tell you how I felt about you.'

'Stop it,' she said, moving away from him. 'I should go in. Oliver will wonder where I am. Don't say any more.'

'Why?' he said, watching her walk away. 'You know how I feel. You've always known. You wait for me to come running and you, I take it, mustn't make any effort at all. And your father. No, I won't stop. Someone's got to tell you. You're driving a perfectly nice man who loves you into a miserable, anxious mess. You want him to say sorry for shocking you. And why should he? You had a wonderful mother, Anna, but she taught you never to ask. And that's terrible.'

'Stop this,' she shouted at him. 'You didn't know her. She taught me to stand on my own two feet. That is *so* different.'

'And taught you nothing about your father. Well, I will. He's a good man. Personally I would have been indebted to Meryl for coming along and making him happy again, instead of so obviously resenting it.'

'It wasn't resentment,' she yelled back. 'It was not belonging any more. I'd lost someone I loved too, remember?'

The door opened and Gio peered out, attracted by the shouting. Giulio strode across and pulled it shut, stopping Anna from going in. 'And so did he, and when the chance came to be happy again – which is rare, God knows, it's rare – he took it because that was the greatest compliment he could pay your mother. And what did you do? You sulked.'

'I did not. It's his life. Not mine. He can do what he likes.'

'Of course he can,' he shouted. 'So why don't you let him and be happy for him instead of hovering in the background like his conscience stopping him? Don't end up like Sophia, Anna, an emotional blackmailer.'

She hit him. A stinging slap with the flat of her hand that sent a shock wave through her.

'Brilliant.' He swore, not even touching where the marks of her fingers were reddening on his unshaven face. 'And that solves what?'

She looked at him, appalled. She thought of the silent lunch at Meryl's. The cheap little gibe at Fenella. Her father. Oh, God, her poor father, with this sulking, unhappy daughter, making it so hard for him to be happy. Meryl must hate her. Meryl, who had taken the burden of a broken-hearted man from Anna's shoulders and let her live her own life, must loathe her. She loathed herself.

She shut her eyes and pushed the heels of her hands into them. Then she looked up at him. 'I'm sorry,' she said, shakily. 'I shouldn't have done that. I don't know what came over me.'

'Don't torture yourself,' he said. 'Go home. Get on with your life. And I mean *your* life, Anna, not someone else's.'

'Yes.' She was so ashamed of herself. 'I must stop hurting people, square it somehow with Meryl, and make it up to Oliver. I mustn't hurt him any more. And I do love him. You might not think so but I do.'

There was a long silence. 'I see,' he said. 'Well, one less thing to worry about.'

She asked Andrea if she could have a photograph of Lorenzo, the one in which he was smiling right into the camera. 'I know he's not my father,' she said, 'but he was my step-father, and I think I would have liked him.'

He gave it to her immediately, troubled because she still insisted she wanted nothing. Sophia had left no will and, in truth, there was little for her to leave. Andrea had already inherited everything. Anna slid the photograph out of the frame and, as she did, a smaller one fell out. She picked it up and saw that it was the one Sophia had carried of her as a baby. 'Look,' she picked it up, 'can I have this too?'

Andrea glanced at it. 'A picture of me? Of course. But I wasn't a beautiful baby. Papa took that minutes after I was born. That's why it's so fuzzy.'

Anna looked at him and then back at the picture. Nothing. Nothing at all.

'Andrea?' she asked abruptly. 'Why do you always call him Papa when most Italian children call their father Bebbo?'

He looked away from her. 'Mamma insisted. In the south,

331

you see, in places like Naples, they never do. You see, it used to mean stupid.'

Oliver was standing beside the kitchen sink, watching Anna step carefully around the dustsheets and the ladders that Aftab Viraswami's decorators had draped across anything that couldn't be moved. 'Here.' She handed him a paint chart. 'Aftab says this is the only possible colour. What do you think?'

He took the chart and looked at it without seeing it. 'Fine,' he said. 'Whatever you want.' He folded it up and handed it back to her.

'Just fine?' she said, bending her head so that she could look at his face. 'Not "amazing" or "perfection"? Or "Oh, my God"? Hey,' she turned his face to look at her, 'what is it?' He wore a look of such anguish that Anna thought he was about to cry. 'Oliver', she cried. She put her arms around him. 'What's the matter?'

'Anna,' he began, running a hand through his hair, 'Christ, this is hard.' Gently he released her arms and moved away. 'I can't ... I don't think we should go on with this.'

There was a small flutter in her stomach. 'You mean the kitchen?'

'No. You know I don't mean that. I mean us.'

She stepped back. The oddest sensation was sweeping through her. 'But why? Because of Sophia? But she's gone now. It's over.'

Even as she spoke she knew that there was another agenda in his life, one that did not include her, one to which he had clearly been referring. It had been there all the time. 'Have you met someone else?' she asked, not taking her eyes off him. 'Truth, Oliver, this is hurting. Don't make it worse.'

He nodded, then immediately shook his head. 'Yes, no. I don't know. Maybe. I just know we're not the same people we were a year ago, six months ago. Oh, God, Anna, I'm so sorry – on top of everything else. But I can't let you go on doing all this.'

It was two weeks after they had returned from Rome. He buried his face in his hands, not trusting himself to look at her.

She said, in an odd little voice, 'Would you like to tell me why? And who? No, don't tell me that. I don't want to know. No, that's not true. I do. You owe me that.'

'I owe you a great deal more than that.'

He said that everything was different. He had seen that in Rome. He had fallen in love with a gentle, compliant Anna, who would be there when he came home. He didn't know her any more, or her family. Oliver had ended up with a girl who, whether she liked it or not, was inextricably linked to all these strange people. He no longer felt part of her life.

'And there's no one else?' she asked, feeling as if this was happening to another person.

'Not anyone new,' he said, and for the first time he looked directly at her. 'I mean, Rachel's around, but I hurt her badly and I have no idea what will happen.'

She knew she would miss him dreadfully. And she did. Loving Oliver had been a part of her, a steady strength that had pulled her along when she only knew how to stand still. It was hard, but the worst was knowing he was right. They loved each other – in different ways they always would – but they were no longer in love. He wanted her to keep her ring, but she made him take it back.

Two weeks later he called her to say he was seeing Rachel again. She would never like Rachel, but that was under-standable: Anna had truly loved Oliver and never under-stood why Rachel had let him get away so easily.

She resigned from her job. Gilbert accepted it with expressions of regret, but Anna knew that that was to spare them both. After the last few weeks it would have been impossible to have recovered her reputation as a driving force, and the truth was she no longer felt like one. The only consolation was that Tania Prowton was not offered her job. She had sealed her fate with Circle by giving a resentful, and entirely truthful, interview to a tabloid about what they called her 'Kinky Love Games with Max the Rat'. All of which did nothing to dent Max's continuing and even increasing popularity since his legion of fans continued to confuse his on-screen persona with reality. Bridget was dropped. The word was that she was going to present a home-décor programme on the cable network. None of it seemed more than mildly amusing to Anna, who lunched with Henry and turned down Charles's offer to return.

In the end she went to stay with her father. Aftab wouldn't allow her home and there was a limit to how long she could stay with Carrie now that her own life was so firmly back on track. 'As long as you like,' Carrie had protested. 'Besides, you're a great babysitter. William says he's never had so many dates without me cancelling or saying we have to eat here.'

Her father insisted she came to him. Meryl only wanted her to be happy too. There would be no problem. Fenella's new baby, a girl to be called Meg, was only a few weeks old, so Meryl spent a lot of time there. It would mostly be just the two of them.

Early one morning she made the decision. And, on the whole, in spite of some misgivings as the plane banked for the descent into Aberdeen, it was not a bad one. They walked across the hills and talked, sitting on the edge of lochs drinking soup from the flasks Meryl left for them before she took off to Craigaithan Heights. Sometimes they took Fiona and Nonie with them, occasionally Corin, and came back with their jeans and tracksuits drenched. Then they raced around to dry them before Meryl got back to berate them for their hideously amateurish way with three small children.

Once when they were on their own, Anna had wept and wept, and Colin had stroked her hair until she had felt calm enough to continue the walk home. 'If you're going to cry,' she said, blowing her nose hard, 'I recommend a forsaken hillside in a howling gale. No one to care about the noise.'

He was happy, she could see that. Even happier when he knew she wasn't without hope that her life would turn around. Meryl had only ever wanted Anna to feel that she was taking care of him properly. Athol and Fenella had been daunted by this career girl with her high-powered job and had tried to emphasize that at least they were good at what they did best, which was being good parents to their children, who were every bit as spoilt as Euan and every bit as nice.

'I perhaps overdid your skills,' Colin admitted, with a sheepish grin. 'It's my fault. But you *are* clever and I am proud of you.' They'd all made mistakes, he said. But Anna wouldn't hear of it. They had tried. She hadn't. Seeing how determined she was to be the major fault in all of this, he gave up. Once Anna decided to do something, no one could stop her. Colin laughed quietly to himself. Not know his own daughter? He was learning. On balance Anna knew she deserved the cautious reception she got from Meryl, the cool one from her step-brother and -sister-in-law.

Before she left to return to London, she stopped off at Athol's new house. It was pretty and welcoming. Her mother would have liked it, she knew that instantly. There was a big scrubbed table in the middle of the kitchen at which the children were drawing and squabbling over who had mixed black paint with the white so that now, Fiona complained, they only had grey.

The kitchen looked out over rolling hills and it wasn't where Anna would have wanted to live, but for a weekend she thought it would be a nice escape. She had arrived as Meg was about to be fed for the third time in an hour and she knew she was not the most welcome sight.

Her housewarming present, of two embroidered cushions, was accepted with some surprise and the bag of presents for the children politely. 'I remembered you said you had pink sofas,' Anna said, refusing to give in to the chill that had descended, 'so I hope these match. It's lovely here.' She glanced around and, to her surprise, knew that she meant it. 'I can see why you bought it.'

'Maybe when we're a bit more settled you'd come to tea,' Fenella said.

She came back to London knowing that several bridges were still to be built. But she'd started.

'You know what you've got to do,' Carrie said, watching Euan stack then knock over a pile of Anna's CDs. 'Anna,' she said severely, taking them away from him, 'will have your knees for breakfast.'

'Not knees,' he said, hurling himself at the back of Anna's legs. 'I bite knees.'

Aftab Viraswami had allowed her back into the house after she returned from Scotland, and if the sun was not actually trapped in the walls, it was a near thing.

'Supposing I get it wrong again,' Anna replied, swinging Euan up into her arms. 'What then?'

'Start again. Like we all do. What did you really want, Anna? I never really understood. Barbara was such a star. You didn't need a replacement for her, did you?'

'No,' Anna said quickly, 'of course not. Never that. In the end it wasn't even because I wanted them to regret giving me up, I just got carried away with wanting to belong somewhere. Not because of someone's generosity or their good nature, but as a right. And then I got to know Sophia and I thought we were so alike – coming from ordinary backgrounds, having to fend for ourselves. She made me feel so guilty. I'd been given this wonderful life, and she had had to suffer for making the right decision about me. Well, that's what it seemed like.

'Sometimes I understand why this young man and I get on so well.' She pulled her face back to look at Euan, who was falling asleep on her shoulder. 'No. Wrong again. He's far more grown-up than me. I tried to redress the balance. And got it all wrong. I should have listened to Guilio.'

'How is he?'

'No idea. Last saw him in Rome.'

'Why haven't you seen him?' Carrie asked, taking Euan from her.

'Because I don't want to get it wrong again. And I might have left it too late. You hadn't thought of that, had you?'

'You might not have. What did your mother used to say? "It's not what you've done, it's where you're going." Hard to beat that. I know what I'd do.'

'Tell me?'

'You're not stupid. Go figure.'

Chapter Twenty-seven

Anna walked up from the tube station, along Holland Park Road, and turned off into the warren of streets that lay behind it. Under her arm she carried a brown bag of shopping from the deli on the corner. It was just past eight in the evening. She knew her mother would have liked him. That was odd, too, because she had never felt certain that Oliver would have been her choice. As she turned into the square she deliberately, but not entirely successfully, ignored the scuffle her nerves had started in the pit of her stomach. The house was in darkness.

'Shit,' she muttered.

That had never occurred to her. The steady drizzle had turned to rain. She was about to walk away when a car swept round the square and started to back into a space against the park railings. She swallowed as the driver got out. He wasn't looking as he walked across the street, head down. It was wet and cold, and her hair was suffering. It wasn't until the last moment as he was about to go in that she said, 'Er . . . hello.'

He turned his head and just stared at her, not quite taking her in and then seemed unable to shift his gaze.

She cleared her throat and began again, unnerved by his silence. 'I thought I'd come and say hello and tell you I've sorted some stuff out.' Nerves always made her sound stiff and formal.

He moved to look past her. 'No. It's all right,' she rushed

on. 'No one's with me. The thing is,' she rambled on, knowing she sounded rehearsed and unconvincing but it was too late, 'you see,' she said, shifting one of the packages so that it sat less heavily on her hip, 'I've been jilted, and I'm out of work. Which means, quite possibly, I'll soon be homeless. My father says I can live with him in Scotland, and Eamonn is used to the homeless, which I'm likely to be at this rate, so I could go there. Only, I thought ... maybe we could talk. I mean, I know you might not want to, but I just wanted to talk to you.'

'About what?'

'Finding out what matters. Actually, I know that bit. It's where I go now that I'm having trouble with.'

For a long moment he just looked at her. 'Say it again.' He was leaning against the door his hands stuffed in his pockets.

'Which bit?'

'Any of it.'

'Oh, my God,' she begged, 'don't make me. That was so hard. Look, I've come straight from being interviewed for a job and it's not much – not like *Newsbeat*, social issues, one-offs, that kind of thing – and I don't know whether to take it or not. It's a friend of Henry's and they've got no money. And I'm getting desperate for a cup of tea. And I thought you might give me that recipe for pasta – look, I've got the ingredients,' she said, patting the bag. 'And, oh, yes, you could teach me how to set a sleeve in case I ever have to give up the day job.'

He began to smile, a crooked, crumpled smile, as though he didn't know whether to laugh or cry. 'You haven't met my family,' he pointed out. 'You might not like them.'

'But I like you,' she said. 'In fact, I more than like you. And, as a Sicilian, that's a lot to admit without any encouragement. So that's a start, isn't it?'

He put down his case and walked towards her, stopping just in front of her, saying nothing, just looking at her.

'Don't,' she said nervously. 'Don't just look at me. Do something.'

He reached out and pushed her hair out of her face. Then he wrapped his arms around her and held her, her wet face against his.

'In which case,' he released her, took the groceries from her and said, in a voice that wasn't quite steady, 'you'd better come in and talk.'